THE BIG HEART

The Lokayata edition
of the novels of
MULK RAJ ANAND

THE BIG HEART

MULK RAJ ANAND

ARNOLD-HEINEMANN

© *Mulk Raj Anand*
First Published May 1945
Reprinted   June 1945

New Revised Edition 1980
Edited, with an Introduction by Saros Cowasjee

Published by Gulab Vazirani for Arnold-Heinemann Publishers (India) Pvt. Ltd., AB/9, Safdarjang Enclave, New Delhi-110016 and printed by Sunil Composing Co. at S.P. Printers, Naraina New Delhi-110028 (India).

(In a speech on Luddites, the Nottinghamshire weavers,
in the House of Lords, February 27, 1812.)

'But whilst these outrages must be admitted to exist to an alarming extent, it cannot be denied that they have arisen from circumstances of the most unparalleled distress : the perseverance of these miserable men in their proceedings, tends to prove that nothing but absolute want could have driven a large, and once honest and industrious, body of the people, into the commission of excesses so hazardous to themselves, their families, and the community. . . . But the police, however useless, were by no means idle : several notorious delinquents had been detected; men, liable to conviction, on the clearest evidence, of the capital crime of Poverty; men, who had been nefariously guilty of lawfully begetting several children, whom, thanks to the times ! they were unable to maintain. Considerable injury has been done to the proprietors of the improved frames. These machines were to them an advantage, inasmuch as they superseded the necessity of employing a number of workmen, who were left in consequence to starve. By the adoption of one species of frame in particular, one man performed the work of many, and the superfluous labourers were thrown out of employment. Yet it is to be observed, that the work thus executed was inferior in quality; not marketable at home, and merely hurried over with a view to exportation. It was called in the cant of the trade, by name of "Spider's work." The rejected workmen, in the blindness of their ignorance, instead of rejoicing at these improvements in arts so beneficial to mankind, conceived themselves to be sacrificed to improvements in mechanism. In the foolishness of their hearts they imagined that the maintenance and well-doing of the industrious poor were objects of greater consequence than the enrichment of a few individuals by any improvement, in the implements of trade, which threw workmen out of employment, and rendered the labourer unworthy of his hire. . . . But the real cause of these distresses and consequent disturbances lies deeper. When we are told that these men are leagued together not only for the destruction of their own comfort, but of their very means of subsistence, can we forget that it is the bitter policy, the destructive warfare of the last eighteen years, which has destroyed their comfort, your comfort, all men's comfort ? That policy, which originating with "great statesmen now no more", has survived the dead to become a curse on the living, unto the third and fourth generations ! Are we (then) aware of our obligations to a mob ? It is the mob that labour in your fields and serves in your houses,—that man your navy, and recruit your army,—that have enabled you to defy all the world, and can also defy you when neglect and calamity have driven them to despair ! You may call the people a mob; but do not forget, that a mob too often speaks the sentiments of the people.,

Lord Byron.

Although human conditions have changed much since Lord Byron spoke in the House of Lords, his words might still have some relevance to our time.

M. R. A.

Introduction

The Big Heart (1945) is Anand's seventh novel, but the first to have a factory hand as its protagonist. Ananta, a coppersmith, returns to his home-town of Amritsar after having worked in Bombay and Ahmedabad. He brings with him Janki, a young widow, whom he loves and who is now slowly dying of tuberculosis. In Amritsar, Ananta resumes his hereditary trade, but like most people of his brotherhood he has difficulty making a living. The introduction of the machine has thrown the artisans out of work. Though Ananta suffers from the introduction of the machines, he can still see their usefulness. He knows that the machines are there to stay, and he draws an interesting analogy between machines and dowry while talking to Janki : 'Like the fashionable Vilayati bride, we have accepted, we ought to accept the dowry of machines she has brought, and make use of them, provided we keep our hearts and become the masters'. Ananta urges the workers to form a union to bargain collectively with the factory-owners for jobs and keep the old brotherhood alive. In this he wins the support of the poet Puran Bhagat Singh. But he is unable to muster sufficient enthusiasm among the jobless who are carried away by the demagogy of the student leader, Satyapal. Events take an unexpected turn when Ralia, one of the castaways, starts wrecking the machines. Ananta tries to stop this wanton destruction and is killed by the raging Ralia.

Untouchable dealt primarily with an out-caste who begins to have glimmerings of the lowness to which he is condemned. *Coolie* is about a young boy uprooted from a paradisal landscape and thrown into the whirlpool of 'civilisation'. *The Big Heart* touches on both these problems, showing how each acts and reacts upon on the other. But in this novel, the hero,

Ananta, is not a passion sufferer but is shown capable of protest against degradation :

> He (Ananta) saw a man utterly naked, his buttocks wrapped in a paste of sweat and dung and urine, rolling about the edge of a ditch in a hissing agony, lifting his neck with an aching stupor and then slipping into his filth.

The Big Heart draws on *The Sword and the Sickle* of Anand's peasant triology, as well. *The Sword and the Sickle* concludes with Lalu realising the need for brotherhood as a prerequisite of success. *The Big Heart* opens with Ananta already possessing this knowledge, but it goes on to show the difficulty of applying this knowledge in a world torn by hatred and suspicion.

The basic conflict in *The Big Heart* is between the forces of tradition and modernity, and this is evident in the setting of the novel—Billimaran or the Cat-Killer's Lane :

> It must be remembered, however, that Billimaran is not a blind alley. Apart from the usual mouth, which even a *cul de sac* keeps open, it has another, which makes it really like a two-headed snake. With one head it looks towards the ancient market, where the beautiful copper, brass, silver and bronze utensils made in the lane are sold by dealers called kaseras, hence called Bazar Kaserian. With the other it wriggles out towards the new Ironmongers' Bazar, where screws and bolts and nails and locks are sold and which merge into the Booksellers' mart, the cigarette shops and the post office with the spirit of modern times.

The Ironmongers' Bazar stands for the machine, and thus modernity, while the Bazar Kaserian stands for tradition. The fettering images by which modernity is symbolised—'screws and bolts and nails and locks'—show the author's ingrained partiality against tradition. But time has wrought a change, and time is moving with every measured stroke of the 'gigantic four-faced English clock,' which vies for attention with the shrine of the Goddess Kali in the shabby lane.

The temple and the clock also represent tradition and modernity respectively. And though the author and his spokesmen Ananta and the Poet see the evils of the machine age and the benefits of the old way of life, they realise that the older order is obsolete in a country on the verge of a vast social, economic and political change. It is indeed clever of Anand to disclose through gossip that his hero is by no means perfect, and yet leave it to the reader to uncover that the foul appellations used to describe Ananta have no basis in fact. The reader sees him as a kind, generous person, fond of children, and concerned about the welfare of his brethren. His hearty, bluff and casual manner hides a sensitive soul. He has been acquainted with pain early in life, but has 'almost conquered it with his great capacity for happiness'. Of the characters present in the book, he is certainly the best qualified to organise the brotherhood, and his experiences in Bombay and Ahmedabad are an additional factor in his favour. There is, no doubt, the poet Puran Bhagat Singh, but he is too exalted and abstract to be a man of action.

Ananta's failure stems partly from his own shortcomings. He believes that man is wholly responsible for his own destiny, but the manner of his death ironically vindicates one of his sacrilegious jibes—'God works in a mysterious way'. In a society as hypocritical as it is orthodox, his liaison with Janki is frowned upon. Ralia, who beats and starves his wife, is more acceptable to the thathiars than Ananta, who genuinely loves Janki and has given her a new lease of life. His reputation as a whore-monger and a drunkard, though false, deprives him of the moral authority demanded of a leader in a tradition-bound society. His agnosticism is looked upon as another facet of his immorality, and he is—through no fault of his—suspected of being in the service of the hire of chattel slaves. But, above all, he is unable to dramatise his cause and he is hence unable to offer an immediate remedy for the misery of the disinherited. To the starving men, who want immediate gain, he offers a post-dated cheque for a better life in the distant future :

> The Revolution is not yet. And it isn't merely in the shouting. Nor is it in this single battle in Billimaran, brothers. It is only through a great many conflicts between the employers, authorities and the workers, in a whole number of battles which our comrades elsewhere are

fighting, that there will come the final overthrow of the bosses.

Sound logic—but not to the hungry. Opposing the Union is Satyapal,—the man of indiscriminate hatreds. He hates the English and the Russians, the Communists and the Capitalists and much else besides. He is in favour of immediate action— seize the factory if you can, wreck it if you can't. Satyapal, Anand informs us, 'seemed to have an uncanny awareness of the irrational desires of people'. As the basis of his militancy lies in the common suffering of all those present, his words have a stronger impact on the people than do those of Ananta.

It is significant that Ananta should die at the hands of Ralia, who is carefully drawn by the author for the thoughtless crime he commits. Of those laid out of work by the machine, Ralia and his family suffer the most, and Ralia is shown ranting at the machines early in the novel. During the political discussions he is for the most part shown drunk or asleep, and he kills Ananta unintentionally while wrecking the machines. Ananta is thus a victim of rage and insanity, not of a religious or political creed, and his sacrifice is the sacrifice of the unselfish man for humanity. Violence may be necessary against an entrenched enemy, Anand seems to say in *The Sword and the Sickle*, but in *The Big Heart* he is against all killing. To have violence without murder is a problem that confronts most revolutionary humanists, and this problem remains unsolved in Anand's mind.

There are many things about *The Big Heart* which are attractive. 'In no other novel has Anand so attempted to organise a whole social, economic, and political picture', writes Margaret Berry. The problems of caste and class are complex, and they cannot be solved separately, for they are often linked together and influenced by cash nexus. The coppersmiths are kshatriyas, the second highest caste, but their profession has lowered their social status. With the coming of the machine and the enrichment of the few, a sub-division has appeared among people of the same caste : the rich look down upon the less prosperous of their brethren. Money is the great God, and in novel after novel Anand repeats that there are only two types of people in the world in our time—the rich and the poor. In the final analysis,

Money decides both caste and class; it also decides one's political affiliations. The factory owner Murli Dhar has as little choice of being a Communist as Ralia or Ananta has of being a Capitalist. The struggle for national freedom, too is essentially a struggle for freedom from want.

No student of Anand can miss noticing that the author's view of life has become more comprehensive and that he can now include in his circle of sympathy, things for which he formerly had no tolerance. British rule was evil, but there was much good in British institutions; Capitalism is another name for exploitation, but there are Capitalists who have the welfare of the workers at heart; Gandhi's aversion to machines is as unacceptable as his espousal of an unplanned, individualistic, profit-making industrialism, but he is right that 'Violence breeds violence'. In this book there are no unmitigated villains. Even the police, who appear as the instrument of British power and oppression in *Coolie*, *The Village* and *The Sword and the Sickle*, are treated with comparative leniency and come near being human. The whole of man's nature is governed by the new god Money power, and when Anand attacks individuals he never lets us forget that these people themselves are victims of unjust inheritances.

Anand's perceptive treatment of the Indian confusion in a little over two hundred pages is an achievement, especially the action is narrowed down to the happenings of a single day. The author distinguishes the old hero Arjun in the *Bhagvad Gita* whose choice to act is made by the God Krishna from his new heroes who choose under pressure of their own consciences. *The Big Heart* is symbolic of Anand's urgencies in so far as he wants men to become more than themselves.

SAROS COWASJEE

Author's Note

Already, before the beginning of the second world war, I had begun to feel that there was need in the novel, even when dealing with the raw life (specially when dealing with the raw life) for what has been called the 'human reference'. Implicit in the human reference as an important value are some new questions : What it can enable man to face the world's realities ? And can he in our machine world develop a new myth for himself—'Change upon all the Eternal Gods had made, and make himself, rise to his full potential ?

I had tried in every theme of strain in my fiction of struggles, beyond the first novels of miseries to suggest how the hero grows to awakening, when he ventures into an area of experience, where, urged towards fruitful action by his love of life, he finds himself, among others, who are unequal to the intensities he desires. Thus cut off from his fellow men, who are shut in the old shelters, even though ill at ease with them, the hero pays by ostracism, contempt and even by death, for his will to rise above his birth place.

The tragedy of Ananta, the boundless, is thus the inevitable doom of a man raised from his surroundings by vitalities, above the two mouthed lane of Billimaran, to the heroic pitch of action.

The fable of the machine coming into the handicraft world, is not inspired by schoolboy enthusiasm for gadgets, but conceives machine as a new tool, which was to take men further into the life process, if it did not fall into the hands of greedy men. The hero died, as 'Virgil died, aware of change at hand'.

I have lent myself here to many echoes of the old life, which perennially float below the underlayers of the Indian body-soul. I have allowed myself to be swept by heterogenous currents of discord. And I have ventured to rescue from myriad feelings, the regenerating breath, which we are often too ashamed, in our time, to breathe into each other's ears.

The Big Heart was written from the torment of living between two worlds 'one not quite dead and the other refusing to be born'. And it is precious to me for the shelter it gave me as a half way house before facing other storms.

I owe to Professor C.D. Narasimhaiah and Dr. Saros Cowasjee the impulse to reissue this novel. In fact they advised some revisions and cuts, which I have gratefully accepted, as the impetuous first draft of *The Big Heart* was written in a great hurry prompted by the publisher's scurry.

Khandalla
January, 1980

MULK RAJ ANAND

1

OUTWARDLY THERE IS NOTHING TO SHOW THAT KUCHA BILLIMARAN in the centre of Amritsar has changed very much since the 'age of truth', except that the shadow of the tall Clock Tower built by the British, falls across it from a few hundred yards away, and an electric bulb glows faintly from a post fixed by the municipality in the middle of the lane. But, of course, a lot of water has trickled through its open drains since the 'age of truth' : the pure, holy water (if it ever was pure !) of the ceremonies of the 'age of truth' ; the dirty water of the 'Middle Ages'; the slimy, asafoetid water of the 'iron age' and many other waters besides. The fact about water, like Time, is that it *will* flow : it may get choked up with the rubbish and debris of broken banks; it may be arrested in stagnant pools for long years; but it will begin to flow again as soon as the sky pours down its blessings to make up for what the other elements have sucked up; and it will keep flowing, now slowly, now like a rushing stream . . .

But though water keeps on flowing, the earth crumbles. And those houses which stand cheek by jowl on both sides of the fifteen yards width of Kucha Billimaran have been corroded by Time.

Dating from the 'age of truth', whenever that may have been, there are about thirty to forty of these houses, large and small. The large ones are mainly the tall ones, belonging to the few well-to-do coppersmith families who, rising from humble beginnings, have prospered in the 'iron age' and built one storey on top of another, gradually, on the fourteen to twenty square yards of the earth on which their old hovels stood. The small ones, inhabited by the bulk of the coppersmith community of Amritsar, jut out of each other in curious shapeless tangles. They show that architecture, specially for the craftsman, called thathiars, who belonged to the second highest caste and were yet degraded for following a dirty profession, was not the strong point of the 'age of truth'. Or, maybe, this lane was the particular hell to which the coppersmith families were consigned by Karma because someone in the community once killed a cat, which is why the lane is called Billimaran—Cat-Killer's Lane. But, crumbling and rickety, the hovels rest on the firm foundations of the earth beneath them. For the earth rests, according to legend, on the horn of the primaeval bull, and gives very little sign of any corrosion, except that the bull, finding one horn strained and fatigued after a century of bearing the burden, shakes a little and transfers the weight of the earth on to the second horn. These earthquakes may have displaced some of the bricks of the outer walls of these houses, or knocked the plaster about, but they have left them intact. Only, it would be absurd to call these ramshackle buildings by the respectable name of houses when they are really dilapidated hovels, blackened by the soot of the coppersmiths' furnaces and foundries, greased by the mustard-oil saucer lamps which they burn to illumine their nights (and yes, sometimes even their days), dirtied by the spittles, the nose-blowings and sweat of the men who hammer metal into shape, day and night, night and day.

Of course, there has been some renovation here and there, if only as a kind of revenge on the destructive processes of Time. But only the hard-headed and the hard-hearted, who trudged with vibrationless feet in the streets of the 'Cities of Gold' and made the middle man's profit, have been able to add anything new ! And this has really meant subtraction, for those who amass gold believe in cutting down their expenses to a minimum. One or two of these prosperous families have, therefore, had the walls of a group of houses, which they bought up in the middle of the lane, knocked down, and have recently set up some machines in the resulting shed. But the spirit of time has not quite assimilated this innovation. And though Billimaran manifestly remains all of a piece, all one and one all, even as is the ultimate belief of the inhabitants, however various the gods they worship, men pass by the factory gate, their faces knitted into frowns like question marks.

It must be remembered, however, that Billimaran is not a blind alley. Apart from the usual mouth, which even a *cul de sac* keeps open, it has another, which makes it really like a two-headed snake. With one head it looks towards the ancient market, where the beautiful copper, brass, silver and bronze utensils made in the lane are sold by dealers called kaseras, hence called Bazar Kaserian. With the other it wriggles out towards the new Ironmongers' Bazar, where screws and bolts and nails and locks are sold and which merges into the Booksellers' mart, the cigarette shops and the post office replete with the spirit of modern times.

And just as it has two openings into the outside world, so it has two or three great neighbours. One of them, at the Bazar Kaserian end of Billimaran, is the shrine of the Goddess Kali, mother as well as dread destroyer who must always be appeased. Another, reached by way of devious lanes, is the Golden Temple which was built three hundred years ago by a Sikh saint with money donated by Akbar, the Great Mughal, around a tank which gives to the whole city its name Amritsar, Ocean of Nectar. Here the more skilled coppersmiths were employed as hereditary artisans for some generations, embossing reliefs of religious scenes on gold-washed brass and silver plates and making the pinnacles which glisten on the top of the pure white marble. The other neighbour is the Clock Tower, the monument which ushered in the 'iron age', with the fancy weathercock on its steep needle which talks to the sky and records the evanescent moods of the winds and the spheres, and with its gigantic four-faced English clock from which the families with the two-or three-storeyed houses in Billimaran can read the movement of the two hands of the new god, Time.

In the midst of this jumble of the old and the new, the men and women of Billimaran, children too, have assumed a different hue. They are paler and sallower, where grime and dirt does not hide their bodies. For they have to work harder, they say, to buy the new gadgets of the 'iron age'. Also, they feel that the price of flour has been rising for some unknown reason. Caught in the mousetraps where they are born, most of them are encaged in the bigger cage of Fate and the various indiscernible shadows that hang over their heads. And they do not know the meridians beyond the length and breadth of Billimaran until the day when they are carried out, feet first, to join the elements. Some of them have done the trip to somewhere away by rail, but come back after losing everything except their loincloths to the sharpers and touts who abound. A few stolid men, blank in appearance, have ventured open-mouthed to the 'cities of gold', and have come back tight-lipped with a new suffering to avenge in Billimaran. A very small number, the sons of the rich, have gone out, however, and become Babus or Sahibs, but then they have never returned to the old lane, and their lives revolve round other constellations which are like the Sun, the Moon and the Stars to the folk who have been left behind. Only, most of the boys, who have found jobs in the machine shop or the factory, have bought cheap Road Master bicycles and, with shrill mouth-organs adjusted to their lips, they make daily excursions into the civil lines of Amritsar for an airing on the stifling, hot evenings of summer. And they bring back a new aura of romance with them from the cinemas, though their lives are as yet rooted in the old commune. There is this change in their fancies, however, that they are bicycle-minded factory workers, while their elders remain merely pedestrian coppersmiths; they work in the glow of small electric bulbs gleaming under the lustre of great arc-lamps, standing over polished heaps of intricate machinery, with pulleys and wheels and handles before them, while the older members of their community bend like gnomes before the fires in mature furnaces, soldering the joints of household utensils or crouching in the doorways, their lined faces groping for light in a world where, they say, the 'darkness is spreading'.

Altogether, a spirit of unrest broods over Kucha Billimaran, like the doom promised on the judgement day at the end of the 'iron age'. And already the convulsions of the sad lands across the black waters are shaking this old lane with the thunder of the machinery implanted in its midst, which is said to be making tools for the greatest war on earth that is rumoured will be in progress at the ends of the horizons. The leaping tongues of fire, which were said to have singed the beards of their headmen while they were planning with the Devil to start the roaring monsters of machines and to rob the coppersmiths of their living, are supposed to have given warning of the devilry that would spread from a ray of the flaming sun and encircle the earth. The swarms of crows, which blackened the sky like the harbingers of famine, and which are now spreading over the countryside, with droves of vultures around them, spell the surest disasters. The rats, which are frequently emerging from their holes and collapsing after they have performed their dance of death, betoken the coming of dread plagues. The brooms which begin to walk and follow the housewives about are the faceless messengers of death which will sweep the whole hungry population before them. The sudden cramp, which has got hold of the souls of men ever since the ragged rhythm of the machines in the shed began to drown the hammer-strokes with which the coppersmiths were used to smooth rough metal into shape and imprint the polish of gold on finished pots, augurs ill for them as a caste. Heaven has sent them messages in their dreams, messages which have chilled their bones for a long time—this is the 'iron age', the age of Death, which is to culminate in the doomsday.

Only Ananta, the rogue who has returned from Bombay, knows a little about the war and calls the Sun's maturing a Ray of Revolution. He thumps his big chest with his fist and shouts, 'There is no talk of money, brothers; one must have a big heart.' And the young men in the factory, who know him to be a man of heart, in spite of all the rogueries and devilries attributed to him, echo after him, laughing and with mock heroics:

> 'This is the machine age, sons,
> This is the machine age.
> We are the men who will master it,
> We are the new men of the earth of all the
>   evil old ages!'

And, of course, everyone joins in the fun and scoffs. . . .

2

'THAK, THAK, THAK. . .' THE HEAVY METALLIC CLANG ISSUED from the half-open doors of Ananta's small shop in the middle of Kucha Billimaran by the new factory into the sombre half-dark of the dawn.

Ananta was imprinting evenly spaced rows of bright moon-strokes on the clean, pink, acid-washed surface of the copper pitcher in the light of the electric street lamp. With his left hand he revolved the huge vessel ever so gently on the long iron anvil, adjusted between the boulder-like legs of the wooden horse, while he wielded the polished hammer with an easy precision with his right hand. And his giant frame towered over the eight by six yards room, littered all over with anvils, wooden hammers, iron hammers, pincers, huge iron scissors and other tools, except for the square yard of the corner by the door of the inner sanctum, occupied by the open furnace.

But within him there was the surging of a peculiar 'ghaoon maoon', a kind of disturbance spreading like knife-edges from the bits of the dream he had just before he came to work. He had awakened in a sweat and since then the perspiration had been cascading down his body in streams, both through the 'hoom' of airlessness and the pressure of the nightmare.... Stark silence had brooded over the cremation ground, and his mother, his dead mother, had stood burning, even as she was exhorting him to look after his step-mother Karmo. And then, suddenly, he had seen himself—was it on the platform of the railway station or the base of the Clock Tower ? He couldn't remember now.... And then there was a considerable crowd before him and he had begun to speak. But Janki, his mistress, had interrupted him with a wail, and as he had turned to go towards her in a garden which looked like Guru ka Bagh, the crowd had become like the masked men he had seen in the dacoit films in Bombay. ... And they were following him, while he had run, their hands dripping with blood. He had been frightened and had tried to run faster, but behind him there was a voice calling, 'I am hungry, I want blood,' and he had felt almost overpowered. ... He had looked back and found a black woman with a trident in her hand standing on the cremation ground, stamping upon corpses and dancing as she shrieked again and again, 'I am hungry ! I want blood !' And he could hear the dead moaning under the feet of the woman, whom he soon recognized as the Goddess Kali, for her tongue was bulging out red, and her eyes were like two sharp glint-discs, shining like diamonds from the coal-black face. He had tried to shout for help. But no words had come from his open mouth. And he had to stand there, dazed with horror at the massacred bodies, till he saw a policeman with a machine-gun coming towards him, and he had turned— to wake up in a sweat which even now trailed down in crystals off his forehead.

He did not stop to wipe the sweat. He merely struck the hammer in a measured movement as though he did not want to admit even to himself that he had been afraid. An artist, over and above the craftsman, his hand moved with an easy grace in spite of the disturbance within him, even as he imprinted a pattern of moon-strokes by way of finishing touches on the vessel before him. But the swirling uneasiness inside him rose in sudden bursts of sickness and slowed him down as if he were face to face with the black death.

The clock in the tower struck five strokes and enveloped the atmosphere with a dim fear, so that Ananta hurried, though he was soaking with sweat. He knew that soon he would finish this job and then deal with the perspiration. Afterwards he must go and see whether Janki's fever had abated. And if his sweet-heart was a little better, he could go and have a bath in the rest-house of Sant Harnam Das by the Golden Temple, and get a change of clothes. O, for a drink of cool whey! But the milk shops had had no milk for several days now, and if you did not have milk, you could not make curds and beat it up into whey and skim the butter. As for butter—there was no talk of it in times of scarcity! It was fifty rupees a tin in the black market.

His mouth watered at the thought of the fried puris he used to eat with kara and black carrot pickle. He could feel the saliva gathering under his tongue and felt slightly ashamed of his enormous appetite and his well-known greed for food and drink. Until recently he had never felt a pang of shame about his love of good things; in fact he had gloated on his reputation as a 'flesh-eater and drunkard'. Partly this was because he was as stubborn as a mule and delighted in the bad name he had earned from the people he did not like, although he was tortured in secret by a conscience which grew more and more like a cancer inside him, from the failure he felt he was.

A turbulent spirit and wanton in reaching out after life, he sensed now and then the poise of a furious calm in himself, like that of a leaf suddenly come still in a storm, specially after he had been struggling like a tormented beast in the cage of his soul. At such times he rose above his sense of doom and looked on himself as a person whose lusts were the reaction to other people's envy of him, whose depravity and drunkenness were a fight against the debris of broken idols in his mother's home, whose hotheadedness was a protest against the decay around him. And then he was dimly aware that his sudden love of 'Revolution', that had burst out like a red flower in Bombay, was due to the disgust he felt for the selfishness of his youth. But all the moral self condemnation of himself, and his attainment of the splendorous heights above the spurts of sulphurous regrets in him, did not prevent him from succumbing to the abysses of devilry in the volcano below his stomach.

For the 'Revolution' was as yet some distance away and, meanwhile, he had to balance himself almost on his head in the narrow alleyway of Billimaran among the gaping hovels and the half-men before his eyes. So he drank liquor, as well as the brackish blood of his own liver, and supped on the putrid sweat-sodden world around him. He lounged about the cookshops, defiant against life, gourmandizing, singing ribald folk songs, throwing his money about, without any respect for God, the Sarkar or the orthodox men of his caste, a crazy rebel except against those who were his comrades in filth and against the children who found his presence intoxicatingly rich to their naive sense of sight and touch.

'There was quite a thick crowd of hooded men in the cremation ground,' he muttered to himself, 'almost like the shadow of—' He dared not name the awful thing. So he phewed a hot breath without relaxing his vigilant stare at the vessel and continued to imprint the moon-strokes on it.

The spring was entering upon the summer through the impetuous dawn, and the 'hoom' was rushing the blood up to his head. In Bombay, he recalled, one could feel the cool breeze coming from the sea. O for the days in Bombay when he had worked in the Royal Naval Dockyard foundries ! If only Janki's fever had abated somewhat they would still have been there with the comrades ! O even for the days in the cotton mills of Ahmedabad, though the heat there was simply unbearable and the company unions all-enveloping ! O for the big hell, where there was life because there was struggle, where one's head was swimming in gaiety with the intoxication of meeting comrades in the Madanpura slums ! O for the life where a broken heart could seek out other broken hearts and fight together with them ! O for those comrades in the midst of these stubborn asses, the thathiars ! At least in Bombay there was no rumour-mongering and malicious gossip, even if the comrades disapproved of his drinking bouts.

He smiled to himself even as he groped for more light to adjust his eyes to the moon-strokes. And he thought how his return home to Amritsar had been an anticlimax. He had been refused a job in the new factory ten yards away, because the headman of the coppersmith brotherhood, Murli, who had founded the firm in partnership with the headman of the utensil sellers' community, Gokul, regarded him, a cousin, as a rival to his son and sons' sons. He wondered if there was anyone in his dream who looked like Murli. 'But no, I must not be superstitious,' he said to himself. And then he gurgled with a laugh and muttered: 'I don't care. I could sell the whole lot of them and drink away the money ! They cannot ever imagine the glories of abandon, and they haven't the courage to do a thing though they prate about Murli Dhar —Gokul Chand's achievement in getting a Government contract.'

'Thak ! thak ! thak' !—he struck the hammer with a greater deftness and agility as he got more excited. And it seemed to him as if he were emerging from the monotony of the craftsman's habit to a new rhythm like that which he had felt in his body when he had to make papier-mâché masks for the effigy of the ten-headed King Ravan of Lanka for the Dusehra festival in his youth, or when he had made wooden and earthen toys for the slum children in Bombay. The rising pressure of the strokes sharpened the edges of his bones with a new courage until he felt as if he were Raja Rasalu, the proverbial hero of the Punjabi legend, setting off on his adventures, seated on a white charger. But even as he felt exalted he heard the soft tread of steps behind the doors of the inner sanctum and felt as if the shadow of the forms in his dream was descending on him in the eerie dark.

Then he shook his head and called himself a fool for being so disturbed. He knew it was only his mother.

'Vay Anantia, vay son, you are up early !'

Karam Devi's voice came from the dark cavern behind the shop, shrill like that of an ogre. And, following it, came a tall old woman with a bent back, dressed in a greying black skirt, a grey head-cloth over her straggling wisps of white hair and her drooping shoulders. She advanced slowly, gingerly, watching each step, for the light of her eyes had waned many years ago and she groped around through the debris and implements.

Ananta did not answer her through sheer mulishness, nor did he raise his eyes to look at her, though he had felt kindly towards her since he came back from Bombay. She was a fussy old woman, his step-mother Karmo. He kept his gaze fixed steadily on the rows of bright moon-strokes he was imprinting. The light of the electric bulb in the lane was now failing in the glow of the waxing dawn, and he could hear a hubbub of voices at the door of the factory up the lane, as of an altercation. Someone—he knew it was Ralia—was shouting: 'Open the door! Open the door!' He wished he could get up to see what was happening, but there were only seven more rows of moon-strokes left to do and he thought he could hold on till he had finished the job.

'I couldn't sleep, son, for thinking of it,' Karam Devi went on muttering all on her own. 'All these eaters of their masters have ruined us, son, ruined us! The low thathiars!... You mustn't associate yourself with the scum against the elders of the brotherhood, as I still have hopes.... It is such a good match. If only they don't spoil everything by spreading rumours about you!... Why do you drink, son? And why do you go about with gamblers? These eaters of their masters will not let us be happy. They even say that old Lala Gagar Mal used to tease me when I used to go to scrub the floors in his house. May the boats of their lives never float in the sea of existence! And then about you and Janki—they tell such tales!... You could keep her as a first wife till she dies of her consumption and the new girl will be a second wife. I wish you would meet those gentle folk from Jandiala. They will give us the offer of their daughter if only you will see them and if I can persuade Aqqi to give her daughter Puro in exchange to one of their boys!—They are gentle folk, both the brothers, Ram Saran and Binde Saran, of Jandiala. They haven't a tooth in their mouths, son, nor evil tongues.'

'There isn't a fang in your mouth, either, but that doesn't make your talk sweet,' Ananta said, and then ignored the old woman. He had a bad conscience about her, and was fond of her in a queer way, though he suspected that, deep inside him, he resented her for being a substitute mother and longed for the dead mother whom he had seen burning in his dream so often, always burning.

'They say the girl is so pretty—oh, so pretty,' Karam Devi continued unperturbed. 'And how happy I should be to look at the face of your bride with the last little light left in my eyes I shall not expect her to serve me, son. I shall serve her and you.... And you can have her all to yourself after Janki is dead. And you can take her wherever you go....

They say she has read up to the fourth class, too. I am sure she will get on with those silk-saried girls in Bombai. Son, you don't know how happily I shall go if I can see your wife before I die.... I have saved a little money, too, from my service at the house of Lala Gagar Mal, and I have made inquiries about the rates of cloth and gold thread. As for the jewellery, you know they can make brass look like gold with the help of Bijli nowadays. The wife of Ralia—you know she brought a whole dowry of such ornaments and no one knew until later.... There will only be a question of money for the marriage party, but then you can raise a loan. Haven't you had any luck at gambling lately? If not, perhaps I can ask someone for a loan. But you must see these people. They will be in our lane some time today. Now, look out for them. They have to cast eyes upon you and they are sure to give you the offer. But only....'

'Oh, go and sleep your dreams off, mother,' snapped Ananta, and cut her short. And he spat the bile in his mouth into the black sooty corner of the furnace, beyond the goats-skin bellows. Then his ears pricked at the sound of filthy abuse up the lane, which came mixed with the devout outpourings of a hillman bathing at the well beyond the doors of the factory.

'Son, you can say anything to me you like,' the old woman persisted, wiping the tears from the wrinkles of the pale shrivelled face, 'but you are a trust given to me by your mother and my husband. I have never regretted not having had a child from my own womb, especially as your mother was so obedient to me when your father married a second time. And before she died....' And suddenly she could not help sobbing at the memory of his mother's passing. But equally suddenly she stopped, wiped her face and continued: 'You don't know how I have waited all these years, begging this person and that person for a match for you, going now to Jullunder, then on to Ludhiana or Philaur, eating the dust of the roadway, drinking the blood of my liver—just to secure a bride for you. And I will be so happy!'

'I thought it was my happiness you desired so much—not your own!' Ananta mocked, shaking his head and then concentrating on his job. Then he relaxed and smiled, saying: 'You are like me, wanting a little more of something than you can get. Only you want a wife for me, and I....'

'Han, son, it is all for you; only for you. So don't be hard on your old mother. I have cried my eyes out for years waiting for your bride. You don't know what it will mean to me. The women of the brotherhood will come to beat the drum, and the young girls will sing, and there will be the bridal party. . . . Oh, then shall the gods bless us and your bride will come home and fall at my feet. And I shall pat her on the head. . . . All this could be if you see the folk from Jandiala. Only. . . .'

'Only what ?'

'Only don't go to them with the smell of liquor in your mouth. And don't take the side of these low thathiars. Then, the folk from Jandiala will consider us as good as the family of Murli Dhar.'

'Oh, go, go, and rest, mother!' he said impatiently.

But she was persistent, and held fast to her instinct even as she kept a grip on his life. She knew how to talk.

'The wife of Sadanand—have you heard about her and her father-in-law ? . . . Gauri, wife of Ralia, told me she saw them together yesterday.'

'One up to the old man for that,' said Ananta. 'He shares with me a desire for happiness. Lalla Murli Dhar ! He even winks at my Janki. Only the rogue won't give me a job in his factory.

'As I was telling you, son, they are gentle folk, Ram Saran and Binde Saran', Karmo said, ignoring his reference to Janki.

'Go, go, mother, you have told me; I am not interested in your gentlefolk,' said Ananta good-humouredly enough as he dropped the vessel aside with a sigh of relief after the last stroke. Then he heaved himself from his hobby-horse, brushed the sweat on his forehead, face and cheeks, into the cupped palm of his hand and threw the contents on Karam Devi. 'There, now, go, I have purified your soul with the nectar that oozes from my body.' And he stretched his body to ease the cramp in his rump, yawned and laughed an involuntary laugh: 'Ho, ho, ho, ha. . . .'

Suddenly he was brought to attention by a veritable storm that seemed to be mounting outside the factory where the voices of the crowd were mounting above the hum of the machinery.

'I must go and see what they're up to,' he said.

3

> 'This is the machine age, sons,
> This is the machine age. . . .'

ANANTA INTONED THE REFRAIN IN AN EXCESS OF GOOD HUMOUR, half consolingly, half mockingly, as he came up to the crowd which stood about in knots outside the gates of the factory shed. His song sprang from the relief he felt at having finished the day's work before the break of dawn; but as he approached the men and saw their drawn faces, yawning with the fatigue and the stale breath of a heavy night, as he saw their sagging bodies leaning by the half-open door, some crouching on the hump of curved, small brick platform before it, he felt a tremor of shame at his lightheartedness. He knew they were waiting for the foreman, Channa, because there had been a rumour that the factory was going to take on one or two more men. And ever since the rate of piece-work for making utensils had been gradually lowered, most of the coppersmiths had been shutting up shop and were anxious to secure jobs in the factory where their nephews and one-time apprentices were earning a rupee or more a day.

The men listened to Ananta's gong-like voice and turned away their faces, except for tall Ralia, an ex-drinking companion of Ananta's, who fixed him with a hard stare. But even Ralia did not look at him for long and hung his head down. His once handsome face with the hawk nose and strong chin seemed to have visibly contracted in the last few days. Ananta knew that the insidious torment of worklessness in a world where it was difficult enough for Ralia to buy food for his wife and two children, even if he had had money, had been eating into his healthy, hot-blooded body; that Ralia, the stubborn, masterful giant who knew no thwarting, was up against it. Perhaps Gauri, his shrewish wife, was making matters worse, for always there was a tug of war on between them to decide who should govern whom : Ralia resenting her pettiness and possessiveness, subduing her with an occasional beating followed by soft words; Gauri relentless and hard against his stubborness in not submitting to her constant and changing wants. Ananta wanted to contact Ralia and to assure him in some way, to cure the sickness of

Ralia's soul, but was a trifle afraid of his friend's inflamed obstinacy.

'Oh, go and eat the fresh air, brother,' Ananta ventured. 'Do you think that that wretch Channa will give you a job?'

Ralia straightened his head sullenly like an angry dog from where he was sitting, and gazed not at Ananta but at the fringe of sunlight which dappled the leaves of a pipal tree which jutted out of the roof of the factory shed. He had come to realize in the depths of his being that if anyone got a job here he certainly wouldn't, for both Murli Dhar and Gokul Chand were afraid of the freedom of his massive, untamable body.

'You talk as if Murli is your mother's lover and has told you all about these jobs,' he muttered between his closed teeth.

'Actually, I shouldn't put it past old Murli being my stepmother's lover,' Ananta answered with a smile. 'They might begin to fawn on each other, because he feels the vitality of old age and she, because she wants to secure for me the match that is coming from Jandiala for his grandson Nikka.'

The men smiled sterile smiles from claying faces, stricken with the inertia of heat and hopelessness.

'Then how much do you know, Ustad Anant Ram?' said Dina, the pale, reedy, limping clown, the bosom friend of Ralia, who was known as 'Timur Lang'.

'I know as little as you about this workshop, brother,' said Ananta, 'but I know something about the rate at which souls are sold in the markets of Bombai and Ahmedabad.'

At the mention of Bombay and Ahmedabad, the legendary cities far away, where fruits of gold were said to hang down in the orchards of the houses of big Seths and silver coins were hurled every year over the head of the blessed Aga Khan, the small knots of men turned interestedly towards Ananta, whom they usually ignored or treated as the prodigal son. Ananta knew that he could win them over all together far more easily than break down the suspicions of each of them individually. So he piled it on thick, exaggerating wildly, with the emphasis of his voice, what was really true but seemed melodramatic at this distance from the shores of the Arabian Sea.

'I tell you,' he continued, 'I have seen children sold for a handful of rice by parents too weak to walk. And you could buy a young girl and run a brothel for what you and I still give here for a midday meal. Oh, and as I watched the wailing children who had been separated from their parents, some really abandoned by their folk, I tell you, a fire swept over my body like ripples of scorching flames across a forest. And for days I burnt in myself with a slow anger which would burst into flaming tempers, till I was really running amok, shouting : "If only I could get hold of the illegally begotten scoundrels who had started this hunger I could gore them with the knife-twinge of my conscience !" '

'Oof... bale, bale, really ?' the crowd whispered as one man. 'And that in Bombai ?'

Ananta knew he had roused them and that he only had to give them one stirring call and they would be ready to go and murder. As an agitator in the Trade Union Movement he knew how to feel the pulse of the crowd. But, apart from the feeling of power he derived, he had learnt to be generous and not abuse that power.

'It is easy to get excited,' he said, 'and to run riot, because the fire of one soul catches another, and can set the whole world ablaze. But look how the ferungis have arrested the steam generated by fire in the engine. Their cool brains have controlled their passions so that they are able to imprison us all in a prison without bars. I understood this and tried to let the fires of hate in my body burn themselves to ashes. I knew that what was wanted was a militant passion against the wrongs which I saw in the Madanpura chawls, the cool heat which comes from knowledge and which alone will bring about 'Revolution'. But my Punjabi temper would burst out at the mere sight of those who not only tilted the scales and measures, but thieved large profits from foodstuffs while corpses lay in the countryside.... That is another story.... But when I want to tell you is the lesson of it. Don't let your sullen hatred simmer in the cauldron of this congested lane on this hot morning. If you have asked Channa whether he can give you jobs and he has said no, then resolve to get together as men. It will make us brothers and make our voice irresistible.... Now, Ralia brother——'

As soon as he uttered the very last words, he knew that the spell was broken. He had singled out one man from the crowd and the unaccountable reactions of this man would ruin the unanimity of their hushed listening.

'Did you, when at Hardwar, promise to give up wrong-doing ?' asked Ralia with a bitter sarcasm in his voice.

'Han,' said Dina Timur Lang, unable to resist the occasion

for the display of his particular talent for mockery. 'Did you resolve to practise self-denial during the last pilgrimage to the holy places of Hindustan?'

'Ohe, ohe, he had a sudden inspiration from heaven this morning,' said Viroo, alias 'Black God', a small, dark, elderly coppersmith with the bristles of white beard on his face.

'Ohe, Shanti! Shanti!' muttered Viroo's younger brother, Bhagu, blacker than the 'Black God'.

'Live as good neighbours,' said Arjun, a lanky, walrus-moustached thathiar.

Ananta knew that Viroo and all the older members of the coppersmith community were hostile to him because of his open liaison with Janki, but he had thought that he could influence Ralia and Dina with his talk. Now he realized that he had struck the wrong note after making a good beginning. They had been all attention at first but had then turned away in a kind of silent dissent. Their passions had apparently needed a spark from the hearth and not the mouthfuls of cold water moralizing. Their situation was certainly much more serious because they hadn't had a job of piecework to do for weeks, and, in some cases, months. And, obviously, the fact that he had been thak-thaking at a cauldron this very morning while they were waiting in vain at the gates of the factory shed to see Channa, made them much more bitter against him than they would have been. He cursed himself for the good luck which, through the friendship of the Kasera boy Khushal Chand, of the firm of Lal Chand-Khushal Chand, had secured him the only piecework he had had for a month, but which had singled him out as the enemy.

'Brothers,' he began.

'Oh, ja, ja, Ustad,' said Ralia impatiently. 'You went on a long journey, and you spent a great deal of sweat in going and coming, but you did not really perform the pilgrimage. You have come back flabby and spiritless from those parts. You talk like a schoolmaster when our blood is boiling.'

'There is that rape-mother Channa,' Dina Timur Lang said. 'Look at the way he is poking his sparrow's beak at us from the window in the door! Come on, open the door, traitor!'

'Go away, go away and don't sit there,' came Channa's squeaky voice, and then the aperture in the gate closed.

'How did he get in there?' asked Viroo. 'He certainly did

not pass this way through the gate.'

'Don't you know that there is a back door to the factory in the Ranwater Lane?' said Ralia.

'Like the maze of the Nabob who used to play hide-and-seek with the girls—this factory,' said Dina Timur Lang. 'Now that bastard has disappeared from the window. What shall we do?'

Ananta had stepped back from the gate and stood with his hands on his hips, a colossus, weighing up the tension in the air, as the clamouring voices of the coppersmiths rose in the stifling hot morning like whispers of doomed men asking for a reprieve from Channa, the angel at the door of hell. In the hollows of his own body and in the pockets of air through, the shimmering uncertain haze before his inner and outer eyes he could see the all-pervading word FOOD written large like the smoky letters drawn by a practising aeroplane over a cantonment. He had missed catching the glimpse which Channa had given the crowd and wondered what the foreman was up to.

'Knock at the door,' he said half in answer to Dina Timur Lang and half because he wanted the suspense of the silent resentment which possessed the men to expand itself.

Dina picked up a brick from the crumbling wall of the house by which he was standing and threw it at the gate.

'Ohe, take care!' bellowed Ralia, as the brick rebounded and landed near him on the curved platform.

Only the sharp screech of the machines and the monotonous hum of the gyrating belts came echoing across the shed, the death-rattle of the new song of the machine, urgent but already fixed as a conventional folk tune in Billimaran.

'I said, Dina Nath, brother, knock at the gate,' said Ananta.

Dina Timur Lang walked up in the curious goose-step he had invented to get over the defect, his shrivelled right leg forward while his left hand held his left hip and balanced his frame. He approached and knocked at the gate.

'Ohe, what do you want?' came the squeaky voice from behind the small window in the gate again.

And, immediately, the worried red little sparrow-face of Channa, the foreman, appeared in the aperture, a pair of steel-rimmed glasses on the small eyes, beads of perspiration on the sharp, beaky nose and the pink-white skin, fascinating like a Sahib's and horrible like a leper's.

'Come out,' said Ralia.

'I will not,' Channa said, waving his head so that the streaks of thin hair on his head fell over his forehead lined prematurely, by worries, for he was only thirty-four.

'Come on, ohe,' said Ralia vulgarly, imitating his voice. 'I am a married man, you need have no fear on that score.'

'There are no jobs here.' Channa said, opening and closing his thin lips in an indignant little pout. 'We are taking on the only man who is some use to us, Mehr Chand, who has been to a technical school. And he closed the aperture of the window forthwith and disappeared into the machine shop.

Dina knocked automatically at the gate with both hands. And Ralia rushed at the gate with his giant skeleton. But the great wooden door, with brass knobs on the squares designed by a clever carpenter of the last century, had been specially fixed so as to make the factory immune from such attacks.

'Where is this rape-mother Mehru? Let me rape the——. Where are you?'

Ralia turned from the gate cursing obscenely and raced towards the platform of a dingy shop opposite the well where Mehru generally slept. But the string bed, suspended from the shop door like a hammock, was empty.

'He has probably gone to perform his ablutions,' said Dina Timur Lang. 'He has certainly stolen a march on all of us.'

'He was here a moment ago,' said Bhagu, the sallow-faced younger brother of Viroo, as he adjusted the string which held his broken glasses on his ears.

Ananta could see the red-hot coals of fire which glowed in Ralia's eyes, if Mehru had been there, he might have been badly knocked about.

'I shall murder him!' shouted Ralia.

But Ananta knew that his friend was only boasting, for he knew that the flesh of all the coppersmiths had been aglow with rages and riots, though their spirits followed their bodies like shadows, helpless and broken, miserable in the face of the empty days and nights.

'This is the machine age, you know,' he said, 'in which each man is for himself, till he learns to unite with the others.'

'This is the machine age, the machine age,' Ralia repeated. And he seemed to go mad at the sermonizing tone in Ananta's voice. 'This is the machine age...' And then he began to mimic a wild caricature of the movement of machines and to rave: 'Yes, machines, machines, machines—phuff, phuff, phuff, grrr .... Yes, may I rape the mother of the machines inside there the, machines! ... Grrr ... They roar and they spit. They squeak and they squeal! They talk chapper, chapper like Channa.... They are the machines! Each one of those men there is a machine! That chapper chapper Channa and all those boys working in there are machines!'

Ralia's face seemed contorted with malice as he ground the words in his mouth and waved his hands towards the factory. And then he seemed to work himself to a flaming fury of vindictive passion: 'Han, but we shall live to see those machines crush the bones of that chappar chappar Channa as well as the boys. They were so eager to go to work in there.'

'By Parmeshwar, those boys will be crushed and broken,' shouted the Black God Viroo suddenly. 'I'll change my name if they do not break under the weight of those machines, as Mahatma Gandhi said they will, all those who trust themselves to the machines.'

'But I thought,' said Ananta, 'that you yourself wanted a job there! "Foxes finding the grapes sour"!'

The truth of this charge infuriated Ralia intensely and he writhed with maniacal bursts of hatred, foaming at the mouth, red in the face and shouting at the top of his voice.

'Han, han, our bellies drive us to want to dash our heads against that door!... See!.... Otherwise I, for one, wouldn't spit on the faces of people who leave the hammer to wrestle with those machines. Rape the mother of my luck!'

'Those boys are in the same position,' said Ananta. 'So why rave against them?'

'Ohe: leave your cleverness!' taunted Ralia. 'We know you have been to Bombai, but we are not impressed.'

'After all, the son of the shopkeeper came back and settled down in the shop,' said Viroo. 'Lecher!'

'Ohe, Ralia! Ohe, Viroo Mal!' said Dina Timur Lang. 'Ananta is our brother!'

'I don't know whether he is our brother or the brother of those traitorous boys there,' Viroo replied. 'But, by Ishwar, they shall all see, Ananta and those illegally begotten, who is stronger, the devil engines or them!'

'These fools think they can dominate the engines,' said Ralia. 'Use them, pull the lever, push, twist and turn handles and become Sahibs in the process and put on kot-patloon and oil their hair !'

'But, by Ishwar, they will see who is stronger,' added Viroo 'You can call me the son of an ass if they are not strangled by those monsters. If they do not break, if the bodies they have built up on the wrestling-pitch are not sucked away by the demons !'

'We shall see who will have the last laugh, chappar Channa and the boys, Ananta or myself !' said Ralia.

'Han, we shall see who shall have the last laugh,' Ananta said, as he saw the ridiculous figure which Ralia cut, possessed by all the sound and fury while the other coppersmiths looked on uncomprehendingly. The Clock Tower struck six ding-dong bells in the distance, and he felt a panic in his soul, almost as if he were in Bombay and late for the factory.

'Han, we shall see who shall have the last laugh !' Ralia raved with a resurgence of his pride and anger as he raced up to Ananta because the latter was drifting away. 'Bahin-chod, we shall see ! Look, look there, and, if you have had your ears cleaned of dirt, listen to what they are saying !' And he seemed to go mad again. 'They are laughing at you. Do you hear what they are saying ? "Chappar chappar... Cheekh... Phuff... phuff... Chappar... chappar... Cheekh." Fool, listen ! They are drinking the blood of those boys in there. They are swallowing their bones, masticating, crunch, crunch. And they are—'

And he began to dance the wild dance of a clown in a circus as he ran up to the gate of the factory and began to knock at the wooden frame hard, hard with his fists.

As Channa's ill luck would have it, he opened the aperture of the window at the moment and poked his head out. Ralia caught hold of it and slapped his face hard, so that Channa shrieked with terror.

'Father ! Father !' cried Ralia's little son Rhoda as he came up and stood watching the spectacle. He was frightened at his father's behaviour. 'Mother is calling you,' he said, clinging to his father's legs.

'Ohe, leave the foreman and go and attack the boss !' Ananta shouted.

'Come, come and calm yourself, Ralia Ram,' Dina said,

dragging at the lapel of Ralia's shirt. 'And go and show yourself to Gauran, or she will——'

'Get away, all of you !' Ralia raved. 'Get away, swine !'

But Viroo and Dina dragged him away, even as he still shouted after the receding figure of Ananta.

Little Rhoda's message from Gauri reminded Ananta of his duty to Janki.

'This is the machine age, the machine age. . . . I will rape the mother of this machine age !' Ralia shouted after the receding figure of Ananta and began to follow him.

'Ohe Ralia !'

'Ohe Ustad !'

'Ohe brother, come to your senses !'

The men shouted as they got hold of him.

4

AS HE THREADED HIS WAY THROUGH THE TENSE ATMOSPHERE created by Ralia outside the factory gates, to the cross-roads where Kucha Billimaran met Bazar Kaserian, Ananta affected a studied nonchalance. Partly he was overwhelmed by the spectacle of the wretchedness that had burst through Ralia's hysterical outbursts, and partly he was aware of their contempt for him going up to see his keep Janki. The violence of a vague hurt knocked between his ribs, and his heart palpitated at the tension among the men who had been part of the scene and his fear of them. Inside him his awareness of a poverty which spread from Madanpura to Billimaran burnt in a dark cloud, heavy and oppressive, and all he could do was to curse the country in which there was always an endless scarcity, punctuated every now and then by a famine. 'Lord God, what a land !' he muttered under his breath, as he withdrew his wincing eyes from the stares which followed him. And he felt as though an enormous shadow was creeping up to his neck from behind him.

When he got to the square and was about to cross the road to go upstairs to the room above the shop of Viroo, the tobacconist, where he lived with Janki, he looked back at the men in the lane. They were still following him with their gaze, even as they whispered to each other.

He thought he would hoodwink them by buying some cream cakes to make a cool drink for Janki while he waited to put them off the scent. He felt panicky and wondered why his conscience had suddenly become active, why his heart was taking up the accusation of immorality in their stares and giving way to a sense of shame which he had seldom felt before. After all, he tried to reassure himself, there was nothing wrong in putting the head-cloth on a widow's head, especially as her life would have remained a long series of insults if she had been condemned to mourn the death of an elderly husband to whom she had been married by arrangement. And he wished that the hearts of these men whom he loved, and whose humiliations he shared, would melt and smile at his misdemeanour and forgive him for his words outside the factory. In Bombay few people worried about illegal liaisons. But in small towns like Amritsar, where everyone knew everyone else, they were narrow-minded and malicious.

Another surreptitious glance at them and he was going to dart up the stairs, but he found Black God Viroo scowling at him. For a moment, waves of fury swept over him, burning his ears, and he muttered: 'Oh, may you die, filthy, stupid wretches!' Then Dina Timur Lang called out humorously, 'Ustad, you have dropped your loin-cloth behind you!' And everyone smiled. Ananta roared with laughter at the joke and his rancour against their censure evaporated, even as the edge of their contempt for him had withered and become a smile. Now there seemed to him to be something touching in their taboo, something even beautiful; even like the beauty of that rippling warmth which spread out of him for them. He showed his thumb to Dina Timur Lang cheekliy and, turning his back, raced up the creaking, wooden stairs.

Janki lay fast asleep on the superior Nawari bed which occupied almost half the room, a Kashmir shawl over her body. Her calm, fair-complexioned face, which tapered to a pointed chin across high cheekbones and a sensitive nose, seemed waxen, as if she were half dead. The image of her as he had seen her in his dream came back to him and he felt perturbed.

Ananta discarded his red native-style shoes at the top step and began to tiptoe towards her. He felt a faint nausea in his stomach with the fear that her temperature may have risen.

Long before he had met her at the shrine of the sages in the village of Kanowan in Gurdaspur district, she had been consumed by this insidious tuberculosis. He did not know when the disease had begun to eat into her, whether before the death of her husband or afterwards. But it made him impatient with apprehension, for if she died on his hands he knew what people would say about his having dragged her to ruin. And the accusation would have a particle of truth, because in his love for the cause, in the service of the trade union movement, he had often neglected her.

He bent over her to see her face more clearly in the half-dark of the room and he was reassured by the delicate dilating nostrils. He sat down on the edge of the bed and gently put his hand on her broad white forehead. It was warm like an underbaked earthen pot. He felt that in this way he could not tell how acute her fever was. So he searched for her wrist to feel the pulse. The limp curve of her feeble arm, with the drooping hands at the end, sent a curious thrill through him, almost as though it was the same limb which, leaping eagerly from the pillow, had in Bombay caressed him when he had come home tired. And, as he drew the arm out of cover and her mouth half opened with a moan, and he whispered tenderly to her, 'There is no talk, child,' he felt the nostalgia of those moments when, her hand in his, and his big chest heaving against her pigeon breasts, the moist pressure of her lips on his own, he had first had her on the terrace of the shrine at Kanowan, the day after all the other pilgrims had gone. In the confusion of the times through which they had lived since, with the mealymouthed advice and gossip of people rattling in their ears, and the constant search for a peaceful abode, that experience, right under the shadow of the presence of the gods, had remained most poignant.

The beat of her pulse was irregular, and he knew that still the slow silent fever clung to her, and came on at any time of the day or night, like a thief waiting for the opportunity to steal a little of her young life, evaporating into air to hide only for another opportunity to assail her. They had both got used to this robber and had accepted it as shadow which fell between them, constantly reminding them that it would, if and when it wished, part them for ever. And yet every time Ananta sensed its presence, he felt torn as though he were suspended by the tuftknot over the edge of the burning-ground in the hands of Yama, God of Death, while this hideous deity was flinging Janki on to the funeral pyre, the whole tension being heightened by the premonition that he would survive his beloved, to be pursued by yet another shadow, the unappeased ghost of Janki.

'I feel warm under this' Janki muttered as she opened her eyes; and then, stretching her limbs, she said: 'Is the sun out?'

Han—long since! Ananta said. 'But you must keep the covering on, even if you feel warm. You must sweat out this fever.... And I shall open a window to let in the light, if not the heat, of the Sun.'

Janki took Ananta's hand to her breasts and looked tenderly at him. But unlike the old days, he withdrew his eyes and hung his head down.

'What is it? What is the matter?' she asked.

'Nothing,' he said, 'nothing, Jankiai.' And he looked away at the room and the confusion of clothes, cooking utensils, faded flowers and fruits that were about. He was irritated by the disarray and wanted to clean up and set things in order. He was surprised at this impulse in him, for he had always reacted against his stepmother's love of cleanliness and had liked Janki because she believed in leaving loose ends about her.

'What is it? Tell me?' she importuned.

The half cry, half moan, of the voice affected him, so that his eyes welled up with tears and his face was covered with the flush of tenderness. He tried to ask himself what was wrong with him, because all his responses were evading him this morning. He knew the despairs of the lives around him; but he had taken the spineless curve of the gestures of the coppersmiths hitherto so much for granted that when he had been shaken out of his torpor by Ralia this morning he did not realize it immediately. But as Janki probed him with her insistent gaze, he became conscious of strange stirrings in the depths of his being, waves of self pity mixed with a deep remorse for others. Bathed in the shadows of the room, chained down to the life of this woman by invisible strings of emotion, his helpless frame twitched at the recollection of the hopeless crowd in the dull grey light of the narrow lane before the gates of the factory shed. He felt he had suffered with those men in the few moments during which Ralia assailed his experienced will with his stubborn ravings and beat up the foreman Channa, and that for all the tension between them he was involved with them as a piecework employee of the middle men, and as a person who had also been refused a job in the factory. All the gestures, looks and words with which they had expressed themselves were the cover of a breathless emotion that had often welled up in him too, before he tamed it, his thathiar conscience, a stupid, absurd, uncanny, instinctive passion which had often come on and possessed him even in the midst of the struggles in Bombay. It was an undisciplined, impulsive, simple reaction which said, 'It isn't right!' though he knew that that judgement did not apply in the complex hell men had made of this world. The audacity of the adventurer, the rogue, the lover, the rebel, the man who bore his life on the palm of his hands, as it were, and judged each situation as it came along, had only thrust this ball of smoke down into his belly, but not scotched it altogether. For the silence of the soul was not a sign of its disappearance, as the inactivity of a volcano is never the index of its extinction.

'Tell me,' Janki pleaded again.

'Childling,' he said, 'I didn't want to worry you, but things are bad out in the country. The shortage of food was bad enough when we were in Bombay, but now it has spread, so that, that, they say, in places men are rotting on the roadside. And, in Amritsar, larger purses have bought up big hoards and the grain has run out of the market. And the thathiars are in a worse predicament than the others. Not only have they no money to buy the little food they could get, but the Kaseras have not been giving them piecework to make utensils. The, factory which Gokul Chand and Murli Dhar have opened has taken in the men they want to make gadgets for the army, leaving the rest of us on the doorstep. This morning while I was maturing the cauldron which Lal Chand-Khushal Chand commissioned me, our dour Ralia and others were shouting for Channa, the foreman, and knocking at the gate ready to break his head——'

'What were they waiting there for if there were no jobs—a declaration of war?'

'No, they didn't expect an invasion from that sparrow Channa, they were eager to wage war against anyone they could get hold of.'

'What have we done?'

'Ralia and company think that I like the machines which have come into the lane and that these machines are the cause of their doom. They say that the teaching of Mahatma Gandhi is against the machines. So everyone should be against machines. And I don't know which way to begin to make them see that it is no use blaming the tools, but it is a question of who is master of machines—we or——'

'I am not sure,' Janki cut in, 'that these toys of Shaitan are not to blame!... Look at the slaughter of those men by the police in Bombai with machine-guns.... I heard their poor wives moaning all night. And I am terrified of those "flying ships"....'

'That has nothing to do with it,' Ananta said impatiently. And, for a moment, he brooded in silence.

'Tell the truth and be shouted at!' said Janki.

Ananta bent tenderly over her and pressed her head.

'I am not abusing you, childling,' he said coaxingly. 'You don't understand that when one is married off to a girl and she brings a bed in her dowry with her, one does not refuse the bedstead because it is too high to get on to easily. If one has a heart and is really capable of love, one likes a bridal bed better than a broken old string charpai. Like the fashionable Vilayati bride, we have accepted, we ought to accept the dowry of machines she has brought, and make use of them, provided we keep our hearts. Machines don't think or feel, it is Men who do.'

' "There is no talk of money, one must have a big heart!" ' Janki said in a mock heroic voice, quoting Ananta's pet phrase. And then she added with a faint, teasing smile, 'Sometimes you seem to me like a machine man or man-machine, puffing and blowing and talking and spluttering as though there was an engine inside you and not a heart. And your big hands and feet and rumps are just like the hands and feet of a machine—never getting tired.'

'You can abuse me as you like, childling,' he said in the manner of a conventional poetic lover.

And he got up and went to open the window to let the light in.

'There is something about you,' she said with serious concern in her voice, 'which makes people either your worst enemies or your best friends.'

'I am a much misunderstood person,' he said with a nervous laugh. Then he yawned and added: 'I think, Jankiai, I better get you some sherbet to drink instead of the whey that I was going to beat up with the cream cakes I have bought.'

'Hai!' she protested like a whimpering child. 'I would have liked some other taste than that sherbet of Banafshan all the time.'

'But, childling, think of your fever,' he said authoritatively, and proceeded to pour out the sherbet from a bottle by her bed. Then he tilted the cool earthen pitcher which rested on a wooden stand, and handed the tumbler to her.

'So you think this of me in secret,' he said, laughing a loud laugh to cover his embarrassment at the accusation latent in her frankness, for his ego was somewhat touchy this morning. It was true that he had the reputation of a selfish rogue, a scoundrel, that many more people hated him than loved him, and that he had always defied them with his untamed spirit, ignoring them with a contempt for their death-in-life, attitude, happy in his own resilient love which did not seem to exist on earth at all or even in the kind of heaven men believed in. For it was a love which lay in the hilariousness of his generous gong voice, casting jokes, laughter and talk with the abandon of a prophet of happiness, a love which came through the filthy endearing abuse he uttered and the quarrels he picked up when he was drunk, a love which was more than the contempt he felt for his elders, for his stepmother, the priests, and all those seemingly lofty people, a feeling which was much more anterior and which expressed itself perversely through the devotion to this lovely, withering widow, to whom he was not married according to the sacred custom of the seven gyrations round the ceremonial fire. And he also knew that though most men were anxious to hurt others, the people around him only talked about immorality and poured cold water on the warmth he exuded with stupidity rather than malice; and that they were more sinned against than sinning, more victims of the world's scoundrelism than scoundrels, even as he was more a victim of the world's roguery than a rogue.

For a moment he looked at Janki and hoped that he could see her faith in him written on her face. But Janki's visage was ubiquitous in its quivering deathly pallor, heightened by a rosy flush, as she drank the sherbet; her eyes were pathetic with the blue shadows that surrounded them as though they were the reflection of a message from the other world; her long black hair fell loosely about her as that of a frightening, though fascinating, witch.

'Have you taken that medicine that Hakeem Jalal Din gave you?' he asked paternally.

'What is the use of medicines,' she said with a muffled voice as though she were unnerved by the flush on her face.

'You must look after yourself, childling,' he urged, almost as if he were remonstrating with a naughty child.

'You can throw the powders on the bonfire of my body!' she said. 'Then I shall be cured for ever and enjoy good health in the next life.'

'If there is another life,' he mocked. 'And as no one knows, you had better not take any chances. Anyhow, death is repulsive.'

Janki tilted back her head and lay looking at the crooked beams of the ceiling.

In order to quieten the agitation of his nerves, Ananta began to beat up the cream cakes before him with a tin churner. He seemed to be absorbed by the querulous jerky motion of this miniature machine in his hands and thought of telling Janki how he liked the toy. Giddily he revolved the wheel attached to the handle, fast, fast, faster until the cakes splashed up to the neck of the small earthen jug. He waited for a moment and, turning his finger round the neck of the jug, collected the little grease that had got stuck there and licked it. Then he bent down and took a draught of the cool whey. But finding it a little too thick, he began churning it again. At that instant, however, there was an uproar in the street, a shrill hysterical wail, interrupted by moans and abuse.

Ananta rushed to the window which overlooked the square. He saw Ralia dragging Gauri by the hair, while she staggered after him alternately protesting and striking him with a broom in her right hand.

'Oh, leave go!' Ananta shouted.

But, knowing that such counsel would be of no avail to the couple, he rushed downstairs.

'Rape the mother of your mother!' Ralia roared. 'I will drag you to that drain, until you drink urine and eat dung for arousing me!'

'Vay! May you die! May you die!' Gauri whined as she

ran with short jerky steps. 'Look, folks, he is going to murder me! Look, brothers, he is going to murder me! This nasty man! Look, folks, for the sake of my children, save me, oh save me from his clutches. Folks, he is going to murder me!—'

'Ohe, let go!' Ananta said peremptorily to Ralia, as he got abreast of the couple.

Ralia relaxed his hold on his wife's hair.

In an instant Gauri struck out with her broom, hitting him on the chest, on the thighs, even as she protested: "The nasty man! Eater of his masters! He is so frightened of Murli! And he wants to murder me. Folks, he is going to murder me!'

At this Ralia pulled her hair in a fury of chagrin and shame and struck her on the face. The dread quarrel flashed for a moment in the shimmering early rays of the sun like dagger-thrusts in the heart of the morning.

Rhoda came weeping from Billimaran, his little baby brother in his arms, and stared at his parents locked in a shameful duel.

'Ohe, for the sake of your children!' Ananta said. 'Oh, come to your senses! Ohe, Bali, Hiroo—come and help me to separate them. Ohe, Dine!'

A crowd rushed forward from all sides, passers-by and shopkeepers and the few straggling coppersmiths who had not gone back to their hovels to try to arrange life a little.

Bali, the sherbet-dealer and grocer, jumped up and held Gauri, while Ananta tore Ralia away. Dina Timur Lang came limping along and tried to calm his friend: 'Come and have a shower of cold water at the bunga of Harnam Das,' he said. 'It is the heat, you know—spring has started early this year. That is why you are so violent this morning.'

Meanwhile Gauri had rushed to her children and, picking up the littler one, stood bleeding at the left ear while she shouted: 'Look, folks, the darkness has come. No food in the home. The rent owing. And he wants to murder me for telling him! The lazy scoundrel! Why doesn't he go and do a day's work? Drunkard! The brother of drunkards! And of whoremongers!'

Ananta knew the last words were aimed at him. And he didn't know what to say to her about the reasons for Ralia's not being at work.

'Ohe, ji,' he said. 'Go, good woman, and rest.'

'Eaters of your masters!' she answered, hugging her child. 'Even a sheep will defend its young....' And she retreated into Billimaran, the victor who had got the last word in.

They had no answer for her.

Ananta felt that they must all go and consult the poet, Purun Singh Bhagat, for advice before he could organize the coppersmiths into a union and plan a campaign on their behalf. But who were they to fight against? Who was the enemy? Gokul Chand-Murli Dhar, the dealers who used to give the coppersmiths piecework, or the Sarkar? He felt dizzy with the violence of the battle of wills in the shimmering airless morning. He felt he should go immediately and get a cold shower on his head. But first he must make Janki comfortable.

'Go Diney, brother, take him to the bunga for a bath!' he said to the sweating Timur Lang. 'Sardar Purun Singh is there—I shall join you soon! We should talk this out with a sensible man and then do something.'

5

LALA MURLI DHAR DIPPED HIS FEET GINGERLY IN THE DIRTY water of the small trough on the right-hand side of the Misri Bazar gateway to the Golden Temple. A heavy-bearded Sikh peasant near him was splashing the muddy liquid more vigorously to clean his feet before stepping down the sacred marble stairs of the holy of holies. Murli's ivory-coloured face flushed vividly against the silver grey of his neatly trimmed moustache and beard. He looked disapprovingly at the Sikh and winced a little. And yet he did not hurry away but only looked askance at the peasant as if he were demanding respect for his old age from the man and rather shocked that the Sikh wouldn't even keep his distance. In a moment, however, a female form brushed past him with a demure look under the shadow of the head-cloth on her forehead. That was his daughter-in-law. He edged away from the trough and followed her with the urgent gait of a youthful heart-squanderer.

The young piece-goods seller at the end of the Misri Bazar, who like all the people in the area knew of the old man's fondness for his daughter-in-law, teasingly sang to himself

the ribald duet which someone had composed, in the form of a plea from Murli's old wife for comfort:
'O Grandpa, press my limbs with your hands,
   I have been gathering spinach in the fields . . . .'
'Ram Ram Lala Murli Dhar,' a voice called out a more devout greeting from behind.

'Ram Ram ji, Ram Ram !' the old man said, turning back automatically, and felt panic-stricken to think that someone may have seen him following his daughter-in-law. And yet he was anxious not to lose sight of her. Everything seemed to be going wrong this morning. At first he had heard that scoundrel Ananta hammering away in the little shop opposite his big house, when he himself had tried his best to see that no dealer in Bazar Kaserian should give him work. Then Channa had come and told him of the threatening attitude of the thathiars as they had crowded round the gateway of the factory and of how Ralia had made a scene and beaten him. And, to cap it all, a stinking hill-man bathing on the platform of the well in Billimaran had splashed water on his neatly starched muslin clothes as he had emerged to go and perform the circumambulation round the Durbar Sahib. And then the Sikh peasant there had splashed muddy water on his legs. And now the boys were calling after him, especially when Seth Gokul Chand had appeared, for it seemed like his partner's voice. How could one keep one's prestige in these days !

He turned round and saw that it was, indeed, Seth Gokul Chand. Behind the facade of the courteous smile he put on, Murli felt impatient because he would now be plagued with all kinds of matters concerning the works which he would rather have left alone until after his visit to the temple.

'You are out early today, Seth Gokul Chand !' he said, trying to be casual, though his face was pale with guilt.

'You know how much work there is to do nowadays, Lala Murli Dhar. What with auditing the accounts ! And then I have to go to the station to get news of the goods, the sheets of brass, which seem to be held up somewhere. Traffic conditions are impossible nowadays. . . . I hear the railway workers are going on strike in various parts of the country, demanding bonuses and "dearness allowances". I wish we could both put a little more energy into the works. We want young blood, you know, Lala Murli Dhar. If only your son Sadanand would put in a little more time ?'

'No, brother, Sadanand must carry on the family craft as long as possible—we have connections with the courts of the hill princes and old clients everywhere. How can we drop them when people are turning silver into utensils ? And isn't Channa at the works all day ? And my grandson Gopi is there in the office. Of course, I am going to send my grandson Nikka to the factory as an apprentice.'

'That boy needs looking after. He is so small and pale.'

'Han, han, I know; but what can I do in my old age.' He is my youngest grandson and his mother is so fond of him.'

'And you are so fond of his mother,' mumbled Gokul Chand, with a mischievous smile on his elegant face adorned with a full upturned moustache. And then, having dipped his feet in the trough of dirty water, he pointed towards the entrance of the temple and said : 'Ao, come.'

And they both proceeded past the confectioner's shop, where devout Sikh pilgrims from distant cities were busy buying little baskets of kara parshad to offer at the shrine, past the stall where a burly Sikh was lifting the shoes, which people discarded before entering the temple, with a stick and putting them in neat rows all round him, past the beggars who sat on the edges of the marble stairs wailing for money and offerings in monotonous tones, and the hereditary musicians who played devotional songs to groups of pilgrims on the pavement. In a minute or two they had entered the vast courtyard at the foot of the Akal Takht, where hundreds of worshippers sat listening to a recitation from the holy Guru Granth.

Ordinarily Lala Murli Dhar was in the habit of sitting down here for a while, because it was here that the proudest mothers-in-law of Amritsar brought their youngest daughters-in-law to listen to the gospel, or rather to eat ice creams, sweet-sour potatoes, gram curry, chilled papadums and round, bubbly gol-gappas, filled with tamarind sauce, which were a speciality of the stall-keepers around the temple. Therefore it was the best hunting-ground for the young gallants, as well as for the old and tried hands, at the art of talking with the eyes. But the company of Seth Gokul Chand, who was middle-aged and intent on making a fortune, prevented old Murli from waiting even for a moment by the corner where he had a date with his daughter-in-law. Instead of relaxing for a while, out of sight of his prying family, to feast his eyes on beauty, he had now to put on the pose of the brave old man who, having gone past the age of pleasure, was now dedicated to the things of the spirit, the transcendental ideals, the realization of which was the prescribed last stage of life for all good Hindus.

'There are a great many people out here today,' Murli said, to put his partner off the scent as he cast a surreptitious look round. He felt the passion of old age tingle in his flesh at the sight of young faces and at the sound of young voices on the warm morning. The fact that he heard that Lala Ram Saran and his brother Lala Binde Saran had arrived to offer him the match of the latter's daughter for his grandson Nikka had elated him with the knowledge that, with his wealth, his prestige was rising; and the strange stirrings he had felt in his body at dawn showed that, apart from a few wrinkles and occasional tiredness, he could still feel the same urges as twenty years ago—when he was fifty. Only, he was afraid of a jerk, one of those sudden jerks which had happened to him at about forty-five, when he had begun to feel as if he were going down the abyss.

'The weather has been very hot,' said Seth Gokul Chand, disturbing Murli's ruminations. 'Suffocating it was last night— I couldn't sleep very well for thinking of those goods held up in transit, and the "hoom".'

'Hey Sri Wah Guru!' Murli mumbled with a forced piety, even as he joined his palms in obeisance towards the gates of the inner shrine which stood across a marble bridge in the middle of the square tank, the gold-plated holy of holies shining with a rich splendour in the bursting sunshine.

Then the old man resumed his steps, surveying the faces of the moving congregation for the figure of his daughter-in-law, because he hoped she had seen him and would make for the rendezvous which was in the garden, Guru Ka Bagh, out of the precincts of the Golden Temple, on the way to the pillared shrine of Baba Atal.

What is holding the goods up, Seth Gokul Chand? Surely the Sarkar wants us to make the parts, doesn't it?'

'No one knows. The Babu at the Goods Office says that the stuff is held up at Bombai. He wouldn't lie, because I tipped him generously the last time he secured delivery. Now we have enough for the next week, but I am afraid of a shortage of materials. Of course, the Sarkar has given us orders for a year. But you know, Lalaji the Sarkar's left hand does not know what the right hand does.... My only fear is that if we can't get any more materials, we can't employ any more unemployed thathiars. And that may create difficulties for us——'

'Han,' said Murli. 'I am the Chaudhri of my Panchayat, and they are already up against me for joining hands with you. They gathered round the factory gate this morning and became really nasty, so Channa tells me. But we can only take on a few of them if ever we do take any. I am taking on one, Mehru, whose mother is my wife's cousin. Things are very bad for them all, I agree, and they are my kith and kin, but——'

'I am for employing them all, though I think we should try and find room for the more experienced hands first.'

'No those who have opposed me at every step,' said Murli, stiffening with an ardent hatred of opposition, as though the will of his youth was welling up in him. 'We shall employ only the good gentlemanly sort among them, not rogues like Ananta and Ralia.'

And having said this, Murli frowned till his face wrinkled deeply. The irritation seemed to dry up the springs of emotion in him and he yawned with the fatigue that came on him so suddenly and made him feel as if he stood at death's door.

'Don't be angry with me, Lalaji,' said Gokul Chand. 'Only most of them are workless and hungry.'

'As they look on me as their father-mother,' said old Murli, 'I naturally want to see them happy.'

A little beggar-boy came from behind them, singing to the tune of the iron bangles on his hand, and put his bowl forward with a 'wilking', abject expression on his face.

Murli frowned again, gave him a pice and waved him away with the splendid peacock feather fan he carried in his hand. But as he looked back he caught sight of Ananta.

'If only you knew how I hate these low thathiars!' the old man began. 'They are eating my life up. Especially that Ananta, the scoundrel, who has come back from Bombai. There, he is behind us. He is corrupting the whole lot of them!' And he put his fan on his mouth by way of a signal to Gokul to talk softly.

'I should treat that man more gently myself,' Gokul said.

'I was going to ask you if we might offer him a job in the works.'

'Seth Gokul Chand ! He is a confirmed rogue, a drunkard, a whoremonger, who has abducted a widow from Batala and is living with her in the chubara above Hiroo the tobacconist's! He is leading the men astray.'

'I should employ him precisely for those reasons. A wild bird is better in the cage than flying about and tempting the caged ones with the fruits of the garden.'

'There are no fruits in the garden nowadays,' Murli said, withering to ashes with the fading fires of hate in him.

'Just as you like, Lalaji. You know the thathiars best.'

They walked along self-consciously for a while, the tension between them increasing with the noise made by the beggars, blind men and ascetics, reclining against the whitewashed walls of the surrounding houses, singing shrill hymns, chanting and moaning for a pice over their begging-bowls.

'Ohe look, ohe look at the old man—he is dressed up as if he is going to his wedding !' a child's voice called out from behind.

'And the other one, the son of Mishtar Marcado—half Sahib and half bania with his moustache !' another voice joined in.

'Didn't I tell you that he was a rogue !' protested Murli. 'It is Ananta putting those little thathiar boys up to make fun of us!'

Seth Gokul Chand looked back to see if he could recognize any of the mischief-makers. Only Ananta was coming along, his flanks swaying like those of a Brahminee bull. And there was nothing furtive above his approach either, as he came up and bawled in a respectful but slightly impudent tone : 'I fall at your feet, Seth Gokul Chand. I fall at your feet, Lala Murli Dhar !'

But somewhere from among the crowd came the lilt of the duet about the difficulties of love between Murli and his old spouse :

'O Grandpa, press my limbs with your hands,
I have been gathering spinach in the fields. . . .'

'I will beg your leave,' said old Murli hurriedly to his partner, irritated by the teasing tune to the pitch of desperation. 'I have to go round quickly, for there are some gentlefolk from Jandiala coming to offer a match for my Nikka today.'

'May your tribe increase!' congratulated Gokul Chand with a faint trace of mockery in his voice.

As Murli walked away, Ananta repeated his respectful greetings to the old man.

'Come, bai Anant Ram,' said Seth Gokul Chand with a show of cordiality as he stood to take off his clothes on the pavement of the tank in preparation for a dip in the holy water. 'Whither?'

'Oh, just for a stroll around and a bath, Sethji. I have been wielding the hammer half the night.... And how is your exalted temperament?'

'I thought I would come here and have a dip in the tank, son.'

'Not just a tank, but the ocean of nectar!' said Ananta, pointed to the green scum that spread in the corners of the muck and water that gives its name to the city of Amritsar.

'As you would say, those are the sins of rich people like me floating about,' said Seth Gokul Chand with a laugh at himself. 'Still, I can skim them with my arm, and have a dip to purify myself.'

Ananta softened to the astute Seth, and was on the point of inviting him to a cool, pure shower at the well in Sant Harnam Das' bunga. But he thought that would be too familiar, though he was a friend of Gokul Chand's younger nephew, Khushal Chand.

'You must enjoy yourself,' he said.

'No, no, every time I meet you I feel guilty,' Seth Gokul Chand said.

'Then I shall remove myself from your sight at once,' said Ananta with a jovial smile. 'I fall at your feet.'

'Oh, wait, where are you going?'

'To the bunga there for my bath,' said Ananta. And he strode along, both because he didn't want to make Seth Gokul Chand feel more guilty at present and because his little cronies, Ralia's younger brother Rama and little Rhoda, who had been cheeking the two headmen of the Kasera and thathiar communities respectively, were likely to show up from between the legs of people, where they were playing hide-and-seek, spoil the atmosphere of cordiality between him and Gokul Chand.

6

THE ROGUE IN ANANTA WAS ELATED AT THE CONTACT WITH THE two old rogues who, he felt, were soon going to be pitched in a dire struggle against the unemployed coppersmiths. He felt as if he had gone like a decoy horse into the enemy camp and gauged the strength of the hostile forces, as they used to do in the old days, when a king, wanting to fight another, sent a decorated steed across the frontier to see if the next Rajah would molest it. And he thought he knew, from his instinctive reactions to both the bosses, who was for the thathiars and who was against them. This knowledge, he felt, was a great gain, for he would be able to do what the Angrezi Sarkar always did to perfection, divide his enemies. He must think out the strategy at once, some trick which would appeal to the stubborn Ralia and the other thathiars, and which may also be sanctioned by the local political leaders. In spite of everything, however, he liked the two old men, and the sheer exhilaration of meeting them like this prevented the strategy against them from maturing in his head. If it had been Ralia or Viroo, they might have decided to state their grievances against the factory owners with their fists or called them filthy names and accused them of being dirty old men, who came eyeing young damsels in the Durbar Sahib; but he himself felt (partly because of his own unconventional way of living) that to call names and impugn the sexual morality of your enemy was to prove by lust something against greed, a passion completely dissimilar and one which arose from quite different causes. True, he had put up the two little boys to make old Murli uncomfortable, but that was merely fun. But he almost felt a fellow-feeling for the old men, especially for Murli, who preserved a young heart through all the scandal-mongering that went on about him and his daughter-in-law. Where were the little boys, though ?

He stopped walking and, turning, looked around among the throng. He wished he hadn't raced ahead and hadn't had to ask the little ones to stay behind and not show up before Murli and Gokul, because he wanted to go and buy them some fried bread to take home to Gauri by way of appeasement, as he knew that there was no flour in Ralia's home at all. He called :

'Ohe, Rhode ! Ohe, Ramia, ohe !'

There was no sign of them and he became slightly anxious, as the hands of the clock in the tower ahead of him stood at a quarter to seven, and he felt he had so little time to do all the things he had to do, bathe and see the leaders before he could go and deliver the cauldron and collect his wages from Lal Chand—Khushal Chand & Co. He thought it was lucky that business hours for the rich shopkeepers in Amritsar didn't begin till nearly midday.

'Ohe, Rhodia !' he called again, cupping his hands over his mouth.

There was no answer. And he began to stroll back on the slippery edge of the tank to get on to the promontory of a terrace from which he could look back, though he did not want to go too far back and meet Seth Gokul Chand's eyes again, for that would be an anticlimax.

This was the curious thing, he asked himself, 'Why do I feel so tense ? I, who have always done what I liked and not cared a fig for the elders, betters, or even my own kith and kin ? Why do I feel so concerned, suddenly ? I, who didn't care for what the world said, believed in no God, law or principle except my own will ?. . .' For a moment he felt that he was probably tired after hammering half the night. Then, suddenly, it occurred to him that he had a disturbed night, for he had awakened in a sweat through the nightmare, as he had lain by Janki's side.

But now behind him his legs were in the grip of little Rhoda, who was shouting alternately with Rama :

'Eh, Lala Ananta Mal !'

'I fall at your feet, Lala Ananta Mal !'

'Ohe, ohe'. Where have you been ?' Ananta laughed, as he played hide-and-seek with the little devils. 'Come, I am in a hurry !'

'What is the great hurry, Lala Ananta Ram ?' asked Rhoda cheekily.

'Ram Ram, Lala Ananta Ram ! Radhe Sham !' said Rama, continuing the inane greetings.

'Where have you been, pigs?' Ananta said genially.

'We have been trying to get donations of kara parshad from the rich pilgrims by the temple, Ustad,' said little Rhoda mischievously.

'And from the look of you, you don't seem even to have got a morsel.'

The boys smiled sheepishly, their eyes filled with a sly appeal.

'Come on,' he said. We will go up to the bhai Sikh confectioner near the house of Sardar Gurbax Singh Barishter, and see if he is frying any puris.'

And he sped along with the kids running little capers of joy behind him. For the rogue and scoundrel that he was to the elders of the thathiar community, he was the idol of the youth of the craft. Partly it was the contagious warmth exuded by his well-knit body, the rounded proportions of a frame which seemed to combine a tiger's fury with the casual dignity of an animal who did not need to throw his weight about. Also, there was the air of the rebel about him, the man who worshipped no God and feared no mortal and had travelled further by train than anyone else in the neighbourhood. And there was his large, expansive, generous manner, the open, frank, hearty speech which endeared him to those whose impulses were yet free from restraint—a remnant of childishness in the mature wine of life with which he was intoxicated, but of which no one knew very much, and of which even he himself had had only a few glimmerings.

'Oh, uncle, there is someone distributing kara parshad in the lane there,' Rhoda said eagerly.

Before the boys had moved, Ananta tied the extra loin-cloth which he carried in his hand into an untidy knot on his forehead, rolled the shoulder out of his tunic, so that the sleeve dangled forlornly, and darted into the subway which led, by the platform of the Clock Tower, into the little street before the house of Sardar Gurbax Singh, Barrister-at-law.

Assuming an abject, beggarly expression, he rushed towards the donor of gifts, a rich merchant with a Peshawari slate-coloured silk turban on his head, and said over the heads of the other beggars who crowded round:

'Sardarji, may the Gurus bless you, may you prosper——'

'Get away, scum, get away! the pilgrim said. 'I haven't yet made the offerings in the temple. Go inside the temple!'

'Oh, give,' Ananta simulated the whine of the oppressed. 'Give in the name of Wah Guru to one who is a Sikh at heart, but is not allowed to beg inside the Durbar Sahib, because he looks like a Mussalman.'

The rich pilgrim fixed him with his stare for a moment.

'Give, Master, for the sake of these orphans I have picked up.'

The halting realism of his histrionic display of the honest beggar wronged in the temple of a religion which had been founded to reconcile Hinduism and Islam touched the donor to the quick. He put one of the three baskets his servant carried into Ananta's hand and proceeded.

'May you prosper, Sardarji!' Ananta simulated the beggar's blessing manner. 'May your family prosper for three generations. . . .' And he began to dig under the greasy leaves which covered the hot halwa for chunks to give to Rhoda and Rama.

But the youngsters and female beggars in the subway crowded round him, crying and wailing, thin, wheezy little gasps of cries, moaning and 'wilking'. 'Oh, Baba de, oh, give, for the sake of God, give!'

Suddenly, impetuously, in order to get rid of them, he threw four loaves of fried bread in the air for the youngsters to catch. And when they all raced towards it, he gave a bit of halwa to each of the women. Then he handed the basket to Rhoda and Rama and told them to go away.

As his two wards fled with the basket, he found himself standing in the middle of the passage, alone, bereft. For all the beggars, young and old, were now scrambling over a stinking rubbish-heap on which the four puris had fallen. They fought each other with loud curses and abuse, sweating and straining and tearing each other's rags, while those who were nearest the food beneath the little mountain of bodies shrieked to get out.

He rushed to the heap and began to drag the beggar-boys away forcibly. Partly out of fear for him, partly out of sheer fatigue and weakness, they did not resist his strong arm.

'Oh, forgive my son and do not beat him,' one mother cried from the mouth of the subway. 'Baba, forgive, he is only wanting it for his little sister who is here. Oh . . . !' And she beat her head and her breasts crazily.

Ananta removed the more guilty and separated those who had gripped one puri below, their faces bespattered with the dog-dung and the slime of the drain which covered the rubbish heap.

'Ohe, don't eat it,' he said. 'I will get you more.'

But the two youngsters still remained locked in combat.

'Ohe, look,' Ananta said. 'There are three others there, not soiled.' And he lifted them in his hands and ran into the Line ahead.

At that instant an eagle swooped down like an arrow, snatched the food out of his hand and left a track of spurting blood on his forefinger.

'Oh !' he shouted, and then became dumb with anger and frustration.

For a moment he stood like that, thoroughly ashamed of himself for swindling the rich donor and then creating this riot among the poor beggars who were much more desperately in need of a morsel than even Rhoda and Rama or the bitch Gauri. He did not know how to face the beggars. And for that reason he felt a revulsion of hatred against them. His eyes fell on little heaps of refuse all along the edge of the drain. 'The dirty Bikanaries !' he muttered, lifting the end of his loin-cloth to his nose. And he began to walk back towards the marble pavement of the temple, cursing himself for abusing the wretches.

Behind him the two boys who had been fighting over a puri abused him in common :

'Sala, elephant !'

Their mothers, sitting further up now, also vent their spleen.

'Like a bull, the swaggering fool, fighting those who are younger than him !'

'If only my husband were alive to teach him the lesson of his life !'

'Oh, don't talk of those who are gone ! I can't bear to think of my little one dead !' another woman said, raising her head-cloth to her eyes.

Ananta's heart was knocking with self-pity as with the remorse he felt for the kids who he had robbed on the dung-heap. Tears welled up into his eyes and a cloud covered his sweating face, while within his stomach the bile of a terrible sickness rose. He tried to beckon the salt under his tongue to stop him from vomiting into the 'ocean of nectar' and walked along in a recalcitrant void, filled with forebodings from the nightmare he had had and possessed with a superstitious awe such as he had never acknowledged in himself before.

The classical tune, which a hereditary musician was playing on a sitar to an audience by the Clock Tower gate of the

Golden Temple, filled his heart with a feeling of deep sorrow and released in him a view of the impermanence of all things. As soon as he realized this he hurried away like a thief in panic.

7

THE CHARITY HOUSE OF SANT HARNAM DAS WAS A BUILDING overlooking the Golden Temple on one side and adjoining the Clock Tower on the other. A large, three-storeyed house, it was a centre of worship, established under the last will and testament of a holy man named Harnam Das, to provide a place for communal prayers and community singing, smaller than those in the temple courtyard, and to house itinerant 'men of God' when they came to Amritsar from different parts of the country. The vast rooms of the three upper storeys were so designed as to make devotional contact as fervent and contiguous as possible, and the acoustics of the rooms were suited as much to the delicate strains of the classical musicians who came and played their old instruments here for comparatively larger congregations. The people who were in charge of this *ashram* were life members of a new Sikh society, attached to the place in the spirit of *bhakti*, devotion through work and service. But, although it remained a Sikh shrine in spirit and practice, like many other such houses round the Golden Temple, the arrival of a new warden called Puran Singh Bhagat, an itinerant poet and scholar who had been to Russia, China, Japan, and Britain, and who was known to be a devotee of a new kind, had led to the place becoming a centre of the city's political organizers and workers like Ananta. The latter had initiated all the other thathiars to the shrine. And, as the compound of the house offered social amenities, such as a well with the public bath built round it and a wrestling-pitch, the place had become very popular and led to some pouring of the old wine of the Sikh ideal of service and devotion into the new bottles of the minds of men, who came here robbed of all content of belief in the holy books without being filled with another faith. Also, it had led to the breaking of many old bottles which were tightly corked and refused to open, as well as to the spilling of a great deal of liquor down the drain ! In fact, the place was the centre of a great deal of heterogeneous life, and many varieties of experience, among which the only connecting thread was the curious Indian acceptance of all and sundry, without any attempt on the part of one person or another to impose his own peculiar vision on the rest, except that every one objected to the plain-clothes members of the Criminal Investigation Department, who frequently came to lodge here and were, when discovered, thrown out by the scruff of the neck by the voluntary effort of the habitual visitors.

When Ananta came in, the multiform, multi-tongued throng of bathers, the mud-bespattered wrestlers and the pilgrims were all listening to the Black God Viroo, who was holding forth from the platform of the well where he crouched, while Ralia and Dina were both rubbing oil on his body. Puran Singh Bhagat, a gentle-eyed, hefty man of great height, dressed in clothes of homespun khaddar, stood with a newspaper in his hand as though just about to leave. The miscellaneous crowd sat about in the courtyard. Some of the men were chewing the twig brushes with which the devout are wont to clean their teeth, some were gargling, some rubbing soap on their bodies after they had dipped themselves under the lion-mouthed jets of water, which were attached to reservoirs filled from the top with bucketfuls of water drawn from the well.

'... a demon took a monkey to wife, Sardarji, and the result, by the grace of God, was the Angrezi race,' Viroo was saying to Puran Singh Bhagat. 'And they will be consumed in the same fire which they have started.'

His eyes fell on Ananta as the latter entered the courtyard and went towards the verandah to disrobe, and he greeted him aggressively, even as his body sank under the hands of the masseurs. He enjoyed being massaged because in this way he could get the illusion of being a wrestler, necessary to offset the feeling that the ugliness of his body gave him. The triumph of the athletic frame helped to drown the sorrow of never having been offered a wife by any member of the coppersmith community and confirmed the frog's soul into the respectable pose of an old uncle.

'I fall at your feet, Anant Ram ! So you have come back to our fold, safe, unscorched !' he said.

'"Unscorched"? How do you mean, unscorched ?' Ananta whispered, turning surlily towards the old man.

'Why, unscorched by the fires of hell that you are helping to light, the leaping flames of which have licked the very heavens, until God sits uneasily on His throne in the sky. Don't you see that the flames are enveloping the whole universe, and even spreading to the sacred city of Amritsar!'

'I can't even buy a box of matches nowadays,' Ananta said with a melancholy humour, 'and you talk of me setting fire to the universe!' And proceeded to disrobe on the verandah.

'Kamma, a poet of my youth,' parried Viroo, 'made a song about those matchboxes which you as a poet will understand, Sardar Puran Singh.' And he recited in a hoarse, high-pitched voice:

> 'Two matchboxes for a pice—oh, Lala
> Take two for a pice, Babu . . .
> Buy two for a . . .'

'And,' he continued, 'the fable of this matchbox shows how the white race has set the whole world on fire. The matchbox was made in Vilayat and brought here in ships——'

'Matches are also made in Japan, and in our own country,' put in Puran Singh Bhagat with a laugh, his huge dumpling of a nose enlarging with his smile. 'I have seen them being made in the factories of Japan.'

'But they began to be made in Vilayat, by the scions of the monkey race, and were transported here across the seas, Sardarji. The merchants here were eager to buy them up and sell them at a profit. And, with the profits, came this "Mine" and "Thine". And the monkey race thrived and were happy. And the big Seths in this land, too, rejoiced. But the greed of profits on the matches set fire to the hearts of the poor in Hindustan and burnt them up until they have been reduced to ashes and cinders.'

'That is why uncle Viroo is so black, brothers!' said the irrepressible Dina Timur Lang, leaving off the massage and crouching by the old man. 'He got covered with the smoke of the fire, the ashes and the cinders!'

'If it is the profits that hurt you, brother,' said Puran Singh Bhagat with a gentle smile, 'then, like Ananta, I am with you. But you will agree that the matchbox is a blessing, even when made by Kruger.'

'Who is Kruger?' Dina asked in a mock English accent.

'Never mind!' protested the Black God. 'If he made profits, he was the Devil's own son! He will reap his reward!'

'That he did, brother,' said Bhagat. 'He gambled on the lives of millions and then got so entangled in his swindles that he crashed and committed suicide. But whatever the poet Kamma says, there is nothing wrong about matches.... They make a light even as they burn a fire.'

'Oh no, Sardarji, he would rather light a fire by striking one stone against another,' said Ananta. 'And he would leave the rest to God.'

'Oh no,' mocked Dina, 'to be correct, he would rather take his pair of tongs to somebody else's hearthfire than spend a pice on a matchbox.'

A ripple of laughter went through the crowd.

At this, Ralia, who sensed that the feeling of the throng was running against Viroo, and who felt that the Black God had been rightly indignant at the iniquity of the factory owners and of machines, left off massaging altogether, twisted his lips and waxed ironical:

'Ah, what to say, electricity is such a boon! The whole world was dark before it was discovered. There was no sun, no moon and no stars. You couldn't see the "hills from the mounds", or the copper under your nose until electricity came to the city of Amritsar! Oh, and as for the phuff-phuffing Rail Injan, why, it never gets tired, though it always sounds as if it is out of breath and hungry, even after devouring all the grain on the land, or at least burning it and ruining it with its soot! And, aha, what to say of that engine of destruction, the bird of steel, which excretes bombs and urinates bullets! All made in Vilayat! The guns! The rifles! The machine-guns! All the Devil's instruments for destruction.'

'All made by the scions of the monkey race,' said Viroo.

'And installed in our midst by the worshippers of Bhairon and Hanuman,' mocked Ananta, referring to the millions of Indians who had readily accepted railways and telephones.

'All for profits,' insisted Viroo. 'Against the will of God!'

'Shared by the cousins of the monkey race here,' insisted Ananta.

'That is the point,' said Puran Singh Bhagat, caressing his beard, even as he twitched his head, in the nervous manner he had, before beginning to explain. 'Men look to meanings as fools to deeds and children to their mothers' love. And, brothers, we should see who is to blame before condemning a dead instrument. Nothing is worse than active ignorance.'

'And in apathy lie the seeds of rot,' said Ananta.

'Two boxes for a pice, brother,
Two boxes . . .'

Viroo sang the refrain stubbornly.

'You are right in a way, brother,' said Ananta to win him over. 'But now you can't even get a box for an anna! . . . listen to Sardar Puran Singh.'

'Your heart sinks within you that you can't buy matches to set fire to your soul !' said Ralia.

'Smoking those Vilayati hukkas such as you have brought from Bombai. Son of the devil ! Cousin of the white monkeys !' raved Viroo, insulted and sticking to his stand. 'The student Satyapal has told me where you get your money from—Sarkari spy that you are !'

'Uncle !' protested Puran Singh Bhagat. 'Guru Nanak Deo has said, "Evil-mindedness is a low woman, anger an animal without direction, whereas in love and understanding men are equal." Such sharp words against one of your own cousins are not worthy of you.'

'No cousins of mine, but a drunkard and a whoremonger !' retorted Viroo, rising from where he crouched, the whites of his eyes bloodshot. 'No cousin of mine who is seen talking to Murli and that Gokul ! The traitor—shitting in one place and urinating in another !'

'Oh uncle !' Dina counselled, as he saw knots of men rushing up from all over the courtyard to see the fun. 'Come to your senses.' And he repeated one of Ananta's pet phrases : ' "There is no talk of money : you must have a big heart !" '

'It is me you ought to abuse,' said Mehru, thrusting his blinking, pupilless eyes to the sun as he came up dressed in an open-necked cotton shirt and muslin dhoti after his bath. 'My mother has got me a job in the factory and I am going there now.'

'And I shouldn't be ashamed of taking a job there, brother,' said Puran Singh, patting Mehru affectionately on the shoulder. 'These are bad times. There is little to eat. And the Sarkar may be oppressing us, but the people of Vilayat are the friends of the peoples of Roos and Chin, and on the side of truth against falsehood.'

'What, the white monkeys ? The devils—they—on the side of Truth ?' said Ralia. 'They shot us down there in Jallianwala Bagh as if they were the "doots" of hell reaping a harvest of death. . . . And now they come asking us to make gadgets for bombs in Murli's factory.'

'Don't you take any notice, Sardarji,' said Ananta to Puran Singh. 'They all wanted to eat dung and drink urine in that very factory this morning !'

Ananta was suffocated with rage and bit his lips with the torment of their distrust and his own lack of argument, in defence of the evil Sarkar. And he stood and shook like a tree as though testing its power to withstand the storm. 'They really ought to have some light to illumine the darkness around them.'

Puran Singh Bhagat sympathised with Ananta, but tactfully did not speak.

'You'd better look out and not put your tail on fire and get burnt, my son !' exclaimed Viroo. 'And don't drink and smoke those cheroots and sleep with that whore of a widow whom you have not wed !'

'Ohe, uncle, don't behave like the Black God,' said Dina Timur Lang. 'Cast-up dust doesn't hide the moon, and Ananta is one of us.'

'Ohe, uncle ! Don't be a fool ! even Ralia protested.

'Peace, peace and patience,' said Sardar Puran Singh Bhagat. 'You trust me and I shall explain what Ananta means to you when I come back from the court.'

'What is the quarrel about ?' asked a pilgrim.

'They nearly beheaded me, Ananta brother, before you came,' said Mehru. 'But I willingly offer my head to you.'

'Go, your mother must have slept with Murli,' said Ralia. 'Go.'

Ananta shook with fury, his mouth frothing at the corners of his lips, his body sweating, his temples bursting, and the ball of smoke he had sensed in his stomach all this morning smouldering as if the solid matter in it was being ignited slowly by the sulphur of those matches that they had been talking about. He felt that the breath of foul calumny had reached its limit when such abuse was hurled against Mehru. And he writhed in an agony of frustration as he gasped in a vain attempt to find a way of communicating to these men the core of his tenderness, the despair and the hope which he felt for them inside him, to tell the roughnecks of the possibilities of joint action in their difficulty, to assure them of the world of Roos beyond the world of Amritsar, so that they could see with the help of the flame inside them as Puran Singh Bhagat could perceive the Truth so clearly and with such humility. At last, he clenched his teeth, swallowed the pride of his body, and said :

'Test a friend in trouble, brothers. And I beg you with my joined hands to see that if we want to prosper we must not fight amongst ourselves. All the world is in a whirl in whicц men and women are devastating each other, while delirium burns the cities and villages of Hindustan. I tell you there is no hope for our land except in Revolution. But that requires devotion and thought. Perhaps it will be achieved throughs Uncle Viroo's belief in Karma; if not, by reciting the verses of! Karma. "Sow good deeds and you will reap good deeds— only I believe you get your reward here on earth and not in heaven !" Let us go and consult those who know how to organize for the struggle against the employers. See, come and meet Mishtar Latif with me. And wait for Sardar Puran Singh to come back from the court, where he has to appear because he is on bail. You know that he is a Bhagat, a devoted one, who is not covetous or greedy, who has entered our struggle because of his love for the poor even as he turned his back on family life once to search for God.'

'A thief who has to appear in court can't help those who have never stolen,' said Viroo primly. 'I put my trust in my *Kismet* and my God !'

'Eh, Sardarji,' Dina Timur Lang said, apologizing for Viroo's bad temper, 'Uncle is rude because he has had nothing to do for days and he was so used to work.'

'There is no talk,' said Puran Singh Bhagat, touching the feet of the Black God. 'Now you all go with Ananta and see Mr. Latif. Finish your ablutions and go. . . . And I will see you as soon as I can get away from the court.' And he joined hands in obeisance to them, twitched slightly as he adjusted his turban, patted Ananta on the back, gazed at the giant hands of the clock in the Clock Tower overhead and gasped, 'Nearly eight o'clock ! And I have to be in the court at nine !'

'Come on,' said Dina Timur Lang, clowning to relieve the tension. 'A shower from the mouth of those lions there will cool the tempers of all the fools and leave wise men wiser.'

8

ALL THE ELEMENTS SEEMED TO HAVE CONSPIRED AGAINST ANANTA this morning, for he found himself eating the dust of the road outside the bungalow of the famous Amritsar leader Sheikh Abdul Latif an hour and a half later. He had overcome the hostility of his friends and persuaded Uncle Viroo the Black God to come with him to see Mr. Latif, while he had given Ralia and Dina a rupee to go and buy some puris and pickles to eat for breakfast. On arrival here he had been told that the leader was out eating the fresh air. So he had waited patiently with Viroo facing the board which advertised the great leader to the world as Sheikh Abdul Latif, M.L.A., M.A. (Cantab), Barrister-at-Law in both the English and the Urdu alphabet. But after a while Viroo had got tired of looking at the lurid inscription and left to join Ralia and Dina in the food queue. And then, with the heat of the sun pouring down on his head and the dust of Kutchery Road rising to his nostrils, his own patience had been exhausted. On making further enquiries from the same ubiquitous servant who had told him Sheikh Sahib had gone for a walk, he had been told that Mr. Latif had gone to Lahore early this morning and wouldn't be back till the evening. The bottom seemed to fall out of Ananta's soul. He got up and began to walk away from the exalted man's doorstep. But he did not know how he would justify to his coppersmith brothers the great faith he had built in the superior wisdom of this elusive leader. He decided to brave it, however, and to go and find them in the food queue, and headed towards the yekka stand outside the Amritsar Railway Station a quarter of a mile away. But, for all his attempts at bravery, the shadow of a strange oppression seemed to be descending on him, like the doom which the old thathiars talked about, a demon of fear projecting itself on him as though from the back of his head through memories of his nightmare—or was it the collective weight of the men's grievances which loomed large above his eyes, a cruel good, exacting and stubborn as a donkey.

He felt alone and his heart palpitated like a wild bird with flapping wings, as though he had been caught in the trap spread by some wily invisible hunter. The prim, elegant hedges around the bungalows and the perfume of the sweet peas in the garden bowers on the roadside seemed to make his isolation more complete. For though he did not see one white face the grim weight of the reticent Sahib's frowns hung over the atmosphere of the Civil Lines, a bigger cloud of oppression than any other. His body sweated profusely and his pace quickened.

As he sped past the General Post Office he thought of the days when he used to come to the cinema opposite, and felt a little easier. For this was the borderland between the Sahib's world and the 'native' city into which he had often ventured as a youth. Then he had felt like a wild bird, with his flock of companions, flying giddily with him, away from their little nests in the town, reeling, somersaulting, freewheeling into the open spaces beyond. Often he and Ralia and Dina and Bali and Khushal and the younger boys from Bazar Kaserian and Kucha Billimaran had gone playing hide-and-seek all the way, changing the face of the town, pulling the turbans off the heads of the dead-in-heart respectable shopkeepers, cheeking the 'burnt-up' pedestrians, eating and drinking, playing pranks, gay and carefree. Gone were those days now, he felt, gone for ever ! For good fortune seemed, nowadays, to come at random, while misery knocked unfailingly at the doors of one's life. Would he ever be able to laugh again ? he asked himself. Would he be able to untie this tangle in which he and the other thathiars had got entangled and be the carefree, wild bird again, who did not have to do anything but fly ?

For a moment he felt, elated with memories of his adventurous youth and glanced from side to side at the peasants going in small bunches towards the court. Apart from the worried faces of these lean and swarthy men, with their sunbaked brown legs and feet covered with dust, the whole atmosphere of the Civil Lines was peaceful, the sunny stillness exuding a rich warm smell as of bursting spring through the overheated grass and flowers.

But as he took the corner into the Queen's Road and walked beyond the Y.M.C.A. Church towards the Railway Road he seemed to travel from the heaven of the Civil Lines into the hell of the native city.

For here were swarms of women and children, running after tonga and yekka carriages, with outstretched hands, begging for a pice, their faces contorted into smiles which were the composed expressions of abject hopelessness, a grim mockery of utter despair. They would run along halfway up to the crossroads where the blue-and-red-turbaned policeman stood on point duty, and then suddenly edge away and join the broken heaps of those who were tired of begging and had sat down to await their fates, as if the last vestiges of strength in them were exhausted.

Ananta had seen beggars before, but today they seemed to him to have sunk to the lowest depths of degradation. He recalled his experience with the destitute kids in the alley by Durbar Sahib two hours ago, and he found the bile of a strange sickness emerging in his mouth, even as he noticed the soiled crumbs of a chapati mixed with lentils in a bowl shared by five children. Was it his own disappointment which was colouring his vision so that nausea filled his belly?

As he proceeded towards the Octroi Post, however, he saw whole crowds of women huddled together, the whites of their eyes glued in empty stares from hollows deep like those in unburnt skulls on the cremation ground in his dream last night. They bent over the fleshless skeletons of their children, looking, just looking, without moving their heads, as if they were waiting for something, they knew not what. They had bowls or pieces of coloured rags spread out for alms, but they were not begging. For they seemed too weak even to lift their head and accost the passers-by with their stares.

The old-time rogue and scoundrel impetuously struck the upper part of his chest and coughed up a rupee from the pouch he had made inside his neck with burnt lead, as criminals and prisoners do in India, and he went and bought a betel leaf to get enough nickels from the Pan-Biri wallah's on the corner of the Octroi Post to distribute among the women and children. He decided not to go by carriage to Hall Bazar but to trudge it, giving an anna to each group of famine-stricken creatures as he went along.

As he threw the first coin into the earthen bowl of a family, a mother with two muddy-skinned boys, he was overcome with disgust for them and muttered to the older youth: 'Why aren't you manly enough to sit up and beg?' The boys only turned their imploring eyes at him, while their mother pointed to their wasted backs. Ananta stood to contemplate them for a moment and found that starvation had bent their spines till they were doubled up like circus clowns, only without the gift that excites laughter.

Here and there a few children ran up to him, but mostly, along the whole length of the road, they just sat, listless and weary.

Because they were too ill to come swarming round him, Ananta even stopped to look at them with that fascination of horror with which he had often contemplated the ascetics and sadhus, who mortify their flesh in order to realize God at religious fairs. He saw a man, utterly naked, his buttocks wrapped in a paste of sweat and dung and urine, rolling about on the edge of a ditch in a hissing agony, lifting his neck with an aching stupor and then slipping into his filth.

Unable to bear it all, he turned his head towards the footbridge by the petrol pump station on the corner of Railway Road and Kutchery Road.

Klang, klang, the bell rang in his head, the knell of heat and pain, like a soundless alarm announcing the dissolution of the rogue who had lived in the kingdom of abandon too long. Klang, klang, klang, it struck the roots of his senses, and around his vitals, to gnaw into his thick-set, bull-like frame, as though awakening it with a twitch from some long yawning sleep, till he could do nothing but stare emptily again at the twisted bodies on the roadside.

There was a huddle of women concentrated like hens on a rubbish-heap on something in their midst, while two of them held the ends of a rag in the form of a canopy to protect them all from the angry sun overhead.

'A child is born,' one of them said, and waved him on as they noticed his probing eyes.

He threw two nickel annas and proceeded, striking his tongue against the roof of his mouth.

A women hugged a small skeleton of a girl to her breast farther up. But, looking inwards, he felt he had no sympathy left to offer to this mother whose anguish neither talked nor sang the tune of beggary, but stood fixed, placid and sagging in despair.

'O God, O God, O God,' he cried out in his soul through force of habit, and only realized afterwards that he did not believe in any God, had indeed never prayed for years, and therefore had no right to call upon such a Being if one such existed. Gautam Buddha, too, he remembered from the story in the scriptures, had called out like that as he had contemplated the misery of Kapilvastu before renouncing the evil world.

Dizzy with the heat, spluttering a heavy stale breath and spitting the rich gore of his betel-leaf saliva into the dust of the roadway, he saw that the more fortunate citizens of Amritsar were walking along like himself, or riding in carriages, hurrying, hurrying towards their work without spending any time to pause and see the spectacle of this ruin. In the past, he felt, he too would have gone by without blinking an eyelid at those hapless people, but now...

But what was the use of merely looking at this putrescence? He must do something! But what could he do? He had heard of worse misery in the towns and villages of Bengal and Bihar. How could one man's sympathy surge up and spread the balm of pity over the rotting flesh of the whole of Hindustan? How could one make one's flesh feel their torment? He could only fell a smothering wordless feeling for the man kneaded in his own filth, for the others whom he had seen, and still more for the kith and kin who had turned upon him this morning and called him a traitor, as well as for the men who were being maimed, wounded and killed in the furnaces of the wars beyond Hindustan, of which a poster, calling for recruits on the board by the footbridge, reminded him.

The legions of men at the ends of the horizons were marching in military formations to unknown facts in conflicts a million times bigger than that of Mahabharat in which the Pandus and the Kurus fought at Kurukshestra. During the last war he had been too boisterous a youth to care very much. And during the days of Jallianwala Bagh he had looted some of the cotton from the Imperial Bank in Hall Bazar for the mere fun of the thing. But his experiences in Bombay through the changes and turns of this titanic struggle had taught him to look at the map for Chin and Roos which had formerly been mere rumours to him, lands where rivers of blood had been shed by men like himself who had upset the peacock thrones of kings.

On his nerves and tendons, pulled as it were by jagged and contradictory feelings of an unyielding guilt, a bitter hatred for the lies and infamy of profiteers like Murli Dhar and Gokul Chand arose. The swell of an eager passion to hurry away possessed him. Where he wanted to go he didn't know.

And as he walked like a bull charged with madness, the passers-by edged away and made room for him. He smiled at this spectacle of himself frightening others and tried to infuse his face with kindliness. But the confusion and smoke of his embarrassment in the face of the tenderness that possessed him made him fearsome. And, as he caught a glimpse of the hurt that he willed behind his yearning to help others, he felt he saw a certain contempt for himself, for the devilish, disobedient son he had been to his stepmother. And arising from that contempt he felt the emergence in his bones of a boundless monster's energy to undo the harm he may have done, and to gather all the thathiars around him by curbing that pride in his own nature which he could see in their stubbornness.

No God, he felt, could make such a world and consign it to such suffering, for if He did so He was not a good God. But that was not the question, and if his friends believed in Fate, he would let them. Only he must convince them that they could not win bread separately but together, and that if they believed in their own manhood and were patient, and held on to each other, he would form a union and help them to come through. And then he felt calmer.

He did not know whether it was this overpowering feeling which made him feel a little more at peace with himself, or the fact that he had now ascended the footbridge and felt a whiff of breeze cool his body swollen with heat. He stood with his hands on his hips and cast a cursory glance on the engines which were shunting wagons in the goods yard of Amritsar Junction. He wished that by some miracle so much brass and copper may have arrived in the godowns that Gokul Chand-Murli Dhar & Co. would be forced from their own needs to employ all the workless thathiars.

'What a hope!' the cynic in him answered.

But as he began to move down the steps on the other side towards Hall Gate, he recalled how once, when he had been despondent about Janki's future in Amritsar, Sardar Puran Singh Bhagat had told him : 'Never surrender to fear—never, never, never. . . . For if the mountains should break and the rivers flood and lightnings crash, so long as you go on, through weariness, exhaustion and doubt, in the spirit of devotion to work and service of others, holding fast to the light which is in you, you will be so strengthened that you will go a long way—even if you don't get there.' 'And where does one want to get to?' he, Ananta, had asked. 'Oh, not very far,' Puran Singh had answered with a laugh as he twitched his head and brushed his flowing beard. 'To oneself and others.'

'A long pilgrimage that—to oneself and others!' Ananta muttered to himself, 'in the midst of the dishonesty, false pride, cruelty, selfishness and the injustice of the world. Difficult to know what to do and what not to do! To know the good and the evil!... Especially with the world against one because one did not act according to its customs——'

And as he jerked along to avoid the Pussyfoot Johnson Temperance Hall, and almost walked into the array of a quack's panacea for all ills, and then nearly tripped up on an anchorite who was sitting on a bed of nails to accustom himself to the thorns of this world and the next, Ananta felt as if he were walking on a tightrope like a clown trying to balance himself on his head.

9

'BLOW, BLOW, NIKKIA, BLOW, FOR GOD'S SAKE BLOW THE BELLOWS and don't look round! There is no "nautch" going on in the alley there!'

Sadanand screwed his lean black face till the ugly twist of his chin, which permanently pointed to one side as though it had been struck a blow from which it had never recovered, jutted out menacingly towards his son.

Nikka's thoughts had been wandering: his heart was with Rhoda and Rama, who had gone to bathe with Ananta and had feasted on delicacies, and the older boys, Mhenga and Daula and Shibu, who would now be at their jobs in the works like the Sahibs, while he was blowing the old bellows. His grandfather had scolded him and sent him back at the corner of Billimaran while he himself had gone to meet Nikka's prospective father-in-law at the Yekka stand by the Clock Tower. His limbs were listless in the airless morning, over which ran the heat of the furnace in almost tangible layers. He had to lift the two goat-skins alternately, one with the right hand and the other with the left, open them through the strapped brackets at the top till they filled with air, close them and press them down, till the wind went rushing through the hole into the mouth of the furnace. Then his father held a silver tumbler, by means of a pair of tongs in his left hand, even as he applied the mixture of zinc and powdered silver with a prong, soldering one end of the silver tumbler to the other. Nikka had to control bellows, not press them too hard with the right hand nor too slowly with the left, in order to produce an even heat. He had learnt to do this, as every thathiar child learns from his infancy, for few coppersmiths can afford to employ a full-time bellows-blower; and the children are always near at hand, anxious to play about with the bellows, especially if they get a pice for giving a helping hand, so that by the time they are growing up they have learnt to blow perfectly. Still, the Almighty did not make the two hands of man equally strong, and even the most practised right hand can press a little harder than the left hand. And the unequal wind sends sparks of charcoal fire flying all over the place, and the solderer's eyes, not being protected by any goggles, are always in danger of not being able to see again or at least being dimmed for life. Nikka was frightened of his father's voice and got confused.

'Steady, seed of an owl, steady!' shrieked Sadanand as he swallowed a whiff of smoke. 'I tell you, blow the bellows evenly. How will you be able to master a wife if you haven't got enough strength in your arms to blow the bellows for half an hour?'

Nikka looked pale, paler than ever, except where the glow of fire lit his face with a rosy warmth and showed the delicate features he had inherited from his mother. His big, sad brown eyes were half closed, his lips were half open and his chin drooped with the heat that seemed to overpower him, making his face a wilting flower.

'Just one more stitch and then we shall have finished,' said Sadanand, relenting a little. 'And then you can go to the factory.' As soon as he had said this he corrected himself. 'Oh no, of course, "they" are coming, though I hope that Baba and "they" don't arrive before we are through with this job.'

The father was intent on his job; he was a hard-working and careful craftsman, and possessed a kind of mechanical energy which seemed to be automatic, for there was no glow of physical health about him; and he seemed to derive a compensatory strength from the attempt he made to infuse an unnatural dignity, or rather pride, into his emaciated, angular, little body—a conceit not of the 'body', however, but of a grandiose manner, the swagger of the *nouveau riche*.

Nikka's eyes had already welled up with tears, but luckily the irregular pressure of his bellows sent two clouds of smoke swirling across the barn-like shop, where there was no chimney to eject the smoke, and his misery was curtained off from his father's gaze by the black shroud.

'Sadananda, son, you might have prepared a better reception for our guests than this smoke,' came Lala Murli Dhar's voice from the Ivory Sellers' bazar end of Kucha Billimaran. 'The whole lane is full of smoke. Here "they" are Lala Ram Saran and Lala Binde Saran from Jandiala.'

'Ao ji, ao, come on my head, come on my eyes,' greeted Sadanand even as he accelerated the soldering. 'Come and grace us with your presence.' But he was red-hot with embarrassment and flustered to be found at work, especially at the low occupation of soldering, which made him the equal of the visitors as a brother thathiar, when he felt he had risen to superior heights of splendour by becoming a partner in new factory with the Kasera Gokul Chand, a man of a slightly more pretentious caste.

Now that the guests had come, Sadanand tried to calm himself by thinking of the bright side of it, they would form a better impression of Nikka seeing him at work than if he had been merely sitting around in the shop, all dressed up for the occasion. Anyhow, if they were badly impressed with the soot and grime here, Baba could take them to have a look round at the factory, where his elder son Gopi was a manager, and where Nikka was ultimately destined to go. If they were still not impressed, then let them take the offer of their daughter's hand elsewhere, for he was not going to deck himself up in finery to greet them or get his son to look like a doll in order to impress them with the new prestige the family had acquired through the factory.

'I fall at your feet, Lala Sadanand,' greeted Lala Ram Saran, the enormous turban on his small pukka brown face shaking a little.

'I fall at your feet,' echoed the feeble, wheezy voice of Lala Binde Saran, his more docile twin brother.

'Come and sit down,' said Lala Murli Dhar, leading the way. And he began to drag a dust-laden strip of carpet from the side to the wooden platform which projected from the shop into the lane.

'Acha, my son, stop blowing the bellows. I have put in the last stretch,' said Sadanand to Nikka, now all tenderness to the boy.

With one last gasp Nikka relapsed and fell back, exhausted.

'Oh, my son, my lion,' said Sadanand, rushing to him. He was afraid that the boy might faint and then everything would be ruined because the folk from Jandiala might think the boy was an epileptic or something and may withdraw the offer. And that would be the most terrible blow to the pride of the family. But, luckily, the boy was only tired.

'Come, my son, go and get some puris and kachauris for the guests and yourself,' said Murli Dhar. 'Here is some money.' And he took a wallet out of his pocket and deliberately exposed the face of some rupee notes in order to impress the guests.

'No, no, don't be formal, Baba Murli Dhar, how could we eat here, considering——'

But the host was just showing off his wealth and knew full well that a prospective father-in-law never eats at the house where his daughter is to be wedded, lest he be violating the Hindu principle of giving a daughter away freely rather than for a token or a bribe. But pride could not live without showing a great deal more to the credit of the proud, as power cannot be sustained without an exaggerated show of strength.

'At least sit on the clean carpet and not on the bare boards of that platform,' said Sadanand with a deliberate humility whose deliberation was emphasized by the ridiculous 'clean'.

'Give them a cushion or two,' said Murli. 'The one that came from Kashmir—that cushion!'

'No, good hosts, no, don't trouble,' protested Lala Ram Saran. 'We are villagers and not soft-bottomed city folk. Besides, where God is, everything is, comfort as well as rest.'

'Acha, where is your brother Gopi, ohe Nikka?' said Sadanand. 'Go and ask him at the factory if he will leave work for a moment and get some sherbet or soda-water—which will you have, Lala Ram Saran, Lala Binde Saran: sherbet or soda-water?'

'No, kind hosts. whose food do we eat every day if not yours, and whose drink do we drink?' said Lala Ram Saran formally. 'Don't trouble. . . . But we would like to see the boy.'

The war of courtesy ceased and Murli Dhar and Sadanand went pale. They had heard that the girl was slightly older than Nikka and they were afraid lest the prospective fathers-in-law of the boy should notice the boy's poor physique and withdraw the offer. Apparently she was so much older than Nikka that her uncle and father had not considered the little boy before them to be their prospective son-in-law.

'Come son,' Sadanand called to Nikka. 'Say "I fall at your feet" to your elders.' And then, in order to give the boy confidence as well as to impress the guests, who seemed embarrassed, he continued: 'He is already learning all about book-keeping at the works. I put him to blowing the bellows today only because I couldn't get any labour this morning, otherwise he is always at the factory. We are hoping to make him a Babu Manager there, soon. . . .'

'How big is the gap between being taught and having learnt, son?' said Ram Saran with the villager's characteristic sense of humour.

Nikka was overcome with shyness as he arranged his sweat sodden tunic into shape and wiped the soot off his face with an end of his loin-cloth. But even in his pani he felt a secret thrill at the idea of being married off, though he hung his head down and felt his face grow hotter and hotter.

'Oh, come on,' old Murli urged him. 'Come and say "I fall at your feet" to him.'

'Come, son, don't be shy,' coaxed Lala Ram Saran. 'After all, you are like a son to us, and you are going to be much more than a son. Come . . . .

Nikka went forward through the tangle of hammers and anvils and tongs, his nose covered with sweat, his head and heart throbbing, his eyes dimmed with the warmth of fear and excitement, his legs possessed of a queer strength, as though the thought of his bride had filled his loins with the will to conquer. He laid his head over his joined hands on the boards of the platform, not knowing who was the prospective father-in-law, though he had a vague idea from his mother's talk at meals that it was Binde Saran's daughter who was to be his bride.

'Beautiful boy,' said Lala Ram Saran.
'And so gentle,' echoed Lala Binde Saran.

'Though we must send you some clarified butter,' said Lala Ram Saran. 'That would put colour into the boy's face. They say, "Where a husband is strong, God is pleased...."'

'There is no want of anything in our house by your blessing, especially since we have started that factory and have secured lots of orders,' said Murli Dhar, 'though, as you know, the ghee in the town is adulterated. Still, we get better food than anyone else in the thathiar brotherhood from the shopkeepers here, as they all want me to lend them money, you know. But, of course, food is scarce these days.'

'Ah yes, and the prices are rising!' said Ram Saran, who knew about this family's tight-fistedness, especially their legendary niggardliness over spending anything on clothes or food except the barest minimum.

'There may be famine, brothers,' said Sadanand, aware of Ram Saran's insinuation, 'but we have, by your blessing, enough contracts at the works to tide over any bad time. We are doing better than anyone else, by your grace, as we still have our contacts with the courts of several Maharajas and Rajas through the silversmithy.'

'Perhaps the boy can come over and live in the fresh air at Jandiala for a while,' said Lala Ram Saran with an obvious tact to smooth things over and pave the way for the more concrete talk.

'Actually, he goes to the wrestling-pitch every morning,' said Murli, who had even this morning rebuked his grandson for going to the wrestling-pitch with the other boys. 'And he is my favourite as far as money is concerned. Come, son, here you are—two shining rupees for you. Go and get yourself some puri-kachauri.'

'But come back soon, son,' said Lala Ram Saran, whose mind had been made up about the match long before he came here, because he knew that even though old Murli and his family were mean, they had money, and that was what interested him both immediately and in the long run. 'We shall have to be going soon, and we would like to kiss your forehead before we go.'

Nikka made obeisance with joined hands and made off like a lark flying to liberty.

'He is a very dutiful son,' said Sadanand, commending the boy with an artificially polite, self-satisfied smile. And he continued: 'It is all the blessing of God that he was born into a house where there is no dearth of anything. He has only got to go steady. Diligence makes money as that fan the wind.' And he pointed to his father's peacock hand-fan.

'May he live long,' said Lala Ram Saran. And he took the opening supplied by Sadanand: 'Acha then, what do you feel about his—marriage?'

'Han,' echoed Binde Saran. 'What do you feel?'

'Whatever you say will be done,' said Murli Dhar, fanning himself and his guests with his hand-fan. And knowing that the match was as good as Nikka's, he tried to impress the folk from Jandiala with more information into which the importance of the new factory could be reflected. 'Of course he is going to inherit the works one day, as I can't live for ever!' As the last words became exclamatory in his mouth a terrible hush fell on the company, for it was true that his chances of imortality were certainly getting dimmer every day.

After a pause, Lala Ram Saran cleared his throat and strained his husky voice. He had got the proud Murli and the prouder Sadanand into exactly the right shade of grandiose exuberance through which he could extract from them what he wanted.

'You know, Baba, that there is a scarcity of foodstuffs in the towns. Well, there is a famine of cash in the villages. Add to this the scarcity of metals everywhere.... The life of a coppersmith is like a water-bubble nowadays.'

'To be sure, brother,' admitted old Murli, 'things are bad.' But then he sought to change the subject and added positively: 'Life is short, but hope is long.'

'It is the hoarders in the villages, you know,' put in Sadanand. 'And somehow, there is so much malice about, and covetousness—and oh, the beggars!' Robbery in daylight.'...

'We don't know what has happened,' said Lala Ram Saran. 'But while you can at least feel the heat of your furnaces and foundries, our furnaces are lying cold and empty. I have had to apprentice my two sons to a man in the building trade and leave the family profession. Woe is me! I don't know what has happened. Some say it is the wars in Vilayat, some say that the end of the world is near. I don't know.'

'It is this Amrikan machinery—the toys of the Devils!' said Binde Saran. 'And the only people who could keep an eye on the Sarkar are in goal—at least, so says Sohan Singh Josh!'

'The traffic is difficult,' said old Murli evasively to bluff them, as Binde Saran seemed to be having a good guess. 'We ordered some steel for the works from Vilayat. And though it has come to Bombay, it is lying there in the godowns because the railways are too busy.'

'Han brothers, so we will do straight talk,' said Ram Saran, who knew that the old man was now going to cry havoc when previously he had been boasting of being richer and better off than anyone else in the world. 'We are villagers. Our need is so bad that we have come to selling our daughters!'

At this his brother, Binde Saran, hung his head down and flushed red with shame and bitterness, for obviously he had a sense of dignity in his melting eyes.

'Oh, don't talk like that, Lala Ram Saran,' said Sadanand. He was hurt by the fact that they should be offering the hand of the girl to Nikka only in their hour of need, for what money they could get and not because they considered his son the best and most handsome boy in town. And yet he was cornered, because he could not now refuse the offer.

'I feel ashamed that you should be in such a plight, brothers,' said Murli in an undertone. 'But, Lala Ram Saran, why don't you send both your sons to the factory for training? I will see to it that they have the best of everything.'

'The shame is ours,' said Ram Saran with an uncanny sense that Murli would try to slip out of the bargain to which his pride had already bound him. 'We don't want to take advantage of our future relationship like that. What will the world say?'

'We have heard that you have turned away so many of the thathiars,' added Binde Saran. 'No, that wouldn't be fair. You have opened a factory and not an agency for securing jobs for everyone.'

'To be sure, brother, if everyone talked like that we would be saved a great deal of trouble,' said old Murli. 'Instead——'

'Rest assured that we are not what those gossiping, slanderous enemies of ours have made us out to be,' protested Sadanand. He knew that he and his father were caught in the net they had helped to spread. Therefore he was inclined to get the best of the bargain now from the folk of Jandiala by making them believe that the notoriety he and his father had earned, by ousting the members of the coppersmith brotherhood from the piecework market and not employing them in the factory, was not deserved. 'We have been buying jewellery and clothes—what for ? Not to keep in the house, but to bestow on the bride of our Nikka. And we will spend to our capacity on the marriage.'

"And may I tell you that I have had your daughter in mind ever since I held her in my lap when she was a baby,' said old Murli, trying to pour oil on the troubled waters and to smother all this straight talk under a gush of sentiment.

'You are kind—but I don't know what to say,' put in Binde Saran. 'They say he who covets another's property will go to hell, but—'

'Let me tell them, brother,' interposed Ram Saran. 'They will understand. . . .' And he turned to his hosts : 'Brothers, you are heads of the thathiar community and you know how badly we have all been affected by the shortage of metal and the coming in of the factories. The truth is that we haven't anything more than the loin-cloths we walk about in.'

'But that is nothing to be ashamed about,' said Murli, fanning himself vigorously even as he summoned the courage of his pride to come to his aid. 'What is modesty among such near relations as we shall be ! Sadanand, bring two bags of a hundred rupees each from that safe so that they can get the girl's trousseau.'

'Are you sure that will be enough to prepare the girl's trousseau with ?' said Sadanand, giving Ram Saran a significant look.

'Why, Bindu?' Ram Saran turned to his younger brother.

'Oh, don't ask me, I am melting with shame,' said Binde Saran. 'That it should come to this ! There are a thousand miseries in one daughter.'

The gloom of the bride's father communicated itself to the others and they were all still, so that the noise of the jig-jigging, scraping and turning in the factory further up in Billimaran reverberated in their ears sharply and jarred on their nerves.

'Give them three bags, Sadanand,' said Murli, for he saw in the reticence of his guests about the sum offered an occasion to clinch the bargain on the cheap.

'Acha,' said Binde Saran. 'We take the bags only on the understanding that if times are better——'

'Times will never be better now for us,' said Ram Saran,

who had made up his mind to sell his brother's daughter and wanted to give no promises for the return of the money. 'What is more, I am thinking day and night of the future of my two sons ! Without wives they shall never have any homes. Oh, brothers, you have no conception of our misery in the villages !

The tension mounted to a crescendo.

Neither Murli nor Sadanand spoke for a moment. Ram Saran was evidently grasping for more money. And yet he knew that if they didn't accept the bargain now the disgrace would be unbearable, as the whole world would know that the folk from Jandiala had sold their daughter. On the other hand, Murli and Sadanand knew that if Nikka didn't get the girl, the weakling would probably never get another offer. But neither side could go on bidding for a girl as if she were a slave on the market. What if any one of their enemies in the brotherhood got to know ? Especially Ananta's stepmother, because she had been known to have asked for the hand of Bindu's daughter.

'There are two girls in the house where my granddaughter, Parvati, is married,' said Murli, putting them off the track of more money and getting very hot and bothered in the attempt to do so. 'And I did mention the names of your boys to Paro's father-in-law.'

'We will see about that when the ceremony of Nikka's marriage takes place,' said Sadanand, helping the old man out. 'You know, brothers, the atmosphere of marriage is contagious. And I am sure they will be fixed up, your boys. Meanwhile, Baba, give me the keys to the safe. And perhaps you can give our relations some sheets of metal when they arrive from Karachi.'

'Oh, brothers, where is this boy, our Nikka ?' said Ram Saran, unable to restrain his glee at the huckster's profit he had secured by his restrain. 'We want to give him the ceremonial offering and go. The sun is rising high overhead.'

'Oh no, you can't go just yet,' said the old man, 'you will have to stay the day now you are here.' And he turned to his son : 'Sadanand, ask your mother and the mother of Nikka to inform everyone concerned that we will have the betrothal ceremony in the afternoon, as is fitting for the dignity of our house.'

Just at that moment the gong-like voice of Ananta could

be heard greeting someone at the door of his shop across the lane.

Sadanand got up with his hands joined to Lala Ram Saran and Binde Saran and, saying, 'Wadahi, Maharaj, May your tribe increase!' walked across the tangle of implements towards the stairs in the corner of the shop, looking like a weather-beaten scarecrow at a harvest dance.

'I will get the keys to the safe,' he said to the folk from Jandiala with great emphasis, even as he turned to see if he was out of audible distance of Ananta should that rogue be eaves-dropping on the bargain they had struck.

'Some people would like to cut our throats, you know, Lala Ram Saran, Binde Saran,' said Murli, turning his eyes away from the direction of Ananta significantly.

10

WHEN ANANTA RETURNED FROM THE GRAIN SHOP HE FOUND THE poet, Puran Singh Bhagat, waiting for him.

'Where are the comrades?' the poet asked anxiously. 'And did you see Mr. Latif?'

Ananta told him with a smile that Ralia and Dina had probably gone to drown their sorrows at the liquor shop and that Viroo, Black God, had gone home; but he did not answer the last part of Puran Singh's question.

'So Mr. Latif was "not at home" ', the poet said in a falling voice, rather ashamed of belonging to that category of men who were called leaders but were never 'at home' when wanted.

'But how did you manage to get back from the court, Puran Singhji?' Ananta asked, evading an answer to the poet's repeated reference to Mr. Latif.

Puran Singh Bhagat presumed now that Ananta had made an unsuccessful visit to Mr. Latif's bungalow. So he refrained from probing any further and tried to communicate that, though of all leaders he alone was available, he had little faith in his capacity to lead.

'I felt like a cheat going away to court this morning without being able to tell your cousins anything which could help them. Luckily my case doesn't come up until the late afternoon. So I thought I would come back and have a talk with you all. But I believe I am being shadowed by a C.I.D. man.'

'As my brothers are all scattered, you need not expose yourself here if the plain-clothes man is following you,' Ananta said. 'I have to go and see how the woman of my house is.' And he hesitated to ask the poet to accompany him lest, like other respectable people, Puran Singh Bhagat may not want to be seen going to visit his kept woman.

'I shall come to see my sister—Janki,' said Puran Singh, warmly catching hold of Ananta's hand and pressing it.

Ananta was moved by the poet's cordiality and he led Puran Singh towards the chubara, his head bowed in gratitude.

Janki had got up from bed and was sitting down on a low chair crocheting a bedcover as both the friends came in. She shyly drew the head-piece of her dhoti over her forehead.

'Our brother, Sardar Puran Singh Bhagat,' Ananta said. O 'my spiritual guide and mentor.'

Janki joined her hands and whispered the Sikh greeting.

Puran Singh Bhagat went over to her and patted her head affectionately, saying 'I have been wanting to come and see you, sister, all these days.'

'I will make you some sherbet,' Janki said, almost rising.

'Oh !' exclaimed Puran Singh, jumping with pity at the pallor on her face, and resting his hand on her forehead. 'But you shouldn't be up at all—your head is burning with fever !'

'Janki !' Ananta reproached breathlessly. 'Why did you get up, my life ? You go back to bed.'

'Don't be harsh with me,' Janki said. 'I get so tired of lying down all day. And I am really no worse.'

'Acha, then, sister, please sit back on the bed against the pillows,' the poet suggested, the tenderness choking his voice.

'I will, after I have given you some sherbet.'

'No, a cup of cool and simple water would be nectar to me,' Puran Singh said, aware that there was in her attitude the characteristic Indian woman's personal devotion—the first attribute of selfless devotion.

'I shall look after the Guru,' Ananta said. 'You go and sit up in bed. We have need of wisdom today and he will tell us what to do.'

Janki obeyed docilely enough, her ivory face flushed a vivid red, more through the fascination that Puran Singh had for her than with the consumption inside her. And she wondered whether it was his presence, his wisdom or his poetry that attracted her.

The poet went towards the window, ostensibly to give the woman privacy to arrange herself, but really to see if the C.I.D. man was about in the square. 'May I open this window to let the air come in?' That, he thought, would be a good excuse to secure a position from which he could look out for the detective.

'Han Sardar Puran Singh, do,' said Ananta almost guiltily, because he knew that the poet may have been concerned about the need for fresh air for Janki. But he casually went on filling the bronze cups with water from the slender-necked pitcher.

As the two men began to drink water, Janki insisted on their having a bit of dough cake each to eat, and they had to assent for fear of exciting her too much. And, for a while, they ate, Puran Singh Bhagat still walking about tensely as if he expected the detective to walk right up to the room and handcuff him, while Ananta sat at the threshold of the alcove which spread mysteriously like the inner sanctum of a temple into the darkness.

'Do sit down, Sardar Puran Singh,' Ananta said as the poet came to fetch the bowl of water after eating his portion of the dough cake.

'I'd rather not,' the poet said with a deliberated pressure of the will, though he looked at Ananta at the same instant with the utmost gentleness.

Ananta understood, but to Janki, fighting against her own shadows, there was something strange in the obvious fears of these two statements. For a moment there was a strange hush in which they could hear the flies buzzing, round the crumbs which had fallen from the poet's morsel of the dough cake. Then Puran Singh Bhagat spoke:

'Anant Ram, brother, you were wrong to tell Janki that I am your spiritual guide. Actually, you are my Guru and I am your chela.'

'Don't mock at me, Sardarji,' said Ananta; 'I am a "fool" in this house! Besides, think of your learning and experience—you have been round the world while I—there is no talk!'

'No, I mean this,' said the poet. 'Because it is not

wisdom which is wanted by the thathiars so much as faith—a new faith. And you have it. I am not being modest. I really mean it. I found it confirmed for me this morning. You see, I have often felt that each day one learns more about human nature and each day one knows less. And to a learned man, action is difficult. But you may know by instinct, and from the heart, and act upon your knowledge, while I may just be dithering.'

He seemed to become vague and cloudy and his words were so faint that they seemed to get lost in his beard. Then, with that strange twitch of his head which betokened the release of some pent-up god in his nature, he spoke aloud: 'You know I ran away this morning. Because, knowing what little I do know about this tormented world of ours, I yet could not, from the truth in me, advise you thathiars about the right course of action. I had to go to the court, of course, but I was a coward nevertheless, because my manhood seemed to desert me in the face of their arguments.'

'They wouldn't take anyone's advice,' Janki put in, 'from what I know of them.'

'But surely we have to form a union, Sardar Puran Singh,' said Ananta. 'It is the simplest thing to do, isn't it? They are like children and they lack confidence——'

'Han—but it isn't really so simple,' said the poet. 'And you know it, otherwise you would have formed that union some days ago . . . . In spite of the fact that you share the suffering of the thathiars and can act as I can't, it isn't so simple because——'

'Because they haven't been able to make up their minds, Sardarji, whether they hate machines too much to take jobs in the factory or whether they are really looking for jobs there. And we ought to make up their minds for them.'

'That is it,' said the poet. 'Though they don't know it, they are torn inside them, even as the whole world is rent today about whether to use the machine or to scrap it and go back to the age of the spinning-wheel. And this quarrel in men's minds is going on in spite of the fact that the machine is there and can't be refuted. The bulk of men are rooted in custom and hardly yet born, while there are some like us who are only half alive. As Uncle Viroo invoked Mahatma Gandhi this morning, the truth must be faced that not only have many people listened to the Mahatma's gospel but they themselves feel that machinery is bad. And if one sees the spectacle of those beautiful and ingenious products of science, the modern aeroplanes, dropping thousands of tons of bombs and distributing Death to the poor and rich alike, one has to make up one's mind about the machine——'

'Life can defy Death,' said Ananta, 'and if we come alive, if we control our fate and take it all in our stride, why should we be so afraid?' And he winced in his bravery as though slightly terrified.

'I think you are talking with only part of your being—the brave part!' said the poet. 'Because, like me, you too are afraid. A bomber——'

'That is how Janki was talking this morning,' said Ananta laughingly, 'and she called me a machine man.'

'Poor hen-pecked husband!' said Puran Singh Bhagat ironically.

'Weeping eyes and laughing teeth!' commented Janki. 'I will make him some tea to soothe him.' And she proceeded towards the corner of the room which served as a kitchen.

In the ensuing silence the poet thought of his fear, and of the reasons for that fear. And though the rational part of him failed to come to his rescue, his mind was filled with an atmosphere in which one oppressive fact was incandescently connected with another, as though he felt that all the misery of one part of the world sprang from another. And the horror that he felt hanging over the universe, and which he ascribed to the machine, seemed to shape itself into the future form of that perfected death machine, the sinister robot aeroplane and rocket, hurling a twelve-hundred-pound bomb on a row of houses and burying people, most of whom had done nothing to deserve death. And that image rose before his eyes like a cosmic disaster which seemed to darken life altogether. 'Am I a coward?' he asked himself. The answer came that he was frightened mainly because he knew too little, because he knew that even though he lived his own life and had not done anything to provoke war, he bore some responsibility for the fact that a child anywhere should be mutilated by a bomb splinter, the responsibility of being part of a huge, intricate and frightful world in which vast forces had been let loose by proud, greedy and power-crazed weaklings frightened to be themselves, even as he himself was afraid to acknowledge his own weaknesses, uncontrolled by the emergence of an enlightened will in men which could give history another direction.

'Don't you think,' said Ananta, concentrating on the poet's gracious greying beard, 'that it is those respectable people who, having no strength, enter Government service who are responsible for oppressing people everywhere ? They look so meek and mild but I am much more concerned about those "doots" than about the "doots" of hell !'

'I said you were my Guru !' exclaimed Puran Singh Bhagat, walking away from the window, where he had been peering into the square again.

'What have Government offices to do with machinery ?' asked Janki between a series of puffs at the fuel sticks in the oven before her. 'I thought it was people like Murli Dhar, who ran factories——'

'But men like me, the "machine men", also want to introduce machinery,' said Ananta with a smile. 'For instance, Jan, I would like to persuade the Municipal Committee to lay down gas pipes or electric power here, so that your green cat's-eyes could be spared for me, from that smoke in the oven where you are blowing your precious breath away. Come, may I sacrifice myself on you, let me blow; your life is dear to me.'

'No, I am all right,' Janki said in the paroxysms of a protracted cough.

'Yes, Janki, sister,' the poet said. 'Look at the souls trapped in the airless kitchens of the old houses, think of them sweating before the uneven fires of wood-sticks and cow-dung fuel, think of yourself, and then, rubbing the metal utensils with ashes to clean the soiled pots after every meal—not souls but slaves. The unuttered songs of your lives is choked up by the smoke of this evil homeliness and never gets a chance to burst out ! And then think of the women of Europe released from the dark prisons which men's blindness has made of homes everywhere. At least those European women are getting to know that they are half dead and are trying to come alive. If you think of those things, you would prefer to use the gas or electric cooker. In fact, if you knew that there is an electric kettle which boils water, I am sure you would have got our tea ready long before the time it has taken you to light the fire. Though, and I must not lie to you, all those conveniences are the sisters of other evils, unless you use the extra time you get to scratch your head.'

'Han, my fear is, brother, that once you start using these eaters of their masters, machines, you don't know where to stop, said Janki. 'You would end by electrocuting the whole world, and there will be no life left.'

'That is because the machine has become entangled in the mesh of several desires, each pulling a different way. On the one hand there is, as Ananta said, the Sarkar—Authority. Certainly it was the Angrezi Sarkar which first brought the machine into this country; in fact it was the Angrez log who first brought about what is called the Industrial Revolution. They brought the rail gadi here, with the steam-engine, the telephone, the bicycle, the motor-car, the pistol and the machine-gun——'

'Especially the machine-gun!' interrupted Ananta.

'Han, for good or ill, Authority and Law are bound up with the evils of the machine,' continued the poet. 'And then there are the rich merchants of our country, people like Murli Dhar and Gokul Chand, who are profiteering with the help of the machine, because they want to adorn their dead bodies in expensive shrouds. And then there is the machine itself, a death-trap which alters the whole character of man, especially if he handles it without knowing something about it!

'When we thathiars begin to handle the machine,' said Ananta, 'we shall soon show them!... We need not become slaves to the profiteers or the machines. We are men. We will make a Revolution!

'So I am on the fringe of this new and terrible world,' said the poet with a smile. Then he looked out of the window ever so furtively and immediately withdrew his head as if he were a frightened bird seeing the reflection of danger before it. 'Certainly I am involved in the despair of those who do not know whether to take the plunge into the dark whirl or run back to the shores of the past and sit brooding on the white lotuses in the ponds of this ancient city. And I am not sure even that I know what suffering means. Brother, it is one thing to imagine pain in words, another thing to——'

'Speaking for myself,' said Ananta with the impetuousness of the Punjabi extremist, 'I would take the plunge into the ocean. After all, men have gone to their deaths with a song on their lips, and here is the promise of an abounding life, certainty of struggle. Let the storm rage, I say!'

'Ah,' said Puran Singh Bhagat, 'you are young and have

hope. And your enthusiasm is infectious. And the poet in me is always dreaming, planning just like you. And I know that our will can smother our fears. But we are a tired people and have no tradition for using complicated things. And that means that we must be responsible and weigh up this matter. Also, we have to think of our stubborn elders. They are quite wise in their orthodoxy, you know.... My own grandfather, who was a painter in the Court of Maharaja Ranjit Singh, thought the English were devils, and he hated the whole bag of tricks they brought with them. And he declared that the Sikhs lost their hold on the Punjab because Rani Jindan was deceived into using the big guns of the Ferungis and abandoning the sword of the Sikh Surmas. My father, too, died hating the English because, apprenticed to the family craft of painting, he found he could not compete with the European machine-made pictures. I began by thinking that through our religion we could restore all the human ethics to labourers and craftsmen which the Westerners have tended to lose for a hundred years. So I worked for our freedom movement with Lala Lajpat Rai. But since then I have learned a great deal. For instance, I learnt to love English people. And I realized that there are many Englishmen who are as tormented as we are by the present age.'

That was a revelation to Janki, that Puran Singh Bhagat could love the English while hating the Angrezi Sarkar. She looked at the inscrutable, kindly smile that played on his face, and thought how like Ananta he was, how quick to make friends and enemies, except that her own man was more reckless and prodigal both in his generosity and harshness.

'The tea is ready,' she said. 'In the Angrezi tea-pot!

'I should like to go to Vilayat one day and see what conditions are like there,' Ananta said, lifting his eyes dreamily under the thick eyebrows. 'I should like to see those steps which walk, and the railways which run in the bowels of the earth. I should also like to go and see the giants of Roos. Comrade Khan told me that there they have learnt to grow wheat in the snowfields and to extract power from coal in the earth without anyone having to go into the mine. In all those things the earth is coming to be more and more like heaven. The Roosis must have courage!'

'I hope you do have a chance to go, brother—maybe the giants will still be there after all the violence and death.'

'So you doubt that there will be any men left?' asked Ananta, his ears pricking up. 'You are in a bad way today, Sardarji. I wish you would forget all about that detective out there. I shall deal with him. After all, one has only to die once and after that one is immortal.'

'No, perhaps I shouldn't have put it that way,' said the poet. 'Actually, no one can wipe out the whole of humanity. Only, certain men can destroy the will of other men by piling terror upon terror. Look at me crumbling slowly inside me for fear of that C.I.D. man, and perhaps he isn't even there. Also, these powerful men can kill the poetry of life, the beauty and strength of it. For instance, before these wars people in Europe were just learning to explore their minds, to get to know themselves and each other a little, because they had already learnt to control nature to some extent. They were only half alive, but they were moving to some extent. But now they must have been pushed back to the crude lumps of human experience, to spritual death and stagnation. They——'

Again the poet seemed to have flown away to some remote region as he looked out of the window and talked aloud to himself. Neither Ananta nor Janki interrupted him when he paused, for they felt that the earlier tension in him was mounting to a mad desire to unburden himself and talk himself out.

'They were fast losing their grip, even when I was there,' continued the poet. 'They seemed to me to go sleep-walking through the streets of their cities, or to wait and watch, looking, looking, looking through empty sockets at indifferent faces, not hating, not loving, only looking for they knew not what. And neither grief nor the warm suns of August seemed to melt them. They expected no sympathy from anyone and certainly did not want to give it to anyone. They could buy every material comfort, so they worshipped money and would die for pennies. I went to a hospital with a friend whose child had swallowed the broken top of a bottle. And we were kept waiting filling up forms for hours for the doctor. And when he came he seemed less than human, so casual he was that. . . .'

'The same thing happens at our civil hospital in the Ram Bagh,' interrupted Janki. 'I shall never go there again. Why, the nurses move almost with automatic hands to help the doctors and make the beds ready for new patients even before the relatives of the last corpse have removed their kin.'

'The decline of sorrow,' continued the poet, 'helped by the lack of faith, seemed to have hardened their faces and emptied their souls.'

'And yet you are for importing machines from Europe into this country ?' Janki challenged. 'They are probably tired of doing the same job all day and every day.'

'There were many people like us who were horrified at the prospect of the coming years of ruin. They were harassed by the changes that had brought them from the horse-carriage to the motor-bus and they were frustrated because the motive, power seemed to them like the remorseless wheel of Jagannath, directed by some invisible God and trampling on their lives, tearing them from their roots in the soil, destroying their old life, their old way, as well as their homes and throwing them ou the rubbish-heap, after they had been used to swell profits. And they were in revolt against this civilization even as Gandhiji and his followers are against the "Satanic Western Civilization". Even as Mahatma Hans Raj——'

'You speak of the learned,' interrupted Ananta. 'Some of the people there may be weak enough, like our own folk, defeated by the machines and the masters, and accepting the worship of the rich docilely as a decree from heaven, as their kismet. But this is not so, surely with the real men who are together ? And what about the new idea of brotherhood ? I saw the Bombay strike of 1939, and when the miserable little Southerners joined hands, I can tell you, something new was born. Perhaps your new religion—that is what togetherness can do for us. I know because I have felt it in my bones. I know that a few people feel that the old religion will help us, but I know that the old kismet idea is played out. Only I don't know what is the new fate which is preventing men from trusting their hearts. Perhaps it is weakness. For I, too, am afraid.'

'Confusion ! turmoil ! Selfishness ! Greed ! Lust for power ! Above all, hypocrisy,' said Puran Singh Bhagat. And he took a large gulp of tea and swallowed his bitterness.

'What panacea do you offer, then ?'' Ananta asked breathless at the poet's denunciation of Europe, at which he himself had always looked through his romantic dreams and the glamour of travellers' tales.

'For a long time I have felt timid and thought it would be

presumptuous for me to tell you the cost you may have to pay for the machine.'

'I think we are already paying it without even having the advantage of using it.' He paused and laughed at his own joke.

'You mean, Sardarji, that the thathiars . . . ?' began Janki tentatively.

'They might lose their manhood, their place in the thathiar brotherhood, their sense of community,' answered the poet.

'I tell you the machine is already there!' protested Ananta. 'And we have got to decide to go and work it rather than sulk because we can't get piecework. We must force the owners to employ us. After all, men are better men when they are working than when they are idle. After all, neither these bosses nor the Sarkar dare slow down production if there are wars on! And we will try to take things in hands as soon as we can get in, then form a trade union and prepare for the Revolution.'

'But what is the Jinn that has possessed the bosses and is holding them back from loving you?' Janki asked.

'Because, gentlewoman, each is for himself,' said Ananta. 'The dead ones spite the living as in Vilayat.'

'The failure of the Angrez log,' said the poet, explaining it all in his own way, 'lies in their reduction of man to a mere cipher. Their politicians did not realize that the power of the State to rule should come from the striving people rather than from a small group of old families. Their rich did not see competition and mass production of cheap goods are not worth having if these are to be attained at the expense of death and degradation. The rich were for keeping the poor in their places, and they accepted the help of any gangster who came along because he was keeping the rich where they were and degrading the poor. And when the gangsters got their own way they openly trampled upon men. No wonder the skeleton was their symbol. And then there were wars. Their spiritual leaders and guides built their homes in a barren, hard orthodoxy and clung to the shells of old myths rather than evolve Ananta's faith in a new togetherness. And the people seemed to grow more tired and cynical, inured, as Viroo said, to "mine" and "thine" as their religion. So that when you ask me what is this new Jinn which keeps the rich from loving the poor, the inexorable demon which is destroying them steadily, and will crush us all if we don't look out, I shall say it is the Nemesis of no care which parades itself in the coquettish disguises of a sensational make-belief, declaring itself to be Life when really it is Death. That is why I am afraid for our brothers—that they should lose the loyalty and grace which, in spite of the quarrels, they still have for one another in the thathiar brotherhood, especially if they are coerced into tackling the machine.'

'Then what is to be done?' said Janki, while Ananta sat spellbound in the dimly comprehended exaltation of his own strength against the poet's fears.

'Sister, this is not an incident by itself, it is an incident in the Revolution, a new development in which men will have to measure their strength against the new world, and either realize their power or be destroyed,' said the poet. 'When I was in Vilayat, an Indian friend of mine lived in a small cottage over a garage. Space is very limited in that congested world, even more congested than it is here. As the Nemesis of war daily came nearer, my friend's wife had some adjustments done to her place to make it proof against poison gas and bombs, for they had a baby daughter. The lady decided that she would take shelter in the small passageway in the middle of the house, if and when the bombs began to fall. And she had that hall reinforced. One day she discovered that the switch of the electric boiler in the bathroom was not in the house but down below in the lock-up garage, which the owner of the place had let to a gentleman with a car who lived some distance away, and who kept the key with him. Suddenly all her precautions seemed to her useless, because if the boiler should burst with the blast of a bomb it was certain, she felt, to scald her and her child to death. She told the landlord this and tried to make him install a separate switch for the boiler up in her flat where she could control it. The landlord, of course, refused to see the need for it. But she had the switch put in all the same. And in that story is contained the truth: if you have the *controlling switch* in your hand, you can make the machine a slave rather than your master. It is that switch or destruction.'

'Ah, that is it, the switch!' exclaimed Ananta. 'There is no talk of money; one should have a big heart!"'

'But what if people don't learn to use the switch?' said

Janki. 'And, anyhow, what about the main switch in the Power House ?'

'I'd rather that all men had a switch to their hearts,' said Ananta, 'as well as the right to appoint an expert watchman to control the main switch at the Power House. They have done that in Roos and they are—'

'The trouble with you folk is that you are always talking of Roos and not about your own country' Janki gibed at Ananta. 'I can understand why the thathiars won't listen to you. They have nothing to eat, and the machine has come and taken their jobs away from them, and you talk of Roos to them.'

'All this is necessary,' declared Ananta, 'because in our country the difficulty so far has been that, with their eternal belief in *maya*, our people often do not know what we are fighting for and against. And though it is good to live on doubt, one must believe in something, specially at moments when it is necessary to act. Puran Bhagat, there, has at least sifted the grain from the chaff.'

'And yet I doubt,' said the poet, 'if there is much grain in what I have said to go and feed the hungry with. That is one of the reasons why I said I was a coward. And the second reason is that it is difficult to be a man in the process of working the machine, to avoid being churned up by it and by the forces which it releases.'

'The people here are God's, the land belongs to the King, the machinery has just been installed by Murli Dhar and Gokul Chand—but we are Men,' Ananta answered Janki ironically. 'I think it is possible for me to see what the next step is. We must organize that union. If we control our own weaknesses and struggle for a share in the control of the main switchboard, we shall go further. Otherwise——'

'I said you were a machine man !' taunted Janki.

Puran Singh Bhagat smiled at their exchange and sat down at the foot of the bed to collect himself before taking leave.

'Tell him the right thing to do, Sardarji,' Janki suggested. 'He is merely a barker and rushes about without much sense of direction.'

'I told you the checker at home is equal to lentils !' said Ananta with a laugh. 'But you realize, Jankai, that while Puran Bhagat, like all the learned folk, is trying to think out the best way of living, I can hardly evade those wretches. I admit I am not as sure of my thoughts as Puran Bhagat.

Sometimes I feel that I too believe in the faith in which the thathiars believe, and at other times I feel I could change the whole world.'

'Braggart!' Janki said.

'No, Janki, he is right,' said the poet. 'I wish I had his courage, his love of action—even a little of his roguery.'

'Certainly you wouldn't have been so afraid of that C.I.D. man if you had my roguery,' said Ananta.

'Maybe being on bail makes one feel faint-hearted,' said the poet. 'And I have had a recurrent dream lately that I was going through a dark tunnel, a river-like sewer, and that the people I held on the strings in my hands were all breaking loose and being swept away by the stream.'

'So you too believe in your dreams,' Ananta said. And then he bellowed: 'If I can be the Guru for a moment, let me tell you that if others can dispose of our lives, we can also dispose of our own lives—and deaths. So there is nothing to fear!'

'Brother, there are a great many forces disposing of our lives today,' answered Puran. 'And the trouble with me is that I have to take account of them all. I am very afraid. Like dolts we tread the crooked streets of a bad time, drained of pity and unable to hold each other's hands. Those famished men in the streets of our cities, for instance, come from their villages to this world built upon pain, their few belongings on their shoulders, their families behind them, trekking the dusty way to the gates of nowhere, where the jaws of hell await all newcomers. Irretrievably they leave their native fields in ever-growing numbers; the red sunsets close about them, and they travel through the nights, the poet's moon braying over their heads, and the hounds of big houses at their legs. And in our cities of death they breathe their last breath. And there they sleep, with others like them. And our words cannot wake them. This is a story with murder in it, of slow mutilation and prolonged torture. And the tragedy behind our tragedy is, that though we have not made it, yet we have made it.——'

'That is no solution,' Ananta said impatiently. 'You force yourself to fear the truth by talking aloud to yourself as if you were making an effort to believe that you can do something. And all the time you want to do nothing! The trouble with you learned folk is that you spend so much of your time looking at your own feelings and at the end you are too weak to act.'

'Why are you sitting there, then?' taunted Janki. 'You yourself?'

'I have no doubt that I want to do something,' protested Ananta. 'But I was not sure until now what to do.'

'Now that you are sure of what to do, I should go and do it,' suggested Janki with the woman's instinct to see things done.

'Han, and I must do my kind of action,' said the poet, rising. 'Pen-pushing. I will look in at the shop before going back to the court, and if you can get the men together I should like to talk to them.'

'When I come to think of it myself,' said Ananta, 'I think it is going to be a rough crossing. When I go to deliver my cauldron to the dealers, I shall see if they have any metal sheets to give all of us enough work so that we can gain a little time.'

'Go and see if the coast is clear for me, at any rate,' said Puran Singh Bhagat with a gentle smile.

11

'NI, WHERE ARE YOU, NI?' GUJRIAI, THE WIFE OF MURLI, CALLED as she walked ahead of her husband into the alley past Ananta's shop, almost facing their own family mansion. She was dressed in a colourful pink head-cloth and a fawn skirt, which she had put on for the ceremony of the betrothal of her grandson Nikka. And she looked happy for once as she led the head of her house to collect rents from the inmates of the hovels which she had let to her coppersmith cousins in the alley, as well as to inform them of the increase in her family's prestige that was to accrue from the betrothal of her little grandson.

No one answered her call. For there was an old feud on between the patriarch Murli and the other indigent coppersmiths. And the wives of the thathairs in the alley recognized the voice of the quarrelsome wife of the head of their brotherhood and secured the latches of their front doors, apprehensive at the renewed demand for arrears of rent that Gujri's voice betokened.

'Ni, where are you?' Where? Gujri raised her voice so that it resounded through the lane like a shrill penny whistle. Like most Indian women, she was deeply wrinkled at sixty and was visibly crumbling because of a lack of sympathy between her and her husband.

'Is there no answer?' asked Murli impatiently, fanning himself against the heat and the flies with his splendid fan.

'Ni mother of Dina, ni wife of Ralia, ni mother of Mehru, ni dead ones, where are you?' Gujri raised her voice, till it seemed to penetrate the narrow length of the alley, across the layers of damp, musty hovels festering like stinking cesspools in the vapours that rose from their dark dungeons at the touch of the all-pervasive heat of the sun.

There was still no answer, except that a little obscure beetle hummed in some subterranean hole, a gloomy buzz as if it were announcing its own doom at the hands of a nearby frog.

'Why don't they answer?' said old Murli, harsh on his wife since his personal vanity as a poohbah was at stake. 'I don't want to get angry on this auspicious morning, but we must have the arrears of rent if we are to prepare for this marriage, with everything so dear nowadays.'

'Acha, father of Sadanand, you go back to the shop and I shall go up to each of these bitches,' Gujri suggested. In spite of the humiliation of being a cast-off Hindu wife in full knowledge of her husband's peccadilloes, she only thought of his ease, believing in the unspeakable blessedness of offering worship to the lord and master.

But before Murli could answer, came an ash-smeared, matted-haired ascetic, clanging a pair of long iron tongs in one hand and iron rings in the other, even as he shouted: 'Bham, Bham, Bhole Nath! Bhum Bhum!...' This dithyrambic repetition of the other name of God, Siva, with its shrill accompaniment, penetrated the dwellings in the sub-lane where the voice of Gujri had merely fallen on deaf ears. Bhole Nath, alias Siva, the destroyer, the wretched women felt, was angry with the world, and appeasement was called for if they were to save themselves from his wrath. Also, poor as the wretched tha-thiar women were, they gave alms to the beggars as though that would bring merit, because thus they would have denied themselves in giving and atoned for their evil deeds, and because they believed that if you gave anything it came back to you tenfold.

'Vay, wait, Bawa, wait Bhole Nath,' called Gauri, wife of Ralia, from the first floor of the house which belonged to Murli. 'I want a charm for my baby, who has fever.' Then, seeing Murli in the lane, she drew the end of her dhoti demurely to half-screen her face.

'Has he gone, the mother of Mehru?' asked Buddan, the mother of Dina Tamer Lane from the second floor of the same house, leaning like a witch with straggling hair from the window.

'No, sister, he is still here,' Bhago, the mother of Mehru, said, opening the door on the ground floor by a small balcony. 'Take this snuff, Sadhuji. I have kept it for you. And pray that my son——'

'Ni, all of you, so keen to do charity, why don't you answer me?' said Gujri, advancing to the balcony beside Mehru's mother.

'Mother', said the Sadhu, 'resent not those who, immersed in life, yet know that they are not of this life and do good deeds to earn a higher incarnation in the next. . . .' And he raised his voice again with 'Bham, Bham, Bhole Nath'. He was angry at Gujri's intrusion, for even those who had left the world needed a crust of bread to survive long enough to practise the mortification of the flesh to earn release from the trammels of existence.

'Ohe go, Bawa, go away,' snapped Murli, his face red with the heat in spite of the peacock fan in the narrow stuffy alley. 'You beggars will not let anyone rest all day.' He was not against charity or holiness: he went to the temple every morning, but he felt that everything had its time and place in these busy days. 'Business first, family second and beggars afterwards—' that was his motto.

'I call in the name of God,' said the ascetic. 'May Ishwar meet the true measure of his love or anger to everyone.' And he turned his back on the old couple with fiery, bloodshot eyes, chanting in a broken voice: 'Bham, Bham, Bhole Nath!. . .'

'And on this auspicious day too! What if he should pronounce a curse on us! The curse of an ascetic can bring disaster! You shouldn't have spoken to him like that!' protested Gujri.

'Ni, where are you menfolk?' Lala Murli Dhar challenged the tenants, angered by his wife. 'I should like to face them.

No talk that the rent has been delayed for three months now ! And we can't make ourselves heard when we call !'

'Vay ja, ja, go away, eater of your master,' shouted old Buddan from her window. 'Don't you come riding on at us, imagining us to be as enamoured of your charm as your daughter-in-law !'

'What is she barking ?' Murli asked his wife, as he was rather deaf.

But Gujri was very vulnerable on this score and said, 'Nothing. . .'

'Gujri, sister, ignore Chachi Buddan. I was coming round to congratulate you on Nikka's betrothal just now,' said Mehru's mother ingratiatingly. 'Wadahi, sister, wadahi brother, may your tribe increase !'

'I want the rent and not congratulations,' said Murli, petulant now. 'Where are these boys, Dina and Ralia ? I can talk to men, but not to these women.'

'Vay child,' Ralia's wife called to her one-year-old son Rupa as she now uncovered the whole of her face deliberately. 'Tell Grandfather that your father has just gone out to the flour shop. Vay, where are you ? Hai, Hai, again eating the earth on the stairs, Vay may you die, you will die if you eat dirt and dust. What with your fever.' ...

'What does she say, mother of Sadanand ? He is gone to the flour shop ? Well, I am not going there looking for him.'

At this instant, Buddan emptied some slops on the slab of stone at one end of her floor, and in the absence of a pipe to carry the water away, the dirt, splashed all over the two yards width of the alley just where the landlord and his wife were standing in their whitewashed raiment.

'Ohe ! Ohe, look, folks ! Ohe, have some sense !' the old man spluttered with excited squeals of anger as he looked at his muslin tunic splashed with dirty water.

'Ni Buddan !' called Gujri indignantly. 'How dare you do this to us ?'

'This is just to remind you, we want a pipe built,' said Buddan, leaning over the window. 'And don't you come shouting for rent till you have done something about that or given me a groundfloor room somewhere so that my son's leg is not strained coming and going up steep stairs. See ?' And she disappeared again.

'I said to you, father of Sadanand, you go and rest and I shall talk to them. Go now and change your shirt. They are not worthy of talking to the head of our house. May I become a sacrifice for you. Go.'

'They have no shame !' the old man muttered under his breath. 'They have no respect for anyone ! Keeping the rents pending for months and then insulting us when we come round. And I shall be late at the factory now. They have enough money to drink with. And they can go to prostitutes, the rogues, but their mothers die when I ask for my dues ! Low people ! Shodé !'

'What about you and your daughter-in-law ? Call yourself names, not us,' protested Gauri, wife of Ralia.

'Acha, you don't stay here, Gujri,' coaxed the old man, frightened of Gauran's sharp tongue. 'It is not becoming to our dignity to stop in this smelly lane and exchange abuse with them !'

Murli coughed with the choking passion which possessed him, flushed red and pale by turns. Then, fanning himself to calm his fury, he turned to go. But before he had advanced a yard, the children of some hill-men coolies, who had been stealing apple-peelings from the doorstep of Karam Devi, came rushing into the lane like a host of locusts and crashed headlong into the legs of the old man. Ordinarily very affectionate to the young, he burst with irritation now :

'Ohe, rape-mothers ! Ohe pigs ! Ohe !'

The children fell aside, scampering and scattering with shrieks of fear and laughter and then, seeing no way out of the blind alley, scurried back in the direction from which they had come, only to crash into old Karam Devi, who suspected that they had stolen apple from her basket.

'Vay ! May the vessel of your lives never float in the sea of existence !' Karam Devi shouted as they slipped out of her grasp.

Murli coughed to control his bitterness and, flustered but anxious to preserve his dignity, lifted a lapel of his dhoti to his nose, partly to guard his nostrils against the putrid smells that rose from the hovels as well as the dirt and slime in the alley, but mainly to hide his face from Karam Devi, the mother of the hated cousin Ananta. And thus he scraped along.

'Who are you abusing ?' Gujri called out to Karam Devi, because she had not seen her chasing the children and thought that Karmo was abusing her husband and herself.

'Grandma, is it you?' greeted Karam Devi cordially. 'Wadahi, wadahi, congratulations on Nikka's betrothal. I saw the folk from Jandiala arrive. And I thought I would catch you here and tell you how happy I am. Though, when will my son Ananta get a match? Without a wife, is anyone's home a home at all?'

'I have no time to arrange other people's affairs on such an auspicious morning,' Gujri said. 'The head of my house and I came to collect rent but, instead, we have only got insults. Just when I was thinking of distributing sugar-plums to you all to celebrate the betrothal of my Nikka. And now what about the rent? We were leaving you and your son to the last, because we didn't want to see your face the first thing!'

'Ananta will pay up, Grandma. Ever since he has come back he insists on paying for everything. He is a good boy at heart, whatever people might say against him. And, oh, it breaks my heart to see that he will never get a bride, while —'

'Now don't think that we are breaking your heart. It is your son and his deeds! Don't you come weeping on my shoulders. He lives with a prostitute up there, and you know it as well as I do. Besides, he is stirring up trouble against us!'

'Mother, whose shoulders shall we weep on?' put in Karmo.

Mehru's mother, who was patiently combing wads of wool into fine pads, joined in at this and, wiping the sweat off her ape-like face said, 'We have brought forth these sons of ours from our bellies. And we have to find them brides from somewhere.'

'And now the times are bad,' said Karmo, encouraged by Bhago, 'and the boys can't even get any jobs. Who shall we look to if not to you and Grandpa?'

'I know you are jealous,'! said Gujri. 'And you have all joined together against the owner of my house. What can we do if your sons are drunkards and whoremongers and——'

Ja, ni ja!' yelled Gauri from her porch now. 'You can't go on abusing us—you, with your husband living with his son's wife and making eyes at me! Look, folks, the darkness has come. The thief threatening the sheriff!'

'Now, didn't I tell you so, Mehru's mother,' protested Gujri, stunned and breathless at this outburst, even as the sweat rolled down from her thin hair over her knotted forehead and parrot's nose. 'Such is the filth they talk about the noble owner of my house. And it is sheer jealousy. Don't think I don't know about all the gossip that goes on about my family. And what for, because we have opened a factory and can't employ everyone.'

'Sister,' said Karam Devi, docile and beaten and sad. 'When death is near one doesn't bother about anything but to see that one's sons will have sons and carry on the family. One doesn't worry about the wealth of other people. One only thinks of loving one's own folk and dying peacefully. And who are we to compare ourselves with you? Our deeds in the past life were bad, yours good. But if only you masters will employ our sons!'

'You all talk the same meek talk when you want anything from me,' said Gujri. 'Don't I know how you hate us, really, bitches! Greedy low thathiars!—Don't I know that your mouth waters to see my progeny flourish! And then you go and accuse my husband of——That Buddan has thrown filth on his white head and Gauri has attacked his honour! Perdition on you! May the curses of heaven descend on you! And I pronounce this curse in the full faith that the house which an old devout woman curses will perish. You have troubled my heart so!'

'Ni, ja ja, call your daughter-in-law names,' said Gauri, roused. 'You are the bitch and not I, nor Aunt Buddan, nor Aunt Karam Devi. Yes. Go, if you value your skin, or the master of my house will come and drag you by your thinning hair!'

'Don't quarrel, sister Gauran,' appealed Mehru's mother.

'You take her side, because they have given your son a job!' said Buddan.

'Sister, keep quiet, aunt, patience,' said Karam Devi, who felt guilty about her son living with Janki and thought that they all deserved their bad luck as the price of their evil deeds, that they were all in the grip of a superior destiny which rewarded joy and sorrow justly.

'Then, we can't blame them, Buddan,' said Mehru's mother. 'It is our lot to suffer. God alone knows the things that pertain to God!'

'Yes, when God wants to give, He will give us through the roofs,' said Karam Devi. 'And what do we know of His mysterious ways?'

'Acha, now you are trying the sob-stuff—that one threatening like a tiger, the other mewing like a cat!' said Gujri, inconsolable.

'Let them mew like cats,' said Buddan, emerging at the foot of the stairs, 'but you are no pigeon. And I know that you will not clear out till I remove all the remaining hair on your head.'

'Hai ni dohai!' Gujri shrieked as she ran. 'Hai ni, they are going to beat me! Hai, they are going to loot me! These shameless witches! Vay Sadanand, Vay Gopi, my son!'

'I will give her the rent when she comes again,' said Buddan in a hoarse voice, mistress of the situation. 'I tell you, Karmo, Mehru's mother, Gauran, they don't love you. These swine. They give you these smoky houses to live in and think that you should crawl out like worms before them. They strip you of your clothes and strangle you and then they come asking you for the rent. Gloating over the bride that is coming to their house while our sons are growing impotent for lack of wives. I tell you, they have never loved us and never will love us——'

'It is our past sins, Chachi,' said Karam Devi.

'Patience, sisters, patience,' said Mehru's mother. 'Don't defy God or an old woman. Patience and love—for love brings love and hate brings hate.'

'Ni, don't cringe before them with your "patience, sister",' said Buddan, her shrivelled face contorted with spite. 'I tell you, they won't even throw a crumb at us And it is not us but they who are greedy. They want to grab, grab, grab— piling up a fortune by hiring young boys for low wages, never mind if our sons are reduced to skeletons. I tell you, when anyone is bitten with the gold lust as that Murli is bitten, he loses his soul. And they have no conscience left—they will do anything to make money, even eat dung, these eaters of their masters!'

Her words rang down the alleyway and silenced the other women for a while. But the damp Fate which enveloped the dark corners, the nooks and the crevices of the festering lane, the destiny which had played havoc with the mouldering walls of the houses, reasserted itself as the two fatalists, Karmo and Bhago, began to moan over their misfortunes, resuscitating their belief in Karma, recognizing and accepting their role on earth as due to the faults they and theirs had committed in their past lives and, overcome by self-pity, they shed tears and cried:

'We belong to suffering, sister. We belong to suffering! This life is not worth living! All we can do is to do some good deed : and prepare for the next——'

12

> Ohe, the bull is coming! The bull!
> Ohe, the bull!
> Ohe, Ananta, the bull!

THE CHILDREN LAUGHED AND SHRIEKED AS THEY CAPERED ASIDE from the path of Ananta, who hurried with the finished cauldron lifted in his two hands over his head.

'Ohe, get away, sons, get away!' he shouted.

But by now they were clinging to his legs, laughing and shouting as they stopped catching live wasps from the puddles on the terrace of the well in Kucha Billimaran and ran to him.

At that Ananta began, playfully, to sway and snort like a bull. The children only laughed the more and would't leave him. So he lifted the cauldron, put it down on the wooden platform of a closed shop, rolled his eyes like a tired bull, phewed hot breath from his mouth and leaned back.

Immediately he had done that, he could hear the clock in the tower striking huge gong notes of the hour—what was the time? Ananta wondered. And he answered, 'Eleven,' from the way the shaft of sunlight was falling across Billimaran. And for a moment he applied his attention to the gong notes and listened, keeping the children at bay with one hand, while his eyes stared with a rapt expression into the void before him, as though, right at the moment that he had been caught in the world of time, the timeless world had pulled him back to the eternities before watches and clocks had come into Hindustan, before all the hurry and scurry had begun to dominate his life. The nostalgia for the past occupied him, the longing for the chaotic world in which one could make day and night one in work and then play about like these children on the money earned from piecework. He felt that to some extent he was still doing that, though he was more conscious than other thathiars that the coppersmith's trade and other handicrafts could never overtake the wastage of the new life with its quick changes of fashions in utensils, just as the rule of Maharaja Ranjit Singh could not come back, with its absence of trains, canals, machines and its ease and luxury. All this occurred to him in a flash. But, almost as soon as the feeling came, he dismissed it impatiently and turned to the children.

'Chacha Anantia, give me a pice,' said Rhoda.

'Chacha, give me one too,' said Durga, the little daughter of Bali.

'Chacha, oh, Chachaji, give me one,' said Rama, the younger brother of Ralia.

'And me,' said the son of a hill-man coolie.

The other little girls and boys stood round the cauldron, fingering it and making smudges on it with their dirty hands.

'Now lay off me and that deg, children,' said Ananta. 'Have you ever known of anyone being paid a pice for doing nothing in this world of ours ?'

'Han me,' said Rhoda. 'You gave me two pice on the day of the Spring Festival.'

'And the basket of puris this morning,' said Rama, shy because he was older.

'Han, but festivals are another matter,' said Ananta, assuming a child's tone of voice. 'And, as for the puris, they were charity from someone who wanted to go to heaven. But I mean on an ordinary working day ?''

'You gave me one only three days ago,' said Durga. 'And Bapu told me off for taking it from you.'

'And you gave me one for buying dry mango juice too,' said Rhoda.

'Acha, what is done is done, friends,' said Ananta. 'But now I am making another rule. You will get a pice only if you do something to earn it.'

'Can I run an errand for you ?' Rhoda said.

'Oh, I will go,' Durga said with a coy expression.

'Nahin, I will go, let me,' Rama offered. 'I am bigger than you two.'

'You will all go,' Ananta said. 'You will all help me to carry this deg and you will get a pice each for doing so.'

The children shouted and jumped for joy and began pulling, pushing and tugging at the cauldron.

'No, not like animals,' said Ananta. 'I will put it on the wheelcart of the pickle-makers there and you shall push the cart.'

He raised the cauldron from the platform and headed towards the shed where the pickle-makers kept their little carts, with the children trooping behind him, excited, happy and hilarious.

'They want to push this cart with my deg on it, Munshi,' he said to the clerk of the pickle factory. 'I will bring it back——'

'Take it, brother,' said the Munshi, 'they will make less noise about the place and I shall be able to do my figures in peace. What with the noise of the factory there—this lane has become an unrelieved hell !'

Ananta settled the cauldron on the cart and then negotiated the vehicle on the rough surface of Kucha Billimaran, against the noisy, rasping protests of the children, who wanted to push it all by themselves. As soon as they had got into the square where Kucha Billimaran cut into the Bazar Kaserian, Ananta withdrew and left it to their mercy, thinking of Munshi's words about the factory and realizing how, inside him, if he was to be honest, he felt as frightened of the consequences of the factory's coming as everyone else, in spite of the optimistic way he had been talking, in spite of the enthusiasm he had worked up in himself.

As the children's enthusiasm to push the cart was more forceful than their physique, he had to help them after they had been straining in vain for a moment. But he made a show of exerting his full force, so that they got the feeling that it was mainly they, and not he, who were pushing the vehicle.

The Kaseras were arranging their wares of brass, bronze, copper on the boards of their low, narrow shops, murmuring, 'Om, Om Hari Shiva, Radhe Sham, Kali Mai, Radhe Sham, Krishan, Ram, Ram,' and the various names of God, joining hands to the little effigies of Ganesha, the Elephant-headed God of Wealth, showing the incense of half-incandescent thup to the tawdry-coloured oleographs of saints, putting garlands around them, or splashing holy water into the depths of the caverns, on their greasy cushions and their shop-fronts.

The shrill laughter of the children pushing the cart burst upon this solemn, airless world like fresh gust, of wind. Ananta was afraid that some Kasera or other might object to the racket the children were kicking up if he took them too deep into the Bazar. So he halted and said.

'Now you have earned your reward : you need not come any further.'

'Oh, we want to push it, we want to, Chachaji !' the children cried. 'Please let us.'

So he let them carry on till he reached the shop of Lal Chand-Kushal Chand. Then he stopped, banged his throat with his fist and coughed up a four-anna nickel piece.

'Change this into pice,' he said to Rama, 'and distribute it equally among you all.'

All the children eagerly stretched out their hands for the money and began to suggest the various shops where they could change the nickel coin.

'Go away, boys, and don't make such a row,' said Lal Chand, the dealer, turning the short, muscular neck of his handsome fair-complexioned face from where he sat on the platform projecting from his shop, engaged in adding figures in an ochre-coloured ledger-book.

Seeing the children scatter suddenly at Seth Lal Chand's rebuke, Ananta stared at the dealer for a moment and stood still trying to control his rage. The fellow had been his pupil in the wrestling-ring for a few days, but had ceased to come again because his younger brother Khushal, who was also Ananta's pupil, threw him too easily. And now, Ananta felt, the coward had grown up and was putting on airs. It seemed nowadays it certainly didn't matter if you were a coward or a brave man so long as you had money and could hold your head high, higher than anyone else. He felt mad that the pressure of Lal Chand's weakness, refurbished into a show of strength by his wealth, should give the lie to his pet phrase, 'There is no talk of money, you must have a big heart.' He gritted his teeth hard and vowed that he would no longer remain one of the broken wrecks of the thathiar community, that he would refuse to become a shadow or a wraith in the obscure background of the doom that hung over Billimaran, that he would get the men together and fight them rather than fade out. He lifted the cauldron and put it on the projection of Lal Chand's shop.

13

'I FALL AT YOUR FEET, LALA LAL CHAND,' ANANTA GREETED THE dealer in the familiar manner.

Ananta revolved the cauldron and pushed it lightly forward on the platform. Then he glanced at its base to make sure that the jolts in the cart had not done any damage to it.

'Are you looking to see if those brats have dented it?' said Lal Chand, lifting his jowl so that his regular features were covered with a frown.

'No, only admiring my handiwork for the last time?' Ananta lied. 'It is a pity I can't keep it to have sweet rice cooked in it to distribute at my wedding.'

Lal Chand resumed work on his ledger almost as if Ananta were not there. Ananta secured a precarious hold on the edge of the platform with his rump and waited, fanning himself the while with an end of his greasy, sweat-covered tunic.

'Are you going to do any wrestling at the big akhara, Ustad Ananta Ram?' asked Allah Bux, the tinsmith next door, whose own broken ears betokened his addiction to the wrestling-ring.

'Ohe nahin, brother, I can't get the time even to wash my bottom properly,' said Ananta. 'I have been at this deg since dawn.'

'That explains why you are here so early,' said Lal Chand ironically.

'Where is Lala Khushal Chand today?' Ananta asked. 'Perhaps he could take delivery of this. Could you call him if he is upstairs?'

'It is early morning, you know, and we haven't even earned a pice,' said Lal Chand, undoing the upper button of his muslin shirt. 'I don't know what time the shops open in Bombai, but here we still start business about midday, you know.'

'We thathiars have to work all hours, Lala Lal Chand, especially nowadays.'

'Don't you think anyone else works? I have been at this ledger all night.'

Lal Chand screwed his face tighter with annoyance so that his high cheekbones stood out like the shining blades of a well-polished chopper.

'Ah, but every figure there means wealth, while every star on that cauldron means only the hope of a modest wage.'

For a moment the dealer deliberately restrained himself, with a view to asserting the dignified calm which was his ideal of a superior dealer in negotiations with low thathiars. Then he said: Han, there is a debit side as well as a credit side in the ledger. But what can a thathiar know about figures?'

'Where is Lala Khushal Chand?'

Ananta wanted to bring the conversation discreetly to the question of his wages.

'He has gone to the station with Uncle Gokul Chand to get delivery of some goods.'

'Oh, I didn't know that you had shares in the new factory too, Lala Lal Chand!'

'If you want information about the factory from me, you have come to the wrong quarter—I don't know what things are coming to! Everyone is anxious to know all about the factory.'

'You need not be surprised at my inquiry, Lalaji. After all, we are workers and you are employers, and we can't get on without each other, as things stand. But I have been refused a job at the factory. So it doesn't really matter to me who runs it. I would like to go on making these degs for you. Perhaps you could give me the wages and also some sheets of copper for all those thathiars who are unemployed. We will——'

'Put that deg on the scale there.'

Ananta jumped up to the platform and hooked up the scales which stood in the corner, put the cauldron on one pan and the iron weights on the other.

Lal Chand came over and began to adjust the scales and count the iron weights, mumbling the figures under his breath the while, his contempt for the dirty tunicked coppersmith making him withdraw a little.

'Fifteen rupees seventy paise,' he said.

'Hain?' said Ananta, taken aback. 'Fifteen rupees, seventy paise.'

'I have told you counting and adding were never a coppersmith's strong point,' Lal Chand said, with an irony which did not disguise his embarrassment. And he had to repeat, 'Fifteen rupees, seventy paise,' as though to assure himself that that was the price he was going to offer and stick to. 'And don't tread on that white sheet on the platform with your paws.'

'Are you joking, Lala Lal Chand?'

'No, I am not. That is the wage for a deg in the bazaar today. Go and ask any Kasera. We have had to reduce wages because there is no demand for these utensils now. People haven't the money to buy utensils. And the market for this kind of work is contracting everywhere.'

'You have reduced wages'.... That is a strange thing to

happen in these times when everything is so dear.'

'I have told you that I haven't sold a thing this morning, and I don't want a row over the first deal. So—'

'Oh, Lala Lal Chand, open the case and give me the fair wage which you have always given me, and—another sheet of copper.'

'Fifteen rupees, seventy paise ! And you will agree that you are lucky to get work, when every one of your brothers is workless.'

Lal Chand repeated the sum he had already offered curtly and sat down to open the cash-box beside him. Then he took the money out and, counting it, put it before Ananta.

'But, Lalaji !—'

'There is no talk of but, that is the wage in the market, I tell you. And you ought to realize I am being very considerate to you for old times' sake.'

'But you can't reduce an established wage. Give me what you have always given me. It is not a mere figure in a ledger. It represents work, labour, the three days I have spent on it—this deg !'

'I say you should think yourself lucky that you got work at all. Think of your other friends, Ralia and all the others. We believed in your craftsmanship and we gave you the copper to make a deg. It is dead stock and won't be sold for years. Now take the money or throw it away—that is your own lookout.'

'But Lala Khushal Chand gave me the copper sheet and there has surely been a mistake, for he never mentioned that wages have been reduced.'

'There he is, I can see him by the banyan tree, talking to someone. I will ask him what wages he promised you.' And he flushed a vivid red with heat and anger, and beads of perspiration gathered on his nose.

'Han, I will call him. . . . Eh, Lala Khushal Chand !'

'He is coming, he is coming, don't be impatient.'

Ananta scooped the sweat on his forehead in the palm of his right hand and threw it on the damp earth of the bazaar under the shadow of the banyan tree. Khushal Chand did not hasten back at the call. And the tension between Lal Chand and Ananta grew to breaking-point, because each of them was sure that Khushal Chand would give evidence in his favour. Ananta was sure that no revised wage had been mentioned and that, therefore, the old wage stood. Lal Chand was certain that the younger brother had passed on the collective decision that the dealers had arrived at : to reduce wages for piecework below the level of the standard wage in the new factory in which the most important dealers had bought shares.

After waiting for a few moments, doubt assailed Lal Chand's mind that Khushal Chand may have forgotten to mention the revised wage. He ducked his head forward and called to his brother.

'Ohe, Khushal !' And before his brother had ascended the steps to the platform of the shop he said : 'You did tell this thathiar that the wages for piecework have been reduced, didn't you ?'

'Han,' Khushal said, rather flustered. 'No'—he corrected himself. 'I am afraid I didn't.'

'But you had it in your mind to tell him, surely !' Lal Chand suggested.

'Nahin,' answered Khushal, going pale. 'I didn't discuss wages with him at all.'

'You knew, though, didn't you ?'

'Han, but I forgot to mention it.'

'If you had the new rate in your mind, and that is the rate being paid in the whole market, that is good enough for me, and I shall pay him that rate.'

'Acha,' said Khushal, taking his hand to the end of his dhoti, where he kept his money tied in a knot, 'I will pay him the balance between the old rate and the new rate. It is my fault.'

'Oh, there is no talk,' said Ananta, responding to Khushal's generous gesture. 'I don't see why you should have to pay the penalty for a mere trick of the memory. If that is the new rate, I will take that money.'

And he picked up the fifteen rupees, seventy paise.

'That is the wage,' Lal Chand said, with a sigh of relief. 'And I tell you we have been very considerate to you.'

'Did you get delivery of the goods, Lala Khushal Chand ?' asked Ananta, evading Lal Chand's explanation and getting ready to go.

'Whether he did or not we are not giving away any more sheets of copper for piecework,' said Lal Chand. 'Don't let there be any mistake or forgetfulness about that. The factory needs all the supplies we can get.'

'Acha, if that is the talk, then I had better go home and change my profession,' said Ananta bitterly. 'And thank you for showing me all that consideration.'

'That is your lookout,' said Lal Chand, 'if you feel the time has come for you to change your profession.'

'Ananta Ram, you must take this extra money,' said Khushal Chand. 'It is only fair that you should.'

'Nahin, brother, there is no talk of money; it is a question of the heart, said Ananta with a laugh, making a show of heroism, though he was raging inside.

And he laughed an embarrassed laugh to control his bitterness, put his hand on the handle of the pickle-maker's cart and walked away.

14

'OH—S-O-NN, ASK HIM THEN—ASK HIM FOR—ANOTHER BOTTLE, ask him!' said Ralia drunkenly, as he sat with Dina on the platform of Bali's little grocery and sherbet shop in the square where Kucha Billimaran cut into Bazar Kaserian.

'Let us go,' answered Dina, and hiccupped before completing the answer. Then he belched and said, all in a mouthful: 'Let us go back to the Drink Shop . . . . Come . . . .' He had only had a small quantity of drink and was comparatively sober.

'Oh putar . . . . ohe putre, your Chacha Gauran will beat me. . . . . I don't want to go . . .' said Ralia, his eyes rolling sleepily. And . . . I am thirsty! . . . Do you hear, son, I am thirsty. . . . I have been thirsty for a week and you have kept me from drinking.' He raised his hand almost threateningly and Dina cowered. But Ralia was only making an extravagant gesture. 'Oh, son of Timur Lang, I am thirsty like that Sun in heaven now, and—where is he? That son of a bitch?'

'Not Sun—that is the Moon!' protested Dina, lifting his eyelids from the stupor he clownishly affected just to keep in tune with his drunken companion.

'You take a bet on it—that is the Sun!' Ralia shouted 'I know it is Sun because you—didn't let me have a . . . . I hope Gauran is not listening. But I should have liked to have a whack at one of them, see!'

'I don't see—and that is the Moon, not the Sun,' said Dina, burying his head in his arms. 'I am—sleepy! . . .'

'Ohe putar .... I have—won my bet, now get me the money and I can buy some more liquor from that son of a bitch!' insisted Ralia, shaking his friend till the latter nearly fell.

'Don't you call me son of a bitch!' Dina protested.

'Ohe it isn't you ... it's that——'

'Now, then, brothers,' said Bali, approaching with a slab of ice in his hands from a cart in the square. 'Scram.'

'You, Bali Seth, you decide—is it the Sun or the Moon up there?' said Ralia. 'He says it's—''

'I have no time for such trifles,' said Bali. 'Cold ice in my hand. Get away!'

'I have a bet with him—brother, a bet,' said Ralia ingratiatingly. 'If you say it is the Sun, I shall win and buy that liquor off you!'

'There is no liquor here,' said Bali peremptorily. 'Go to the shop where liquor is. I don't want Gauri to come shouting at me for harbouring you. Already your son Rhoda has been here asking for you several times.'

'Oh, rape-mother everyone!' said Ralia, swaying dangerously, his face swollen with drunkenness. 'I don't—care for anyone. Not even for the Tunda Lat!' And nudging Dina Timur Lang's elbow, he said: 'Why, ohe Choohe Shah, speak!'

'Don't!' shrilled Dina, red-eyed and excited. 'Don't call me Choohe Shah!' And the rest of his words were drowned in a huge belch which rose from his inner good nature, struggling against the little liquid which had soured it. 'I am no mouse, even if you fancy yourself as a wrestler!'

'Ohe hacha, ohe hacha, ohe hacha!' answered Ralia, abject now where he had been boastfully proud and haughty a second before. 'Ohe hacha... Get us another drink. He has—he surely has some bottles hidden away there....'

'Nahin, I haven't any, Ustad Ralia Ram,' said Bali, trying to flatter the tough's vanity. 'Besides, the woman of your house sent Rhoda here asking whether you have got any flour for the household.' The grocer's pale respectable face was tense with embarrassment.

'There's no flour—anywhere.... See!' Ralia said, sobering at the mention of his wife and the flour, and angry with frustration. 'She can eat dung.... And she can drink urine! See! She can eat dung and drink urine as I eat dung and drink urine!'

'Ohe, come to your senses,' said Dina, lifting his head from the hollows of his intertwined arms, a gentle light in this buffoon's eyes.

'Give me urine! Now give it to me,' said Ralia, almost putting his arms round Bali. 'Choohe Shah—no, Seth Dina Nath, Dina there, will pay for the bottle. It isn't his money anyhow—' He stole it from his mother.'

'If you say that I will really make you eat dung and drink ——' The hiccup made his protest ridiculous again. And he seemed to have lost his sense of humour.

'Give me the urine—it isn't his money.... It is his mother's,' Ralia repeated, violent and nasty. 'And he has stolen——'

'Shurrup!... Bastard!' shouted Dina, as he sprang from his seat. Abominable fellow. 'If you say fire, it will not burn my mouth. I am no thief.'

'Ohe, brothers! Ohe...' said Bali, as he came between them. 'Go your separate ways. It is no use for fire and cotton to be together. Go. Have some respect for my customers. Look, there is Mahasha Hans Raj coming.'

'What are we if not customers?' said Dina, sitting back very much on his dignity against the grocer now and forgetting his quarrel with Ralia.

'We are not the lovers of your mother!' taunted Ralia, backing up Dina. 'All we want is more——'

'Ohe chup kar!' Bali said, cautioning him. And, twisting his face deliberately, he put on a meek expression and joined his hands respectfully to the august person who was approaching.

Mahasha Hans Raj was a stocky, middle-aged man. His beautifully-modelled visage was like that of the god Krishna, with a complexion like that of the cowdust hour, though the horn-rimmed glasses he wore seemed to give a somewhat sinister concentration to his small eyes, and his face seemed to have been hardened by the excess of moral energy which inspired him. He had been brought up in the reformist Neo-Hindu Arya Samaj, hence the appellation Mahasha, but not finding enough room for his religio-political beliefs in that society, he had joined the Congress. Certainly, no one could call his patriotism 'the last refuge of a scoundrel,' for his sincerity was patent, but his priggishness was, nevertheless, frightening to the two drunkards, as indeed even to the grocer

Bali, and everyone else. For, apart from the fact that he was a hundred per cent for Mahatma Gandhi's programme of reviving the Golden Age in India, and his keen interest in the wrestling-ring and the idea of brahmachara, celibate life, not much was known of his outlook on life except that he was one of the accused with Puran Singh Bhagat in the case which was being argued in the court of Mr. Silver, First-class Magistrate of Amritsar, on the charge of making seditions, anti-war speeches to the cotton-workers at Cheharta. Like the poet Bhagat, he was out on bail, and his sudden appearance here seemed surprising to Bali, who knew that there was a hearing on this morning.

'Don't you shurrup me!' protested Ralia, resisting the pressure of the leader's will that advanced like a shadow of righteousness before the leader. 'And I don't see—why I should join my hands to anyone. I—I am a man . . . of pleasure . . . not . . . duty!'

'I fall at your feet, Mahashaji,' Bali said.

'I fall at your feet, Baliji,' the Mahasha acknowledged the grocer's greeting formally. Then he paused, contemplated the two drunkards with a stern and vigilant eye, and asked Bali with a mild laugh: 'Why are they so sad today, our two thathiar brothers?'

Bali didn't answer, but smiled. And, of course, neither Dina nor Ralia were feeling well disposed towards the world to answer.

'Why, brothers?' the Mahasha Hans Raj probed, anxious to solve their problems. For he had heard about the trouble in the quarter and had, in fact, come specifically to preach a solution of the issue facing the thathairs. 'What is the trouble? That student Satyapal there tells me——'

'Our mother has died!' said Ralia, making a solemn face. 'You ask Babu Satyapal . . . . He knows.'

Dina couldn't help bursting into laughter at this, though generally he laughed only at his own jokes.

Satyapal, who was buying some matches at Hiro's the tobacconist's came up in the midst of this laughter. A tall, thin young man with curly hair, his oval face was scarred with pockmarks, and wore a self-righteous hauteur and insolence.

'I am surprised that the death of your mother makes you so happy,' said the Mahasha with a gentle smile.

Unable to maintain the permanent scowl of seriousness into

which Satyapal had willed his face—he laughed, though he kept silent.

'She was a very [hiccup] old woman,' answered Dina, to keep up the joke.

'So you are celebrating her demise,' said the Mahasha. 'I see. And who is going to look after you now?'

'The only girl the bachelor thathiars could have had,' said Bali, 'the daughter of Binde Saran from Jandiala, is going to be betrothed to Nikka, the grandson of Lala Murli Dhar.'

'Han,' said Ralia, trying to be serious, 'I am said in my heart. Our old mother is dead. And the new girl has gone into the household of that beti-chod.... But we are men of pleasure. And we don't care for the Tunda Lat!'

'But the Tunda Lat is very concerned about you,' began the student Satyapal.

'Oh, don't you joke at my expense, Babu,' protested Dina. He was often called Tunda Lat, Limp Lord, by his friends, on account of the limp in his leg.

'He means the Angrezi Sarkar,' said the Mahasha.

'Don't you see,' said Satyapal, 'that they are flooding the country with the instruments of destruction? At first they brought railways, telephones and telegrams; now they are bringing that engine of death, the aeroplane. All for profits, and because they are hungry for markets. Big monopolies wanting big contracts. And the lackeys of imperialism here—'

'For ought we know,' mocked Ralia, 'Murli Dhar and Gokul Chand are making parts for these steel birds in their factory at the bidding of the saab.'

'Never a truer word said in jest,' said Satyapal.

'I don't know about the intentions of Murli Dhar and Gokul Chand, who are sympathetic to religion,' said Mahasha Hans Raj, the spiritual leader, hedging.

'But I hear there are some who want you to take up jobs in these works of the Devil,' Satyapal came to the charge. 'All I came to tell you is that these men who are advising you are Communists. If you do what they tell you, you will be run over by them and their machines, broken and pulped and ground into dust.'

Both Ralia and Dina were puzzled at this talk, which exonerated Murli Dhar and Gokul Chand and seemed directed against Puran Singh Bhagat and Ananta. Not inclined to religion, however, and sensing a sympathy for the bosses in

Mahasha Hans Raj, they turned a deaf ear to his gentle voice, but pondered uncomprehendingly over Satyapal's acrimonious insinuations.

'It is true what Mahashaji says,' said Bali, persuaded by the superior visitor, though he had no views of his own.

'Man wants but seven hundred yards of earth to live and seven feet to die,' Hans Raj said. 'And I agree with Babu Satyapal when he asks why you go in for all these contraptions, but I don't agree with his kind of revengeful politics.'

'Our dharma says that this Vilayati mixture of iron and leather is evil,' said Ralia. 'To be sure Babu Satyapal is right.'

'Han, but it is a question of the soul, of the spiritual satisfaction which is lost in working machines, said Mahasha Hans Raj, trying to persuade them to listen to the deeper reasons which he had for rejecting the machine.

'Too true,' said Satyapal, taking advantage of the doubts about machines raised by spiritual leader and working up for a harangue as he found the two drunks suppressing their yawns.

But Mahasha Hans Raj asserted himself for a moment by raising his hand and saying: It is a question of good and evil, of the age of truth against the age of falsehood, of the world when there was light against the world of darkness, of the India in which we had a great civilization and everyone was a peasant who ate a bellyful and the machine-ridden India we are threatened with by those who want to reproduce here the conditions of the atheistic West——'

'Of Bolshevist Russia,' cut in Satyapal, 'where the party in power wants to mechanize the very soul of man to produce machine-men with their mass-production and their five-year plans! I tell you, as I have told Uncle Viroo, that the white race want to bait us with more money and to harness us to the chariot of their wars, which will just smother us under their wheels and consign us into the abysses of hell.'

'Satyapal,' protested the Mahasha, 'don't talk of the white race and black race. Talk of our differences with our brother Europeans, but not of Asia and Europe, like the Japanese.'

In the fumes of drunken ennui that covered the faces of Ralia and Dina, on the brink of their ruin and before the emptiness of their yawns, these sentiments aroused memories of the altercation between Viroo and Ananta at the bunga of Sant Harnam Das. They could not see the subtle differences between the Mahasha and Satyapal. They clutched at the clouds of heat and stretched themselves as if they were aching with an intense yearning to grasp their destiny between the two poles of their actual desire for a job and their evasive drifting into the nothing of drunkenness.

'Wake up, brothers,' exhorted Satyapal, 'wake up, before you fall into the pit.

That is where they are taking you. In order to ensure that the student Satyapal should not pervert his gospel, Mahasha Hans Raj interrupted the boy deliberately: 'The Western ethos has made machinery the New Messiah. The source of all higher life comes to man from his spiritual mind, but they are for abolishing personality. Mahatma Gandhi has said that it is every man's duty to resist the Sarkar and the evils of Vilayat which are flooding the country. Only the evils, remember, not the good. And the sage knows that our happiness lies in the acceptance of this duty—the mysterious God who is greater than all petty considerations of want and family demands. We are men. And men owe obedience to some God, or Higher Power, like Duty. We must submit and sacrifice everything to this higher thing which lives and acts through us, otherwise we are doomed.'

The Mahasha's face was strained even as his words became more and more abstract. He seemed to be consumed by an inner tension, between the man of religion who believed in the ancient spiritual splendour of the Vedic age, and yet knew that most of the other members of the revivalist Arya Samaj, as well as the Congress, were the very men who, contrary to their religious ideals, were hastening the machine age for profit. So he had resolved all his doubts about the loss of spiritual satisfaction portented by machine work to the labourer, by the monotony threatened by civilization, by beckoning a dark 'something'.

'We are not oxen,' lashed Satyapal, so that his pock-marked face contorted into a pitiless, ugly scowl.

Excited by the excessive priggishness of the student leader, and half persuaded of the truth of what he had said, Ralia was overcome by a maddening wave of hysteria against Murli and Gokul.

'What about those pious Arya Samajis of yours, Murli and his family?' he bawled at Mahasha Hans Raj. 'They are destroying our homes. Why don't you blame them squarely as Babu Satyapal does ? They have brought the engines.'

And then, before anyone could control him, he closed his mouth and simulated the sound of steam bursting and the phuff, phuff of an engine in a violent caricature of the factory in Billimaran which soon gathered force and became the forward drive of the belt and the backward pull of the pistons as, jumping off the platform of the shop, he went with short, sudden steps up to the middle of the square and back. 'Chappar Chappar Channa !' he shouted, as he had done outside the factory this morning. 'Cheekh Cheekh . . . Phuff . . . Phuff . . . We are not oxen ! . . . Chappar Chappar . . . Cheekh . . . Phuff . . . Phuff . . .'

The mock-heroic dance of Ralia's representation of the machines in Billimaran demolished the gentle attitude of Mahasha Hans Raj and made it a joke. Satyapal felt embarrassed at the disrespect implied in this and tried to control Ralia's orgy by a shriller and louder exhortation which would swallow up the joke and mould it into a serious stand.

'It is no joke, but a question of life and death !'

At this Mahasha Hans Raj began to justify his kindness to Murli and Gokul :

'The merchants and dealers who have opened factories have no hand in the arrangement of life in our country under the present dispensation, just as you have no voice in it today. The Angrezi Sarkar arranges life, and it has multiplied infamy and plunder and murder by starvation. . . . Those who belong to the Arya Samaj at heart believe that every individual has a soul, an enduring essence in him. And they seek to purify life by giving charity and honouring the duty they owe to their dharma.'

'A single pea will not burst the oven !' mocked Dina.

'They may feed the yellow-robed priests in the Samaj, but they certainly prefer to see us hungry,' taunted Ralia bitterly.

'Han, they seem to leave their religion behind in the Samaj on Sundays and only worship money on the other days,' said Satyapal, backing up his protégé.

'You do not know the number of men who were put out of employment in Vilayat,' said Mahasha Hans Raj, 'and the numbers of those who were condemned to the workhouses. I tell you it is not our Indian brothers who are so much to blame as the devils who deny God and the spirit.'

But the spiritual leader's defence did not satisfy Kalia.

This gave Satyapal the opportunity to extend the argument of the soul to his own oppositional temper. 'Down with the liars, the slanderers and persecutors of our brothers ! Down with the whites !' And he lashed out harsher and harsher with every sentence and brought the vehemence of the demagogue to bear on his audience.

'Stop it !' roared Mahasha Hans Raj when he couldn't bear Satyapal's provocations any longer.

And then a brooding silence dominated the square, spreading on the layers of shimmering heat and smothering the wills of all those who gathered round to see the fun, till, for a moment, it seemed that Time itself had stepped in the nothingness of the void, emptied of all illusion by Satyapal, who had taken upon himself to tear each sheath before the eyes of men.

'There is Ananta,' Dina said, breaking the spell of the magician. 'Please do come, Lala Anant Ram, but bring something !'

'Let him answer now, the big heart that he thinks he is !' said Ralia.

'Oh, the machine man !' said Satyapal, with a laugh. 'If I get into his way, he might run me over. So for my safety I shall get off his track.'

'I haven't been home since I came back from the court,' said Mahasha Hans Raj, excusing himself. 'Our hearing is in the afternoon.'

'Have some sherbet, Mahashaji,' offered Bali.

But Mahasha Hans Raj waved his head and his hands.

Satyapal took advantage of the dramatic moment for escape which offered itself.

'I am sorry I have to go,' said Hans Raj to Ananta, 'but I am coming to collect Sardar Puran Singh Bhagat at your shop on my way to the court in the afternoon.'

Ananta joined his hands to the spiritual leader formally.

'Ananta—steam-engine !' commented Ralia, 'puffing and blowing and snorting !'

'So did you a moment ago,' said Dina Timur Lang. 'He has been getting his wages. I wonder if he will stand us a drink.'

The talk of the leaders seemed to have perplexed Ralia, so complex and abstract it was, against the factories, and yet for Murli and Co., against the white race and yet settling nothing, proposing no course of action.

'How much did you get?' he asked Ananta, inclined to be very friendly and giving him the benefit of the doubt in spite of all the malicious hints in Satyapal's insinuations.

'Fifteen rupees, seventy paise for a deg weighing one maund and a half,' answered Ananta with a restraint that exaggerated his bitterness.

'What?' Dina said, shocked.

'God, that's the limit!' shouted Ralia.

'The rates of piecework have gone down,' said Ananta, with tear-stained eyes. 'Actually, Khushal Chand offered me the difference between the old rates and the new rate from his own pocket, but I refused to take it.'

'The curse of heaven descend on your face!' shouted Dina. 'Why didn't you accept the money?'

'Even the loin-cloth of the running thief is good enough!' said Ralia.

'Give me a glass of sherbet, Bali brother,' said Ananta, ignoring his friend.

'Would you like anything stronger, Seth Anant Ram?' asked Bali importunately, with the obsequiousness of the small shopkeeper towards every customer, soul man or machine man.

'No, I want to cool myself down,' Ananta said. 'Sherbet of Sonf and the arek of Keora.'

He was still shaking with fury as he sat down on the edge of the platform of Bali's cavern and began to wipe the sweat off his face with an end of his dhoti. His temples throbbed violently in the heat and before him the future stood pregnant with the unknown doom of all his hopes and wishes.

'What is to be done, then?' Ralia said, after a while, challenging Ananta for his untoward silence as well as arraigning him in the name of the student Satyapal.

Sparks of fire and flashes of lightning rushed through Ananta's body as the shafts of the sun fell from above the sack-cloth awning on his hairy legs. He did not know what was to be done immediately, for, though he had a long-breathed sense, at the moment he felt too involved in the drama of his own humiliation to offer himself to them, red flag in hand. The track which he felt he had somewhat cleared after his talk with the poet Puran Singh Bhagat was now littered with his own black feelings and the shadow of Satyapal's form which he had seen crossing his path. He knew that a few impressionable young students, hated the poet because of the fine shades and subtleties, the wisdom, of the latter's mind; and that Satyapal despised him, Ananta, because he was known to have been working with the orthodox trade unionists of Bombay. Puran Singh Bhagat, of course, being a man of explanations and arguments, was safe from the speeches of Satyapal, and could even frighten him with the devotion, unselfishness and spirit of sacrifice he retained, though he had renounced religion and was not quite popular with the upperclass Congress leaders like Mahasha Hans Raj, as well as with the various sectarian groups.

But he, Ananta, was vulnerable. For against the religion and morality which Hans Raj championed, he could only offer the rule of thumb built on his instinctive knowledge and experience of other people; and what little theory he had picked up at Bombay was not sharp enough to combat the clever Satyapal, who built all his hopes on a sincere shrill voice and shriller emotions. In spite, however, of the positive aspect of his belief in Revolution as the only cure for the mismanagement of life by capitalists in Vilayat, in Bombay and Ahmedabad, and his belief in the new brotherhood of trade unions which would help to bring about Revolution, in spite of his utter faith in the myth of Revolution, his sense of inferiority arising from his non-possession of much book knowledge made him regard Satyapal as a redoubtable adversary. He knew that the boy had the ability to huckster the indiscriminating by the fire of his eloquence and to whip them up to a moral frenzy.

'Give them some sherbet too, Bali,' Ananta said, as he saw the grocer filling one tumbler.

'Ohe nahin!' protested Ralia and Dina together with characteristic Punjabi politeness. 'Ohe nahin!'

'Come on, have some, friends. All accounts are kept in the heart.'

'They want something stronger, Seth Anant Ram,' said Bali. 'And I can't give them any more liquor after they have emptied the Kalal khana in the morning. Besides, if the poolc got to know, it would land me in gaol for two years. I hear they are tightening up things all round. It is a bad time for us shopkeepers as well as for people. If we take the trouble of getting supplies and charge our price we are called black marketeers; and if we have empty shops, then you folk come shouting at us.'

'Everyone is crying bitter tears,' said Ralia. 'Everyone's mother seems to have died ! I thought until this morning that only we thathiars were hungry and wretched and helpless. Now there comes that Mahasha Hans Raj saying the merchants and dealers are as badly off as we.'

'Poor men, brothers,' said Ananta, 'have several ways of dying. They can choose to work for the merchants and dealers and die off slowly but surely. I call this way of dying "death by the indifference of the rich". But men can choose another way of death. And that is when they band together and say : "You have made such a mess of everything, because you considered profits as your god; so clear out now and let us rebuild the world to suit everyone and not only for a few of you !" The rich answer this demand either by making the workers hate their brethren in another country and thus bring about "death by the wars of the profiteers". Or they shoot down the workers and thus bring about another kind of death —"death by revolution against the rich". I know which of these deaths is best, but we shall have to die many deaths before the final liberation which is life. There is no other solution for us. The merchants are blind and will not voluntarily restrain their greed or give up their profits just for the asking. But just now——'

'You are full of homicidal fury, Ustad Anant Ram,' exclaimed Bali.

'Ohe, don't bark !' said Ralia, his small blood-streaked eyes spitting fire. 'Profiteering on our lives and then crying havoc ! Let him explain what he wants to do for the moment.'

'Ohe, brother, keep calm,' said Dina. 'If the judge says it is death, it is death.'

'There is your son, Rhoda, come to call you, Lala Ralia Ram,' said Bali, anxious to shift these tough customers from his shop. He had accurately surmised what little Rhoda's mission was.

'Father, mother says will you go and fetch the flour, because then she can go and bake the bread in the oven of Mehru's mother,' said Rhoda, all in a mouthful.

'Ohe, run away, rape-mother, I am coming,' Ralia roared

at Rhoda. 'Don't you see I am talking to someone? Go away.'

At the suddenness of his father's rebuke Rhoda began to cry.

'Ohe, go and tell your mother that your "today's meal" is with me,' said Ananta. 'Go tell her to get some flour from Aunt Karmo to bake bread for all of us in the oven of Mehru's mother and I shall cook some meat at the shop. Go on, then, and stop crying; I shall give you a bone all for yourself.'

Ralia felt suspicious at this generous offer, because he had begun to feel like a soul in pawn, believing that if anyone tried to be kind to him it was only another ruse to torture him. But he was much too afraid of his wife not to accept the hospitality, especially as he had no money at all to buy flour with.

'Go away, then, and don't stand in the company of elders, whining son of a pig!' he said to Rhoda in a less raucous voice.

Rhoda ran like a frightened puppy at the growl.

Ralia was overcome with a wave of self-pity.

'I won't eat bread baked in the oven of that blackleg Mehru's mother!' he said. 'I won't eat dung! If the limp lord had only lent me a rupee——'

'But you would only have drunk urine if I had lent it to you,' said Dina Timur Lang tartly.

'Ohe, brothers, don't quarrel,' said Ananta.

'Han, brothers,' said Bali, 'I can see the patients coming from the consulting-room of Hakeem Muhammad Ali there, with their prescriptions. And I have business to do now. So——'

Ananta took the hint and got up, but Ralia and Dina sat sulking, now out of a shamefaced stubbornness against Bali's insinuation.

'Come, then,' Ananta said, putting his hand on Ralia's soulder.

'Acha, hacha,' said Ralia, turning angrily to Bali. 'When I have money to spend I shall go to another shop.'

'Ohe ja, ja,' said Bali, pushing him away. 'Go and eat the air.'

'Don't you touch him,' said Dina, springing up to defend

his crony. Now you think of your bread, then of your pottage.'

'Ohe, look before and after,' counselled Ananta; 'there is an old woman behind you with a prescription. Come, come, away, both of you, and we will go and cook some food in my shop.'

'But what is to be done about the Kasera's new rates?' said Ralia, swallowing his pride at being forcefully shifted from the sherbet-seller's shop.

'I don't know', said Ananta, leading both men across the crossroads. 'Go and ask for jobs at the factory or call a meeting of our Panchayat. Anyhow, we must form a union.'

'We certainly will not go to eat ashes at the factory,' Ralia said.

'We must call the Panchayat together at my shop then,' said Ananta. 'We will eat, and talk the matter out.' And in his heart of hearts he knew that the crisis was imminent, that the events of months had matured into the situation which would confront them at the gathering in his shop, and that if they did not, or could not, resolve upon a common course of action at that meeting, then some catastrophe, some explosion, would happen before the time was ripe for the big explosion of the Revolution, for the depths of utter misery had been reached, and everyone was strained to breaking-point, ready to find vent in something . . . anything——

15

THE PROTRACTED HUM THAT WAS THE UNDERTONE OF THE factory throbbed in the sagging heart of thathair Mehru; the monotonous shrill, rasping whine of the big wheels revolving in a never-ending movement jarred on his fear-torn spirit; the sharp twangs of the small riveting machines plucked the hair from the middle of his knitted eyebrows like a pair of tweezers in the hands of the barber; the dithyramb of the whole ragged rhythm of the workshop aroused his vitals into a sense of alarm bordering on hope pulled him between wan care and feeble no care, enveloped him in the strange aura of the factory's roar.

And as he contemplated, with furtive glances, the rough corners of the stables and outhouses from which the clay plaster was hanging like festoons in the glare of the electric bulbs which made the old darkness into light, he swept up the steel and brass shavings from the floor into a heap by the door. He moved his fingers gingerly, both because he was afraid of cutting his hand with their sharp edges and because he felt the humiliation of being asked to start at the bottom and do an unskilled job before being allowed to go near a machine. He had bent copper ends and brass ends or any useless part of a sheet left over after cutting the patterns for utensils in the old days, but, mostly, he used to set the boys Mehnga, Daula, Shibu or someone else to hammer those odd bits together to send back to the dealer for remelting. But now there were those boys, skilled mechanics who tended the machines while he had been reduced to the position of a sweeper.

The protracted hum that was the undertone of the factory ceased for a moment and dumbly blended into a purple agony as that of a goat being butchered, and then it started with a swish again.

Mehru could see Mehnga at the machine which was washing metal in a milk-white liquid, his monkey-face looking all round for mischief. Fatty Daula, with his round ball of a face, was filing away beyond him. Shibu, the broken-nosed, was soldering small brass boxes by the door, his eyes covered with goggles to protect him against the flying sparks so that they seemed to come out of his nostrils. In fact everyone was at it, standing by heaps of oily grey machines, moving their hands with quick jerks as if they had been born armourers, efficient Sahib workmen or English engineers back from Vilayat like those at the Power House, and not the sons of thathiars who had been wielding hammers on solid anvils, sitting cross-legged in narrow, smoky shop hovels. He envied them and wondered how long it would take before he would be allowed to handle a machine—would he ever get used to the noise, the protracted hum that throbbed in his sagging heart, the monotonous shrill, rasping whine of the big wheels revolving in a never-ending movement which made him so afraid, the sharp twangs of the small riveting machines that seemed to pluck the hair from the middle of his knitted eyebrows like a pair of tweezers in the hands of the barber, the dithyramb of the whole ragged rhythm of the workshop. . . .

He felt as though his soul was torn with the guilt of having taken this job over the heads of the other thathiars, and being suddenly uprooted from the corner of the shop where he used to crouch making utensils, even as the metal before him was shrieking and wailing in the torture chamber of this fascinating new purgatory, where the heat was mounting to suffocation point. The clang of his old hammer had been harmonious, for the rhythm of those beats came from the force of the hand, controlled and yet free, maturing the raw metal into shape, till it became a whole before the eyes in a day; but the grey engines before him seemed to frighten him away, as it were, and the finished thing was nowhere in sight.

He swept the shavings into a huge heap, wiped the sweat from his nose and stopped for breath.

The others looked happy enough. Perhaps he too would get on to it, for after all it was his first day here.

His small, sore red eyes seemed to be swelling with the heat and he wiped them with the edge of his tunic. Then he swept the shavings a little further, feeling useless because the work required no effort.

But then he felt that he was lucky to get the job, to be one of the thirty thathiars to be employed in the factory. And yet this realization made him feel bad because of the treachery it implied to the brotherhood. Why couldn't they employ Ananta and Ralia and Viroo and Bhagoo and Arjun and all the rest?

The feeling of guilt surged up, beneath the fear, above the glare of sunlight which poured cruelly in several shafts through the window with the iron bars in the back wall of the factory.

Ananta, with his experience of Bombay, could have been a wonderful foreman, instead of that bald-headed little bastard Channa, with the pinched sparrow-face. He wondered why Murli Dhar and Gokul Chand, who were both such respectable business men, employed this man, whom people called a shifty crook, though he, Mehru, must not say anything about Channa till he really knew his character, for that would not be righteous.

There he was, the foreman, coming towards him, in the white shirt and khaki shorts—Quicksilver Channa.

Mehru blinked his lashless pink eyes and pretended that he hadn't seen him. Then, wiping the sweat from his neck with his hand, he swept the shavings forward.

'Why, bai Mehru,' called Channa in a squeaky voice, even as he nodded over a machine, 'how are you liking it?'

'Each one is happy in his own skin.'

Quicksilver Channa looked quizzically with his little pinched bird-like face and knew that there was a double meaning in his answer. He felt sheepish and apologetic, knowing that Mehru knew all about him, and he tried to be humorous, though the words that mounted to his tongue were rather cutting:

'You look as if there is mustard growing in your eyes.'

Thinking he had gone too far, he was frightened in his callow, abject soul, however, and walked up to Mehru. The new thathiar worker was equally afraid that his pink eyes might disqualify him for work here and cost him his job. So they both tried to be nice to each other.

'I must have some medicine put into my eyes,' Mehru said.

'Ohe,' said Channa, seizing his opportunity, 'I will sell you some antimony powder which I bought from Kangra Hills.' And he cast a surreptitious glance around lest someone should see him doing this deal, for everyone suspected that he was in the black market.

Mehru had no choice in the face of the foreman's offer and said : 'I will try it.'

'Acha, then I shall go and get it,' said Channa, turning like the quicksilver he was and walking away as if he were a cross-country runner exercising for the races at the Diwali Fair in Amritsar.

Mehru sweated with the tension of this contact with the mighty little bully, and then broke into a fresh sweat at the thought of the price he would have to pay for the antimony when he hadn't a pice in his pocket.

At that instant, however, he found Gopi, the eldest son of Sadanand, and grandson of Murli Dhar, coming towards him, and his heart began to throb at the new threat to his existence.

'Grandpa saw you in the Durbar Sahib,' the boy said with the easy but patronizing familiarity of the boss's young son condescending to talk to an older employee, so that his frame stiffened visibly, his rather feminine, oblong pale face flushed a vivid pink and his wide nostrils dilated a little.

'What, Lala Murli Dhar?—I did n't see him!'

'But grandpa has all-seeing eyes,' said Gopi, trying to put significance into his phrase.

'Being in love with the Omniscient, I am sure he has become omnipresent himself,' Mehru said lamely, though in his heart he felt he ought to have said: 'Your grandfather has stolen the light from everyone else's eyes and left them all to grope around.'

'You see, Lala Mehr Chand,' said Gopi, launching on an uncalled-for apology for grandpa's Omniscience, 'these ignorant, illiterate oxen, the thathiars, do not realize what advantages they would have if they honoured grandfather. He is a Municipal Commissioner and Chaudhri of the Bazar, and now he has joined this firm with Seth Gokul Chand, who is also a Municipal Commissioner, and other wealthy and respectable dealers. If only the thathiars realized how, through him, their status was rising, they would not be joining hands with rogues of number ten, gundas and budmashes. Now we might be taken into the Kasera class, so we are not asking all the thathiars to come to the betrothal ceremony of Nikka today, but only the respectable, decent people among them and in the Arya Samaj. Of course, both grandpa and father have asked me to invite you.'

'You will have to forgive me,' said Mehru instantly, as though he wanted to escape the trap before it was laid. 'I appreciate your kindnesses to me, but I haven't even a rupee to donate to little Nikka on the betrothal ceremony because I was unemployed for months and have only been here a day.'

'Oh, don't you worry about that: some hear kind words by paying, some see splendour by luck.'

Mehru smiled, half amused at the cleverness with which Gopi had wrapped up his patronizing attitude and half embarrassed at the obsequious manner in which the boy spoke.

'Come,' Gopi said suddenly, 'I will put you on to another, more interesting, job now that you have got used to the atmosphere of the factory. There is a press there, a wonderful invention, which bends brass plates into boxes, one a minute. It looks simple, only there are four ways of adjusting the plate for the operation and only one of them is the right way. Come, I know that, with your skill, you will discover the right way quickly. Come.'

And he advanced with his hand cordially resting on

Mehru's back and went towards a press with a revolving wheel on top and began to work the machinery. Mehru knew this promotion was a bribe, but he accepted it and all that it involved.

'If only your eyes were not spitting blood, you could pick up the exact angle in a moment,' said Gopi. 'Now, look, this is how it is.' And he took up a plate, put it on a flat surface by fixing the hole in the brass on a knob and then revolved the wheel on the top with a quick but firm jerk. As the wheel went back the plate had formed into a box under the press. At that Gopi smiled with self-satisfaction and turned schoolmaster again:

'That's the way, that's perfect—just the right jerk does it. You better try it with your own hands now.'

Mehru wiped his hands on his tunic and began to repeat the movements which Gopi had shown him. Nervous, his face sweating, his eyes strained and intent, his teeth controlling his chapped lower lip, he repeated the operation. His hands had the magic of hereditary craftsmanship in them and they caught with a delicate sympathy the exact pressure needed for the crucial jerk. It was so simple and easy that no brains were needed for the job, and he thought that Gopi had made such ado about nothing like a juggler showing off before performing a trick.

Gopi took up the finished box and, hoping that it would be faulty, measured it against a straight file which was lying about, while Mehru waited with beating heart. The verdict was slow in coming, but it came:

'Acha, you have got it. But practice makes perfect. You finish some of them before the break for the midday meal and then ask Channa for some more.'

'Acha,' Mehru said. But he left that if this was all there was to do during the day he would get so bored he would want another more intricate job soon.

'Oh, but I am a fool,' said Gopi, turning back from the direction of the door. 'I might not be here this afternoon as I shall probably have to help with the arrangements for the ceremony at home. And Channa may not be here either. So you ask Lala Khushal Chand——'

'Lala Khushal Chand?' queried Mehru. 'Of Lal Chand-Khushal Chand & Co? I didn't know he was here.'

'Oh yes,' Gopi swaggered. 'He and I were at the Technical

School together, and but for us the factory wouldn't have been founded. I shall tell him to look after you. He is in the office.'
And he crossed the courtyard and raced up the stairs to a low-ceilinged room over the hallway which had been converted into the office.

' "The crow says nothing is so beautiful as my plumage," ' Mehru muttered a proverb to himself as he saw the proud little boy walk away. And then he stood making boxes automatically, while his mind ran riot, thinking of the possibilities of the future, whether he would be happy doing this job which was mere child's play or whether he could do a little of the old craft at nights.

Quicksilver Channa had been waiting eagerly for Gopi to depart and came up to collar Mehru and finish his deal immediately after the manager had gone up into the office. So that before the new thathiar worker had resolved the problem of doing a satisfactory man's job, the foreman stood by him, as if some snarling, shrieking machine had spat him out.

'Here it is,' he said, lifting his eyes. Then, loking furtively and scratching his head as though the itch had got him, he handed a small two-inch bottle of antimony to Mehru.

All the previous qualms about the potency of this powder, its integrity, and about the consequences that would follow his announcement that he had no money, assailed Mehru again now.

'I am afraid I can't pay for it now,' he said by way of getting out of the bargain.

'It's only a rupee,' Channa said.

'But, Ustad Channa—it is a very little bottle——'

Quicksilver Channa was almost as frightened as Mehru and could not bear any suspense during this bargain. So he cut in :

'You can pay me later when you get your wages—I will only charge you a little interest on it, an anna on the rupee.'

Mehru paused and looked at the bottle. It was half full of antimony and half of cotton.

'Say han or na !' Channa said menacingly, urgently.

'Han,' answered Mehru like a curse of defeat.

'You can stay at this machine if Gopi has put you on it,' said Channa with a sudden exuberant cordiality and then rushed away, unceremoniously announcing for all to hear : 'I must go and help with the ceremony at the big house.'

'I see that you have been promoted,' said Mehnga, whizzing past Mehru.

'Han, you look out,' sain Mehru bitterly, 'I will soon be a Foreman at this rate.'

'I shall be a partner in the firm when you become the Foreman,' mocked Mehnga. 'Seth Gokul Chand will offer me his daughter in marriage. And I shall then sell my bicycle to you and buy a motor-cycle.'

'And then you shall fall, like the monkey you are, and break your head,' said Mehru. 'Only Seth Gokul Chand's daughter will not be your widow, because if he hasn't given her in marriage to his partner's grandson, Nikka, who is being betrothed to the girl from Jandiala, then the Chaudhri of the Kaseras will not give her to you.'

'Ohe ja ohe, blind one, go and have some antimony put in your eyes, and if you want a Surmchu slide then——' He made a rude sign and fled, as he saw one of the managers coming.

'Vulgar hound!' said the young Lala Khushal Chand indulgently, as he came down the rickety stairs from the office on the passageway into the courtyard. 'Ohe, is this the respect you show to your elders, the son of Mehnge!'

'Mehru sheds false tears and excites your sympathy, Lala Kushal Chand!' said Mehnga cheekily.

Then he ran back towards his machine, pulling the tuft knot of fat Daula on his way. Daula chased him among the machines, and for a moment they played hide-and-seek in this maze as if they were born sons of the 'Iron age', when civilization could be measured by how near they got to a cable without being electrocuted or how near they could run in front of a lorry without being run over. Their conduct had certainly changed from the docile boys they had been when they were apprentices, concentrating on utensils as they crouched in thathiar shops to the rough-necks. Braggarts and tough-neck sahibs they had now become, looking for any mischief that would relieve the tedium of minding the machines.

The other workers raised a hue and cry to scare them off each other, but, after dodging every one, they ran into the courtyard, where Daula overtook Mehnga and locked him in the wrestler's embrace.

'Ohe, leave go, leave go, fools, mudhosho!' the other workers shouted. But the blood had mounted to the faces of the boys and they were losing their good humour in the heat of a real quarrel.

At this Shibu strolled up with a bucket of water from under the leaking tap and, with an easy and natural grace, splashed the contents on them.

Cursing Shibu they separated from each other and, wiping their faces and their water-soaked clothes, laughed even as they belatedly chased Shibu who had proceeded towards the well.

'The seeds of the devil !' said Mehru, nibbling over his job and rather resentful that he had been done by Channa and furious that the boys couldn't see the sob choking the curses that lurked in the throats of their elders.

'They are full of mischief as they are the only lads in this area who get butter to eat,' said Kushal Chand benignly.

'Where do they get it from ?' asked Mehru innocently.

'Oh, the thieves' kitchen !' answerd Khushal Chand with a smile which descended to the dimple under his chin. 'Quick silver Channa knows all the mysterious ways of securing things.'

'What about the brass plates I am to bend—do they also come from the black market ?' His notions of right and wrong were elementary and he could not believe that the owners could shift so well for themselves in the half-famished world he knew.

'Han, there are heaps of things in the store room, and for all I know, they come from the thieves' kitchen.' said Khushal Chand, laughing.

Then he looked towards the courtyard warily and, leaning over to Mehru, said : 'Will you be seeing Ananta today ?'

Mehru hesitated, imagining that the employers were manoeuvring him into the position to do something wrong and that 'they' had sent Khusal Chand to spy on him or to pump him for some secret information.

'Give him this money which I owe him,' Khushal Chand said. He handed him some notes, and nervously looked at his watch and said : 'Oh, five to one. I must go. Tell Ananta I will get the boys here to join his union if he succeeds in getting the other thathiars.'

Mehru took the two notes and stood with his mouth wide open, confused, afraid and amazed.

Khushal Chand walked away with an easy gait, a strangely mysterious figure.

As soon as the boss's back was turned, Mehru contemplated the bank notes, sceptical and unsure and yet delighted to have been in touch with a person who had not put on any airs. What did it mean? he wondered. Was it a bribe for Ananta or a loan?

He thrust the money into the folds of his loin-cloth and went on making boxes with mechanical ease. If it was as easy as this, why had they not invented an extra gadget to do what he was doing to help to make brass boxes and eliminate all that man's hands could do? But he was grateful that there was no such machine yet, because he would be unnecessary if there was. And he felt that Khushal Chand was a nice understanding kind of boss if he really wanted to help Ananta.

Then his face knitted into a question and he wondered what he should do about the ceremony this afternoon. Perhaps he could ask his mother to go instead. He felt shy at such gatherings.

The protracted hum of the machines that was the undertone of the factory had more or less stopped. And he could only hear the jagged, ragged rhythm of a turning machine and the yell of the wheel before him as he reversed it to lift the box he had made from the brass piece on his side. His eyes chafed like putrid sores, his face wore the leer of a joke as he became bored with the job in hand, and he felt his soul twitching with the anxiety to go out and have another bath.

16

'I FALL AT YOUR FEET, SETHJI,' SAID SADANAND FORMALLY AS HE came up to the counter of Chaudhri Gokul Chand's shop at the far end of Bazar Kaserian, almost opposite the shop of his nephews Lal Chand-Khushal Chand under the shadow of the banyan tree.

'Ao ji, Sadandji, sit down,' said Gokul Chand, as he waved his right had towards a small stretch of platform covered with jute cloth, which was the only space not occupied in a shop chock full of brass, bronze and copper utensils. And he puffed at the little coconut-basined hookah, which he held in his left hand, with short, nervous puffs.

'Nahen, Sethji, I won't sit down because I am on my way

to the Benarsi shops to get silk turban for Nikka,' said Sadanand, excusing himself with joined hands. 'But I thought I would stop for a minute and remind you about the betrothal ceremony in the afternoon. We sent the barber around to call everyone, but Lalaji asked me to ask you if——'

'Congratulations, Sadanand !—may you flourish, brother,' interrupted Gokul Chand. Then he coughed as though the rest of what he had to say got stuck in his throat.

'It is all your blessing,' said Sadanand. 'Our common venture in the factory has brought us luck. And that is a special reason why we want you to be present.'

At this Seth Gokul Chand seemed to be caught in an unending paroxysm of coughs, and, leaning over the platform, he spat three or four times into the open drain which ran under the shop. Then, red in the face through the exertion, he said : I am very worried about the consignment of goods, because I have been to the station and it hasn't yet arrived. And I hear the thathiars are clamouring for jobs . . .' After this he sat back to puff at his hookah again.

Sadanand instinctively knew that there was more to it than that in Chaudhri Gokul Chand's embarrassment.

For a moment there was silence between them, to which the fury of the sun above the banyan seemed to add its quota of heaviness. Someone from somewhere cut the atmosphere, however, by throwing the sun's reflection off a polished brass plate teasingly into the eyes of the Chaudhri and his guest.

'Who is this blinding me ?'

Sadanand was impatient as he looked round the bazar, which was emptying through the excessive heat and because most people had adjourned to their midday meal.

'Eh Lala Sadanand, congratulations, wadahi !' shouted Lal Chand, the nephew of Chaudhri Gokul Chand, across the bazar.

'Ohe, what is this child's game ?' roared Gokul angrily. 'Isn't the sun's glare blinding enough ?'

'I wanted to attract Sadanand's attention, uncle,' said Lal Chand without a blush.

'You are coming to the ceremony, aren't you, Lala Lal Chand—and your brother too ?' Sadanand called aloud.

'You must ask the elders first,' Lal Chand replied, making an easy way out. 'But accept our congratulations.' He hesitated for a moment, looked about himself to make sure

that no one was listening, then cupped his hands and shouted:
'Only I wanted to tell you to beware of that rogue Ananta, because he knows that you agreed with us about the new rates for piecework.'

'Acha,' said Sadanand, discreetly terminating this open discussion.

'He tried to show me his trained biceps!' shouted Lal Chand. And he imitated the movement of Ananta's broad shoulders.

'Ohe hacha, hacha!' Chaudhri Gokul Chand said. 'Have some sense and don't shout so!' And a frown of extreme displeasure gathered on his square jawed face, emboldened by the full moustache.

'I have heard that they had a row over the wages on a cauldron this morning,' said Sadanand, presuming that the Chaudhri would be quite willing to gossip even though he resented his nephew's clumsiness in proclaiming all about his quarrel in public, and that loose talk may create the necessary atmosphere for pressing his invitation.

'It is a bad business,' said Gokul Chand, evading the trap that Sadanand spread before him. 'When we decided among us Kaseras that we were going to reduce piece wages, I had hoped that we would be able to take people like Ananta on at the factory. But you and your father did not want him, for some reason. Now—since he, one of the best craftsmen, has suffered a reduction of wages, the news of our decision has spread among the whole thathiar fraternity. And they are not at all pleased. It strikes me it's going to be a bad business if they all get together.'

'You can take it from me,' said Sadanand maliciously, 'that they won't get together. There are all kinds among them—— As for him, he won't suffer in any way; he is living with that rich widow, Janki, who is said to have brought all her husband's jewellery with her. It is the other thathiars I am sorry for. I wish you had knocked down their wages gradually. Then they would not have known all at once, and and we——'
He did not want to reveal to Gokul Chand that he had a scheming mind, so he hesitated and changed the subject by reverting to the invitation again.

'Anyhow, what is done is done. Now, if only you will grace our home today, we shall all be able to face them together in case. . . . Because we are one of the few thathiar families who are with you in this decision. Later, you will find that if you begin to deal with us in these festivities and ceremonials, most of them will come round, for they are all good Hindus, except for those who openly became Muhammadans when the Aga Khan asked them to be on one side.'

Seth Gokul Chand was irritated because he felt that Sadanand was blackmailing him. He had been forced by the circumstances of the market, where there was little or no money in household utensils, to open a factory and take on Government contracts. In order to assure the employment of skilled workers he had had to choose and select, first, the boys from Murli's family, who were highly skilled silversmiths, and then such other thathiar boys as had been to a technical school or were young enough to go to one and learn to handle machinery. Old Murli was the headman of the thathiar brotherhood. For this reason he had given him shares in the factory on the same footing as to some of his own Kasera brethren. But he had never intended the partnership to involve eating and drinking with the low thathiars, or to be on intimate social terms with any member of this community. For though both the Kaseras and the thathiars were Hindus of the Kshatriya, the second highest caste, they had kept away because the craftsmen, doing dirty, grimy, ill-paid work with their hands, had come to acquire a low professional status in Hindu society. Now he was on the horns of a dilemma, for his solidarity with his fellow partner in the factory, Murli, was in conflict with his affiliations with the Kasera brotherhood. And all these and other fears and doubts tangled up inside him to make his face a knot of worry.

'You know, Sadanand,' he began, disengaging his mouth from the small pipe of the hookah, and dodging the issue again, though more plausibly this time, 'the thathiars still have a bad reputation. I mean—most of them are still said to be devotees of the Aga Khan. Several times I have myself seen the women of your brotherhood going up the stairs of the Aga Khani worship house——'

'No, no, Seth Gokul Chand,' Sadanand interrupted, 'you cannot say that about our house. Nobody from our family has ever looked towards the Aga Khan Jamait Khana ever since my father went and knelt before the Guru Granth at the Durbar Sahib twenty-five years ago, and ever since my sons and I joined the Arya Samaj. And I think the same holds true about most of the thathiars. Of course, there are black sheep. And to be sure, the women—you can't keep a check on the whims and fancies of women ? But if you name any we will raise the question of expelling them from the thathiar brotherhood at the next gathering. I know for a fact that Karmo, the stepmother of Ananta, goes to the Jamait Khana. Therefore, so far as we are concerned, we have stopped his hookah and water and have not asked him to the ceremony. On the other hand, some of our Arya-Samaji brothers are coming. . . .' He looked desperately unhappy as he boasted this empty boast.

'All these matters are your own affair, brother,' said Gokul, puffing away more nervously than ever. He had given a good enough excuse for his inability to attend without saying a sharp, curt 'no'. But he know he was in for it. The sub-caste snobbery he had inherited from generations of his ancestors, and all the lordly taboos accruing to the credit side of his family ledger, had only so far admitted some paltry wages to the menials of other castes for services, rendered, on the debit side. That was the only compromise in the old days. Today, for the first time, he realized that he couldn't open a new account book in partnership with people whom he considered to belong to a lower caste without the risk of losing caste. And he felt unhappy about the partnership. He had much rather have gone on in the old way, for at least then everyone had a place in the system; the lord was the lord, and the menial the menial ; and the lord could even like the menial so long as the menial kept his place. But now he had been forced to pal up with people for whom he had a profound contempt; and religion, custom and convention were going by the board.

'I don't know what the world is coming to,' he continued peevishly, 'it is all a muddle. Everything is so uncertain now-a-days. People have forgotten the highest duty they owe to themselves and their religion. The young don't listen to the old, brotherhoods are breaking up, and no one can keep our ancient customs alive without being called a fool by his children.'

'I agree with you,' said Sadanand, conceding all that in order to win him over. 'The dirty rabble has raised its heads to the sky. The beggars whine. The outsiders from villages moan. And robbery and midnight thefts are raging in the city.'

'That is why I say one must do the right thing,' said Gokul. 'I am not orthodox, mind you, because orthodoxy—well, now-a-days. I suppose I believe we should be like rubber which can be stretched when required but——'

'Han, one must keep a check on oneself and not do things lightly,' persisted Sadanand. 'But one must also keep a check on sentiment. Now stretch a point like the rubber you were speaking about and come. I say it with joined hands.' The saliva of humility gathered on the corners of his mouth. "Please come and grace our house and be assured that our family at any rate has no connection whatever with the Aga Khan. My father goes to Durbar Sahib, as I told you, and he adopted the Mahant of Kanowan as a Guru; my brother, the overseer, at Allahabad is a follower of Radhaswami, and my elder son Gopi and I go to the Arya Samaji. And little Nikka, by the grace of God and your kindness, will grow up to be a skilled mechanic and not a thathiar.'

"Your humility,' said Gokul Chand with an embarrassed smile, 'makes me feel ashamed. But I almost feel like quoting the proverb about the origin of our brotherhood : "To Ram was given an arrow, to Sita a bow, and from them the truly noble order of Kshatriya Kaseras is descended !" And you must realize, Lala Sadanand, that I am the Chaudhri of my caste brotherhood and there are a hundred eagle eyes looking to see what I do.' And he feigned a short gasp of a laugh in order to disguise the fact that he was rubbing in the superiority of his caste brotherhood at the same time as he was being courteously generous to Sadanand.

'Our progenitor, the God Visva Karma, only bequeathed a hammer and a pair of tongs to us, apart from our rough hands,' said Sadanand. 'But, by Ishawar, we are proud to have broken metal into shape and earned our living by the sweat of our brows.'

He realized in his heart that when his family was proud to belong to its own community he had lived on the earth but felt very natural. Now that they had begun to sit on exalted seats they had become buffoons. The fear of the higher castes, generated by ages of patronage, suddenly seemed to lift from Sadanand's mind for a moment and he sat back rigid, hard and proud in the integrity of his thathiarhood, though his soul quavered with fear lest Gokul Chand should refuse to come to the ceremony and he and his family should drop from the heights of association with the upper-caste Kaseras to which they had been aspiring ever since they opened the factory.

'Now, don't be touchy,' said Gokul Chand. 'I was only being funny. You know, you have lost your sense of humour lately.'

This broke down Sadanand's splendid assertion of physical freedom against the superior airs of the dealer, almost as if Gokul Chand's rebuke had melted the quivering, bursting nerves in the thathiar's body with one gracious word. Sadanand smiled and then said obsequiously:

'Acha, you have done a great many favours to us. Now, please, come to the shagan ceremony in the afternoon. Promise you will and, I assure you, no harm will come to your position in your brotherhood. And you will have lifted us from our bitchy brotherhood to something higher.'

'Acha, brother, I will ask some other members of my brotherhood what they feel,' said Gokul Chand, relenting a little. 'I can't say any more.'

'Oh, I put my turban at your feet, Seth Gokul Chand,' said Sadanand, taking his hands to his enormous headgear. He didn't mind sinking to the deepest depths of degradation if only he could realize his ambition. He knew that his family had more than half won the position to which they aspired by entering into an irrevocable contract with Gokul in the factory and that their class status was the same in the eyes of the world. But he vaguely knew that it was only in big cities that high-class Lalas and business men ate and drank together, that the way up to the high prestige which their family wealth assured them lay in Amritsar through exaltation into the slightly superior Kasera caste brotherhood.

'Promise you will come,' he insisted.

'That I can't do, Sadanand,' said Gokul, repulsed by his excessive humility. 'I will do my best. I will try and persuade the elders of my brotherhood that we might have social relations with some of the thathiars now that we are partners in the same firm——'

'Acha, then, I need not go round to the other elders of the Kasera brotherhood to invite them.'

'No, you needn't. If one or two of us come, that will be symbolic of the whole brotherhood.'

'Acha, then I fall at your feet,' said Sadanand, getting up and joining his hands in a formal gesture of farewell.

17

ALL THE TIME HE HAD BEEN SHOPPING AND COOKING IN READINESS for the feast he had promised his friends, Ananta had found himself overcome by a sudden and profound silence through which the various strands of the memories of his childhood and youth had emerged in him, and, particularly, the thought of his lighthearted abduction of the pretty widow Janki from Batala and the complications which this had caused until he had had to take her away to Bombay. He thought how he had got caught up in the struggle of the workers for 'dearness' allowances there, how he had spent himself organizing men in the new brotherhood of the trade unions, and how he had changed, not only from the boisterous rough he had been at home, but the ardent lover he once was. From being a devotee of sensation and following each wayward impulse where it led, he had, through certain sudden jumps and leaps, become aware of other people's desires as well as his own. And then the quality of happiness itself had altered, because it had become for him the service of others and the realization of oneself through such devotion. Meanwhile, however, all this adventuring of the spirit had played havoc with his soul. For, whereas he had been absolutely sure of each impulse he experienced in the days of sensational living, all his reactions had become unsure and chaotic, blurred and deceptive, when he had travelled into regions of feeling where slogans, words, abstract ideas and other men with other wills were involved. There were huge gaps in his understanding of the world. And native wit could not go beyond certain instinctive truths. So that he had often had to ask himself how he could master his destiny with only a heart and the study courses of Comrade Adhikari to go upon. How could one trade the earth, without fear and with dignity? What portion of love could one give to others and to oneself? Who were the enemies—the police, the Sarkar, the millowners, the Germans or the Japanese? All these and other questions had occupied him intermittently. And beneath the apparent ease of his gait he had been learning to balance himself—as if on his head! And he had found the need for caution in achieving such a stance, for, from accepting the world at its face value, he had begun not to accept it at all, save in so far as he could alter it. He had forsaken the lure of easy victories, and knew that in taking the plunge into the struggle for 'Revolution' he had entered an arena where only the hardest search would yield a way among the thorny paths of the tiger-infested jungle of this world. It was certain that the trouble with one's fellows was deeper than that they could not find a way through the tangled undergrowth of the world, with their broken and tortured bodies, and no souls. So one couldn't help them to walk with wooden supports, or by merely healing their skins. No, the trouble lay in the many bonds of custom and habit and superstition which bound them, and in the weakness, fear bred by poverty and the struggle for existence and the pain inevitable to life. What was required was to give them heart and to lift them from the abject, frustrated and terror-stricken creatures they were to the courage of manhood. And that required first that one must become a man oneself, to battle with the despairs which assailed one, and to believe in happiness and the possibility of abolishing unnecessary suffering, to settle one's doubts patiently, in fact to believe in 'Revolution' as a new kind of religion. He didn't know where all the deep urges for the service of others which possessed him had come from, that there were many thieves even in the mind of the rogue he had once been, there seemed to have been some honour among those thieves, and even an uneasy partnership between them and the rogue himself. He had had to keep a vigilant eye on all those cankers in his soul, without finding out much about the mysterious discontents which rose in him from time to time, the waves of disgust and abandon that welled up in him. And one of the reasons why he admired the poet Puran Singh Bhagat, in spite of the latter's pessimism, was because he seemed to have seen through a great many deceptions and falsehoods about himself and others and was ceaselessly straining for devotion and truth, struggling to break out of the trap even as he, Ananta, was straining.

'What a trap to find onself in, though!' he said to himself as he ascended the stairs up to his beloved's room with a pot of meat gravy, dal and some chapatis which he had prepared in the shop for the feast.

'May I become your sacrifice—why did you trouble to bring me this?' said Janki from where she lay crocheting on the bed. 'I don't feel a bit like eating.'

'No, may I be your sacrifice,' Ananta said. 'Childling, you must eat.'

And, drawing a stool up to her bed, he placed the bronze plate on it and uncovered the small brass cups and chapatis. He felt a trifle impatient with her because she was ill and an extra responsibility on his troubled soul.

For a moment she did not move, but just sat pale, looking, hauntingly beautiful as death. He smiled at her deliberately and tried to avert his eyes as though he were frightened of the thing he could so clearly see written on her face. But then he remembered the vision of her that he had seen in his dream last night, and the desire to know if she resembled any of the shapes he had seen, made him fix her with his glance. The silence between them intensified his horror as he caught the reflection of a mask which was identical with the lost soul who had receded farther and farther from him in the garden of the nightmare. She seemed to be wilting like a pale white moti flower under the stress of the afternoon heat and her illness, her head hung down as though she was withdrawing to a world of her own, the dank clammy underworld of Yama where the souls swam with difficulty in the putrid ocean of filth, tormented by vipers, snakes, scorpions, and blood-sucking leeches.

'Chin up,' he said, tilting her face affectionately even as he cupped her head in his two hands, suppressing his impatience with her and exerting himself to make her look happy.

She lifted her sad eyes from which the light seemed to be fading, leaving them a grey-green where they had been vivid cat's eyes, mocking and rather uncanny the way they saw through people.

'Smile,' he said.

'Go away,' she said playfully. 'Don't tease me.' And then she smiled and drew the head-cloth half modestly over her forehead with a characteristic blandishment in the face of his desire.

His senses filled with lust at the memory of her gesture, and he recalled the warmth of that fire with which they had burnt together as they had lain in the sweat of their love, each aching to be both, enclosed in a world where space and time seemed to break into the darkness of a half-swoon. How he had loved her, almost broken her and eaten her up, as if he were not content for her to remain separate. And then he had had to see her withering before him daily and withdrawing, consumed by this dread fire of her own, the fever which possessed her. He had not dared often to notice her thinning face and emaciated body, because he knew that he was partly responsible for her illness. For, having eaten the full fruits of her love, he had plunged into the work for 'Revolution' and left her bereft, alone, helpless, consigned to the subtle despair of her inevitable doom. Sometimes, of course, he had tried to retrace his steps on the dusty road to where she still stood with blisters on her feet, and he had lifted her so that under the shade of some tree they could rest awhile, gather more strength and set off on their journey together once again. But though she had the inclination she had not the strength. And then he had drifted into the bylanes and subways on his own, as though waiting for her to get abreast of him while he groped around. But once he had escaped from the orbit or her warmth, once he was free of his habit of her, they were not the same when he came back, and the love between them seemed to have been destroyed, emerging only in the form of his desire for 'Revolution'. Latterly she seemed to be catching up with him; and the two different worlds of their beings knowing that they might be separated, clung to each other, with a passionate longing to sacrifice themselves for each other. So that the familiar homely Punjabi phrase 'May I be your sacrifice' had assumed the intensity of a poignant though humorous figure of speech between them. But today the looming struggle between the thathiars and the factory owners seemed to overshadow their lives and make them tense and a trifle strange and self-conscious with each other.

'Acha, childling, you eat your meal and I shall come and see you after I have fed my other guests,' Ananta said.

Janki was touched by the gentleness that seemed to have come over him, and she was filled with a respect for this silence which soon became a sense of awe and wonder. She knew how, in the past, the loud-mouthed, open, frank barker in him used to disappear for long periods when he was engaged in work, and become an almost saintly presence, but never had she sensed the same quality of tenderness in his voice.

She was aware, of course, that the crisis he was facing was still mounting and that, in spite of his outward calm, he was today a boiling cauldron of conflicting loyalties, passions and desires, that somehow his dedication to his friends had given him a quite, compelling dignity. She responded to his gesture in serving her the food and fell to.... Unable to swallow the morsel she had picked up, she said:

'You have a little of this with me.'

'Nahin,' he answered softly: And he got up to go.

She remonstrated with him, as the was the only way she could establish her connection with him, across his cool dignity, change his anxiety for the thathiars into love for herself.

As last he bent down, tore a chunk of chapati from the plate, dipped it in the gravy and stuffing his mouth with it, laughed:

'I haven't yet learnt to deny myself for the sake of denial, as Puran Singh Bhagat seems to have done. Nor have I learnt to sacrtfice myself for others really.'

'But why this sudden humility, braggart?' she asked.

'Because I can neither look after you nor really forget you and devote myself to the "Revolution". And I suddenly feel frigntened, Jankiai. Frightened of something I don't know what, almost as if there were ghosts in this room trying to claim us. Perhaps I am a fool.... And it is all the fault of my stepmother, who used to tell me that the ghost of my mother often came and possessed her to see how she was treating me.' He laughed a little nervous laugh at this, and then continued: 'Ever since I woke up in a sweat last night I have felt as if I have been pursued by a shadow; not like the C.I.D. man that Puran Singh Bhagat was afraid of, but something invisible and intangible.'

'I have never known you so superstitions,' Janki said, a dainty morsel in her mouth. 'That witch Karmo certainly filled your mind with queer things.'

'Perhaps one can never get over the fears which mothers put into our minds,' Ananta said. 'Perhaps, also, because we thathiars live in a small world, full of denial and refusal, insults and humiliations, we have begun to feel doomed. With one half of me I too feel I am doomed, and with the other half I feel could fight, to avert the disaster. But it has certainly been a bad day for me. I have been wondering, for instance, why the Kaseras and Murli have fixed on me as their chief enemy when it is so difficult for me to persuade the thathiars to do one thing or the other ? . . . Why, indeed, are the dealers torturing the thathiars at all ? I know full well that we suffer from the day we are born till the day we die, but this cruelty is unnecessary. A little reason could settle this difficulty between the Kaseras and us. Instead ! . . . Oh, it is awful, really ! Not even the relief of the little happiness we had in Bombay ! . . . And I know there will be no more happiness in this darkening world for anyone for a long time to come. . . . And I feel I ought to do something good before I die, so that the others who come after can be a little happier, but I am not even equal to the call of my own torn conscience. . . . The truth is that devotion and sacrifice are the twin brothers of courage and will have nothing to do with cousin cowardice !'

'Acha, now, don't feel guilty,' she said. 'I don't believe Puran Singh Bhagat is addicted to self-abnegation for the sake of self-abnegation. I hope he is not. And I think no one should be like that. What is the use of frowning all the time when you have so little time to live, and everything is transitory and will pass away ? We should be happy while we are allowed to be here and do what is required of us and then go when fate calls.'

'I feel one can fight fate,' he said. 'So don't talk of going.' He realized, however, that it was not because he felt sorry for himself in doing something for others, but because he was too attached to them and felt unequal to the duty he owed them, that he felt unhappy. Also he did not really want a selfless denial like that of the saints, but the achievement of a programme which would build their union, give them strength and bring them food, as well as inner happiness, whereas the sacrifice of the saints was perhaps much higher and certainly unattainable by folks like him.

Only, he was afraid of the thathiar sense of doom pulling him down with its final sense of futility of every human effort. Only, the immensity of the complex hostile world and the pain and wastage going on outside Billimaran robbed him of the belief necessary to fight against despair. Attached to Janki, clinging to his own life with a fervour born of pity for his community and fear of the shadows, he wanted to become unattached and offer as pure a devotion as the poet. And yet he could not think of assuming the greybeard solemnity of the priests in the temple, nor of flagellating himself like the sadhus and rubbing himself with ashes. And, emerging late from a prolonged adolescence into some instinctive wisdom, he was gravely troubled inside him and seized with great doubts about his capacity to fulfil the task of outflanking Destiny.

'I must go and attend to them, childling,' he said to Janki. 'At least we are going to have one more feast before—I will come back and see about your medicine later.'

'Death is better than that medicine,' she said resignedly.

'May I be your sacirifice,' he said, patting her tenderly now. Don't talk of death ! . . .'

But as he went downstairs he felt more frightened than ever.

18

'LET US TASTE A BONE,' DINA SAID FROM WHERE HE SAT IN A leisurely stance, away from the fireplace in the shade of the jute-cloth awning at the doorstep of Ananta's shop.

'Ohe, wait, wait, you have tasted the meat three times already,' Ananta said as he stirred the mutton in the cauldron with a long-handled brass ladle. 'Let me dish out the gravy for the womenfolk in the alley first.

'After all, I ought to get a commission for fetching the meat—there was not a bone to be had in the whole town outside the black market ! And my mouth is watering.'

'Acha, fore, have it and don't cast your evil eye on the meat.

And Ananta dished a ladleful into a bronze dish which he picked up from among the jumble of pots, pans, smoky rags, hammers and anvils strewn about him in the soot-filled corner which he was in the habit of improvising as a kitchen on special occasions.

Dina Timur Lang greedily gnawed at the bone. The meat was hot and he had to throw it back into the dish. Then he began to tear a piece off it with his gnarled fingers. It was still hot, so he lifted his fingers and licked them, smacked his lips and dug at the bone again, with little short moans and cries of pleasure : 'Ah, wonderful ! I could eat my fingers. Now we only need that *potent liquid* ! I wonder where Ralia has gone, the swine !'

'Ohe, come to your sense and don't bark!' said Ananta, significantly referring to the talk about the potent liquid. 'Or those puppies there will go and spread the tale.' And he suddenly turned towards the door and, feigning the accent of the owner of a cookshop trying to drive away some dogs, he began: 'Hut, duray, duray, little puppies, go away!'

But the little children, headed by Ralia's son Rhoda, came swarming round the shop, eager to taste the food, the smell of which had filled the whole of Billimaran.

'Uncle, give me a bone,' Rhoda said.

'Go, go, little pups, how can I give you bones before we have eaten the meat on them?' he roared mockingly.

'Ohe, Chacha, you know what I want, a boti!' Rhoda pleaded.

'Han, Chacha Anantia,' said Rama, shy as ever.

'Go away, dog of Chacha!' shouted Ralia as he came up drunkenly from behind.

Ananta began to dish out the meat in little leaf pots to the children, giving Rama a big portion to take home to his sister-in-law Gauri. The children looked greedily at each other's portions and were barely kept from fighting by Ananta's injunction: 'Those who want more may come back after they have eaten their portions: good eaters will find food here, but selfish hounds will only get bare bones to quarrel over. Now go off and enjoy yourselves'

Having disposed of the children, he filled dishes for Ralia and Dina and himself and began to eat without much ceremony even as he handed the portions to his two friends. 'Here you are,' he said, pushing a leaf pot and some chapatis in a common plate before Ralia.

'No, I don't want it,' said Ralia, tipsy and sullen.

'Oh, of course,' said Ananta. 'I forgot that some people drink their midday meal—some eat it.'

'You smell like the drain outside Lohgarh gate,' rebuked Dina Timur Lang. 'Let me have the bottles.'

'I will have such fun with you,' said Ralia threateningly. 'If you insult me that limp leg of yours will get a companion.'

'Ohe, eat, Dine, will you,' Ananta said, 'because you must be ready to serve the others when they come. . . . Sardar Puran Singh Bhagat is probably coming and also Mahasha Hans Raj. I will give you your portion of drink.'

And he rose, took the bottles from Ralia's cotton scarf,

went into the back room, poured out three china cupfuls of home-brewed wine and brought them out, saying: 'This is the gravy to go with your meat.'

Both Ralia and Dina seemed to be cowed by Ananta's manner as well as the appearance of the leader Mahasha Hans Raj, of Viroo and his brothers Bhagu, Arjan, and some other unemployed thathiars—Bhanta, Mela, Mukunda, Bihari, Buta and others.

'Ao, ji, ao, come and sit down to the meal,' greeted Ananta with the effusiveness of the Punjabi host. 'Welcome.'

'Nahin, brother,' they muttered almost in a chorus, 'No.' They were suddenly overcome by the politeness of the Punjabi guest. And a war of courtesy started, after which Ralia broke the round pitcher of hospitality in a loud voice:

'Acha, don't look as if your mothers have died. The householder is himself in want of sympathy, but the beggars crowd at his door for love.'

'Ohe, keep quite, you are drunk!' said Dina Timur Lang. 'All these days you stretched your mouth for food; now that you have got it you won't eat and fancy yourself as the Prince of beggars!'

'Brothers, don't mind Ralia, come and eat,' said Ananta, and he began to dish out food for them. 'There is a little drink too at the back if you would like it,' he added, just to tease the leader Mahasha Hans Raj, who looked as though he had come here under protest and disapproved of meat-eaters and wine-drinkers.

'I feel my heavy-bladdered stomach within me is expanding like a balloon,' said the rotund Black God Viroo, brushing the sweat off the white bristles of several days' growth of beard on his face. 'And the ball of my belly distended, not because I have been eating but because I have not swallowed a morsel for days. So I for one will eat my fill.' And he sat down on the worn wooden threshold.

'Acha, come then, Viroo Mal, you are like a father to us, come and eat!' said Ananta. 'Come, all of you, brothers!'

All the newcomers settled down in odd crouching positions on both sides of the threshold, except Mahasha Hans Raj, who laughed shortly and, coughing nervously, said:

'I hope you won't win them all over merely by offering them food, Lala Anant Ram!'

'One's own thoughts and one's own deeds are one's constant companions,' Ananta answered somewhat tartly.

The hurt, haughty note in his voice charged the atmosphere almost as though the heat of the afternoon had filled the void before the men. The silence stiffened the texture of their hard faces, and they ground the food as if they were masticating some bitter poison in their mouths.

'It is an unfair tactic, you know,' the leader said, with another embarrassed laugh, as he realized that he had made a *faux pas*.

But the words were lost in his mouth as he heard the tread of heavy footsteps behind him and turned to the tall, gawky presence of Puran Singh Bhagat.

'Ao, Sardarji,' shouted Viroo with a cheek stuffed full of food, 'now there is Mahasha Hans Raj to discuss with you on your own level that question we talked about this morning. You are for the Roosis, aren't you?—so the student Satyapal says.'

'Iron cuts iron, brothers,' said Puran Singh Bhagat, joining his hands to all with a vague, formal obeisance; 'as for wool piled on wool, it becomes more wool.'

'And if someone puts a live coal on this wool!' said Ananta. 'Heaven help the whole town.'

'The student says,' continued Viroo, that Ananta and you are Communists who receive your orders from the King of Roos.'

'Who are these students?' the poet asked.

Viroo did not answer this question.

And there was a tense silence for a moment.

'That is not the talk, Lala Viroo Mal,' cut in Mahasha Hans Raj with his eyes averted from the poet. 'Whatever the student Satyapal says is exaggerated. I say, what Mahatma Gandhi has always said, that man is not all belly but also belief, that whatever you do you must do it in accordance with our Hindu dharam.'

'The student Satyapal tells me,' said Viroo, 'that Communism stands for the ruin of our joint family. Making babies in bottles. A removal of children from their homes to haspatals. No God. So the souls of men with become like wax in the hands of godless folk and man will be destroyed.——'

'In former days, the perverters of truth died,' Ananta cut in indignantly, 'now they don't even get fever.'

'Let Puran Singh answer!' protested Viroo.

'It all depends on how you interpret Communism,' the poet said. 'I certainly don't believe that Communists want to destroy personality or the soul. They wouldn't have beaten the Germans off in this war if they had no souls and had no respect for human beings.'

Then you can tell us what the Roosis are doing about the Machine,' said Viroo.

'Now, first things first—you asked me about the Roosi view of the soul and human beings—'

'To Viroo it is the same thing—Dictatorship of the Proletariat and the Dictatorship of the Machine!' the Mahasha said mildly, looking from where he crouched and feeling that he was in a position of disadvantage in this argument, as he was sitting down while Puran Singh Bhagat was standing. 'And they are not really different, are they, when you come to think of it, Sardar Puran Singh?'

'That is why we are intent on smashing them all!' said Viroo.

'There is no arguing with you, Chacha,' said the poet, cornered. 'You put such emotion into your words that they sound like abuse. As for Mahasha Hans Raj, he knows that two different words can describe the same thing, if you hate that thing or are partial to it. Those who hate the Communists call them "Reds", "Bolshies", "Soulless Machine Men" "Robots"——'

'Ah, but Communists call everyone who doesn't agree with them "Trotskyites", "Bourgeois", "Cannibals!"' protested Mahasha Hans Raj with a laugh. 'Only through religion can one be truthful.'

The poet hesitated and then spoke:

'In no age, brothers, have words been so perverted in the name of truth. Simpler than all things, Truth has become more difficult to obtain than anything else in the world. And yet truth is a force which you cannot hedge. I agree that there are various kinds of opinion which are held with equal sincerity and conviction. But there is such a thing as a truth above personal truth, itself truth. And since you and I are both on trail for making our truth the twin brother of the instinct which is in every heart, liberty, you will agree that we are biased in favour of a higher kind of truth. Our justification for this is that not only we ourselves but a great many foreigners also believe passionately in the freedom of our country. Speaking for myself, a great deal of my belief in truth arises from my love and respect for man as such.' He paused, twitched his head and then continued: 'Man's confidence in himself has been systematically destroyed by various interests for a long time now, so that he might be more easily dominated. I believe in the restoration of man if he is to control machinery at the present time. I believe, in fact, if we can have any religious faith, morality or code at all today, it must arise from the reassertion of man's dignity, a pure love for man in all his strength and weakness. Limitless compassion for man. Unbounded love especially for the poor and the down-trodden. So that those who have been left to rot on the dusty roads can be raised and given the izzat which is theirs by the miracle of their birth in this world. Roughnecks and toughnecks in Delhi have uniformly decreed laws and ordinances, detention without trail, mass imprisonment and—oh, the sowing of a harvest of death among the new ripe generations.'

The fact that Puran Singh Bhagat was standing certainly gave his words the emphasis of a speech from the rostrum. The sound of it got home to the thathiars more than the sense. And though they did not understand all of it except in the vaguest manner they were dumbfounded. Even Mahasha Hans Raj could not argue against the towering oracular poet because his voice was gentler, his soul more tortured through its loyalty to religion and his disgust for modern civilization. He raised his head, however, and spoke:

'That is exactly why I came here to beg you and Lala Anant Ram not to encourage these brothers to do anything which may disturb things. After all, at the moment all members of our nation, whether they be employers or employees, together worthy of respect, are equal partners in the struggle against evil.'

'Han, we are together, brother, in our love for freedom from oppression,' intruppted the poet, jerking his turban again with the familiar nervous twitch of his head. 'But we must be on our guard against those in our country who substitute Brown rule instead of the White. Certainly, if there is anything which has accrued to me through my pilgrimage of the world it is the belief that I must help to change the present order built on profit; that I must devote myself entirely to the poor.'

'That is why he is called *Bhagat*, brotners,' Ananta said enthusiastically, explaining the meaning of the poet's name to the thathiars—'devoted to the poor !'

'If the rich were all that bad, Sardar Puran Singh, how could Gandhiji, who, you will agree, worships truth, accept them as friends ?' said Hans Raj.

'Because Gandhiji always worshipped the kind of truth which was orthodox !' answered the poet, 'Because he really accepts private property. The vicious circle of the old order which can never last in India if it has made such a mess of things in the other parts of the world. We have a floating population of millions unemployed, expropriated peasants and handicraftsmen without enough work to absorb them. So here in this country only an overturning of the old will bring the healing balm of love among men. Only a revolution will complete the information of Guru Nank . . . Gandhiji may have been innocent, but he certainly never realized the meaning of Revolution for our country and went on believing in an unplanned, individualist, competitive profit making the like of which has thrown these brothers out of their jobs. The more fierce the competition, the more use is made of unskilled slave labour and the greater the insults levelled at the human being, be it in London, Tokyo or New York.'

He paused for breath and the dilated nostrils of his big nose trembled a little. Ananta was surprised at the certainty and assurance of his manner as compared with his hesitations of the morning. But apparently the poet had been thinking of a programme since then.

'I don't know why the capitalists are sponsoring their fifteen-year plans for the welfare of the workers then ?' queried Mahasha Hans Raj.

'The cleverness of the capitalists lies in not working the labourers to death. No worker, for instance, is required to kill himself with work. And everyone who is employed gets a day off. And those who are unemployed are given a permanent holiday—only without pay. And neither the Sarkar nor the Gandhists can see the sinister consequences of this capitalist kindness to the employed and the shrugged-shoulder indifference to the unemployed.'

'But the merchants and dealers have no hand in the arrangement of affairs today,' said Mahasha Hans Raj. 'Neither Birla not Tata nor Sarabhai has a voice. Certainly you will admit that if they had a hand they would do well for us.'

'We will see what happens soon,' the poet said, drawing back a little, with another nervous twitch. 'But don't let us forget that for all their sins the English at least had the Bible for their background, and the experience of a century and a half of the industrial revolution from the hungry forties downwards. Our merchants are descended—let us be honest—from a caste-ridden society with an utter contempt for the lower orders ingrained in them as part of their dharma. Besides, they are, after all, the poor of yesterday become newly rich, and they have been so used to living in one-roomed houses in the joint family that they don't see why the coolies should not live ten to a room——'

'Ah—to be sure,' Dina Tamer Lane said, while the other thathiars nodded uncertainly.

'But they have not committed murder and rape nor resorted to refined hooliganism as the ferungis yet!' protested Hans Raj. 'Are they not the people who believe in the policy of the firm when it comes to capturing markets? The respect of our people for the inner side of the soul will win through because we are not dominated by the practical side of life as are the foreigners——'

'Not yet!' exclaimed the poet. 'And, anyhow, not every Englishman is an oppressor. I know a few gentle souls among them. Even those who believe in non-violence, as you do, Mahashaji. And they believe in our liberty.'

'Why don't the gentle souls among them speak up then?' said Hans Raj. 'All I hear is the voice of the United English nation, while here in India we speak with as many different voices as there are people. And I have never heard of an Englishman offering the example of non-violence as Gandhiji does. I have seldom heard of many among them who offered themselves as examples.'

'Stop this talk!' said Ralia, awakened from his drunken stupor. Let us eat in peace.'

He seemed to have spoken for most of the thathiars, as the argument between the two learned men had soared above his heads. So the leaders became silent.

Ananta got up, pot and ladle in hand, to cover the embrassing situation, saying: 'There is no talk, brothers, one must have a big heart. Who will have another bone or some gravy ?' And he gave the thathiars more helpings in spite of their protesting grunts and outspread hands.

The guests did not prevent him after the first polite refusals, and, tearing at the chunks of bread, dipping them in the gravy in the leaf pots, swallowed large mouthfuls, their life-blood flowing into their thickly veined foreheads and turning into the sweat of contenment on their necks.

As Ananta settled down again to eat he found that he could not swallow another morsel, for he recalled Mahasha Hans Raj's jibe about the tactic of winning over the men with food. His face glowed red like the smouldering coals in the even by him, as he perceived that there was a partial truth in the insult. For he had intended to call them together and form them into a union over a cup of wine and some food.

Just as they were all absorbed in thinking their own thoughts, the student Satyapal arrived, his tousled hair soaked in sweat and his face prolonged by a sullen, unhappy look.

'I must go soon, brothers,' said Puran Singh Bhagat. 'All I want ro beg of you before I leave is this : I am not sure that Mahasha Hans Raj and I are not in agreement over many thing. If only he will believe that we all love our country and wish the best things for it, however we may differ in our views about religion; he will agree that we have got to get together *to guard* our rights——'

But before he could finish his sentence and get up, Satyapal took advantage of his sense on the platform of the shop and, turning with a flourish towards Puran Singh Bhagat hissed :

'There is no getting together with those who support Roos and the evil Sarkar.' And as Viroo nodded assent, he raised his voice : 'Our beloved leaders were not lying. They looked at the whole circle of the earth with its flaming longitudes and they knew who has set the world on fire. All these ferungis brought the Devil's tricks into the world and now they are destroying each other. We are not going to let our Hindustan be tainted by their Satanic designs, nor by the lackeys of Russia. And we must do something immediately to show them this is no uncertain terms.'

'I want to dissociate myself from such talk, Sardar Puran Singh,' said Mahasha Hans Raj. 'This boy is deliberately invoking the names of our leaders and my views about machines for his nefarious purposes.'

THE BIG HEART

'I know what he is after, brother,' said Ananta. 'But, as I told Viroo this morning, it is not a question of accepting or rejecting the machine, at this late hour when it is already there, it is a question of the heart. . . . And if our hearts are sound, and we are pledged to make a "Revolution", there is no question about being tainted by the Roosis, the Chinis or ferungis.'

'There are traitors in our midst,' began Satyapal, 'who are disrupting our ranks!'

'It is indeed a question of being tainted,' put in Viroo. 'Ask your caste brethren! Would they like to break caste and eat with the Malecha beef-eating Sahibs?'

'We will have some blood-letting soon, and shoot all the traitors who have joined hands with the Sarkar,' raved Satyapal, very red in the face.

'Satyapal!' exclaimed Mahasha Hans Raj. 'To kill others is to destroy oneself ultimately! Don't lose your head.'

'I must say, Satyapal brother, that the talk about blood-letting is strange coming from your mouth,' said the poet. 'All this hatred! Considering you were just indicting the Communists for believing in violence. And Viroo Mal, surely even Gandhiji, who believed in caste, did not believe in untouchability. As Mahasha Hans Raj will tell you, Mahatma often declared his love for the English. Surely there is no question of Hindustan and Vilayat in this shrieking world whose every corner is affected by war and revolution. Our destinies are linked up with the ferungis and with everyone else, for good or for evil. And we sink or swim together or we shall all be drowned by the deluge. There is no escape by isolating oneself.'

'You are ashamed of inciting men to hatred, but I am not,' cut in Satyapal, stepping forward. 'And I am really for the Revolution now while you prate about it and really believe in compromise. I am for a clean sweep of all the filthy scum now.'

'Why object to our age-old division of men according to their *karma*?' said Viroo.

'Because out there at the grain-shop of Mohkam Chand, in Misri Bazar,' said Ananta, 'the conflagration lit by hunger in men's hearts is raging. When I went shopping there before noon at least a hundred men were waiting for Mohkam to open the shop. And it is not a question of what caste your employer belongs to, it is a question of who he aspires to be.'

The thathiars nodded enthusiatically at this, except for Ralia, who still sat asleep with his head in his hands.

'If you knew that not one of us of the thathiar caste has received an invitation to go to the betrothal ceremony of Murli Dhar's grandson, Nikka, there,' said Dina, pointing towards the lane, 'but that Sadanand has been putting his turban at the feet of all the rich dealers, begging them to grace his house on this auspicious occasion, then you would know if it is caste which counts or money.'

'To be sure!' said Puran Singh Bhagat.

'To be sure, I too haven't been asked,' said Viroo. 'But Murli will surely get his reward, as soon as he goes before God.'

'Leaving aside the treatment anyone gets in heaven, what about ensuring a job now?' Ananta pointed the finger of an agitational challenge to the knot of thathiars. 'Will you join the union?'

Han,' they all muttered with one voice.

'There is no time to form the union. You must act if you are to make an impression,' said Satyapal.

'Ohe, son, you keep out of this,' said Ananta. 'Don't incite them. We have suffered long, but we can still suffer in patience till the moment arrives.'

Han, Satyapal. Men live and work for a cubit of stomach,' said Mahasha Hans Raj. 'But it is a question of their souls. Try compromise first.'

'The pomegranate is ripening, brothers,' said the poet. 'And it will burst if you have patience.'

'Men live and "work for a cubit of stomach" in our time,' shouted Satyapal. 'And yet they can't earn enough even to subsist on the margin where life hangs on to death. I say death to the traitors who join hands with outsiders in the name of internationalism and betray their own countrymen. Act now for your race and religion and country. Why, these men have been put in a position where they can neither earn a wage by piecework nor by being employed in the factory. If you agree that they could always be robbed of their just share under cover of caste superiority by the dealers, who regarded them as cattle fit for nothing else but to go round and round the oil mill blindfolded, then you know that if they get into the factory there they will perish !'

'I say,' urged Ananta, 'that we will form a union to ensure their right to a proper wage until they are strong enough to displace their exploiters and seize the factory, which by all the rights in theirs.'

'And then will begin the era of the Dictatorship of the Proletariat in India !' mocked Satyapal. 'And the Dictatorship of the State Machine ! State capitalism and all the old tricks of propaganda and advertisement. And the betrayal of the Revolution !'

If only Satyapal wouldn't lose his temper, there is some truth in what he say,' urged Hans Raj. 'The huge and mammoth five-year programmes will dehumanize man. I feel that the capitalists at least leave some room for initiative and independent thinking among the people, whereas in the Communist utopia—a good steamroller will liquidate all intelligence and then fill the vacuum of men's minds with the filth and muck of the films and the cheap thrills of the arena, the morals of gangsters and the method of dacoos. And the worship of the great God War !'

'Better anything than foreign rule !' shouted Satyapal. 'I am not frightened of making a Revolution today. Away with this obscene Sarkar and away with all who stand between the workers and bread.'

'You mean anarchy ?' said the poet. 'Be sensible, Satyapal.' And then he turned to Hans Raj. 'There is certainly a danger of what you say happening, Mahashaji. But I only hope that by the time the new age comes, men will learn to love each other.'

'Make wage slaves with love then get them killed off in the war, make the survivors into tame trade unionists, then call them men and betray them !' said Satyapal. 'What a programme !' His mouth frothed with bitterness and the pockmarks on his face became darker and bigger.

'It is godlessness which is more dangerous,, said Hans Raj sagely.

' "A well-fed man needs religion",' Ananta quoted the proverb. 'Mahashaji, it is a question of the belly ! The soul is with us all the time, because we are ourselves according to the Hindu faith.'

'Having been a Yogi myself,' said the poet,' 'I believe that some faith is necessary, though there is no need for a belief in God. I think there will emerge a new kind of brotherhood, a new sense of devotion like the *Bhakti* which our saint Kabir preached and practised. I have seen glimpses of this religion already in my travels and——'

'Sit down Sardarji, and tell us more,' said Arjun, his walrus moustache weighing the possibilities of this strange creed where there was no need for a direct relation between man and God.

'Han, han, do sit down,' entreated Viroo, now that the talk had drifted to religion.

'No, I must go,' said the poet.

He gazed at his wrist-watch and burst into an expression of horror. 'Half past two—nearly quarter to three!' And he turned his back without even the ceremony of joining hands to the thathiars by way of farewell.

'O Sardar Puran Singh, all talk apart, are we agreed on its common action?' said Ananta after him.

'I have told you, get together, brothers,' the poet said, returning. 'Form the union here and now, with the factory boys in it.'

'So that the real aspirations of the men can be contained and they can be betrayed all together!' commented Satyapal.

'Wait, I am coming too, Puran Singh,' said Mahash Hans Raj. And he dragged Satyapal away with him, saying: 'Come, I want to talk you, son. Come and see us off.'

'Ah, it has been like a marriage party, this feast and talk and even the quarrels,' Viroo said after the leaders had receded from view.

'And we are the marriage party, are we?' said Dina. 'Old uncles and elderly grandfathers?'

'Oh no, you are the bridegroom,' Ananta mocked at him. And pointing to Ralia, who was snoring, he said: 'Look at your best man.'

'Of course, I am the bridegroom,' said Dina Timur Lang.

'There is no scarcity of brides in the house of the rich,' Viroo said. 'We are all bridegrooms in that sense. Only, don't let us accept that machinery as our dowry.'

'Ohe, look at your white bread!' Viroo's brother Bhagu said soberly.

'To be sure,' said Arjun, 'there is no talk. Have a shame ! We have daughters of our own. . . . As for the dowry, anything would do, so long as we earn it through honest labour and according to our dharma.'

'Han,' said Ananta, wiping a little cold gravy in the dish before him with a quarter of chapati. 'We must not let our bitterness force us to rape or bigamy. Nothing will dry quicker than our tears once we get work. Meanwhile, drink the wine and don't care a fig for the limp lord.'

'But Lala Ananta Ram, we can't indulge in an orgy of happiness when we have no money, no job and no bread,' said Viroo. How can we forget the limp lord just because we have eaten meat and drunk wine for one day ? That boy Satyapal's advice is good : If the factory catches fire by chance, then we can at least get piecework from Kaseras. And we will have made an impression they won't forget.'

'Look, wait—can you hear the band of Jehangir playing the music of gladness to celebrate his grandson's betrothal ?' said Bhagu. 'They are using the back entrance to the house for celebrations, the swine !'

'And they haven't sent the barber round even to ask us to come and pay a donation to little Nikka,' said Arjun, 'And I have still two daughters and a son to marry off ! Who will treat with us if the Chaudhri of our brotherhood shuns us !'

'They are all very thick with each other, Gopi, Lal Chand and Khushal Chand,' said Mela. 'They eat together in the office of the factory, they go to the same whore and drink in the same cluff.'

'I should like to kill the whole lot of them,' Ralia said, awakening suddenly. 'The thieves and robbers who have gathered together and deprived us of work. Look, folks, the darkness has come ! Where is that boy, Babu Satyapal ?'

'The dyspeptic swine !' exclaimed Dina, lunging forward.

'Why can't we go and face Murli ?' . . . I could kill Murli !' shouted Ralia.

'Killing, like everything else these days, is cheap for the Sarkar but an expensive game for the poor,' said Ananta with a smile. There were echoes of the voice of Guru Nanak in his head, but he did not want to turn preacher. He waxed cynical. 'So there is no question of fellows like ourselves indulging in it, because we just can't afford the price. We can only cultivate the disgusting virtues—perseverance, patience and pain, look after our health and think clear thoughts if we are ever to get together.'

'Your cold calculations are at the mercy of my temper,' said Ralia. 'Don't you come preaching all these virtues to us just because you have treated us to a bit of food!'

'Ohe chup, ohe chup, silence!' roared Dina. 'You were quarrelling with him this morning, now you are fighting with him again! What devil has taken possession of your head!'

At this Ralia averted his face, his eyes more bloodshot than ever, his head hung down out of shame at turning against his benefactor.

Ananta was certainly by no means non-violent, but he believed in conserving his strength—till he was finally aroused. And then he could be something more than mere sacrifice and bitterness; he could hack his way across the jungle. But now he felt far too much for these men to answer back.

But to complicate his position with them, just then arrived Mehru, and, unable to see Ananta at the opening of the shop, called: 'Ananta Ram, Lala Ananta Ram, where are you?'

'There comes the bridegroom,' said Dina sarcastically, 'but his mother runs an oven!'

'He is the newest inmate of that mousetrap!' commented Viroo. 'He is no bridegroom!'

'Ohe, don't torment him,' said Ananta. 'He is a thathiar brother, and when a thathiar brother gets a job it is a festival for us as well as for him!'

'Thathiar brother! Traitor more like it!' Ralia shouted. 'No man could have gone near Murli knowing how his other brothers were being treated.'

'From his silence he seems godly,' said Bhagu.

'I looked in,' said Merhu, addressing Ananta, 'to give you this money which Khushal Chand gave me for you.'

'So that is the game!' said Ralia.

'All eyes may be black but they are not alike,' said Viroo. 'I didn't think Ananta could be speaking to us and be winking at the dealers at the same time.'

'There is no unanswerable riddle in this message. It is the wages they owed Ananta,' Mehru said. 'He was sorry his brother behaved so badly this morning.'

'Oh, and I suppose that Murli has sent a message for Ananta to come to the betrothal ceremony this afternoon,' mocked Ralia.

'Ohe, listen, brothers,' said Ananta; if I am richer than you I shall share my money with you, if I am poorer you can spit at me and go your ways. But let us wait and think, not hit out blindly.' If our brains leak and the dealers, or Murli, or Satyapal, can spread the smoke of confusion among us we shall disappear like vapour. If we belong to hunger and suffering we belong to it together. . . .'

'What are we going to do then?' said Viroo, in the grip of Satyapal's incendiarism.

'Let us dixide this money and buy ourselves the peace to think of our sorrow,' said Ananta. 'And then perhaps we can plan to cure it. Go, take this money and buy some flour for yourselves at Mohkam's shop. It may have opened by now.'

'I suppose you want to gain time so that you can promise to one and perform to another,' said Ralia.

Ananta's heart grew heavy with the silent oppression of heat and suspicion that now surrounded him. In vain he had tried to prove to these bitter and maltreated men that he was with them. But now the outer composure which sprang from his inner certainty broke and he burst out:

'Go then and eat your masters! Go—for heaven's sake, go! Of course, they do not love you or me, and we don't seem to love each other, even in our despair! Go and fall into the graves which Satyapal is digging for you with the knives of his talk ¡'

'Let us go and see if Mohkam's shop is open,' said Dina.

'Let us,' said Viroo. 'Come, Ralia.'

'Acha,' said Ralia.

Weighted with misery, they shifted from where they had enjoyed a wholesome meal and began to walk away, confused at Ananta's sudden out burst.

19

CLAD IN A WELL-STARCHED MUSLIN TUNIC AND DHOTI, WITH AN enormous silken turban on his head, Lala Murli Dhar sat on a white sheet spread over a carpet across the verandah of the store-room on the top of his house, talking to Ram Saran and Binde Saran, who had brought the offer of betrothal for Nikka, and the immediate members of his family. A thick canopy, like an awning, stretching from the ceiling to the terrace which overlooked Billimaran, protected the space before the company from the burning rays of the sun. The Chaudhri was waiting—waiting for Jehangir's band to arrive and strike up a note of jubilation, waiting for the guests, long overdue, waiting for something to happen. And his usually calm, white-bearded face was flushed red with the excitement and the strain of this waiting, the worry of it. Ordinarily, he would not have been perturbed, because he himself and his coppersmith cousins had not much respect for time, especially on such ceremonial occasions, but today he was not certain who, from among the choice guests he had invited, would arrive and who would not.

'Ohe, Sadananda!' he called to his son, who was arranging some cow-tailed cushions he had borrowed for occasion along the walls of the verandah, his cotton sadri and muslin dhoti sticking to his reedy black legs with the sweat. 'Send Gopi to remind Lala Gokul Chand and the others that we are waiting for them.'

'Why not send the barber around to remind the members of the brotherhood?' asked Lala Ram Saran, the uncle of the prospective bride. He did not know that the barber of the brotherhood had not been sent round at all to invite the thathiars, but that only a few respectable men from the Arya Samaj and a few choice workers at the factory had been specially asked by Gopi.

Murli knitted his brows uncomfortably and repeated: 'Sadananda, go, son. And, ohe Nikke, take that hand fan and give us all a blow of air; there is such a "hoom" here.'

Sadanand proceeded towards the stairs and began to put on the shoes he had discarded on the top step. Nikka took up the hand fan, as big as himself, and began to move it with all the force in his body.

'Not so fast, son,' Sadanand said. 'I wonder where Gopi is because I could send him round to get the band at least while I go to remind Chaudhri Gokul Chand and the other guests.'

The attempt to ingratiate themselves with superior people seemed to Sadanand, after his interview with Gokul before noon, to be doomed, and there was an element of panic in his behaviour. He was confused and tired as he stood ready to go, his twisted black face crumbling with the fears inside him.

'They are coming, father, they are here—Lala Gokul

THE BIG HEART

Chand and his nephew Lala Lal Chand,' Gopi called from downstairs.

'Ao ji, may I fall at your feet,' Sadanand said, looking down the dark, narrow stairs towards Gopi and the guests.

'May you flourish, Sadananda' called Chaudhri Gokul Chand. 'But you, you look like a bellows-blower, dressed in that sooty sadri and dhoti, and on your son's betrothal too ! Wah !'

'Namaste ji !' said the high priest of the local Arya Samaj who followed, a fat, clean-shaven man dressed in orange robes, with a carbuncle on his forehead.

Lala Devi Datt, a dark school-teacher, through whom the family had originally been initiated into the reformist neo-Hindu society of Arya Samaj, appeared after him.

'Sadanand, son, go and change,' said old Murli, beaming now that the much sought-after head of the Kasera brotherhood, and the prosperous Arya Samajis, had come. His world glowed and he felt his arteries swelling with a new song he had never heard before.

'I have to see about the band, father,' Sadanand said, and waited for the honoured guests to come right up before descending.

'At least put a clean turban on,' Murli said, expansive and hot. And seeing the guests, he got up, went forward and joined hands to them all with profound cordiality. Then he seated them against the cow-tailed cushions and called : 'Gopi, bring some sherbet.'

'But where is your brotherhood ? asked Lala Gokul Chand, striking a discordant note.

'They are coming,' said Murli Dhar hurriedly, an apologetic self-reducing smile on his face that deflamed his heart.

'Grandfather !' blurted out Nikka. 'They are not coming, because father says we are not going to ask them as they are mostly low people. Also, even if they were asked they would not come, because they say we have only asked the dealers, who have cut down their wages——'

'Don't bark but move the fan,' shouted Murli, red in the face. 'What do you know about all this ?'

'But grandpa !' the boy protested, and tears come to his eyes at the rebuke.

'If we had known this, Lala Murli Dhar,' said Lala Ram Saran, shocked, 'we wouldn't have stayed. After all, if our thathiar brothers are not coming, how can we celebrated the ceremony ?'

'We will be turned out of the brotherhood if we don't honour our kith and kin with invitations on this sacred occasion,' said Lala Binde Saran, echoing his brother's concern.

'I think, said Lala Gokul Chand, 'these folk from Jandiala are right. If you don't have the men of your own brotherhood, who will you have ? The Kaseras are not coming. And if possible our visit here today must be regarded as secret.'

'We Arya Samajis have no such scruples, brother Gokul Chand,' said the high priest in orange robes. 'We do not agree with the orthodox Sanatani Hindus in keeping the old caste and sub-caste divisions We have come here openly, and I wish more of us had been informed. We must form a new community based not on caste prejudice but the revival of the true ancient Vedic religion.'

For a moment it seemed as if under the pressure of the high priest's words the atmosphere relaxed. Murli Dhar breathed a sigh of relief, the faces of the guests hung down in deep humility, the flies fluttered happily and a big black wasp sang a song like an incantation before the mighty Sun.

'Han, there is no need to worry, uncle,' Lal Chand said to Gokul Chand. 'We live in new times. Lala Murli Dhar can celebrate this occasion with a few friends and his intimate family circle. Why give sugar-plums to sweeten the mouths of those ungrateful wretches ? I stand by our Arya Samaji brothers.'

'That is indeed what my grandson Gopi says too,' put in Murli, sweating profusely. 'But, of course, we have asked the more responsible members of our brotherhood as well as our Kasera brothers, because we can't break age-old bonds. Certainly, never in my life time shall I renounce my position as Chaudhri of the thathiar brotherhood—sometimes I think that these boys go too far !'

For all that the high priest of neo-Hinduism might say, the opinions of Gokul Chand and the folk from Jandiala had affected him deeply, and he knew that he had blundered in excluding the coppersmith brotherhood from the ceremony. Instead of his dreams of rising into the upper class, he now experienced a subtle pleasure in allying himself with the low thathiars, as a twin brother of the men he hated. And he hoped against hope that even a few of them would come, the new cells of his body exhuding the sweat of confusion on his face and neck.

'Rest assured,' he said to the guests, 'the thathiar brotherhood is coming—What will you drink, sherbet or whey?' And in himself he called for peace in his blazing body.

'I know Lala Lal Chand prefers soda-water,' said Gopi, coming up the stairs. 'So I have brought iced soda-water for all.' He held a bucketful of bottles in one hand and a number of glass tumblers in the other. He proceeded towards the terrace and began to press the balls in the necks of the soda-water bottles with the thumb and forefinger of his hands.

Just at that moment the band of Jehangir struck up a bastardized version of 'Tipperary' and the whole atmosphere became surcharged with a sudden noisy hilarity as if the clarionets had suddenly lifted the misery of Billimaran from abysses below abysses into a faked happiness at the height of this house. Like a child Murli responded to the sound immediately and beamed with smiles as his fears were suddenly drowned in the noise.

'This is indeed a blessed occasion in the last years of my life, to see my youngest grandson betrothed,' he said. And he sat confident as if the strange music had suddenly infected the blood congealed by anxiety in his smallest veins and brought him to the bursting point of happiness and faith in life. For during the past few minutes, beneath the suppressed irritations of expectancy, beneath everything, he had been aware of the thing he had been always trying to avert by going to the temple every morning and evening, the gnawing fear of Death, which often asserted its hold on him and made him hot and cold in the same breath. Now he felt the growing cells of his cancerous fear, which had been multiplying in him for years and which suddenly attacked him now and then, close up like the lids of an inner eye and leave him, the flourishing patriarch of his family, only aware of his enemies, the thathiars, and triumphant above them on the heights to which the music lifted him.

'That will create some "ronuk" and bring the guests from the bazar and the other lanes,' he repeated, straining his throat to raise his voice above the noise of the band. But his throat filled with phlegm and, glancing all round for a spitoon, he got up at length and went towards the corner where Gopi was and spat himself hoarse as though he had had an attack of asthma.

Almost at that instant, as if the elements had conspired to upset everything about the ceremony, the gas in one of the overheated soda-water bottles shot out while Gopi was pressing the ball in its neck and the cherry-coloured liquid spurted all over Murli's clothes and the white sheet on the carpet.

'Ohe, look out, careful son,' the old man said mildly, as though he had instinctively prepared himself for the worst beneath his facade of equanimity and was not at all surprised at this accident. 'Did you give all the boys in the factory leave to come ?'

'Not grandpa, I didn't close the factory,' Gopi said. 'But I told various people to come.'

'Acha, go and call them, son,' the old man said.

Gopi took the four tumblers of soda-water he had poured out and, resisting the 'Lady of Killarney'', which the band had struck up, came and served the guests. He had done the right thing in buying soda-water, he thought. Gokul Chand and the Arya Samajis may have been embarrassed by having to drink sherbet or whey made in the house of the thathiar colleague to whom, they supposed, the taint of a lower caste still stuck in the eyes of the various exalted Hindu brotherhoods. This machine-filled water was neutral. Also, the folk from Jandiala, who conventionally, would not partake of a morsel of food or even a drop of water from the house of their prospective son-in-law, could drink the water brought from a shop !

As Gopi was serving the soda-water, Lala Devi Datt, the school-teacher, looked impatiently at his watch and said :

'It is ten past three : I have to go to give private tuition to some students.'

'Strange tuition you are giving them, Babu Devi Datt,' said Lal Chand, nephew of Chaudhri Gokul Chand. 'I hear that boy Satyapal, who once belonged to our Arya Samaj, and some thathiars, are determined to destroy us all with a bloody revolution.'

'But I sent Mahasha Hans Raj, a dignitary of the Samaj, to advise the thathiars and ask them to accept a compromise, said the high priest of the Arya Samaj for Devi Datt.'

'I too suggested to Hans Raj to encourage them to compromise with both the Chaudhris, Gokul Chand and Murli

Dhar,' said Devi Datt. 'As for Satyapal, I have not seen him for months. He seems to have lost his head since he began to listen to the Free India Radio.'

'I am afraid,' said young Lal Chand, 'that some of us may lose our heads too if he is allowed to preach his doctrine of murder. What with the Communists—Ananta and Puran Singh Bhagat, inflaming the thathiars, and then Satyapal ! . . . At least we might have kept the members of our Samaj from meddling in this affair. Instead !—'

'What has happened, then ?' asked Lalas Ram and Binde Saran with one voice.

'Nothing, nothing,' said Murli Dhar, waving his hand. 'Only a slight misunderstanding between us and the ruffians Ananta, Ralia, Viroo.'

'Han, only a slight misunderstanding !' added Murli's partner Gokul Chand ironically.

'Why, then, are the thathiar brotherhood not here ?' asked Ram Saran bluntly.

'Oh, they are coming soon,' answered Murli. 'Go, Gopi, son, call the boys in the factory !'

Gopi rushed downstairs, his heart drumming against his chest, afraid lest the whole pitcher of his family's complacency might burst suddenly.

Mehru's mother came up after Gopi had gone.

'May you flourish, Baba,' she said as she drew the end of her head-cloth modestly on her judgelike, shrivelled old face. 'I was with Gujri downstairs and thought I would come and pat Nikka on the head. Maybe the magic touch of his forehead imprinted on Mehru's face will bring my son the offer of a bride too.'

'Come, sister,' said Murli. 'Where is Mehru ? We have been expecting him.'

The old woman sat down in a huddle on the shoes by the top stair, sighed deeply and did not answer. The high priest and the school-teacher who lived in a world of abstract ideas were embarrassed and itched to go even as they wiped the sweat off their faces.

'Lala Murli Dhar, we shall have to be going soon,' said Gokul Chand. 'You know I promised to go back to the goods godown at the station this afternoon to see if the sheets have arrived. The Babu said I should look in in the afternoon. . . . Now, I suppose, I will have to telephone.'

'O Ishwar ! Hey Parmeshwar ! where are these people ?' said Murli, with his hands stretched out as he lost hold on himself again. And as the image of the unemployed thathiars gloating over his chagrin wove itself into his mind, his irritatation sharpened into a mounting horror and he vent his spite on them by using Mehru as a scapegoat : 'Look, folk, I give them jobs, I listen to their tales of woe, and this is how they show their gratitude to me. Where is that boy Mehru, for instance ? I specially asked Gopi to invite him here this afternoon.'

'The crows are not pigeons and the pigeons are not crows,' said Mehru's mother with a metallic ring in her voice. 'But even if they were all the same they wouldn't dare to come here because——'

'Because what ?' Murli asked angrily, sensing now that the whole of his design had collapsed.

'Because they were not asked, Baba,' she said mildly.

'Some of them are rogues and I won't have them here,' Murli said.

'Well, they have all become as one,' said Mehru's mother in a respectful whisper. 'Because the wages of most of them have come down to nothing and only a few of them have got jobs in the factory, they are getting together. And even the boys who are working in the factory dare not come here lest they should be stoned to death by Ralia and Dina.'

'But two men of the same trade can never agree,' said young Lal Chand cockily, 'If only they can be kept away from Ananta and Satyapal.'

'Ohe, son,' said Gokul Chand. 'Times have changed. They know that a single soul will rot in hell but a hundred or two hundred can storm the heavens !'

'Brothers,' said Lala Binde Saran, 'you are lions, and yet you wear coats of mail and go forward to wealth and honour together. We thathiars have been like so many scabby goats, each going our own ways so long. . . .' His rugged villagers's face was clean and frank and honest as he said this. 'And I rue the day when I thought of coming here to offer——'

'Be patient, Lala Binde Saran,' Murli said with joined hands to assure him.

The terror of disgrace weighed on his head, for in the shadowy, death-haunted soul of old Murli despair came easily. He knew now that the ceremony of his grandson's betrothal would be ruined beyond repair. For he had proudly turned his back on his old community of coppersmiths without establishing deep and intimate connections with a new brotherhood. As he anticipated the shocks that would lead to ultimate disaster he felt relieved and rested back on the cow-tailed cushion, the temples of his head throbbing violently, his eyes half closed, as though in the silence of his mind he could see the half-guessed possibilities of doom project themselves, like the shadows of the shrill avenging angels of eternal shame on his memory, as he guessed how he would be damned by generations to come for despising his fellow thathiars.

As though these torments were not enough, Jehangir, the Jemadar of the band, came up, dressed in his gold-braided blue uniform, and said with a great show of authority:

'My band has played for quarter of an hour according to the contract. Will you give me the fees of thirty rupees, please, as we have to go to play in Dhab Khatikan for a birthday.'

'Jehangir Padshah, please play another five minutes at least so that we can actually get the ceremony over,' Murli said.

'No please', said Jehangir, wagging his henna-dyed beard and smiling politely. 'That band costs me more per minute than I have contracted to play for here.'

'His time *is* important, Lala Murli Dhar,' interposed the teacher Devi Datt.

'Acha, let Sadanand come and he will give you the fees,' said the old patriarch, defeated.

'I can't wait here all day,' said Jehangir.

'Shanti! Shanti!' remonstrated the high priest, fanning himself with a lapel of his tunic. 'Patience, brother.'

'Look, folks, the darkness has come,' commented Mehru's mother. 'One could have the mirasis and bhands in the old days to play for a whole morning for a rupee and some rice.'

'Those days are gone, mother,' said Jehangir. Don't do "tictures" and pay me so that I can go to my next appointment.'

'Ohe, Sadananda, where are you? Murli called in a feeble pained voice.

'Coming, Lalaji, coming,' said Sadanand from the stairs.

Murli didn't even wait for his son to report the failure of his mission to get some more guests, for he surmised that failure from the nothingness that spread before him now.

'Give the bandmaster his money and ask your mother and wife upstairs, so that we can have the ceremony at once.'

'Those rogues and scoundrels, Ralia, Dina, Viroo, are picketing the lane and won't let any member of the thathiar brotherhood come here—I am sure that that illegally begotten Ananta is behind them.' As Sadanand said this he took a wad of notes out of his sadri and doled out Jehangir's fees and threw the money at him. The bandmaster went downstairs grumbling.

'I suppose Ananta is taking it out of you because I refused to pay him the rates he wanted,' said Lal Chand. 'We shall curb his pride. I shall put Satyapal on to destroy his hold on the coppersmiths if only I can meet the boy!'

There was a moment's silence and then Sadanand called: 'Mother, the mother of Nikka, come up and take the token.'

'If our brotherhood is not coming,' began Lala Ram Saran, 'We had better——'

But Murli didn't let him finish his sentence. He had ceased to hate his own brotherhood now, though in his heart there coursed a wild tirade of curses, imprecations and abuse for them at the humiliation they had inflicted on him just at the moment of his triumph. He bent forward in a posture of supplication and raised his turban with two hands and said:

'Listen, brothers, I have put my turban at the feet of all of you. Save this ceremony. I have sinned. I have erred. You can beat my old head with your shoes. But let us have this betrothal. Those boys of the brotherhood are my dear ones and near ones. If I did not invite them it was because they felt bitter with me about the factory and the loss of their trade. A crow tried to strut like a peacock, but, seeing his feet, wept and cried. That is my condition. Forgive me and let us go through with the ceremony.' And at this his eyes filled with tears and he began to howl, 'O God, O Guru Nanak, please forgive my sins—' The wrinkles of his finely chiselled old face gathered into a terrible knot of misery.

'Acha, grandfather, be patient, here is the offering of the hand of our daughter, Kausalya,' said Ram Saran.

'Sit down and put it in your lap, ohe Nikke,' said Sadanand.

Wadahi! Wadahi! Congratulations' everyone whispered. And Gokul Chand and Lal Chand, Devi Datt and the Arya Samaj priest presented Nikka with a shining silver rupee each.

Gujri, and the mother of Nikka, standing demurely at the top of the stairs, began to sing a ceremonial song in which Mehru's mother joined.

The high priest of the Arya Samaj began to recite a Sanskrit hymn, his eyes closed and his face set as if in a blind effort to infuse into the company the sense of seriousness of the ritual of neo-Hinduism as against the old. As he half opened his eyes and saw the company anxious to depart, he began to mutter a sermon to those present on the necessity of belief in the new community. 'Brothers, sisters, rich or poor, this auspicious ceremony of the betrothal of little Nikka, held according to the rites of the Arya Samaj, heartens us. For we Hindus of all castes and creeds have united through the belief in the ancient holy books. Welcome, all men of all faiths who come to us. But remember, we who have insisted so much on the inner experience of the Spirit have forgotten to be practical. Now we must support each other in this task by bringing about harmony among us, so that we can help each other to fulfil ourselves. . . . Om Shanti ! Shanti ! Shanti !'

This injunction for getting together in religion rose vaguely on the crest of the thup smoke before him.

But from downstairs came to the loud raucous hum of the satirical tune :

'O grandpa, press my limbs . . .
I have been gathering spinach . . .'

with which the thathiars were wont to laugh at the head of their brotherhood.

20

AWAKENED FROM HER SIESTA BY THE SOFT TREAD OF ANANTA'S feet, lifting her startled eyes in the semi-darkness of the room, Janki's mouth formed the question, 'Now, what has happened?' though she did not articulate it. During his earlier visit he had been silent but not so livid with rage.

Ananta hesitated for a moment on the doorstep, poised in thought even as he sought to get used to the dark.

He was not thinking so much as he was in a trauma, torn with indecision, and in the grip of an indescribable nameless anger; a compound of sadness, frustration and a passionate disgust at his incompetence in scattering his friends before he was able to get them together and lead them in a procession through the Bazar Kaserian.

'You are so far away, I can't even see you,' Janki said. And then, with the directness of a wanton, she patted the edge of her bed and said : 'Come and sit here !'

Ananta advanced and then stood shyly, his eyes drowned in the pools of her uncannily bright eyes, so open and inviting they were against the hangdown look he wore.

He breathed a heavy sigh and tried to shake himself out of the torpor of his unfathomable mood, but he found himself still weighed down under the shadow of the great rage that possessed him.

There was the tremor of a pale rose on the delicate curve of her lips, accentuated by the gash of her face, at once desirable and tragic. And to the mounting fumes of anger-pity that he felt for the thathiars there was added the rustling fear of the weird visions that had terrorized him in his dream.

'Oh, take me on your breasts,' he wanted to say, 'and rock me in peace. Oh, heal the pain that I feel at this betrayal. . . .'

But like a drug addict he just stood by her bed, as though craving for the intoxication of his love-hatred, unable to explain to her the lack of pain between his sense of duty to the ideal of brotherhood in which he believed and the thirsting woe of his thathiar brethren which fed on his liver.

She lifted herself on her elbow and stretched her right hand towards him, but he merely sat down on the edge of the bed away from her, absorbed, silent, asking himself : 'What has happened ? . . . What ? . . . What ?' And he remained suspended in the tension as a wounded bird which pauses to discover a direction before fluttering away with flapping wings.

In the silence which spread out before him, in the silence of his body listening to every sound and the agony of tight-stretched nerves, delving deep down for peace, Ananta felt the barrier between the looming chaos of his cremation-ground nightmare and the stormy scenes of the day breaking in tempestuous music of stranger prognostications. Somewhere between the agonized dream of the early morning and the bursting tempers of this day someone was doomed. 'Was it Janki or Karmo . . . or he himself?' But he dared not think fo the final reality. He knew it would come some day, but he did not know the date on which he would have to face it. Anyhow, it was not so imminent, he felt, in his case as in the case of Janki. And out of his love of life he felt himself immortal. Only he could hear the lilt of a haunting refrain about parting, deep in his throat :

'O mother, one day we have to go . . .'

Lest he should be drowned in the strange immobility of this despair, lest he should be consumed by the fears that burnt in his face, he got up and said : 'Everything is going wrong today ! When I came with your meal I had felt hopeful enough. I thought I should enrol them in the union and then march them up to the shop of Chaudhri Gokul Chand and demand piecework for all if there are no jobs in the factory. But Khushal Chand sent me some money he owed me by Mehru, and it was delivered in the presence of Ralia, Viroo and others. And now they think I am in the pay of Gokul Chand and Murli Dhar.'

'That shouldn't make you hang your head down !' Janki said. 'Have faith in God !'

'O misery of the parched, sighing earth !' he shouted. 'O agony of damp dwellings on the narrow alleys ! . . . O put some pity in the souls of these people ! Pity, not "faith in God !"'

'Are you going mad ?' she said.

'Nahin,' he said, shaking his head. 'No. But those who hear the guns roaring on the distant corners of the earth and call them thunderclaps in heaven; those who hear the rumour of catastrophe and call it prescience—do not know the affronts they offer' to the love of men.' And he looked at her tenderly. She had been his comrade in Bombay and had shared his difficulties' even though her knowledge of the outside world was fragmentary. And, as his comrade, she had come outside the shell of her own self. So he had approached her for advice, purely as a comrade. They had had something that enriched, enlivened and elevated their physical love for each other, and gave it an extraordinary meaning. But ever since their return to Amritsar she had been too ill to share his preoccupations. And now she didn't seem to understand at all, and he felt impatient with her, as though they had already parted company or been separated.

He edged away, grinding his teeth and muttering to himself as though talking in his sleep: 'Down lonely streets in the villages men walk like phantoms, their hearts lacerated by the scorpions of regret. . . They gather under the banyan tree over the hookah. The cowdust hour settles into the dark. And they look into the smoky horizons and ask: "O silence of earth and sky, what is the cause of this blight and what is to be done?" They do not know! They do not know! They cannot understand! And there is no answer from heaven.'

'God Almighty will answer them surely, one day,' said Janki, disturbed. 'He will destroy those who have brought this on us.'

'God works in a mysterious way,' said Ananta ironically; 'in such a heartless way that the ominous owl alone has so far taken pains to answer the peasants in the night. God seems to have deserted the world—if ever He were there, helping it along!'

'Don't blaspheme, proud Ananta Ram!'

'I tell you there is famine in this land,' Ananta shrieked. 'And there are wars raging on the edge of the farthest horizons. And yet my friends here will not stop extracting pain out of each other. Pain, pain, pain—there is such an orgy of suffering in the world! And they torture each other!'

Janki looked at his demented figure and realized, almost as though it were a new revelation to her, that she had really never known the experience he was talking about that from her comfortable childhood onwards she had suffered only from the arranged marriage to a man older than herself, and that, otherwise, she had gone on, not knowing what she wanted or where she was going, expecting others to be responsible for her. Inside herself, of course, she had experienced many a pang of heartache, the irritations of a surface existence as well as a sudden jolt at the knowledge of the disease that was ravaging her. And all that had made her imagine the cruelty of life in many ways. But always she had suffered in secret, and then, before she knew what was what, she had come to the end of her own experience with the certain knowledge of her impending death. And since then she had built a shell of self-protection round herself and tried to save herself from hurts.

Ananta had made the acquaintance of pain early, having been left an orphan. But he had wrestled with it and almost conquered it with his great capacity for happiness. And for a time he had regarded it only as a part of experience, something which made one grow, as when a person was ill his pain became merely the urge of his body trying to get well. Since his mature years, however, he had seen it as the constant undertone of life, almost omnipresent whether he happened to be in Amritsar or Lahore, Gurdaspur, Mandi, Delhi or Bombay, a kind of grim joke, a leer, a putrid sewer running like an invisible drain across the earth, devouring rats and cats and dead dogs as well as human beings in its even sweep, and then flooding the earth in sudden eruptions every now and then and laying it waste for generations.

'As I saw mothers sitting with their hungry children in the dust of the roadway this morning.' he said in a soft tone, as though, having spat his anger out, he was only talking aloud to himself, 'as I saw the beggars whining on the footbridge, I decided that if I have never done anything in my life ever before, I shall help my kinsfolk.

"Akh, God grant you never to suffer so," the beggars cried. I resolved that, since I have been luckier than them, I shall do something useful. All of us have the gift of this short life, for I do not think there is any hereafter; and I felt that if only I could give it to others, rather than keep it for my own self, I should feel happier. And who could I have served better than those men whom I used to despise at one time and to whom I came back from Bombai full of love, and with a sense of their izzat as men—as my brothers.'

'Are you really sure that you respect them as men or is it your inflated ego that desires pride and satisfaction and power through this bhakti ?.'

Janki realized after she had said this how it would hurt him, and she was ashamed of her words. Ananta turned to her with a half-suppressed indignation and said with a smile :

'You too, Janki ! Does no one believe in me because I was once a goonda ?'

She felt sorry for him, and yet his righteousness had filled her with a sense of mischief.

'You know,' she said, 'I saw so many people in your movement in Bombai who were suffering from swollen heads that I am rather sceptical of everyone's sincerity—including yours. I don't mean Comrade Joshi or Adhikari, but a great many of the small organizers with their love of power and small hearts, coming lording it over the coolies in the chawls, flagellating the poor with words as though to make up for their physical inferiority.'

'You can hardly accuse me of that, what with my biceps !' Ananta cut in with a smile quickly.

'Oh no, how stupid of me to forget !' Janki mocked. 'Yours is a mental weakness—isn't it !'

'Of course, you brought all your knowledge of the *Gita* to bear on the wonderful work you carried out in organizing the women of Bombai, didn't you ?' he parried, with a biting mockery.

Janki sank back with a laugh. Then, her eyes fixed on the ceiling, she sighed and said :

'Somehow my illness has torn away all the sheaths in which I used to wrap myself as a woman, even as it has left my bones bare of flesh. And I can see through all the disguises and pretences of my life before I make my peace with God. As I lie here day and night, I think of my childhood, which extended over twenty-five years, and over the last three years of my youth with you, and now of my bedridden old age. And, though I try not to think of people bitterly, I have certainly begun to think clearly of all those who deny us freedom. First of all my parents, who created me not because they loved each other but because they considered it a duty, and who regarded me, when I was born, as a curse because I was a girl. Then my husband and his relations, who were more concerned with the dowry I brought than with me. Later, when the owner of my house had died, society considered me as one who should be dead to all impulses and live only to worship the memory of my dead lord and master. Do you remember the things that were said all over the Punjab because I ran away with you ? The followers of the Mahatma in Bombay who believed in freedom, yet despised me because I was not married to you. I admit most of the comrades accepted me as a comrade, but I always felt that some regarded me as a prostitute. The women who came organizing us seemed to me to be devoted to the "cause", only because of some man whom they admired and wanted to obey and for whom they had spiritually substituted the movement for fear of becoming physically attached; and they certainly left me out of everything as a not-very-respectable person because of my life with you ! You will forgive me, therefore, if I began to see through the vanities which made them call by the name of devotion what was the desire to bully people because of some personal grudge they had against life.... Power and trickery and falsehood and backbiting seemed to me to mar what was a struggle for Truth, for giving them their dignity, for teaching them to live by works, as Arjuna in the *Gita* enjoined us.... That is why I failed, why I could not organize anyone at all. And I feel sorry for you because I know that the Truth in you revolts at the petty things your brothers say, because you have the god in you, light and strength and love, and because——'

'And because I lack patience and courage !' Ananta interrupted, censuring himself as though by way of penance. 'I should not have allowed myself to be provoked by their doubts about me. I should have enrolled their names in a book and told them a little about their rights in the new brotherhood. Perhaps I should have begun with you long ago, though with your religion you would never listen——'

'All that talk about hours and wages and bread is illusion, a web woven by spiders to trap the flies if it is not accompanied by love of God. You are right to say we need patience, but all this talk about courage ? . . .'

As she said this, her face seemed a mask of resignation, her body limp as if she had accepted the slavery inevitable to life and was merely waiting for the release which death would bring.

Ananta went over to her and stroked her forehead. Inside him he was straining to get near her, though he thought that her own miseries had tainted her vision.

'May I be your sacrifice,' he consoled her. 'I wish I could take your fever on myself. So that—so that you could be spared to relish a little more than merely the suffering that has been your portion. For, if Arjuna said, "Live in action", then he meant us to fight against falsehood in spite of the odds. Only thus can the balance between "good" and "evil" be kept in this world.'

'For aught I know you may even have courage !, Janki said, laughing gaily. And then she added with a sigh : 'But I have made my peace with God and am ready to go any time He wants me.'

'You almost make me believe in the other world, with your

talk of going away,' Ananta said with his catching, gurgling laugh to drown her sighs and her forebodings of doom.

'I am not worthy,' she said, restraining him with a serious mien. 'And I don't say this out of self-pity. For there is no time to lose if these men are to be saved, however unworthy they are——'

'Or perhaps because we are all unworthy,' said Ananta, rising. He was certain now that his torment was due to his lack of patience and lack of courage. For, as far as roguishness, selfishness, stupidity, suspicion and stubbornness went, he had been no different from the others until lately. And if he had been saved at all it was through his hope for a "Revolution" after which men would find a new way of living, in which they would discover a new brotherhood, away from the pettiness created by the miseries of the present, by the greed of profit-makers and the lust for power of the Sarkar. Essentially, he felt that he had discovered a fresh kinship with his thathiar brothers, especially after his return from Bombay, as though one had to go away to learn to love the world's poor before one could love the poor at home. How happy they had all been eating and drinking together! It seemed to him now like the good old akashti holidays when they were all young together and used to cook goats' heads and drink English port wine to their hearts' content. After all, he realized that was the instinctive brotherhood which united him to them.

'I am sorry now I lost my temper,' he said, purged of all his anger.

'Well then, go and say "I put my head at your feet" to them,' Janki answered, her eyes closing against her will through the waves of heat that floated in heavy sheen-music above her, illusory layers of oppression seeking to drown her while she lay wrapped in acceptance and serenity. 'Rages are wasteful,' she mumbled, as she half opened her eyes, calm and tired.

'Anyhow, I must not strain your health,' he said. 'You must have your siesta. And perhaps I shall go and see whether they have got some flour at Mohkam Chand's shop.

He came towards her, patted her forehead and then tiptoed away.

21

WHEN HE GOT TO THE GRAIN-SHOP ANANTA FOUND NOT SO MUCH a queue of the kind with which he had become familiar in Bombay, but a crowd of men who had besieged the closed doors of the store. Back to back, eager, shoving, pushing and shoving again, swaying this side and that, with ripples of curses and abuses rising from their lips and dying on the edges of the thick atmosphere, they filled the square.

In this land where for hundreds of years men had lived under the shadow of a great uncertainty, where layer upon layer of heat and fear and doubt lay sweating on the faces of the people, men did not respect the bribe-taking policeman and were becoming tired of considering each other. So they trampled on each other's corns and stretched their hands out more and more, for their wants, anxious to grasp the least little remnant of security for themselves in an inclement world where no one expected much help from another, in which the charity of the old world had been broken without being replaced by a new tenderness. And as the Sarkar seldom gave much, except orders and injunctions, asking the populace not to do this and not to do that on pain of conviction, and as the agents of the Sarkar were like accumulations of lice on their heads extracting pain, now slowly, now with a sudden jab, men ran around, hardened into an attitude of despair, from which they emerged either in their prayers to the various gods, who liberated everyone from earthly bonds, or when they were roused into the assertion of their manhood by some impending disaster, and then reached out of each other with desperate curses, imprecations and obscenities. The manners of hell were certainly not improved by the universal fear that gripped men, the fear of tomorrow that spread like the doom of a final reckoning on the wings of a rumour of widespread riots, cyclones, cholera, fever and famine in the other parts of Hindustan. And no one could accept life as a mere habit—as a second nature, for even nature itself seemed to be potentially explosive as at the end of the world.

'Ohe hasn't this flour been distributed yet?' Ananta asked a man on the edge of the crowd as he came up.

'Do you see me eating rice-cakes that you ask me, son of a pig!' said the man peevishly.

'It seems,' said Ananta with a sour humour, 'that the eating is over and now only the throwing up remains ! As for you calling me the son of a pig—well, don't call a Muhammadan that, otherwise there will be a Hindu-Muslim riot !'

'Oh, brother,' said the man, relaxing the tense expression on his perspiring face, 'I am a Muslim, but I wish you no harm. There is nothing to eat here, but if you want to wait you can stand about and see if Mohkam opens his shop. I am tired of waiting for the Judgment Day !'

'There will be nothing to eat here, brother,' another man, an undersized Hindu, muttered. 'The doots of hell have eaten everything !'

'That Mohkam has gone back into his mother's there, at the back of the house, and he will never emerge and open the shop !' said a Sikh.

'You go back into your mother's too, and don't talk so much !' said the Muhammadan.

'I waited here all yesterday morning, brother, and it was the same,' said the midget Hindu. 'So I went away. But I hear that Mohkam did open for half an hour about noon, and a few people got one seer of flour each. So don't go at the bidding of this cow-eater, Sikha !'

'Only Gama got some because of his strong biceps !' said the Mussulman whom Ananta had first questioned, his purple face with its hook-nose relaxing into a pallor of softness. 'And a few other goondas ! He gets food here who has the strongest arms, brothers.'

'Ohe, don't you defame others !' a man with strong biceps called out. 'It is a question of luck.'

'Rape the mother of this luck !' said the bitter Mussulman. 'I am going. I will drink some water and get ready for the afternoon prayers.'

'Ohe, don't go,' said Ananta, challenged out of his stupor by the man's deeper pessimism. Ohe, wait, let me look for my three thathiar brothers, and then I shall see what we can do.'

As he swung his arms there were protests from other arms.

'What can you do—move your buttocks, or break the shop open ?' the Mussulman said. 'We have already shouted to that Mahajan, Mohkam Chand, to open the shop. He has got iron bars fixed outside and he is secure in his house. And one cannot ask for what one cannot demand. That is the law.'

'A rich man's house has a back door as well as a front door,' said Ananta, 'even as words are round but action square.'

'Han, but it is a long way about—the back door to Mohkam's house !' said the Mussulman. 'Anyhow, the man who sells grain and lends money on interest will not give us charity.'

'Ohe, there it is—not far,' said the Hindu midget. 'But there is a poolcia in the square.'

'You come with me,' Ananta said. Then he suddenly caught a glimpse of his friends shouted : 'Oh, there's Ralia. Ohe, Ralia—ohe, Dine—ohe, where is Viroo ? . . .'

'We are here !' answered Ralia, struggling to get out of the crowd.

'Come with me !' shouted Ananta, and led towards the lane. The men he had been talking to remained passive. They had not much energy left and much less faith.

But as Ananta moved swiftly on his feet, his friend Ralia, who believed in the capacity of the rogue to perform prodigies of courage, began to tear the crowd to come to him.

The men now watched the advance in the soft hush of a decisive moment. Then, eager, irking at each other, cursing, talking, shouting abuse, their eyes set on Ananta, they began to hurtle after him blindly, with a grim litheness as though tigers about to leap on their prey. That which was struggling in their jagged nerves, in the twangs to their soul-wants as a possible course of action, seemed to have emerged in Ananta's sense of direction——'Kill Mohkam, the rape-mother ! Beat him !' they shouted. 'Bring him out from where he has gone into his mother's ! Catch him !'

But as the swelling crowd pressed behind Ananta, he knew that the action upon which he had launched would prove abysmal. For the rich do not leave thier homes unguarded, and Seth Mohkam Chand had had an iron gate fixed at the opening of the lane ever since the days when a crowd had burnt his house twenty-five years ago in the Martial Law days because he had condoned Dyer's shooting at Jallianwallah Bagh and taken refuge behind British bayonets in Amritsar fort.

There was a hillman warden with a loaded double-barrelled gun and his 1914-1918 medals standing behind the iron railings, taking aim.

Seven times the swell rose behind Ananta, heaving like a giant shadow with its overpowering crest rolling up and down, pushing forward and backward and then, bending aside as if to unwell before the double-barrelled gun of the warden which fired in the sky, the great whacking wave reformed again and churned up the men who had been caught in the middle as in a splash, till Ananta, falling back on the edge, thought that this was the end.

In a flash he knew that the instinct of the ruffian in him had led him, and the men behind, into a trap. If he had been alone he might have climbed over the gate and collared the warden, or, being discomfited, he would have turned and fled. But with the blind, frightened, infuriated men behind him, facing the warden's rifle on the one hand and the police who would be rushing to the spot soon, he felt he had betrayed himself and them into a position of the utmost danger, from which it was his duty to extricate them. For a moment all the light of the world seemed to be dimmed in his eyes by the shadows of doom that gathered around him.

Then, driven back to his ultimate resources, above the ruffian's deeper instinct with which he had endangered so many lives, he found his feet. He cleared his throat, neighed a forced laugh at the hill-man before him, his right hand raised in admonition as he shouted: 'Ohe, son of a hill-man, fool! Playing with fireworks! This will not win you a Victoria Cross but the gallows! We want to know where Lala Mohkam Chand is!'

The hill-man was cowed by Ananta's assertive manner, made more pompous by his laugh-cough, acrid with chagrin and frustration.

'There he is opening the shop!' the warder said, pointing to the shop.

'There!' Ananta roared as he wheeled. 'There, the betichod shop is opening! Back to the shop, ohe brothers.'

The startled crowd, riven by cries of despair, abuse, curses, as well as the moans and groans of those who had fallen in the rush, moved again with shrill shrieks of horror and expectation. Then, spluttering with confusion, agitated with the eagerness to grab the flour, it surged towards the doors of the shop which were now ajar.

'Wait!' Ananta said, as he tore ahead with his bull's energy blazing in his eyes. 'Think before you act! Ohe, think!'

But the swerving mass had now broken up. And the strongest, quickest and most muscular men were ascending the platform of Mohkam Chand's shop and charging, while the weaker members of the flock slipped and shrieked as they were trodden underfoot.

'Ohe, look—ohe, see what you are doing!' Ananta shrieked.

'Look at wanton greed of those hands! May the curse of God fall on him!' said another man left behind.

'Oh, theft! Ohe, theft! Ohe, robbery in daylight! May Allah save us!' another person echoed.

'Ohe, the poole!' someone shouted. 'The poolcias!'

Ananta could see Ralia struggling over a bag of flour with a swarthy Sikh, and he knew that if the looters were caught they would be in for it. Viroo, the Black God, was trying to scramble up to the platform, while taller men were leaping up and breaking into the shop past him. Dina Timur Lang was restraining Viroo.

Seth Mohkam Chand came out and beat his head and shouted:

'Oh, I am being looted! I am ruined! Ohe, come to your senses, you two! Oh, see, folks, how hooligans have turned on the honest, turning the streets into the haunts of banditry!'

'And the police!' someone completed Mohkam's sentence for him.

As Ralia and the Sikh still pulled at the Khalsa's long hair, Ananta, sensing the arrival of the police, rushed towards the platform in a feverish haste and tugged at Ralia's tunic to release him from the grip of the Sikh. 'Oh, poison of abject want, you have made this land of love into a jungle!' he muttered as he stood helpless and unable to detach the two men. 'Ohe, folks, stop them!'

Then Ralia fell back and off the platform, and Ananta gathered him into his arms. But Ralia still held the Sikh by his long hair.

'Ohe, let go, the poolc! the poolc!' people warned them.

But the concentration of hatred in Ralia's face showed that he was deaf to any cautionary call. For the Sikh, though a comparatively smaller man in build, was a wiry fellow and had apparently been roused by the insult to his religion implied in Ralia's grip on his sacred hair. And Ralia, being the weaker-willed of the two, was seeking to bolster up his faith with all the force of his arms.

After struggling in vain to separate them, Ananta stood aside, not knowing what to do. He had felt the grim litheness of a tremendous physical power when he had led the crowd up to the lane and back, because he instinctively knew and could foresee that they would all follow him, but when it came to two stubborn fighters grinding their teeth and muttering curses under their breath as they wrestled like hill goats, head to head, aiming and hitting and missing, he could not tell what deep wrongs and humiliations against life and each other, apart from the flour, urged them to their furious match. The cruel temper, accentuated by the heat, and 'Devil take the hindmost' attitude of the crowd, oppressed Ananta and he began to move away. But then he heard the footsteps of the policeman and came back.

'Poolice ! Poolcia !' the hushed whisper ran through.

And almost everyone came to a standstill, while some of the more frightened scurried away.

'Oh, Holdar Jan Muhammad, I have been looted,' complained Seth Mohkam Chand.

'Leave go of each other, ohe, and come to the police station with me !' Jan Muhammad ordered Ralia and the Sikh.

The opponents released their hold on each other, though they still spat threats and foul abuse.

'How much have they looted ?' the policeman asked Mohkam Chand. 'And how many have died through that firing ?'

'Nothing has been looted nor anyone killed,' Ananta answered. 'But if he will not open his shop till midday, and there is no flour in people's homes, do you expect them to wait till he has finished making love to his wife before he comes out to serve them ?'

'Ohe, don't bark !' Jan Muhammad snarled at Ananta.

'Who is doing the barking ?' Ananta asked.

As Jan Muhammad's voice had sounded very much like that of a watchdog, the crowd laughed.

'You come with me to the police station !' Jan Muhammad turned to Ananta.

'Ohe what talk is this ! Look, folks !' Dina said.

'He has done nothing!' Viroo protested.

'Your truncheon does not impress me', Ananta said. 'If you want to control people you must first fill their bellies!'

The policeman looked towards Mohkam Chand for further directions.

'I would like a policeman to be on duty here,' said Mohkam Chand, coming into his own, 'to keep the people in a queue when the flour comes. At this rate my life is not safe.'

'You inquire about that at the police station!' said Jan Muhammad, shaking his head.

'What about the flour now? Give us a rupee's worth, Seth!'

'Ohe, give for the sake of my hungry children!

'Ohe, for the sake of God!'

The voices of the crowd were echoed and re-echoed and multiplied by other appeals.

'The flour hasn't come yet,' shouted Mohkam at the top of his voice with a sudden finality. 'Go, and don't eat my head. Come back after five o'clock.'

For a moment a terrible hush fell upon the crowd, a silence between the shocked awareness of the men and the next call to action, the critical word which was to send them hurtling forward to wreak the vengeance that welled in their blazing eyes.

But the expected word never came. Instead the policeman raised the baton in his right hand and said, 'Now go, there is no flour here!' And he began to press them back.

And, as if they were all mesmerized by the uplifted arms of the law in that crucial moment which was the gap between the will and the act, the crowd began to fall back and disperse, impotent with a suppressed rage, purple with the sun's heat, the agony of frustration, and yet disintegrated by the word of command.

Ananta stood his ground for a while out of sheer bravado. Then he felt the shadow of the boundless monster, which had darkened the world before his eyes again and again this morning, hovering over him, this time a compound of animal fear, dim uncertainty, and the demons of superstition evoked in him by his stepmother's babblings and Janki's fever. Dizzily he waved his protective arm towards Ralia and Dina and Viroo and said, 'Come, wisdom's dog smells a kick at the threshold of the house of plenty and goes away! Come.'

'Don't talk so much, and go home if you value your life,' said the policeman to Ananta, before he turned to scatter the other men with the baton raised in his hand. 'And who did the firing? I want that man to come to the police station with me,' he continued as the men were dispersing.

'Oh, Holdar Sahib, forgive him,' and Mokham, 'It was my watchman. And he beckoned the policeman into the shop.

22

'O you who walk like a She peacock
O that I might become the He peacock
To you She peacock . . . Pichoo, pihu . . .

YOUNG LAL CHAND SANG WITH THE LEER OF A VOLUPTUARY'S smile on his face as he emitted a vulgar 'pachkari' sound from his lips at the tail end of the refrain.

The object of his adoration was a bride, decked in a peacock green Benarsi skirt and a pink silk head-cloth, as she walked on her high-heeled shoes behind her mother-in-law. She was one of the first beauties who was passing through Bazar Kaserian on the way to take the air in one of the cool halls of the Golden Temple at the end of the afternoon. For it was getting on towards five when the water-carriers sprinkled cold water on the roads and the devoted sweepers in Durbar Sahib finished washing the marble floor of the temple. And to the sedentary gallants who sat on the worn cushions of their shops she was a light relief from the oppression of clammy heat during a day devoid of customers.

At a cautionary glance from her mother-in-law the bride drew the edge of her head-cloth on to her whole face and went her way.

'Ohe, beautiful ones . . .' muttered Sri Ram, the assistant of Seth Gokul Chand, with an artificial sigh from the Chaudhri's shop opposite.

On being included for praise in this unwanted compliment, the mother-in-law also became self-conscious and, demurely drawing her own head-cloth on to her forehead, waited for her daughter-in law to catch up with her.

'Oh, may I die for you!' Lal Chand called after the women, chagrined because they had not responded to his overtures and with a great deal of rude emphasis in his voice.

'Hai, what blandishments!' sighed the other gallant, Sri Ram. And then he called loudly to Lal Chand across the street by way of an indirect joke: 'What is the price of silk in these hard days, brother? What price?'

'Ohe, behave yourself!' shouted Seth Gansham Das, an old dealer, as he got up from the edge of the drain under the projection of his shop where he had been urinating.

'Look at him shaking hands with an old friend!' said Sri Ram lewdly. And yet sermonizing us.'

'Han, look at him!' laughed Lal Chand. 'Look at the sacred thread round the ears of the killjoy! But lust, fire and itch, these are not concealed!'

'Ohe, is there no one to restrain them from poking fun at other people?' said Gansham Das, advancing towards the shop of Chaudhri Gokul Chand even as he adjusted his loin-cloth. 'Look, folks, they have raised their heads to the sky!'

'Your thread, ohe Khushki!' Sri Ram took up the joke about the orthodox manner adopted by Gansham Das in protecting himself against pollution by wrapping the sacred thread round his ear.

'Better than losing caste as you and the Chaudhri have done by going to the betrothal ceremony of those dirty thathiars!' said Gansham Das. His real objections to their ribald manner was prompted by rumours of their lapse from orthodoxy a litlle while ago.

'Since you have put two hundered rupees into the same factory as Murli Dhar, the head of the thathiar brotherhood, you are equally tainted by contact with the low thathiars!' commented Lal Chand. 'We are all boiling in the same pot.'

'Ohe, I don't want to talk to you! Where is the Chaudhri!' raved Seth Gansham Das, touched to the quick by this reproach, till the wrinkles on his old face cracked the ochre and white lime caste mark which he had imprinted on his forehead in the morning. And the fury of his voice broke the stillness which exhaled from the heat through the length of the Bazar.

Chaudhri Seth Gokul Chand, who had been having an uneasy siesta on the cool marble platform at the base of the banyan tree with some other dealers because of the heat and the abundance of flies, awoke as Gansham Das raised his voice.

'What has happened?' he said, rising, red-eyed with the anger of unquenched sleep.

'These boys have raised their heads to the sky!' said Gansham Das. 'Your assistant Sri Ram and that nephew of yours, Lal Chand!'

Seth Gokul Chand yawned drowsily and gazed at the dull yellow and green foliage of the banyan tree and then at the still dozing men on the platform, which was strewn with fallen leaves like a carpet of dead gold.

This lack of interest on the part of the Chaudhri irked old Gansham Das, who rushed up, cursing loudly and praying devoutly to awaken the other dealers.

'Ohe, awake dead ones, rapers of your daughters, awake and witness the infamy which the head of our brotherhood is practising! Look, folks, how Gokul Chand's assistant and nephew have insulted me and how he sits there without so much as opening his mouth to rebuke them. Live not in the city ruled by those who betray religion! Hey Ishwar! Hey Parmatman! Hey Swami! After spoiling our caste too! Surely you are not going to stand for this sudden business of smoking hookah and drinking water with Murli, the head of the thathiar community!'

The sleepy dealers opened their eyes involuntarily with the suddenness of Gansham Das' outbrust and murmured the various names of God to each other in low, quavering tones of awe.

'I thought, Lala, Gansham Das, that you were annoyed with us about something else,' said Lal Chand. 'So why wake the dead?'

'You are not only lechers but are spoiling our religion!' Gansham Das said, waving his hands furiously. 'Look, folks, one man's home burns down, and they think it is good fun!'

'Ohe, Seth Gansham Das,' cajoled Gokul Chand to appease the old man's wrath. 'These boys are young and foolish. I shouldn't mind them.'

'But what about your visiting the house Murli Dhar, shameless one! Next you will be giving your daughter in marriage to a bellows-blowing thathiar.'

'Oh, grandpa, don't get angry,' answered Gokul with a grin. 'Times have changed.' And then he waved to Sri Ram and said, 'Give me the hookah, ohe boy, so that Seth Gansham Das can have a puff or two.'

'I'd rather drink urine than smoke hookah with one who has soiled his mouth with the food and water of Murli !' The old man's caste susceptibilities had been hurt, and his objection to the lewd jokes of Lal Chand and Sri Ram had merely been bubbles of froth on the surface of a deeper resentment. 'Look, folks, they have spoiled our religion and talk as if lepers have no lice.'

'That is exactly what I was saying to the Chaudhri before I went to sleep,' said another dealer, named Manek Chand, a tall, lean fellow with a nose like the beak of a pelican. 'They are an underhand lot, these coppersmiths. They fairly scare one with their slyness. On the one hand they ask Chaudhri Gokul Chand to eat and drink with them and on the other hand they are thick with those "soshialists" who want to share all property and women.'

'You are talking of two different crowds,' interrupted Lal Chand. 'Murli Dhar and his family are on our side, while that scoundrel Ananta and the other bellows-blowers are on the side of the socialists.'

'Ohe, ooloo, they are all the same !' Old Gansham Das spat the words out of his mouth bitterly. 'The same caste and the same blood . . . . They will smash up everything. I warn you they are thieves, carrion ! I warn you ! Set not your affections on the mean !'

The atmosphere quivered with the half-broken sighs of who were still yawning under the banyan tree. They all rose, rubbing their eyes at the hullabaloo caused by Gansham Das' abuse.

'Ohe, Baba,' said Chaudhri Gokul Chand, scratching his head embarrassedly. 'We ought to make the best of a bad job. The world has changed. Why, we sit together with people of high caste and low caste in the trains. We draw water from the pump which is supplied from a tank controlled by a Mussalman engineer. We walk on roads swept by bhangis. And now the "Municipal Committee", of which I am a member, is thinking of feeding the hungry with tins of food manufactured in Amritsar. Where then is our religion ? We ought to shrug our shoulders at the slight distinction that there is between us and the more well-to-do, respectable thathiars like Murli Dhar and gladly accept them as equals.'

And he sat fanning away persistent flies which buzzed around him.

'Especially as the rogues among them are boycotting Chaudhri Murli Dhar and plotting Revolution,' insisted Lal Chand, standing up on the projection of his shop, his right hand on a chain which was suspended from the ceiling for the purpose of adjusting scales to weigh utensils.

'Thief! Carrion! Traitor!' exclaimed Gansham Das, turning on Lal Chand. 'Have you no shame since you joined these Ayra Samajis, drunkards, whoremongers and kababis!'

'Lala Gansham Das!' cautioned Chaudhri Gokul Chand, shaking his head in the direction of Kucha Billimaran. Then he cleared his throat and, spitting across the street significantly, said: 'There is Sadanand, the son of Murli Dhar, coming.'

'Thieves! Carrion! Traitors!' Gansham Das hissed at the direction from which Sadanand was coming. And he spat to show his utter contempt and howled: 'Spoilers of our caste!' And then he began to walk back towards his shop.

'There is a great deal in what he says, you know Chaudhri,' opined some of the newly awakened dealers, all speaking at once, so that there was a strange hubbub as of a beehive before swarming-time. A beggar-woman advanced with a fly-infested child in her arms and put her hand out for alms while she whined a song.

'Go, go,' Gansham Das shouted at her. 'Go to that Sadanand whose son has been betrothed today. And empty the coffers of that friend of the thathiars, Khushal Chand, who is coming with him, the casteless!'

'Oh, to be sure, Seth Gansham Das is as pure as unsmoked sweets, brothers,' Kushal Chand said with a smile.

'Ohe, come to your senses, leper! Your uncle won't teach you manners—I will!' said old Gansham Das, and raised his right hand to strike Khushal Chand.

'Ohe! Ohe! Grandpa! Ohe!'

The cries and shouts restrained the old man, though he bubbled with anger and muttered, 'Low thathiars.'

'Think of the people we have pushed out of employment suddenly and not of their caste!' said Kushal Chand, confronting the old men. 'That is what I have been saying to Sadanand too. And if you are too used to seeing the thathiars in dirty loin-cloths, think of the misery and sunken-jawed death of thousands of men through famine in the villages. Dogs and jackals are said to be howling over the putrid flesh and bones of carcases in the countryside while we are bickering over caste scruples. These thathiars will soon be feeding on grain picked up from dung-heaps. And then you will have disease spreading to your own homes, for disease is no respecter of caste, and malaria afflicts the rich and the poor alike.'

'Leper!' repeated Gansham Das, and walked away to his shop with a contemptuous wave of his hands.

'I agree with the boy,' said Chaudhri Gokul Chand. 'In the "Munapical Commettee" in the Town Hall, we know a little more than people know in this Bazar and we have to forgo many of our prejudices and face certain questions.'

'I think Seth Gansham Das has caught the itch, but I don't agree with that boy, either Chaudhri Gokul Chand,' said Sadanand. 'Kushal is talking like those hooligans and goondas who call themselves socialists and who go prating about Revolution in Billimaran—Ananta and that Sikh poet returned from Roos. Mahasha Hans Raj is a sensible man and a Congressman. But that student called Satyapal is the devil's own son!'

'Here is another dog barking,' said dealer Manek Chand. 'What has happened to everyone today?'

'All of you are sitting here as if nothing has happened,' said Sadanand. 'True the sun is shining exactly as it did yesterday, but there has been something happening in Billimaran which will disturb our siesta for many days unless we act together.'

'I can't understand what you are all talking about,' said Manek Chand, sleepy and taciturn.

'Equally incomprehensible to me,' said another dealer. 'Have you all drunk hemp or gone mad?'

'I know what he is talking about,' said Khushal Chand. 'And so does Uncle Gokul Chand. You are where your thinking is. Think and decide, not about who is to go to Hardwar to purify himself for breaking caste rules, but what you are going to do for those jobless men there.' The very naturalness of his manner gave him a certain self-confidence and made his words ring through the drowsy atmosphere.

Chaudhri Gokul Chand remained silent. But old Seth

Gansham Das walked up to the banyan tree again.

'That boy is a bloodthirsty hound !' he shouted, brandishing the handle of his small hubble-bubble in the direction of Khushal Chand. 'He is one of those wicked "soshialists" who meet in the houses of prostitutes inside Rambagh gate. They drink wine, commit adultery, trample upon the holy books and spit at the Golden Temple from the windows of the bunga of Sant Harnam Das !'

'Seth Gansham Das is right,' said Sadanand. 'These "soshalists" frequent the lowest haunts. And they are spoiling our children with their wicked ideas.'

Except for Gansham Das and Sadanand, the whole company burst into a spontaneous laugh. Sadanand's strange confirmation of the opinion of Seth Gansham Das, who had but recently startled them out of their slumbers by a vicious attack on Sadanand's father, Chaudhri Murli Dhar, made the whole issue of caste ridiculous.

Lacking the zeal and fanaticism necessary to stick to their superior status in orthodox religion, and equally devoid of the desire to achieve nobility, the Kaseras laughed at the two prigs and even at the part of themselves which sympathized with either of them. It seemed that habit was second nature, but nature was first habit, and when humanity breaks through, laughter is contagious.

When the merriment had subsided, Chaudhri Gokul Chand said simply : 'Brothers, there is a great travail in our land today. And I am not sure that Gandhiji was not right when he said : "If there is war, in its wake will come famine. For war is evil." And, although we have opened a factory and are doing Government work, I, for one, can see that the Sarkar does not wish us well. However, we have to bide our time. A good business is not built on love or hatred, it can only be built by hard work. And we cannot live in a no man's land, doing nothing till the world settles down. That is why I say it is no use talking of caste scruples any more, nor is it any use persecuting those thathiars who have become unemployed through the factory we have opened, but we must give them jobs. I am for giving them piecework, even if we lose a little thereby through the lack of demand for utensils, until we can find room for more of them in the factory. I have been to the railway godown this morning to take delivery of new materials for the factory, and I telephoned again this afternoon, but the goods are held up somewhere on the way. So I suggest that we call Ananta, Ralia and others here and explain the whole thing to them.'

'But Chaudhri Gokul Chand, they are out for our blood!' said Sadanand. 'They are talking daggers and spitting poison. They prevented the few thathiars we had invited to the ceremony of my son's betrothal from coming to our house and now they are planning to ask the boys in the factory to go on strike. I don't know who this boy Satyapal is, but he has lifted his head high and no one seems able to restrain him, not even so respected a person as Mahasha Hans Raj. And that rogue Ananta wants to organize them into a union!'

'Personally,' answered Gokul, with a final wave of the hand, 'I should like Ananta to organize that union, so that we can negotiate with them in the proper manner.'

The realism of Chaudhri Gokul Chand's talk spread the web of a strang silence on all the dealers, till the flames of a white mist covered their eyes, and their temples throbbed with a quickening which had destroyed the ennui.

'That is the true talk,' Khushal Chand drove the dagger home. 'I tell you they have been robbed of the fruits of their labour for years. Their wonderful bodies have been wrecked. Their initiative has been sapped. Their hopes destroyed and with it ambition—their whole outlook on life has been darkened and warped! You can't go on hoping that each of them will go on disposing of his labour separately and remain a slave in your hands. They must get together. And, however much the Goddess of Liberty in our country dislikes the coming together of men, however much you wish to divide them, they will form the union. Why are you so surprised that they hate us? Why shouldn't they talk of Revolution when they have suffered indignities and humiliations at our hands?'

'Ohe hacha! hacha! Don't talk so much and come and do us some ledgers for a change!' his brother Lal Chand interrupted.

The faces of the other dealers were preoccupied, as though assailed by doubts about this new development in their narrow lives.

'I am afraid,' began dealer Manek Chand, 'that——'

'Turn your fear into the will to do some good business and your fear will cease to exist,' cut in Chaudhri Gokul Chand.

'The hounds! Miscreants!' said Seth Gansham Das

irritably from his shop. 'Dragging us through the murk of pollution first and then confronting us with the spectre of Revolution !'

'It is not pollution, Uncle Gansham Das,' said Sadanand, 'it is this talk of Revolution that you should consider. May the lightning smite those raving dogs !'

'If you are really expecting a Revolution, then I'd better go and congratulate the men who are making it !' said Khushal Chand to Sadanand.

Sadanand gritted his teeth and hung his head.

Chaudhri Gokul Chand grinned.

There was a deep and awkward silence. Then the sound of the Chaudhri's hubble-bubble gurgled across the street, split the air, and released the pent-up tension.

Kushal Chand wipped the sweat off his face and, phewing a hot stale breath, walked away in the direction of Billimaran.

23

THE FATIGUE OF THE STRENUOUS DAY AS WELL AS THE OPPRESSION of spring heat had overcome Ananta almost as soon as he had laid down to rest in the cool half-dark of the marble-floored verandah of the small shrine of Kali after the abortive visit to Mohkam Chand's grain-shop. And he had been sound asleep when a little ant whose way he seemed to have barred stung him on the cheek. He had awakened and then fallen off into a second slumber, not so perfect as the first and disturbed by short stabs of dreams. He was trying to balance himself on some telegraph wires outside what looked like Cheharta Station in a position so precariously like the dancer on a trapeze that he was frightened of falling and awoke with a throbbing head. He did not rise from where he lay, and sought to trace back the wisps of dreams that now seemed to have evaporated. There was a bit in which he had been on the point of embracing Gauri, the wife of Ralia, who had been advancing naked towards him. 'Ralia would murder me if he knew,' he thought, and cut the vision.

From where he lay he could see Ralia seated three yards away on a strip of carpet spread right in the street, playing cards with Bali the grocer and Khushal Chand, the nephew of Chaudhri Gokul Chand.

'Wonders never cease,' he muttered, to see the suspicious Balia condescending to play with Khushal. But what was that bit about Dina Timur Lang, flying through the air he had seen—'I may not be able to walk straight,' Dina had said, 'but I can fly anywhere I like. I can fold my legs up and levitate at will.' And, lo and behold, the limp lord was actually soaring. Though, where, Ananta could not remember.... Was it a crowd of people whom he had seen towards the end? He remembered he had walked away in the opposite direction to some people, and then, being pursued, he had mounted the telephone pole and begun to walk on the wire and nearly fallen.

He turned on his arm and saw the giant greasy black image of the Goddess Kali, embossed in the wall in the alcove. She held a sword in one hand, a trident in the other, her tongue was bulging, her eyes red and glaring, while the incense burned before her, wrapping her in a mysterious cloud of smoke and making her seem more sinister than ever. He wondered if it was not his secret fear of this image that had made him dream of her last night. 'How queer!' he said to himself. 'I have grown up to be a man right under the shadow of this image and yet I can't learn to be at ease with her.' But he recalled the evening when his stepmother had sat by his bed when he once had fever as a boy and the fright he had felt when she had told him of the legends of Kali, in her role as the destroyer of the world, specially of how the Goddess loved dancing on corpses in the cremation ground. He had long since ceased to believe in all the superstitious talk of Karmo, and he scorned all the thathiar talk about Fate, the inexorable Destiny which was driving men on and on in the cycle of birth and re-birth and before which man was helpless to do anything. And yet, he felt, there must be a great many remnants of all these beliefs lurking in him because he had always been instinctively afraid of ghosts and spirits and had, all today, been obsessed with the nightmare he had had last night, in which he had been pursued by giant horrors, till he had stood helpless, unable to run, unable even to move, spellbound as though by a looming catastrophe.

He tried to shake off the urge to recall any more bits of his afternoon dream and turned on his side again so that he faced the door and could see the people outside. He yawned and felt that the hold of these uncanny thoughts in his imagination was due to his weakness in planning a clear programme for the struggle here in Amritsar.

As soon as he had made this accusation against himself, his eyebrows knitted with thought and the answer emerged: 'But it is so complex—the world beyond Kucha Billimaran and Bazar Kaserian, the world of the big cities of Hindustan, of Vilayat and Amrika and Roos and Chin. And there is so much happening in the universe, that is it difficult to evolve a programme for action for the afflicted coppersmiths who are trapped in an alley.

'And yet,' the accusation came back, 'you can't swallow the whole of the camel; you must begin by masticating its tail.' These men were important. And, as Comrade Joshi would say in his breathless spate of Hindustani: 'Comrades, the situation in our country demands work and intolerance towards shortcomings, especially in oneself, and the development of the highest qualities. No bureaucracy. No bullying. No mere windbag, wordy lectures. Careful and serious study of the problem. Consultation with other leaders. Go to the root of the question and adopt the necessary decision only after careful thought. Avoid long-drawn-out sessions, consultations, meetings and the like. See that the actual, concrete needs of the peoples are met. And forget yourself. Efface yourself. If need be sacrifice yourself for the good of others ! Remember it is the welfare of the people which counts—that is the goal ! And fulfil it by developing the gift of foresight and prophecy.'

Ananta could almost see the little bespectacled figure of Joshi in khaki shirt and shorts; he could hear him, the quick impetuous words falling one over the other; he could feel the air of utter selfless devotion, the almost ascetic stance of the man. And he felt guilty that he hadn't lived up to the ideal of a leader, that he had neither been able to convince the thathiars of the new brotherhood, nor get them the jobs they wanted. All that he had done was to arouse in the men wild passions which divided them almost as wounded beasts, fear-torn and ready to fall and become a prey to the hunters, in spite of the frothing anger.

Impatient, restless and unhappy, he rolled about like a stallion having a dust-bath to shake off his ennui, and then sat up. He could see the hulk of Ralia in the glare of sun under the huge awning over a verandah and hear him calling with a bravado charged with self-pity as he dealt the cards .

'Come, then, my darlings, come my Queen, King and Joker. . . .'

Apparently Ralia was playing a losing game and two shafts of the now slanting sun fell across his face from above the shadow cast across the street by the verandah of the shrine.

'If I were you I should stop,' Bali the grocer said, mealy-mouthed and furtive. He seemed to have won all the money he wanted to win and now did not want to be seen playing cards with Ralia by his prospective customers.

'Ohe, sit down,' Ralia said, dragging the grocer roughly by the lapel of his muslin tunic.

'I can beat you both, standing on my head,' Bali said. 'So leave my tunic and let me fan myself a little. I will stake fifty rupees without looking at the cards.'

'I haven't got that much,' said Khushal Chand in his deep bass voice. 'So I had better stop, too. There, Ananta is up, and I want to talk to him.'

Ralia shook his head and made a grimace and then bawled:

'You are both frauds; leaving the game just when my luck is turning.'

Ananta felt that if Ralia could not have his way now, after all the day's reverses, he would become violent. And yet he did not want to intervene. For somehow he felt that he was out of it all, rejected, isolated and proud in his aloneness, in spite of the fact that he felt it his duty to go and say something.

'Ohe, play another game with him, the last,' he counselled.

'He has lost enough,' Bali answered. 'He owes me fifty already. And Khushal has lost a hundred in cash——' The grocer was beaming with smiles and yet tense lest Ralia should turn nasty.

'If you are winning, why don't you play ?' shouted Ralia. 'It is only fair.'

'Ohe, let him go, Ralia,' said Ananta. 'Did you ever know a man who behaved decently after he had come in for a lot of money ?'

'I know that you want to make up by gambling what you can't earn by honest work, but I shouldn't hazard any more stakes if I were you,' Bali said, very much on the defensive.

'Don't sermonize me, and sit down and play,' threatened Ralia.

'Brother——' began Khushal Chand persuasively, an embarrassed smile on the dimples of his chubby face.

'Don't "brother" me louse, but play ! Coward ! Sit down !'

Ralia looked terrifying with rage, his eyes bulging and flashing, his face twisted into a most repulsive frown.

Ananta got up and rushed out to them, saying to Bali and Khushal :

'Ohe, play one more game with him, for my sake !'

'Acha, said Bali, sitting down, 'I will repeat my bid. Fifty. I will bid blind.'

'Acha, I will put down five rupees as a token,' said Khushal, crouching.

'Don't treat me as a child,' said Ralia. 'And no bluff.'

'This is a game of chance,' said Bali sternly. 'There is no obligation not to bluff !'

'Acha, lend me ten rupees to stake on this bid, ohe Bali,' said Ralia.

'If that is your wish,' answered the grocer, 'but I warn you that you might lose.'

As Bali laid the ten-rupee note on the carpet Ananta felt the incandescence of the quarrel simmering in the street. And now he was involved in sympathy for Ralia.

'Show !' Ralia challenged.

Bali took up the cards and displayed them. There were three spades. Both Khushal and Ralia saw their combinations. Their faces showed that they had lost.

'Rape-daughter luck !' Ralia mumbled, and then said : Come on another time. But don't cheat this time.'

'Don't be a fool,' said Ananta. 'Nobody has been cheating.' And he got up, scaring the sparrows which were drinking water from the charity bowl on the platform of the shrine.

'You don't know Bali,' said Ralia. 'He knows this pack of cards upside down and back side up. And as for the boss, there, he is in league with the grocer.'

'Hold your tongue,' said Khushal Chand.

At this Ralia ran menacingly and lifted his arm at Khushal Chand, his excitement rising to fever pitch.

'Ohe, ohe, fool !' said Ananta, and caught him by the waist.

'Let me go, lecher ! I will show him what tribe he belongs

to. He may buy up some like you who will take money from him, but I play fair and lose fair and call cheats by their name.'

Ralia's eyes blazed with a wild, murderous glint as he raised his gong-like voice. And almost immediately the whole atmosphere became electric with the pressure of all the thathiars who rallied round from every corner of the temple and the square, bursting with curiosity, excited and voluble, the recreative mass whose eagle eyes were bleary except for the most frightful visions, whose deaf ears could only hear the loudest voices.

'Ohe .. what has happened ?'

'Ohe !'

'Ohe, what happened ? What ?'

'It is my counterfeit Kismet,' said Ralia.

Ananta released his hold on him and restrained the others with the power of his quiet simplicity. The fatigue which had possessed him seemed to be gone as though he was at his best in the thick of things, in moments of crisis.

'Ohe, brothers,' he said, 'rape the mother of Kismet and Destiny. And don't bring God into the question of playing cards or our quarrel with the employers. "Tell me truth," said the sage Manu. And I may add—"face the facts before you". Ralia's anger, like the anger of most of us, has been gathering like a storm for days till he now feels like breaking someone's head or having his head broken by somebody. Now, I agree that a great wrong has been done to us. But if we agree not to dodge difficulties, and spend our energies in private quarrels, but decide to meet, we shall come through.'

He felt that through he had held the attention of the men by the suddenness of his onslaught, he could not rely on the agitator's manner and merely go on shouting louder than anyone else. So he deliberately refrained from mounting the platform of the shrine but merely learned back and began with a wink in a conversational aside :

'God won't help us because, as far as I have known Him, He has always preserved a discreet silence in the affairs of men. And Fate, like money, seems to be a bitch goddess, favouring the few who can invest capital and then call in its aid. . . . You know how many Kaseras offer to the goddess in there. And they are the very people who invoke the arm of the law when God fails to come to their help. Already they are calling us subversive men persuaded by agitators to interfere with their right to divide us and break us up, while over our heads there stands the goddess, with her army of crows cawing the doom of our craft.' And he waved his hand towards the shrine.

'Come to the point and don't beat about the bush like a clown,' sad Ralia as Ananta's jocular phrases hammered on the anvils of their brains.

'All day I have been saying let's get together, brothers.'

'Does the morning break because the cock crows or the dog barks !' commented Dina Timur Lang. Brother, go ahead and form the union.'

'We have heard all that !' said Viroo. We want a little cash. And may the earth open up and swallow the machines in that factory before the cawing crows bring us to our doom. For you know, as we do, why the crows are cawing, brother, and where they come from.

'Angry men listen to no counsel,' said Ananta. But brothers, attend to what I say. For two thousand years our ancestors had been maturing with the magic of their hands beautiful utensils which were part of the dowry of every bride, the decoration for every new home. Then, like the machine-made cloth from Vilayat which ruined our weavers, came the machine and the ready-made aluminium pots and pans, and our wages fell. And rather than melt our own metal in our own foundries we began to buy sheets from abroad. The women-folk mourned that the brass cooking vessels we made were not fit to be given in the dowry of their daughters, as they were in the days of their grandmothers. I love the craft and would rather make the pinnacles of temples which talk to the sky than anything else. But times have changed, brothers, times have changed. And we have to change with the times. . . . That is why the crows are cawing—perhaps Kali's deploring the passing of her reign over this part of the world. That is why they have been gathering together. That is why so many eagles and vultures are about, perhaps. . . . But we are not junglis to be frightened by the shadows of doom which cross our paths, and we are not oxen who will let the crows gnaw the flesh off our hind parts. It is a good thing that we are not like wax in the hands of Destiny, but can choose to do this thing or that. Just as we once delibertely gave up the earthen saucer lamp which burnt a dim little cotton wick in mustard oil and took up the kerosene oil tin lamp instead because it gave more light, and then accepted electricity with its broad glare, so we can now make a choice in this world of evil and destruction, if we have heads and hearts. And, because there is change, and because there is choice, we have the opportunity of saving ourselves through this very Revolution.'

There were whispers of discontent and disapproval: 'Sala, son of Revolution!' 'Didn't we *live* in the good days!" 'Were we junglis then?'

'Ohe, let him speak!' Dina said.

'Listen to what Ananta has to say, brothers,' Khushal Chand raised his voice. And, as though the rich man's son still wore the nimbus of the generations of privilege about him, the crowd listened.

'In the old days,' Ananta took up a heckler's comment, 'all of us lived on the earth and even washed our hands with a bit of earth, but nowadays we all use "Pears Soap"—especially uncle Viroo——'

There was a ripple of laughter because no one had suspected that the Black God could ever have used soap without getting white.

Viroo was very angry at this and protested: 'In the old days all of us lived on the earth and were savages, eh! Now we sit on chairs and make speeches and are civilized! Atheists! Unbelievers! Fear the hand of Fate! It might smite you!

'Now, uncle, we must keep a check on sentiment,' said Khushal Chand.

'Oh, look at the civilized Babus!' Ralia turned on both Ananta and Khushal Chand in a gruff, awesome voice even he poked his head forward like a cobra. 'They believe in charity, of course, they go and feed the hungry and clothe the beggars —the do-gooders!... Bah, I spit on you all!'

'What can a dog know of the taste of butter?' mocked Dina, ascending the temple platform. 'Gandhi brother Ralia Ram, says, self-control, both when, you are out and when you are at home!?[184]

That evoked general agreement.

But as Dina stood in triumph on the platform, Ralia brushed him away with a flourish of his strong arm, saying!

'Ohe ja, limp lord, the son of a Sahib!

'Imitation Sahib won't do!' put in Ananta.

The crowd suddenly brust into good-humoured chuckles of laughter at that.

'No,' Ananta continued seriously when the light-heartedness had somewhat subsided. 'A living, heart-to-heart appropriation of "Vilayati fashions" is what is wanted. The coming of the machine in England, brothers, wrought as much havoc there, a hundred years ago, as it is doing in Hindustan. The bones of millions were ground to dust by machines. Women and children were set to work for a few coppers, so Puran Singh Bhagat tells me—Angrezi women and children, brothers. And there was such hunger as we see in our Hindustan today. The men of property were deaf to the cry of the victims of poverty. How does Ananta know so much about England?'

The men were now rapt. That there had been such things in the land of the Sahibs was a revelation to them; that there were poor Sahibs was almost a consolation; and as for the learned men and saints in Vilayat, there was a frank scepticism. Ananta caught the edge of their curiosity and drove home the comparison.

But the working men of Vilayat themselves took their destiny in their own hands and banded themselves into the new brotherhood of unions. At first they were persecuted and penalized by the employers, and the Sarkar, which was behind the employers. The men stuck together, and struggled and struggled, until today there are few working men and women in factories who are not members of union. They bargain together for higher wages, shorter hours, against bad conditions, for holidays with pay, and defend their rights by strike action—at least they did so frequently until their leaders began to sell them to the bosses——'

'Why don't we go on strike?' asked Dina bobbing up again. 'Ustad, until you tell the men when this Revolution is to be which you are talking about, they will not listen to you. That is the real truth.'

The clown had struck a sincere note. And Ananta sat back to collect himself and began to answer the question seriously, his face set in anxious mould.

'Our people have been living a life of terrible, awful suffering, and poverty, under the relentless oppression of the Sarkar and the rich of our own country. Now we can't cure our headaches by merely changing the pillow. Slight changes can't bring about a new life. What is required is a change, brothers.

But the situation in which it is possible to make a Revolution requires the coming together of many big things. For instance, the rulers and the bosses may get bogged down so that only the workers can carve a way with their giant strides, and lead their masters by the nose. It is possible that the Revolution may break out if the workers and peasants reach a condition of the utmost wretchedness. Or all these circumstances may unite together and the people open the floodgates by a huge final push of their strong shoulders. Unless all these, or some of these, conditions are present no one can tell when the Revolution will be. Until then it is better to lose the wool on your bodies than to become martyrs like sheep——'

'If that is the talk, then I am for setting fire to the wool on my body before the bosses have it,' said Ralia.

'Don't listen to Ananta,' said Viroo. 'Let him be the sheep. Do what the student Satyapal says. Ask the boys who are employed in the factory to go on strike ! Satyapal has got him spotted. Hobnobbing with the employers, whispering into their ears while he breathes honeyed words into yours !'

'I don't know what Satyapal has been saying to you,' said Ananta, sensing danger of disruption, 'but some of these students are foolish with too much book knowledge. As soon as they know anything they must rush and tell everyone to act on their words. I think, brothers, it is the only chance we have now to resolve to get together before our tempers ride away like wild horses. Let us form a union of all those who are unemployed and those who are employed in the factory, and then go in a procession to Chaudhri Gokul Chand immediately from here.... Where are Bhagu, Mela and Arjun and the others ?'

'That is the idea,' said Khushal Chand. 'And I will go with you, even if it means my having to leave home.'

The men were surprised at this strange declaration on the part of a member of the chief employer's family.

'Ho ho !' Ralia laughed. 'And since when has the tiger suddenly become a domestic cat ?'

'There are some people,' Ananta said to vindicate Khushal Chand, 'who recognize that the highest God in this world is to one's conscience and not to one's father or mother or brother——'

'Wait, Ananta Ram,' Khushal Chand interrupted with a wave of his hand. 'I owe our friends here an explanation. It

is the first time that I am speaking my thoughts aloud....'
And then he turned to the men: 'Brothers, you are quite right to be surprised at my conduct and to suspect me of running with the hare and hunting with the hounds, as the Angrezi proverb says. Indeed, I have been living in two worlds: the world of my home in Dhab Khatikan, a miniature palace, with electric fans and baths and lovely meals cooked by our hill-men cooks; and the world of the wrestling-pitch in Billimaran where I have played with thathiar boys, eaten roasted gram with them and shared their life. I admit that I have always belonged more thoroughly to the world of my family, who almost considered me tainted every time I ate with a thathiar boy from Billimaran. But now the time has come for me to make my choice. We have to secure the welfare of our brethren who are in dire distress today. We must join hands with all those who are with us to win the goal. It is clear that if one is to live in the world today, truthfully, and with any honesty, one must break with those who are goaded by their possessions to the side of untruth and dishonesty. I know that it will be difficult for me to expiate the sins of my past, to break with it, and I shall have to suffer. But I also know that it is only by suffering that one is purified and that one learns anything.'

'Shout Lala Khushal Chand ki jai!' Ananta gave a triumphant call.

Bali and a few other men took it up but, for the most part, the thathiars remained silent, buried in their suspicion that a son of the rich could not really be sincere and was perhaps laying a trap for them.

'Look, folks, the darkness has come!' said the Black God Viroo. 'In this iron age the sons revolt against their families, the younger brothers against the elder brothers! This is the result of godlessness and unrighteousness!'

'Han, how can one trust a man who will betray his family?' commented Ralia.

'Ohe, brothers,' protested Ananta vehemently. 'Ohe, come to your senses and have faith in yourself and others. To have friends you must be one. And what stops us from achieving the heaven on earth is your jealousy, distrust and envy of those who are your fellows and feel for us. This is a time of greatness, as Sardar Puran Singh Bhagat says, and much ruin. There is anarchy and unrest in the world today, but there is every sign that the old life is ending and another, new life, is on the way. Fortunately there are men among us who are wise and devoted, and who will help us to measure our strength against the world and learn to realize our own power if we keep our hearts. Our learned men are truly devoted and will not stay aside and wash their hands of the poor as they have done elsewhere, because they seem to have only one religion. They believe in the freedom of our land and they exist for the love of the poor, to fight for the welfare of the hungry, to help to change the way things are now, bring about a new way in the world. And they, and we, shall not be content to let things take their slow, easy course like the Angrezi Sarkar. No, we shall give a push to events with our strong shoulders, as they did in Roos, for only thus can we feed the mouths of the hungry peasants in Hindustan. Well, if such pushing and shoving brings a certain amount of blood-letting we shall have to steel our hearts and take consolation from the fact that the wars which the greed and selfishness of the rich have caused, took many more lives. Out of such a Revolution, brothers, we shall create love and the many new things which we need. You know that we are men of an old brotherhood and religion. We shall not lose our hearts in the love of gold or the worship of money, as did the others. We shall keep faith . . . .

'Faith—what do you know of faith?' taunted Viroo.

' "There is no talk of money, one should have a big heart!" ' a boyish voice repeated Ananta's pet phrase.

'Han,' shouted Ananta and, exploring for the voice, he saw the boy Mhenga, the factory hand.

'But they are talking of another kind of religion up at the works—the student Satyapal and his crew. No compromise they say. And they are telling everyone that you are betraying the Revolution, and that we should all go on strike and have nothing to do with gadgets which are going to be used in machines that will kill our own brethren.'

'That is the right talk,' said Ralia.

'Which students are with him?' Ananta asked. 'Surely there is our comrade Karam Singh there to challenge him!'

Mhenga answered, but his voice was drowned in the hubbub.

'Our brothers, there, talk the right talk, the talk of religion' Viroo, the virulent Black God, said, his small elephantine eyes glinting. 'We'd rather go to them. Come, brothers. If Satyapal does not do anything, we will do the necessary ourselves—make some offerings at the temple! When anything goes wrong it is sent to the maker. When men feel wrong they should seek their maker. The goddess there is our guardian.'

'The goddess there will destroy you—I mean she will let you be destroyed without lifting a hand,' said Ananta.

'Don't blaspheme, or I will break your head', shouted Viroo. Then he turned and let the way towards Billimaran, saying, 'Come, boys.'

And they began to stampede towards the factory, leaving Ananta and Khushal Chand by the platform of the temple with Bali, Viroo, Mhenga and the passers-by who had stopped to listen.

24

AS ANANTA AND KHUSHAL CHAND STOOD WHERE THE OTHERS HAD left them by the shrine of Kali, discussing the best way to reconcile the coppersmiths to the idea of negotiating with Chaudhris Gokul Chand and Murli Dhar, they suddenly heard the babble of voices in Billimaran getting louder and louder. So, without resolving on a course of action, they hurried into the lane, and found that there were several students and intellectuals outside the factory, engaged in what was not so much a debate as a shouting match. Satyapal, who stood on the curve of the round platform before the factory gates, could be heard shrill and resonant above all the other interrupters:

'... instead of telling the workers in the factory to come out on strike in sympathy with the unemployed thathiars, they fall at the feet of that crooked Gokul ... yes-man to the Sarkar, the illiterate Municipal Commissioner. All for jobs... Professor Mejid will tell you all about this....'

'Down with disrupters and spies!' interrupted a student from the opposite camp, who stood at the base of the platform with a knot of other very agitated young men. 'Down with Mejid! Down with *petit bourgeois* intellectuals!'

'Ohe, go and change your name, since you have had your sacred hair cut off, Sardar Karam Singh!' Viroo, the 'Black God' snapped.

'Come, Professor Mejid, and tell them about the wicked deeds of Chaudhri Gokul Chand and Murli Dhar!' said Satyapal. 'Tell these brothers of the crooked deeds of the Communists who say to the thathiars: "We support you but we would like you to rub your nose on the earth before the bosses so that they can give you jobs." '

Satyapal seemed to have gained in authority from his simplification of the issue and his self-dramatization, which made him the vehicle of an extremism that was only prevented from carrying the crowd with him because, unknown to him, the spittle shot through his lips on all sides with every word. Nevertheless, the provocative irritability, of which his thin ascetic frame had become the vehicle, charged the narrow lane with an extraordinary tension, till the contagion of the crisis spread to everyone, even the onlookers, as a feeling of strong sympathy or antipathy and tended to make even the resonable people doubt themselves. Ananta felt a curious affection for him and yet a disgust towards his bitterness.

Professor Mejid extricated himself from the crowd and ascended the platform. He was a discreetly dressed but fiery little man of forty, a hollow-cheeked intellectual with a great forehead, half covered by an astrakhan cap, and large dark eyes shaded by black bushy eyebrows.

'Men do not light a flame and put it under a bushel. Nor have we lit a torch of Revolution that it may be snuffed out by the "phoon phoon" of the compromisers who are toing and froing, like busy bees, gathering honey with which to sweeten their lives. We shall not let this light go out into the shadows of obscurity which envelop the suffering of this land, but we shall fill the bodies of men with this effulgence, so that they can strike one final blow to sweep aside all oppressors.'

The eloquence of Professor Mejid testified to his cleverness. And, again, the impetuous elements in Ananta's body broke into stars of heat at the touch of this comet who talked of blazing a trail to illumine the world. But he reflected on the actual situation through which he and the other coppersmiths were living and felt that he could not merely delight in Professor Mejid's flights of fancy without facing up to the sordid fact that six pice to the unemployed today would mean more than six hours of revolutionary incendiarism with all the fine qualities that it may release.

'... if we want light, we must give light,' Professor Mejid was saying.

'If the light in you be darkness,' Ananta interrupted, 'how can you illumine other people's darkness?'

'The great darkness is in the minds of evil people!' answered Mejid, the ultra-revolutionary. 'The wicked capitalists....'

'And their hangers-on,' added Satyapal.

'To be sure!' said Viroo.

'To be sure!' echoed Ralia.

'If you want to bring a little sunshine into the lives of Billimaran, please don't soar into the heavens,' said Khushal Chand. 'Let us settle this business so that the workers light the torch of Revolution in themselves. Men must learn by themselves, you know, Professor Mejid, and by their own experience, rather than through words poured into them!'

'Han, let the wickedness of the capitalists,' said the student Karam Singh, 'become obvious to all the people. Let this wickedness, which stops the advance of workers, be exposed. For, as soon as they have introduced this kind of industry into our country on a sufficient scale, they will appear in the role of the parasitic rentier class which they have played elsewhere. And they will stop any little progress they may start. But don't forget that there are many capitalists who will desert to our side when the time comes!'

'Like Seth Khushal Chand, eh!' mocked Satyapal. 'The decoy elephant to trap all the others!

His fury knew no bounds now. And, in spite of the fact that he had voluntarily given his place to Professor Mejid, he jumped on to the platform and shouted with a flourish of his hand:

'And they call themselves socialists... these renegades! They join hands with the boss class. Soon they will be saying not only that things should be allowed to take their course and prove the wickedness of the capitalists, but that the bosses are nice people after all, that wealth and prosperity bring freedom to the soul! And they will forget to notice the rotund indolence of the bodies of the employers greasing the cushions of their shops! That the sting of poverty is not in toil, they will say, but in the degradation of the soul under the temptations of socialism! That poverty is quite bearable under trying circumstances so long as you go on eating the crumbs thrown at you from the rich man's kitchen! No, there is nothing inherently vicious in the rich capitalist, according to these people—no, indeed, the prosperity of the capitalists is an eternal torment to their souls ! Why, have we not the example of Seth Khushal Chand ! . . . Hypocrites ! We will show you what it is to believe in *Revolution* !'

There was a biting cynicism in the mockery of this revolutionist, which seemed to be prompted by the courage of despair. And through this courage Satyapal's whole manner seemed, in spite of the obvious histrionics, to become a rather splendid and grandiose assertion of the futility of reason. He seemed to have an uncanny awareness of the irrational desires of other people. And by the mere fact of his emphasis on the most unreasonable expectations he seemed to compensate them for all those suppressions which had never emerged in the monotonous life of the feudal craftsmen, who had laboured for years to a routine undisturbed except by the slowly dwindling darkness around them through the coming of modern knowledge. Deep, deep in Satyapal's nature there were humiliations crying out for revenge, even as the contempt of the slightly higher sub-castes and servitude to dealers was smouldering beneath the kindled ashes of resentment in the souls of coppersmiths. It was said that Satyapal's father had become a convert to Christianity in order to hold his job as a teacher in a Mission School. And perhaps the fact that the boy had been a witness to the subterfuges of his father had made him ashamed. But the alliance between his mood and that of the thathiars was certainly very intimate from the way they stood spellbound before him. And the concentration of all the adjectives, verbs and nouns in the vocabulary of the downright Punjabi seemed to give him the power to excite and be excited like a demagogue. Also, as the basis of his militancy lay in the common suffering of all those present, from the several suppressions, ranging from the terror practised by the Sarkar to the various strata of class and caste and creed and convention, the sanction of his bitterness reached a wider and wider circumference, within the horizon of the Fate that brooded over Billimaran. How much the violent insurrectionism he was preaching derived from his impatience to change India overnight by a bloody revolution, and how much of it arose from the striving for power that was the outer curve of an inner corrosion through his intense sensitiveness to insults from authority, no one could resolve. For though vanity, pride and the flamboyant manner had appeared in him, he had not yet revealed that utter contempt for the people which accompanies to desire to rise, through the depreciation of others, to undreamed-of heights of power.

Ananta withdrew into himself, between snatches of listening to Satyapal, to think of some way of averting the disaster which the orator was breathing into the poisoned atmosphere. But the flood of Satyapal's words was rising.

'Hypocrites, renegades, traitors, we shall show you ! We have lists ready of the traitors who have made peace with our oppressors ! We will save the growing generations of our countrymen from the madness of war, from the horrors of being drowned in the sea of blood, fighting for the Sarkar. We shall show them a bit of our mind. Who says that the wicked capitalists never prospered ? What is history if it is not the story of these wicked men thriving ? And amid all the chaos of the world, can you point to a single righteous man who has prospered against the Sarkar.

'You know,' answered Ananta, 'that if a man cheats he is cheated in the long run ! The retribution may not be immediate, but it comes surely.'

'I have yet to see the killers killed,' retorted Satyapal. And then with his body swaying with passionate indignation, he cried : 'General Dyer was given a purse by his countrymen for murdering our innocents at Jallianwallah Bagh, and Willingdon died of old age, not through retribution for his deeds ! They showed their power, frightened us and went their way; we, too, have to make an impression and *show* that we are not afraid of the Sarkar, or their lackeys, any longer !'

'Balé, oh balé, ohe lion !' said Viroo. 'What wisdom is in your little brain !'

'Shabashe, son, you have justified the seed of your father !' said Ralia.

'Certainly strange seed !' said Dina ironically. 'Scattering death and destruction. . . . Personally, I don't want to hang.'

'Coward !' said Ralia, nudging Dina Timur Lang.

'Oh, brother, killing perverts the character of the killers themselves,' counselled Khushal Chand. 'Listen. Gandhiji has insisted on this all his life : "Violence breeds violence !" And posturing, to make a show of bravery, is as bad when others do it as when we do it—murder will out !'

'And Truth will out like murder !' said Ananta, by way of

confirmation. 'Even if murder is suppressed, the reality will out, brothers. Think and ponder calmly. Do not be led astray. Let us sit down in our brotherhood and discuss the predicament. The Revolution is not yet. And it isn't merely in the shouting. Nor is it in this single battle in Billimaran, brothers. It is only through a great many conflicts between the employers, authorities and the workers, in a whole number of battles which our comrades elsewhere are fighting, that there will come the final overthrow of the bosses. So we must neither be slaves to circumstances nor accept either Fate or unreason, but must rise above them. Now, Babu Satyapal, come down from that platform and let us go and devise some means by which we can win our demands and soar above blinding chance and circumstance to some solid pinnacle of achievement, I beg you with joined hands.'

'You go and stand on the pinnacles of Gokul Chand or Murli Dhar ! Pervert ! Fornicator and abductor of women !' shouted Ralia. 'Go and take money from your boy-friend Khushal Chand !'

'Ohe buk nahin, bastard !' said Ananta, losing his temper.

Ralia rushed towards Ananta but was caught by Dina. 'Now, control the men whom you have aroused with your malicious exaggerations !' shouted Karam Singh to Satyapal. 'Setting brother on brother !'

'Han, brother, you must reserve your energies for something better, rather than fight with each other,' counselled Professor Mejid, frightened of a row.

'Ananta will see the light one day, friends,' conceded Satyapal. 'Don't hurt him. He is really one of us after all.

'The real enemy is hidden there,' said Mejid, mounting the platfrom again, 'that factory, which is going to convert you all from feudal slaves to wage slaves. I have studied a great deal about the astrology of the iron age. And I can tell you that the greatest danger now facing all nations is the wealth of the rich and the development of the machine. Brother thathiars, the evil of usury and the evil of the machine has sapped the life of peoples all over the world. There was a time when, as the poet Iqbal says, Greece and Egypt and Rome were the high points of civilization. But just as the neglect of moral character at the cost of the manifestation of material power brought the Nemesis of destruction of Greece and Egypt and Rome and Babylon, so today we are in the presence of a like material development : skyscrapers in New York, railways in miles of tunnels underground, telephones, cables and wireless and millions of aeroplanes which touch the ceiling of the sky, speaking not a word of cheer to humanity but only death—these will surely bring their Nemesis to this world ! You may ask how are we to be saved. I say : Storm the citadels which are ready to fall like-rotten apples into your hands. Especially the Sarkar ! For if a nation puts faith in extending its commerce, and makes the most sacred things of life a question of a business deal, building its cities on prostitution, usury and greed, adding to its factories then it may expect the fate which attended the nations of Europe !'

'Fate dictates only one thing !' shouted Satyapal, feeling that if the Professor went on being abstract the men would get bored and lose all incentive for action.

'Fate ! Fate ! Fate doesn't dictate anything. I beg you to stop this kind of talk, ohe brothers, all of you, students, Maulvis and Pandits !' shrieked Ananta, desperate with anger and futility. 'Ohe, come to your senses and let us call all our brotherhood together and resolve upon some course for our betterment. Men make of their own deeds, they make of their own character, good or bad; and they shape of their own Destiny ! So come and make your own fate.'

'Talk of character !' said Viroo.

'The lecher !' said Ralia.

'Fate dictates and you must obey !' hissed Satyapal, breathing a great draught of power and inflating his chest. 'We must show the Sarkar. . . .'

At that Karam Singh rushed up to the platform elbowing Satyapal off the curve of broken bricks and began to speak :

'Brothers, let us master this bahin-chod Fate. But let us leave the showing-off. There is no one among us who does not want change. But we have to prepare ourselves for this Revolution. As comrade Lenin said, "Whoever expects a 'pure' Social Revolution will never live to see it. Such a person pays lip service to Revolution without understanding it." '

But before he had uttered many more words there ensued a scuffle between him and Satyapal, who dragged him by the scruff of the neck. And their sympathizers on both sides entered into the arena, first in the role of peace-makers, then as active participants. The result was a free-fight in which, with flashing eyes and grinding teeth, the boys fell at each other, heaping loud abuse and blow upon blow with hard-knuckled fist cuffs and open-palmed hands, swaying in the wrestlers' embraces, till they slipped with half-suppressed moans and muttered curses.

'Ohe, come to your senses, boys, ohe !' Ananta called as he stood away, afraid that his strong arms may hurt someone if he entered the fray.

'Ohe, Babuo, ohe !' Viroo, the Black God, beckoned. 'Ohe, the police might come !'

'The old men for counsel, the young for war !' said Dina Timur Lang, turning to Viroo. 'Now see what your advice has done !'

' "The camels are being swept away, the ants say they float" ', Ralia answered. 'Let them fight it out, for it is the only way to decide the question !' And, while he waited for Ananta to step forward, he called to the students : 'Ohe, let him who wants to fight me accept my challenge ! Let the cowards go and the brave stay.'

But most of the coppersmiths, who had stood ranged while their destiny was being decided with arguments and with blows, did not hearken to Ralia's militant call. Only the little aperture in the factory gate opened and the two heads of Channa, the sparrow-faced foreman and Gopi, the grandson of Murli Dhar, emerged.

'Go away or we will call the police !' Channa shrieked.

'Come out, sons of the police, I will show you the police, if you come out !' roared Ralia.

Channa's face reddened with anger, then paled with fear, while Gopi winced.

'Brothers, stop this needless fight !'

'I will show you the needless fight !' said Ralia. 'I will open your door if you don't come out.'

And, looking round for a weapon and not finding one, he swung his body in a gesture which exaggerated the proportions of his muscular frame.

'Go away, I tell you,' Channa was saying as far as the movement of his lips showed, for his voice could not be heard above the crazy bellowing of students who hurtled down the alley as there was not enough room on the platform to fight it out.

Ralia ran towards the open shop of Ananta, roaring like a

lion, 'Wait, I will show them!' And he came back with a huge iron hammer. Menacing like a Colossus, the image of the God Siva himself in his destructive mood, he charged up the little hillock of the platform and began to belabour the factory gates with giant blows.

Someone inside the works opened the gate just as Ralia was attacking it with redoubled fury. The colossus breathed a large draught of breath and stood for a moment calling :

'Get out, all of you, if you want to save your lives!'

As no one dared cross his path, he walked deliberately into the hall of the factory.

'Follow him and show the whole country an example!' shouted Satyapal in the momentary lull, even as he wiped the blood that flowed from his nose. 'Show the employers and their friends, the Communists!' And he paused to make a declaration to Ananta, but, not finding his face among the crowd, said :

'The jackals have fled before the lion Ralia! Come, boys, follow Ralia.

25

ANANTA HAD SLUNK AWAY AS SOON AS HE SAW RALIA CHARGING the door of the factory to go and fetch Chaudhri Gokul Chand himself. If the employer was willing to put out his turban at the feet of the jobless coppersmiths and the students behind Satyapal and agree to accept their terms, he might save the situation, otherwise the tempers of the men might lead to anything.

A few hill-men and their spouses stood in the doorways of closed shops and at the Bazar Kaserian end of Billimaran, with anxious and enquiring faces.

Ananta fairly ran across the length of the lane, only pausing for a moment superstitiously when he heard the swarm of crows cawing over the shrine of Kali, now perched on a wall above the heap of garbage that dotted the end of the square by Bali's shop. The ominous birds were so near Janki's window that his heart sank. Then he hurried towards the exit, feeling as though he were being driven, not by the hope that he would succeed in his plan, but by that very Destiny which he had sought all day to combat—the Fate which seemed to envelop this grime of the world like a giant cloud of heat. What is the use of struggling against the oppression of the sky? he said to himself.

Then he felt that he would try this last chance to cheat Destiny. And as he hurried, far from the temper of Ralia and the dark looks of Satyapal, the situation seemed it might easily get out of control. He was afraid that Ralia, who had been on the warpath with his friends all day, would certainly destroy half the plant even before he could return.

So strong was this feeling that he stopped suddenly and thought that he would get back. Then he felt that he was being superstitious in foreseeing disasters when all that had happened was a series of incidents on this uncanny day which had, in some strange manner, led to a situation between the Kaseras and the thathiars that was final and irrevocable and could not have been settled without all this happening.

As he got to the middle of Bazar Kaserian he heard someone calling from behind.

'Ohe, stumbling forward and still alive!'

It was Mengha.

'Come . . .' the boy began. And he nearly choked for breath to spit more words out.

'What's the matter?'

'They are fighting,' Mengha said, his face taut, and turned towards the alley. 'Come, Ralia and others have got hammers, and bricks. Ralia is breaking up the machinery. And——'

Ananta stood bewitched. 'What?' he repeated stupidly.

There was blood from a scratch on Mehnga's arm and the boy's dishevelled form told the whole story.

For a moment Ananta hovered on the decision to go forward or backward, feeling like a shadow of the shadow which had pursued him all day, and as if he were going to collapse with regret that the doom he had known to be in his power to avert should now have descended on them all. And he was afraid that a great deal of what had happend was really irretrievable. Then he turned back, as though lifting his head in a deliberate attempt to resurrect the faith that could enable him to control the situation before him.

Mehnga followed.

26

'THIS IS THE KALI YUG, THEY SAY, HAN, THE KALI YUG! . . . Acha, then, I am the destroyer of this madar-chod age, Shiv! . . . Come, brothers, I am Shiva.'

Ralia mumbled as he swung the hammer with both hands and capered like a monkey from machine to machine in the factory, with all the maddened, murderous power of his giant body, while Satyapal and Viroo stood away frightened after they had exhausted themselves breaking the machines. The crowd of workers, unemployed thathiars, students, and other sightseers, with Gopi and Channa at their head, looked on stunned from the verandah. They could all see what was happening, but for a while the wild swing of Ralia's hammer struck a terror into every heart so that no one dared to go forward and interrupt him.

'Ohe, stop now, Ustad Ralia Ram, stop!' Dina called, as he darted into the factory under cover of a machine and stood, his hands joined in supplication, while he rested uneasily on his short limp leg.'

'Rape-mother, this is the kali yug and I am the destroyer, Shiv. Rape the sister of everyone!' Ralia cursed, while the sweat coursed down his body, his distended eyeballs glared red-streaked at the plant and he bent and rose, bent and rose, hacking at the machines.

'Ohe, you have done enough now,' Uncle Viroo said, his small fat body shuddering at the destruction before him. 'God does not permit undue punishment.'

'Nahin! Rape-mothers! Nahin! Fire and steel are good servants but evil masters! And rape sisters. I will destroy them and laugh as they used to laugh—the tricks of the Devil—the machines . . . Ha, ha, ha! . . . I will shriek as they used to shriek! . . .' And he simulated a shrill squeaky whistle as he danced like a machine, swaying his body. 'I will become a bigger machine with this hammer, a bigger master, greater than your. . . . Ho, ho, ho!' And he laughed an uncanny hoarse laughter from the base of his throat as if he were choking with the hatred and vengeance, his face smeared with the grease and dirt that rose from the chaos of black dust, splashing oil and slime that shot out from the broken machinery.

'Thathiars, brothers, come, this is the moment to press your real demands!' said Satyapal, who had gone away to the verandah to look for Professor Mejid, but heard rumours that the police were coming.

Some of the crowd moved away, shaking their heads and blinking nervously as though they were being pursued by the destructive monster Ralia.

As Ralia heard this he stopped laughing suddenly for a moment, wiped the sweat off his forehead, so that his whole face glistened with a savage energy and warmth.

'Now tell me how you feel,' he said, addressing a machine before him. 'I didn't want big money, only a wage with the work of my hand, and you deprived me of it; now talk, may I rape the mother of your mother! I can talk better than you——'

'What is made must be broken, the cause of ruin must become a ruin—then only will the bosses learn!' said Satyapal. 'Brave brother, you have done well. Now come away before the police come. Where is Professor Mejid? Boys . . . come, let us go—all of us, together.'

'I will make it talk, the rape-mother machine,' Ralia said, excited to another bout of futile hatred.

'Let go, now!' said Dina. 'Don't dig up the foundations to finish the roof! Where is Ananta?'

'Han, brother,' begged Gopi with tears in his eyes. 'Spare the rest. What will my father say and my grandfather?'

'Don't weep, Gopi Nath,' Channa consoled him. And then Sparrow-face advanced gingerly into the factory and said:

'Ohe, fool, machines can't talk! Stop it, madman!'

'Oh, can't it talk!' Ralia answered without looking back towards Channa. 'It can talk all right, and it can laugh—at us. Rape-mother, chapper chapper channa!' And he lifted his voice in a hoarse, drunken ghostly cry-shriek, even as he struck his hammer on machine parts and stamped his feet in a dance: 'I want blood! I want bones! I want bodies and sinews! Hoon . . . I want them young! I want them green! Han . . . I want them in a stream so that I can crush them and break them! . . . Han, Han, Han! Don't want the old ones fit for the rubbish-heaps, Viroo and Bhagu and Arjun and Ralia. I drink blood! I drink oil! I drink urine! I like the young best, han, because I am a whore, see! . . . Let them come and pull my hair, let them push themselves up against me, twist and turn and clutch and revolve! . . . I want to be raped! I am a bitch, see! So I want young blood! Let them come and I will embrace them!... I am the bitch goddess machine, han, the Kali of the iron age, the age of machines! ... Hoon, han, hoon, han.... I will wed you—I, Ralia; I am Shiv, and you are Kali....'

'Ohe, stop it!' 'You are going mad,' Daula and Mehru and Shibu, the factory workers, shouted, craning their heads forward.

'The shadow of God is looking on from behind you!' cried Viroo, frightened. 'Fear the Lord ohe! He is watching. Now come away, the just retribution has been meted out to the wicked!' And the 'Black God's' corpulent flesh trembled in panic as the destruction proceeded.

'It was worth a lakh of rupees, all this machinery,' Gopi cried, beating his forehead, uplifted in an adject despair. 'I will go and call grandpa.

'Han, it can talk and it can walk, the bitch!' said Ralia, grinding his teeth and working himself up to a fresh surge of passion by walking rhythmically up and down. 'I will rape it and kill it once and for all....' And he heaved his hammer again and swerved in a semi-circle to attack the machines he had left behind.

'The police are due to arrive, brothers—save yourselves,' said Satyapal, coming back to the verandah, and drifting away, unable to persuade anyone to go back home or to go forward and control the demons he had released.

'Ohe, ustad, I beg you, listen!' Dina cried, coming back into the factory from the verandah again. 'Don't be heartless! For the sake of your children. That Shaitan has gone. The police are coming! Where is Ananta?... Ohe, dohai!...'

'Don't be heartless!' Ralia repeated. 'Food, this machine is heartless too—heartless bitch!... Hoon!... Han!... Whore!——'

And he struck the hammer in a serious of frenzied blows as he walked short steps backwards and forwards in a demonic rage, until the words became the mere reflex action in the larynx. Occasionally he would repeat an oath or mutter a curse, but he seemed intent on finishing his work with the monotonous thoroughness with which he was wont to hammer his copper or brass.

The crowd of men in the verandah hovered like rabbits fascinated by the oncoming killer. And there was a grim silence broken only by whispers and the thud, thud of the hammer and the distant snarls of men in the gully too frightened to come any nearer. And for a moment it seemed as if this eternity of suspense would be prolonged into vaster eternities and become unending, because Ralia went belabouring the most vulnerable parts of each machine, panting and exhausted, but still steady as in a wrestling match where the man with the longer breath and the more resilient muscle can hold out.

'Ralia, son, I ask you, respect my grey hair, the police will soon be here' appealed Viroo. 'Think of your wife and children. Leave off, there is still time.' And he advanced a step or two, but his courage failed him as the hammer shone clear in the air before him and the splinters flew.

As though the mention of his wife and children had drawn him back from his wanton destruction, Ralia stopped and breathed a long breath with his head thrown back and the hammer resting on the ground before him. His eyeballs rolled, however, and he burst out spitting and frothing into more abuse.

'Rape the mother of my wife and children ! I will tackle her afterwards ! Let me destroy these bitches first !' And he began to caper and strike redoubled blows.

'Ohe, have you become a child ?' called Ananta. 'Stop it!'

'Now look at your protege, you who have let loose hatred and inspired these men to rebellion ?' snapped Channa. 'Lala Murli Dhar and Lala Sadanand are coming. And the police is on the way here.'

'Ohe, keep quiet, you !' Ananta said, his heart congealed with disgust for the petty, intriguing, sparrow-faced foreman. And, having taken in the situation at a glance, he walked, with deliberate but heavy steps, into the factory.

Ralia was spitting on the palms of his hand in order to get a better grip of the wooden handle of his hammer, and ignored Ananta.

'Don't go near him, ustad !' Dina warned Ananta at the door. 'For the sake of the shell he will tear down the temple.'

'Han, Anant Ram, some jinn has mounted his head,' said Viroo, now abject in a purple agony.

Ananta ignored the old man and, going up to Ralia, put an affectionate hand on his shoulder and said : 'Break one more machine, brother Ralia Ram, and then come and drink some sherbet and calm yourself.'

'Don't "brother" me, and go away,' said Ralia, shaking Ananta's hand off with a violent shrug of his shoulders. And then, lifting the hammer in his hand, he shouted : 'I shall show you who is the master, those machines or I. . . . I will spit at these engines, I will destroy them, I shall wipe them off the face of the earth.'

'Acha, my wrestler, go ahead,' said Ananta. 'Break them, break as many as you like.'

Ralia looked at Ananta with the hammer uplifted in his hand.

'Go ahead, destroy everything to your heart's content,' Ananta said.

Ralia struck a blow to the top of an electrical drill adjusted to the wall. Then he swung, the hammer back and got into a position to strike at another plant, mumbling, 'Rape—mother.' But somehow he hesitated before striking another blow and stood still with hammer unlifted, as if he had lost the cue for passion which had possessed him a moment ago, just because Ananta asked him to go and break the machines according to heart's desire.

'Go, no,' Ananta said, with a nonchalant gesture of his right hand while his left hand rested on his waist as he stood watching him.

But, instead of striking at the machine, Ralia brought the hammer down and rested it between his feet, almost as though he had been more obsessed with destruction than with the machines and, being encouraged to fulfil his fell purpose, was relieved of his yearning. And yet the intoxication of hatred was upon him, and he turned to Ananta.

'Don't you preen yourself that I have stopped because I am afraid of you. I can laugh at you and spit on your face, trickster, traitor !' And he spat at Ananta.

Ananta's hand rose involuntarily and he slapped Ralias face with a resounding clean slap.

'You will not break my pride,' Ralia cried with tears in his eyes. 'Machine-man, swine ! . . . You are the brother of these machines and machine-wallahs—traitor, blackleg !' And he swooped upon Ananta with his claws outstretched like that of an eagle.

'Ohe, ohe . . . !' The crowd gathered at the door shouting,

remonstrating, begging the two men to cease fighting

Ananta grappled him from the waist and, lifting him, ran towards the door so that the crowd scampered away. But Ralia caught hold of a machine on the way so that they both fell and rolled over each other. The blood rushed to their faces and, sweating, hissing, their soggy clothes caked with earth, mumbling curses, they struggled for mastery. After a momentary loss of grip, Ananta overpowered Ralia and had him helpless under him arms. Ralia seemed exhausted now and his face expressed a calm resignation, as though he admitted defeat, his eyes were closed and the beads of sweat trailed down his forehead and his cheeks.

Seeing him thus, Ananta suddenly gave up as though he thought that the fight was finished and Ralia had recovered his sanity.

At this Ralia sprang up and, gripping Ananta by the throat, overpowered him.

'Now speak, swine !' he roared with a resurgence of energy.

'I will break you and rend you, as I have broken those machine, dog ! Whoremonger ! pimp ! I shall show you !'

And he viciously lifted and struck Ananta's head on the broken part of a machine with a maniacal fury, till Ananta's skull cracked like a pitcher, and a stream of blood shot out in thick spurts.

'Ohe, what have you done ! shouted Dina. 'Oh, horror !. .'

'Ohe ! Ohe ! O Ishwar !' shrieked Viroo, rushing out like a frightened ape. 'Ohe, your own friend !'

'Ishwar ! God !'

The crowd screamed and rushed forward into the factory in sheer bedlam, and Ralia's wife, Gauri, who came calling, 'Where is he ? Where is he ?', uttered a shriek of infinite horror and, with her child in her arms, ran forward from the verandah and fell at his feet.

Ralia stood shaking with fear and excitement now, his face a place blank, with not the slightest trace of anger or pity in it.

'The poolc ! The poolc !' someone called.

'Get out of the way. Clear out ! What's happened !' asked the Sub-Inspector of Police as he advanced.

'Hai ! Hai ! Hai, hai, my lion !' Karam Devi moaned as she trailed behind the Sub-Inspector of Police and, groping, lunged forward. Then with a shriek she fell over her step-son's face and began to beat her breasts, her forehead and her thighs.

Ralia crouched by where his wife lay sobbing in a huddle and rested his head awkwardly on her neck, closing his eyes to evade the angry glaces of the policeman, closing his ears to their abuse, and burying his head in the soft darkness of the luxurious flesh of the woman, as if he were being drawn deeper and deeper into the pit of forgetfulness, away from the danger to his own life and yet on the brink of the inevitable doom.

Ananta's heart had stopped beating, though his flesh was still hot and his flood still flowed and his eyes looked up with an uncanny terror.

The Sub-Inspector of Police separated Karam Devi from his body and felt his pulse and, dropping the hand in disgust, looked round, muttering abuse.

'Take that crouching son of a bitch and handcuff him,' he ordered the policeman behind, while he looked at his wrist-watch. And, mumbling, 'Quarter past six,' noted the time in his book.

Gauri shrieked and would not let go of Ralia, so that two constables had to overpower her before handcuffing her husband.

'What are their names?' the Sub-Inspector said, turning round. 'Tell me, someone!'

27

THE RELENTLESS FURY OF THE SUN HAD BURNT ITSELF OUT OVER Billimaran by the time the Clock Tower struck the half-hour past seven. The crackling fire of opposite wills that had blazed in the tortuous lane had subsided almost suddenly and given place to the ashen calm of the brief Indian twilight. The heat of the day still permeated every nook and corner of the lane, but the shadows deepened the silences that spread all around, between the series of wails, mourning songs and cries which the women of the thathiar brotherhood uttered as they beat their breasts, their foreheads and their thighs, or as they sat head to head in twos, intoning duets, covered by their head-cloths for modesty. The quality of the silences varied, however, from the dead silence that had trembled like a shock of electricity after Ananta's death, the hush when no one could bear to speak except in whispers, to the uncanny silence when silence itself seemed to be listening to silence before being disturbed by sighs of regret and broken words of consolation spoken by the coppersmiths to each other. They now sat together, around the corpse of Ananta, in the shop which had been filled with the contagion of his living breath so recently as at noon-time.

As Puran Singh Bhagat alighted from the tonga carriage at the foot of the Clock Tower and began to walk up to the Ivory Sellers' Bazar end of Billimaran, he sensed from the looks that the shopkeepers gave him that something catastrophic had happened in his absence. The bunch of policemen who guarded the mouth of the lane looked daggers at him, as though they were aching to avenge themselves for some humiliation of their own lives on him.

'So he has come—the poet !' one of them murmured to another.

'Hoon !' the other grunted.

And the others nodded coldly and averted their eyes.

The poet ignored them, thinking that if they were looking for him and had a new warrant for his arrest the onus of responsibility for arresting him lay on them. And he walked into the lane. He was trying to be as casual as he could, but his heart thumped in spite of him.

He had not gone far when he began to see knots of hill-men coolies and their demure wives gathered together at the doors of different houses, tight-throated and furtive and bubbling with the suppressed eagerness of those who have suddenly awakened from the lethargic acceptance of life into a startling awareness of death, known to them through legend and proverb to be near and yet presumed, because of its uncanny and strange knocks at the door when least expected, to be so far away.

Seeing segments of the many mouths of these people mumbling sympathetically their liquid eyes gleamed and fell, while the echoes of weeping came across the lane, he stopped by a group and asked :

'Brothers, what has happened ?'

'Thathair Anant Ram has ascended the celestial heavens,' a hill-man said.

'Killed by that monster Ralia, husband of Gauri,' a hill-woman said.

'They say that Ralia, thathair, broke the machines too !'

another hill-woman said. 'They say it was worth lakhs of rupees ! Look folks, darkness has come upon the world ! These thathiars have raised their heads to the sky !'

'Shut up ! Sardarji knows all about the quarrel between Murli Dhar-Gokul Chand and the thathiars !' said a hill-man, presumably the husband of the shrew who had spoken of thathiars raising their heads to the sky.

Puran Singh Bhagat proceeded, occupied by imperceptible twinges of conscience. He felt numb and his face glowed with that kindly gentle smile which was stamped permanently on the bare flesh of his cheeks, above the greying beard, an altogether happy smile which people took to be the index of a temperament unaware of pain, but which was really the expression of goodwill, born of an inner calm. He tried to beckon the imprint of sorrow by hardening his cheek-bones, but he could only feel a flush of heat gathering beneath the perspiration on his nose, his soul suspended beneath quickly inflating lungs, an emptiness seeking knowledge. 'Why is my blood congealed ?' he asked himself.

Suddenly he hastened his steps, slithering across the greasy uneven surface of Billimaran, restless bubbles of froth in his mouth and the stabs inside him mounting into an accusation, like the beat of the town-crier's drum : 'Why didn't I come back sooner ?' 'But it was impossible,' the answer came back. 'With me trapped in the prison of a promise not to break bail, caged by the laws of the Sarkar !' Protest seemed futile against the Omnipresent will of the Sarkar, the Fate against which he himself was wrestling. Certainly he was not subject to the ancient Fate, which had possessed the coppersmiths and through the acceptance of which they had killed Ananta, the only one of them who had sought to defy that particular destiny, but he felt that he himself was up against another Nemesis, the Fate that throtted freedom and prevented him from breathing calmly through its prohibitions and denials. And yet he felt responsible for the extinction of Ananta's life.

He slowed down and kept his eyes from meeting anyone else's, and reached Ananta's shop with halting steps, for he espied two policemen smoking the hookah as they sat on a bedstead on the platform outside. His own self-conscious hardness was nothing as compared with the callousness of these wardens in the face of death. And then he was in full view of the familiar dishevelled forms of the coppersmiths, seated by the corpse. In a flash the memory of the way in which they had all sat there in the afternoon came to him, the vortex of their dark fears, wild ambitions, uneven determinations rising to his brain above the sense of the tedium of their life, the uneasy, drab and amorphous secret palls of suffering that cluttered up their existence. They seemed a sorry company now, opening their mouths to whisper the habitual 'I fall at your feet, Sardarji.'

Puran Singh Bhagat joined his hands to them and craned his neck forward.

'He had to go, Sardarji,' Bhagu said.

'His end had come,' Arjun said.

'Former days have passed,' Viroo, the 'Black God,' intoned in a sing-song punctuated by sighs, and you have not made your peace with God. What will repentance do when the birds have wasted the field——' And he struck his forehead with his palm and began to weep. But his hoarse moans were drowned in the shrill crescendo of the shouts and cries with which the women in the by-lane began another bout of mourning.

'Ohe, Bhai Sikha !' the policeman on the charpai raised his warning voice rudely.

Puran Singh Bhagat turned on his feet and looked incomprehensibly at him.

'Go away, it is an order that no one except his relations and friends should be allowed near the corpse,' the policeman said.

Puran Singh Bhagat could have said that he was a friend and stayed ; instead he half turned to go.

'Look at him before you go, Sardarji,' said Dina Timur Lang, who sat by Ananta's head. 'Have a last look at him.' And he withdrew the sheet which covered Ananta's head.

Horror !—the triumph of death struck the poet in the face and unnerved him. Puran Singh Bhagat's eyes scanned the twisted drawn features of the bold waxen image wrapped in a purple agony and met Dina's tear-stricken eyes. A tremor of fear and pity rose to his throat and he bent his melting eyes over his joined hands, for he did not want to look at the face of his friend uglied by death.

'Janki has been asking for you,' Dina said, raising his voice a little. 'She is in her room.'

Puran Singh Bhagat revolved uncertainly on his feet,

mumbled a verse of the prayer-book and withdrew hurriedly in case the policeman should insult him. And he began to walk away towards the Bazar Kaserian end of Billimaran, followed by a chorus of 'I fall at your feet' from the thathiars.

He knew that they thought him a gentleman and liked him. And now their triumphant firmness in error seemed to have gone; the egotism with which they had fought against one another had yielded, flooding the bridgeless gulfs between them, and they sat poised, looking now heaven-wards to the trail that Ananta's good deeds would blaze for them and now hell-wards to the flaming misery to which they would have to descend again.

There were two more policemen outside the gates of the factory while a few curious coolies from the pickle factory sat on the edge of the well, peering into the empty court-yard where the murder and destruction had taken place.

The poet reflected that the broken machines, being inanimate had died easily, whereas the man Ananta was really immortal from the memories of him that he had left behind in the hearts of his friends and relations; that in the long run it was, as he had tried to tell the coppersmiths, their manhood and not the machines which was of consequence to them. He wished he had been able to stay among them and console them. But the police . . . And perhaps it was better, he felt, that they should discover their belief in themselves on their own rather than vow impetuously to do something as a penance for the mishap for which they were partly responsible, in the heat of repentance over the dead body before them. Also, for the while, it would be cruel and brutal to breathe one single word about the controversy to those whose respect for the dead was a rigid convention.

The twilight was deepening over Billimaran as though the shadows which had played hide-and-seek with the sun all day, and which had played havoc with the lives of the coppersmiths, had now mingled with the elements and covered the elements in a web of sober grey.

The poet felt easier as he left the dead body further behind him, almost as though the finality of death which the corpse represented had disappeared, almost as though the sharp stabs of Yama's stare which had assailed him had been beaten back by the light in his own eyes, and the momentary fear which the purple agony on Ananta's face inspired had gone out of his bones. 'One man can die,' he said to refurbish his faith in himself, 'hundreds can die, but life can't be extinguished in the world altogether until the very sun goes cold and the elements break up . . .' And yet the inescapable feeling clung to him that each single man is important, that Ananta was his friend, and that with this comrade's going there would be a gap in the world which could not be filled easily. And as the impersonal and personal feelings clashed in him, he was now frightened of meeting Janki.

There was a bunch of policemen seated by Bali's shop, so Puran Singh Bhagat hesitated uncertainly at the door of the stairs to Janki's room.

'Go up, go up. . . . She . . .' they said in a chorus, and some of them winked and made lewd signs such as the procurers make in the market of love.

The poet blushed with anger and wished the fire in his being could become a disembodied force and go and smite them. Then he controlled himself and his gentle, wise face turned with a genial smile and, muttering the Christian words, 'They know not what they do,' ascended the stairs.

Janki was sitting by her bed, crocheting with eager fingers, an unhealthy flush on her face, which created the illusion that her consumption was gone.

She made obeisance to him by joining her hands over the crocheting hook and then, without looking up, said :

"Are they still there ?'

He understood whom she was referring to, and, nodding shame-facedly, as though he were taking on the blame for the misdemeonours of all males, said :

'Have they been annoying you, Janki sister ?'

'They think,' she said, 'that now Ananta is gone I will set up as a common whore and open this house to all. And, being policemen, they think they ought to have the first commission.'

And her face became rigid and red-hot and she could not speak any more. Then, half covering her face with an end of her dhoti, she suddenly got up and retreated towards the alcove.

This effort of hers to control her bitterness and to retreat to a corner released the emotions the poet had kept under check so far. The incarcerated sorrow welled up in his eyes, the saliva gathered in his throat, and the whole of his fluid nature slipped across the rocks of principles and the drifts of ideas, swept over all the languages he spoke and understood, and flooded across his cheeks and his beard in hote scalding tears. The man, whose thoughts embraced the whole of life, became suddenly human; the poet, whose mind had lost some of its warmth through an abstract love for Truth, became the humble, quiet, good man with a direct and personal love for the wronged; the free spirit relaxed and he blew his nose and went to the window by which he had stood this morning like the peasant he was at heart.

Having wiped her tears, Janki returned, her face swollen, and sat down with another effort of will to keep herself from breaking down.

'How is one to control one's kismet if one's life is not one's own to live?' she asked. 'If one is only a woman!... The object of every joke, so weak, so vulnerable!... Just think what they have been saying about me merely because I had the temerity to live with him as his mistress. He was everything to me. And now?' She coughed, as if her grief was stuck in her throat, and continued: 'Because his strong arms are withdrawn, they... oh, they want to paw me about and consider me easy game!'

The poet came over to her and patted her head, almost as if he were blessing her.

'Have a good cry, sister, have a good cry,' he whispered. 'I know.... I know it is hard—especially for a woman. Life is very hard and full of suffering.'

As he said this the words seemed to burn themselves into his brain with a fiery apperception of all their meaning, of all the beauty and ugliness of life, of all the contradictions of the struggle of men and women he had known. And in a flash he saw the deep grooves that were cut in one's soul by the cruelty in this world, the marks from which people never recovered.... What little happiness there was in the midst of the pain in this universe!... But the knowledge of this fact seemed to give him a certain calm, the peace to look at Janki, to understand all about the tragedy which had been enacted and to be the linguist who could mouth words for the silent, without braggadocio or bluster.

'No one knows what a woman suffers,' Janki said, between sobs.

'I know,' he said. Especially here among us 'But nothing in life is irreparable, Jankiai, and, soon, we will fight our way out of the degradation because we have entered into an irreconcilable conflict with evil——'

'You say this in spite of what has happened!' Janki said, raising her face, tear-washed and shoked and hurt.

'Sister, we tried to sow some seeds in Billimaran, and the hot winds that blew carried them into the drains. So the healthiest seed perished without leaving a trace. Some of the seed will take root and flower.'

'How can anything flower in this evil lane,' Janki said bitterly, 'among malicious, murderous people who breathe evil, think evil, do evil!' Her voice rose to a shrill crescendo like that of a wounded bird which does not want to be touched by a healer.

The poet walked away from her, overcome by her indignation and aware of the depth of the wrong she had suffered.

'Certainly,' he said, looking out of the window at the policemen and the mixed crowd that hung around, 'there is evil here. The police are drunk with power. The Kaseras lust for money. The thathiars are stunned with fear and ignorance. But men were not born evil——. Those who say that men are born evil, sister, only do so because they want to assume the power to rule over men in order to keep their evil control, the high caste and high-class people who want to justify their privileges.' He turned to look towards her and, raising his hand in the gesture of a blessing, continued: 'Childling, oblivion shares with forgetfulness a grace without which people would all go raving mad in the streets in face of suffering.'

'I feel mad, mad, crazy!' she shrieked. 'I shall go crazy like the witch-woman in the streets! I cannot bear it! It may be possible for all those who saw him murdered to be consoled, but . . . I can't do nothing but weep.' And she broke down in an hysterical fit of weeping, and moaned: 'He is dead . . . Oh, he was such a noble creature—so much nobler than all those louts! He is dead . . . And all my life has ended with his going. Everything has ended for me in his death. O God, let the earth open up and swallow me! Otherwise they will destroy me, the vultures who are sitting there!'

Puran Singh Bhagat felt that he had been insensitive in preaching to her when what she needed was to be comforted, to be consoled. But the rigidity of his intellectual discipline kept him aloof, isolated, and he stood shaking in an agony of frustration at the awareness of this peculiar detachment in himself, this seemingly heartless reserve that could not break down and which kept him from melting with the affection he felt for this woman. Partly he knew it was his love for ideas and partly the shock of the death of his wife before he had gone on his travels, which had congealed the natural warmth of his heart. And he felt shy even as he contemplated Janki in a huddle before him and went on burbling to himself as if to drown his own embarrassment.

'Sad sad, sad—his going! The awful things is that the blow should have been struck by his friend!'

'Friend!' Janki cried. 'That brute Ralia!... Oh, why did God in heaven not come down and save him from the hands of those! Why doesn't He come down and save this land from itself and those policias, the profiteers and the Sarkar!'

'They are not louts, sister,' the poet said, and advancing nearer the bedstead and leaning towards her. 'They are frightened, suffering, hopeless men. As I came through the lane and stood by the shop I saw how simple and really kind they were in their togetherness. It is no use invoking God to come and destroy them or rescue them, but we must forgive them and try to understand them. I too feel angry with them and with those who instigated them to do all this; there is more blame attached to the buffoons who incited them than to the thathiars. There are many inciters in our country who are pastmasters in the art of directing the simple folk into cheap heroism, till the misplaced energy of the poor begins to seem more disgusting than the wickedness of the deceivers and mischief-mongers. But the only cure for this is to make the men think twice before asking them to lay down their lives for a mere gesture, to encourage them rather to become men, to recognize the dignity of their manhood as against the blind, brutal acts which only feed their own or their leaders' insensate love of glory.'

'How will they learn, Sardarji? When will they learn?... Sermons won't teach them!'

'Perhaps you are right,' the poet said, summing up all the humility in his nature to see that he too had mistaken words for deeds. Perhaps you are right. Because men don't really learn from speeches as much as they learn from examples.' Perhaps the life of Ananta—I mean the way he lived may be ——a greater example for them than any words he could have spoken. Why, they may even recall the wise things he said to them now that he is dead. For what can be more persuasive then the death of a man who love them.'

Those words seemed to console Janki a little. That a wise man like the poet thought her lover so worthy a person compensated her to some extent for her loss. She wiped her tears and mumbled.

'If his death makes a little difference, perhaps it may have been worthwhile. But ! . . . I know *they* don't think so. Not the police, and the heartless gossips of the world !'

The terrible isolation which had made him stand away out of respect for her grief broke down and he came and sat down by her on the edge of the bed precariously, in the dark, and patted her head ever so gently, soothingly.

'You must not be afraid, Jankai' he said. 'You are so sensible and have such understanding. What a great thing it would be if women like you who possess such gifts of sincerity and grace, give yourself to *bhakti*, devotion, to working for others !'

'It is such a short life that I have been vouchsafed,' she sighed, and the tears welled into her eyes again.

'All stories end in death, Jankai' the poet said. 'But, childling, even if one is given a short life, it becomes shorter if it is guarded selfishly. On the other hand, think of the joy of living for others, of helping others——'

'Those who condemn me to be a whore——'

'There are evils bigger than stupid moral condemnation,' he cut in impatiently. There is a life without fear. One day men will understand that there are many whores who have the hearts of saints and many respectable people whose lives are putrid with hypocrisy.' He paused because he felt that he was being cruel to Janki.

'What do you want me to do ?' she said suddenly, with a brave assertion of her face, though large tears stood in her grey-green eyes.

The poet hesitated for a moment. Then he lifted her chin and looked searchingly into her eyes, as though testing her, and said :

'We will go to the shop and sit among the thathairs, sister.

You will become one of them. And you will try to get to know them. For no curtain of fear and suspicion should divide those who have the flame of understanding from those who are in the dark. And though Ananta is dead, and we will have to go and cremate his body tomorrow, the spirit of his comradeship will survive.... And as nothing that springs from effort and anguish and pain can be destroyed, so nothing must divide those who are left behind to share a common suffering. And the ocean of life will rage again. The tides of love will flow and wipe out the waves of hatred——'

'You are too generous to people,' she said sceptically.

'Nahin ! I know that even when the flood of love sweeps across the ocean, there will be enough of the hatred left, festering and poisoning the new life, and that there will never be a complete sweep of all the rubbish.... But what matters is that life makes a fresh start with every change and overturning. And those who have lost faith and been degraded, disfigured and mutilated, become aware of their manhood, and rise become men and learn to stand erect with their turbans on their heads.... Just now, we are so degraded that we could all learn to live a simple and more truthful life with other people.'

'Will they not mock at me for wanting to practise *bhakti*?' Janki said.

'Perhaps they will,' the poet said.

'After tomorrow, then, I will come and live at the bunga of Sant Harnam Das,' she said boldly.

The poet hesitated and then warmed to the idea and said : 'We will look after you there. And when you get a little better, then you can organize the women comrades who come there.'

'Of course the people will say—Janki has taken a lover even before the ashes of her last one are hardly cold....'

'One has to take risks,' he said, rising from the bed determinedly, 'in order to prepare for the new life. That is the only way in which we shall learn to become new men and women.'

'Acha !' she sighted, and sat spellbound in her own words for a moment.

An evening crow cawed his last message of doom before flying away from the window-sill outside the room, and somewhere deep in the grooves of a porch the pigeons cooed in a resonant hum. The darkness spread and obliterated the empty space of the room, so that only the hulk of the bed was visible. Presently Janki got up and lit the kerosene oil lamp and the radiance gradually spread to each nook and corner of the room and dispelled the shadows.

'Come,' the poet said. We must go to our brothers at the shop.

'Oh, my heart will break!' Janki said, as she put on her head-cloth and stood ready to go. And tears welled into her eyes.

The poet spread the shadow of his protective arm around her and, groping in the dim light, led her down the stairs.

THE END
St. George's Mews, N.W. 1.
1944.
Revised, Khandalla, 1979.